"LOOK AT ME, KATE!"

Kathleen heard the compelling insistence of Jason MacAuley's voice, so powerful that it forced her to raise her eyes and view his naked splendor. He stood with his feet braced unashamedly apart, his legs, long and straight and hardened with sinew. She blanched at the fullness of his arousal. But Jason discerned the cause of her anxiety and drew her eyes upward to his own. Kate heeded his expansive chest, the bulk and width of his shoulders, and she quickened at his extraordinary perfection.

She could see why Jason MacAuley could have any woman he wanted.

And even before he spoke, she trembled at his next words.

"I would have thee now. . . ."

THE
WIND-ROSE

Great Reading from SIGNET

THE
WIND-ROSE

by
Mary Mayer Holmes

A SIGNET BOOK
NEW AMERICAN LIBRARY

PUBLISHER'S NOTE

This novel is a work of fiction. Names, characters, places, and incidents either are the product of the author's imagination or are used fictitiously, and any resemblance to actual persons, living or dead, events, or locales is entirely coincidental.

NAL BOOKS ARE AVAILABLE AT QUANTITY DISCOUNTS WHEN USED TO PROMOTE PRODUCTS OR SERVICES. FOR INFORMATION PLEASE WRITE TO PREMIUM MARKETING DIVISION, THE NEW AMERICAN LIBRARY, INC., 1633 BROADWAY, NEW YORK, NEW YORK 10019.

SIGNET TRADEMARK REG. U.S. PAT. OFF. AND FOREIGN COUNTRIES
REGISTERED TRADEMARK—MARCA REGISTRADA
HECHO EN CHICAGO, U.S.A.

SIGNET, SIGNET CLASSIC, MENTOR, PLUME, MERIDIAN and NAL BOOKS are published by The New American Library, Inc., 1633 Broadway, New York, New York 10019

First Printing, January, 1984

1   2   3   4   5   6   7   8   9

PRINTED IN THE UNITED STATES OF AMERICA

To Sylvia Baker, Sharon Gasser, and
Deborah Lazio—for their friendship
and encouragement.

To Marilyn Norstedt—for her laughter.

To Mum—for her wellspring of confidence,

And,

To Brian—for all these things,
and more—with love.

M.M.H.

The Wind-Rose

Before the introduction of the magnetic needle, seafarers navigating the waters of the Mediterranean were forced to find their way from port to port by estimating from which direction the wind was blowing. The mariners of ancient Greece came to recognize the eight winds that prevailed in the Mediterranean and with time set their knowledge down in ink upon their navigational charts. What resulted was a diagram that indicated for any given place the frequency and force of the wind from various directions. Thus, if a mariner could distinguish the specific characteristics of a prevailing wind, he could refer to his sea chart and determine his relative position.

Through the centuries the diagram became known as a wind-rose.

Prologue

The house stood alone, a hoary sentinel amid an encroaching jungle of green, a bleak reminder of former greatness. In a third-story bedchamber the house's lone occupant shifted uncomfortably in his chair, his dark eyes fastened on the smoldering fire.

He had waited a long time, but now the end was near and his revenge would be sweet. Reading the brittle gray vellum for the last time, he carefully overlapped the edges and sealed it with a waxen glob which he imprinted with the family's stamp. Strange how his secret had remained intact all these years. It had been so obvious all the time, yet everyone had failed to make the connection.

Stupid fools, all of them.

Picking up a thin gold chain from the table beside him, he dangled it before his eyes, swinging the trinket attached to its length like a pendulum, slowly and rhythmically. The bauble was wrought in the whitest ivory—a dainty, many-petaled rose whose delicate whorls had graced the throat of a woman long ago. The tiny flower looked awkward hanging from the man's coarse fingers. Impulsively he caught it in the palm of his hand, smothering it in his massive fist.

Katy.

He wanted her to be beautiful. He wanted her to be soft and innocent and afraid. It was so much more exciting when they were afraid. He touched his hand to his bad eye—remembering. He intended that she should pay for all those years of misery. He intended that she should pay dearly.

On the hearth the last log disintegrated, scattering its bones amid the ash dunes. Narrowing his eyes at the death scene, he laughed aloud. After he had had his fill of her, she would undoubtedly beg for the same fate. And his laugh echoed in the hollow room for a long time after that, forcing even the birds nested on the window ledge to seek refuge from its hideous sound.

1

April 2, 1796

Between the years 1775–1815, war raged on the high seas for all but eleven years, and this year of 1796 was no exception. England and France were engaged in a bloody conflict for naval domination, and the United States, recuperating from the economic scars of a war of independence, was attempting to remain neutral in a world that had gone mad.

Unconcerned with the domestic problems of the Continent or the new nation abroad, a young girl reined in her stallion at the edge of a precipice whose tall shadow darkened the waters of the Atlantic below. As her right hand patted the ebony flesh of the horse's neck, her left slid unconsciously to her own neck to finger the ivory circlet that rested in the hollow of her throat. To a seafarer the design of the pendant would not have been unusual, for he would have known that the eight leaflike points studding the circle represented the eight points of a compass. But to the uninformed the necklace seemed both odd and incomplete, like miniature rays surrounding a nonexistent sun. The pendant reminded the girl of another time, in another place, before the ugliness and the dreams began, but memories of that other time inevitably ended in sadness, so she tried not to think about the significance of the bauble, only of its cool surface lying against her throat, where she intended it should always remain.

With eyes the color of green apples, long and almond-shaped, devoid of the extraneous flecks of brown or gray that would mar their purity, she scanned the horizon. Where sky abutted sea, a speck of white like a far-off gull flickered distantly, disappeared, then appeared again and held form. Curious, the girl slid down from her saddle, her long hair intertwining with her palfrey's glossy mane so that she seemed but an extension of that magnificent black beast. What she saw was not a giant bird but the topsails of some sailing ship. Pirates heading for the Strait of Gibraltar? She realized that here, on the coast of Cádiz, she and her relatives were susceptible to attack, but she also remembered her uncle saying that such great wealth flowed on the open sea, the pirates would not concern themselves with petty coastal

11

raids. He had assured them they were safe from the heathen Barbary corsairs.

But could she be assured that she was safe from her uncle?

She scratched the stallion's soft velvet muzzle.

He had touched her today—again. It had been so subtle. A hand placed jovially on her shoulder when there had been no reason to touch. And it had lingered there as he laughed, lingered almost possessively until she felt its warmth penetrate her skin and she had pulled away, terrified.

She rubbed her cheek against the offended shoulder as if that motion would erase any hint of the man's violation. Involuntarily she shivered, not only at the thought of her uncle's touch, but also, as always, at the thought of being touched by any man.

In the distance the miniature sheets of canvas bellied steadily in the wind, speeding the approach of the incoming vessel.

"What are you suggesting?" the man asked his wife.

Carolyn Astruc paced before her husband. "You and I will not live forever, José. What will happen when we are no longer here to protect her? Good Lord, she will be eighteen in June and shows no signs of outgrowing this . . . this . . ." The woman made a helpless gesture with her hand. "She's such a solitary creature. In all the years she has been with us I have never known her to seek either solace or companionship. She smiles so rarely, laughs so rarely . . . I've never even seen her cry."

The man plucked at the threads of his armchair. "As usual, you are exaggerating the situ—"

"Do you think this is the kind of life her mother would have wanted for her? Do you think it's normal for the child to shun every social situation while other girls her age are getting married and bearing children?"

José Astruc deliberately avoided his wife's eyes.

"It is time to end this self-imposed seclusion of hers. We will introduce her to suitable young men, and by the end of the year, I expect her to be married."

At the thought of his niece in the arms of another man, José felt a knot begin to twist in the pit of his stomach and gradually work its way downward until it wrenched painfully in his loins. "Is it not her father's responsibility to find her a husband?"

Carolyn walked to the window and drew aside the heavy drapery. "Her father has shirked all responsibility for her for the past fifteen years. Why should he wish to change his ways now?"

In the oppressive silence that followed, Carolyn saw her husband's image reflected in the glass as he stood and took his leave, too appalled by her suggestion to utter a word in parting. The woman shook her head.

Do you think me unaware of the reason for your hesitation, José? I know why you will be opposed to my suggestion. You want her for yourself. Surprised that I know? You shouldn't be, unless you think that marriage to you rendered me stupid as well as miserable. I can see the heat in your eyes when you gaze upon her. But if you had her all to yourself, what would you do with your other mistresses, José? Indeed, what would you do with me? I deserved better than you, my dear husband. Mary Kathleen will have better.

Mary Kathleen Ryan had been born in Yorktown, Virginia, on June 11, 1778, seven months after her parents, Kathryn Leary and Matthew Ryan, had wed. Two months premature, she was a scrawny little thing, all red and wrinkled, with a thatch of blue-black hair that rivaled the color of night. When her eyes finally opened wider than a squint, she revealed to her family irises that were the most remarkable shade of green. Cat's eyes, they called them, too unnatural to be human. Stranger still, the relatives could recall none of her ancestors who had ever boasted eyes of a similar color.

As she grew into childhood, the thatch of curly hair that capped her head lengthened into a cascade of long black curls, and the eyes that had been round at birth became longer, more almond-shaped, and fringed with thick feathery lashes. Her father spent much of his time away from their rambling tobacco plantation, but when he returned he would usually present her with a stick doll he had whittled, so Katy learned to accept his long absences with childish greed. She never asked where he went, but she noticed that when he was away, her mother often took long rides about the countryside, returning pale and reflective and not at all in a mood for laughter. Once she overheard one of the kitchen slaves whisper, "Musta seed *him* agin," and though Katy had no idea who the "him" was, she knew that behind the door of her mother's bedchamber there were sounds of muffled crying and tears.

By the end of age two she had become quite adept at eavesdropping on the kitchen servants, and one day she learned of Seth Aldrich, the man who made her mother cry. It seemed that when Kathryn Leary was younger, she had fallen in love with Aldrich, a northern ship master who had married the daughter of a neighboring plantation owner. After two years of marriage the captain's wife died, and Seth Aldrich, having no interest in a tobacco plantation or two squalling sons, left the infants in

13

the care of his unmarried sister and took to roaming the high seas once again. On one of his infrequent visits back to Yorktown, he met by chance Kathryn Leary, and the sight of the lithe, translucently blue-eyed blond was enough to send tantalizing thoughts of marriage back into his head. His sons were attending schools in New England, his sister was managing the plantation—there was no reason why he should not marry again.

Kathryn's father, Michael Leary, was not enthusiastic about the proposed union, but he finally agreed to give his elder daughter in marriage to the elusive Captain Aldrich, for if there was one thing that Leary had learned throughout the years, it was that in the end, he could deny Kathryn and her younger sister, Carolyn, nothing. The betrothal date was set for a year hence, an ample amount of time for a Southern lady to prepare for the event, but much too much time for Aldrich to be around his fiancée without having his way with her. He decided upon a short jaunt to the Mediterranean—his last, he promised her.

Months passed.

The wedding day came and went.

Seth Aldrich did not return—not that year, nor the following year, nor the year after that.

After enduring four years of his daughter's bereavement, Michael Leary, in ill health and intent upon having at least one of his daughters married before he died, introduced Kathryn to Matthew Ryan, a young merchant from New Orleans, who, though not wealthy and certainly not the handsome rascal that Aldrich was, was nonetheless ambitious and, at least, Irish. With Kathryn's lethargic approval, another wedding date was set.

Michael Leary did not live long enough to see his daughter married, but he had the foresight to make her promise that she would abide by his wishes and marry Matthew Ryan. Unwilling but dutiful, Kathryn promised and two days later laid her father to rest.

Several weeks before the wedding, a French brigantine sailed into Yorktown harbor with a cargo of wine, brandy, and Seth Aldrich. He was a man changed drastically, a man whose spirit seemed to have been broken by the Algerian corsairs who had captured his ship and made him a slave aboard one of their vessels. His dark hair was streaked with white, his eyes pained and secretive. He stooped forward as he walked, as if he were still crouching away from the lash of a whip. Having been freed by the French, he told Kathryn he had no other wish than to settle in Yorktown and salve his wounds. But before he could discuss his intentions, Matthew Ryan appeared, and if ever two men hated each other at a glance, it was these two. Threats were

14

exchanged both ways—Ryan promising death to Aldrich if he ever spoke to Kathryn again, Aldrich promising revenge on Ryan if he went ahead with his planned marriage.

But the wedding did take place, and seven months later a baby girl was born, a child whom Seth Aldrich did not see until he was sent word that Ryan was away on one of his trips. The Yankee captain paid his respects to Kathryn and the baby, and if, when he left, he was smiling with a smugness that betokened a secret revenge, no one ever mentioned it. After that time, however, the baby was seen to have acquired a new possession—a circlet of white ivory studded with eight leafy petals, the rosebud center of which hung at her mother's throat. The two charms, when coupled on a single chain, formed a seafarer's wind-rose.

Katy never heard the slaves mention the name of Seth Aldrich again—not until the day she found her mother lying at the foot of the central staircase in a pool of blood. Screaming, the child had run to the mother, cradling the blond head in her arms, rocking it back and forth mindlessly. She was not aware of the commotion that erupted around her. Her father raced through the front door, and elbowing his way through the gathering throng of house slaves, came to stand over his wife.

"Who did this to you, Kathryn? Who?"

The woman's lips parted to whisper, "Seth."

Matthew Ryan was like a wild man as he smashed open the glass of his gun rack and grabbed his flintlock rifle and powder horn. At the foot of the stairs Kathryn Ryan died in her daughter's arms while Katy rocked back and forth, back and forth, oblivious of everything except the spreading scarlet stain on her mother's dress.

The inquiry into the deaths of Kathryn Ryan and Seth Aldrich was brief. Although the constable did not condone Ryan's taking the law into his own hands and splattering Seth Aldrich's face into the far corners of the Aldrich stables, he nevertheless conceded the fact of the captain's guilt and acquitted Matthew Ryan of any wrongdoing. In time the gossip subsided and life returned to normal—everyone's life, that is, except Katy's.

Since the day of her mother's death she had not spoken a word. Her waking hours were spent in her bedchamber, her knees beneath her, hands clutched to her arms, eyes fixed blankly, her thin body rocking back and forth incessantly, as if she still held the weight of her mother's body in her lap. Matthew Ryan had said to let the child be, that she would be all right if left alone. But as the weeks passed, she simply drew more into herself until even the servants began to balk at having to serve her, thinking that she had become possessed by some devil spirit. The care of the child thus passed to Carolyn Leary. Often, deep in the night, Carolyn was awakened by the child's piercing screams, but when she attempted to offer comfort, Katy would become cold and unresponsive, not wishing to be touched, only to drift back into the throes of another nightmare and wake screaming again.

By July 1781, with the English Army firmly entrenched at Yorktown and with war imminent, Ryan sent his sister-in-law and daughter south to await the outcome of the offensive, little knowing that by the time General Cornwallis signed the terms of surrender, shy Carolyn would have fallen in love and accepted a proposal of marriage from a young Spanish wine merchant. When she wrote to her brother-in-law, informing him of her intention to become Mrs. José Astruc and of the need for him to send someone to Savannah for Katy, Ryan replied that since Carolyn loved the child, and he was unable to cope with his daughter in her present state of mind, would Carolyn please take the child to Spain with her?

So Mary Kathleen Ryan, at age four, arrived on Spanish soil with a new set of parents and found herself occupying a strange house whose dark wood and heavy furnishings were completely alien and whose inhabitants spoke an unintelligible language. But Mary Kathleen did not voice her misgivings. She merely rocked, and stared, remembering nothing.

Carolyn Astruc turned away from the window, her vision impaired for the briefest moment by a fog that settled over her eyes—a fog that had been appearing with ever-increasing regularity over the past few months. She reached out her hand for the windowsill and only after she had steadied herself did she notice the tiny figure standing in the doorway. She would have to find a solution for Katy soon, or the child's fate would be left to José. . . .

"Katy? How long have you been standing there?"

One delicately arched eyebrow slanted downward in concern. "Are you all right?"

Carolyn laughed off her dizziness. "Just the sun, dear. It blinded me for a moment." Having regained both her balance and her composure, she paced slowly toward the doorway. The look of apprehension distorting her niece's features startled her. "Now it's my turn. Is something wrong?"

"A ship has just laid anchor off the cove. Not pirate," the girl added, responding to the alarm in her aunt's eyes. "They raised a flag. Red, white, and blue—with stars and horizontal stripes. American?"

Carolyn looked bewildered. "Possibly. But what would an American ship be doing in these waters, fair game for the French *and* the British?" She shrugged. "If it *is* a Yankee vessel, it has traveled a long distance to find us. I should imagine we'll learn of its reason for being here rather quickly."

Sometime later, Katy found her aunt and uncle in the study. José was brandishing a piece of parchment in the air while rapid-firing a stream of Spanish at his wife, who looked up and smiled as her niece entered the room.

"I would show you the message from the ship's master if José would stop talking long enough to hand the note to me."

Katy's lips curled in amusement. Her uncle possessed an ego of enormous proportions and would not take kindly to his wife's jibe. He was a man of slight stature, slender-bodied and short-legged, with a face as long and sharp as a weasel's. His dark hair glistened with oil, as did his skin, and Katy had wondered more than once what it was that had attracted her aunt to the man.

José did not dignify his wife with a reply to her comment, but merely dropped the paper into her lap and went to pour himself a drink. Seating herself beside her aunt, Katy held the parchment in her hands and began to read.

The message was addressed to her uncle, by name, and stated that there was a matter of some consequence that the ship's master would like to discuss with him and asked if it would be convenient if he called upon Señor Astruc at some later hour. The note was signed "Jason MacAuley, Master, Ship *Elizabeth*, Virginia."

Katy did not react so much to the message as she did to the handwriting of the man who had penned it. His words were written in bold black script, each letter formed precisely, almost arrogantly, with long, even strokes that, in their simplicity, mocked the curly embellishments that characterized her uncle's script. There was strength in the writing—a strength and power that her uncle would never know.

"Rather cryptic, wouldn't you say?" Carolyn asked.

Katy's gaze stopped at the last word on the page. "Virginia." The implication was obvious. "My father."

"The thought had occurred to me, but I imagine there are many ships originating from Virginia."

"But why would just *any* ship from Virginia moor here?" She handed the message back to her aunt. "I won't go back there. My father sent me away. I'll never forget that, and I'll never go back."

"I doubt that you will ever have to, dear. But we owe it to this Captain MacAuley to at least hear what he has to say."

The master of the ship *Elizabeth* appeared toward early evening, his darkly clad figure detaching itself from the other fluid shadows that roamed the hallway. He stepped into the light of the study with self-assured grace, and after removing his tricorn hat, tipped his head and extended his hand to José, who had popped up from his chair like a frightened bird.

"Jason MacAuley, sir. I assume you are Señor Astruc." His voice was spellbinding, rich and deeply resonant, his words rolling with an easy cadence and swelling the room with mellow, hypnotic sound.

José accepted the captain's hand and cringed as his fingers were crushed in the man's grip. "I had thought the maid would announce your arrival, Captain. You caught us rather unawares." Cowed by the man's presence, José groped for something to say until he was struck by the obvious. "May I introduce my family? My wife, Carolyn." He gestured to the settee where his wife sat very much in awe of their visitor.

Jason MacAuley bent over the hand which Carolyn Astruc extended to him, and brought it to his lips. "Señora." The word escaped in a throaty whisper that left her skin warm from his breath.

José cleared his throat. "And this is my niece, Mary Kathleen Ryan."

That the captain appeared startled by this revelation was evident to no one except Katy, for his look of sudden astonishment vanished almost as quickly as it had appeared.

"Miss Ryan." He grinned, bowing his head. He assessed her with one long sweep of his left eye—the right eye was concealed beneath a patch of soft black leather that slashed across his face like a grisly scar. He stood a head taller than her uncle; probably head and shoulders over herself. His hair was as black as his eye patch, thick and windblown. The dark planes of his face were angular, his chin well defined and impressed with a shallow cleft. The brows that arched above his eyes were handsomely shaped. His nose was narrow-bridged; in profile, straight, thinly boned, and so finely formed that it seemed almost delicate, a paradoxical feature on so rugged a face. His facial features bespoke an ancestry of both strength and delicacy, yet it was his one eye—the eye that was cast in the rich brown stain of warm earth—that frightened her. There was steel and stone in the dark core of that eye, and Katy judged that it would remain cool and unflinching whether its owner was killing a man or taking a woman. She searched for inner calm as the man continued to scrutinize her, but she found only the shadow of fear that had stalked her since childhood.

"If you gentlemen have business to discuss, perhaps Aunt Carolyn and I should leave." Her voice was breathless in her haste to be gone.

Jason MacAuley's voice prevented her from rising. "I think you may have found my message somewhat misleading, Miss Ryan. My business concerns you primarily. You will want to remain to hear what I have to say." Uninvited, he seated himself in the chair opposite her. He was dressed in formal attire—neckcloth and ruffled shirt, coat, waistcoat, and breeches—all in black save for the shirt and cravat. Katy thought him properly funereal. When he wasn't commanding a ship, he probably conducted black masses.

"It has been assigned to me to inform you of some rather tragic news, Miss Ryan." José came to hover behind his wife and niece. "It happened over two years ago—in a fire, I'm told. Your father was trapped inside. I regret to inform you that . . . Matthew Ryan is dead."

Of all the tidings she might have expected, it was not this. She had thought that what he divulged would have some import on her life. But news of the death of a man who was a stranger to her in no way affected her security. "My father is dead? Is that the only reason you are here, Captain? To tell me of my father's death?"

Jason reclined into the cushions of his chair. He had expected a tear or two, a sniffle. What was she made of? Ice?

"Nay. There is more." He reached into the inside pocket of his coat and withdrew a square of gray vellum. "Your father's widow, your stepmother, Pamela, has commissioned me to transport you back to Virginia. I assure you, this situation pleases me not one whit. 'Tis bad luck to have a woman aboard ship, but your stepmother drives a very hard bargain." A scowl passed over his face. "One which I could not afford to refuse." Leaning forward, he handed the parchment to Katy. "This is from Mrs. Ryan. I believe it explains why she thought it necessary to send for you."

His eye lingered on her as she broke the wax seal, examining the girl whose name he had loathed for most of the thirty-two years of his life. She possessed a lovely face, but her body was no temptation, appearing to be that of a young girl. Her gown was high-collared and long-sleeved. Her hair was pulled away from her face and caught at the crown with a long white satin ribbon. She seemed the epitome of youthful innocence.

Katy unfolded the parchment and set it on her lap, her hands shaking too badly to hold it. Slowly she began to read:

My dearest Mary Kathleen,

It grieves me that our first correspondence should be linked with so much sadness. Your dear father passed away before we had finalized the arrangements for your return home, but he would be so pleased to know that I had carried out his final wishes even in his absence. He was in the process of arranging your marriage when he died, and thanks to the groom's kindness (and eagerness, I might add), I have been able to reach an agreement that I feel will be acceptable to all parties involved. I am sure you will find the young man most appealing, Mary.

To see this end accomplished, I have promised Captain MacAuley a handsome purse to ensure that you are safely returned to me. It will be so delightful preparing you for your marriage. Matthew said that it was only fitting that you should marry one of your own kind and not some foreigner.

I look forward to your homecoming with eager anticipation.

Godspeed,
Pamela Ryan

Katy read the missive once, then once again, more quickly. Her stomach bunched into tight knots. Wide-eyed, she stared at her aunt, who, seeing the girl's sudden horror, removed the letter from her lap and read through it rapidly. Katy fought with a lump in her throat that could not decide whether it wanted to go up or down.

" 'Tis a joke." Her voice was barely audible as her aunt handed the parchment to José. "How can she think that I would want to travel to America, much less marry someone my father had chosen for me? I owe the memory of Matthew Ryan nothing, and his wife even less. The woman is mad. And *you*, Captain MacAuley . . ." She turned on him. "How could you be a party to any of this? How could you be so mercenary? Well, I fear that the 'handsome purse' you were promised will remain just that—a promise. I have no intentions of accompanying you. Marriage! Does she not know how absurd that is? I seriously doubt if the arrangement would be 'acceptable to all parties involved.' I seriously doubt if my husband would be thrilled with the wife he would be bound to for the rest of his life. I wonder if he would have agreed to the marriage with such eagerness if he knew that I . . ."

She stopped, realizing that she had already said too much, and rose to her feet.

Politely Jason rose with her.

"I would like to say it has been a pleasure, Captain. But it has not."

"Katy!" Carolyn was mortified.

Displaying no sign of repentance, Katy locked eyes with the captain. "It appears we are all suffering from ill manners this evening, sir. Lest you be exposed to further discourtesy on my part, I think it wise that I remove myself from your presence. Now, if you'll excuse me. . . ." She had reached the portal before he called out after her.

"My ship leaves tomorrow on the afternoon tide, Miss Ryan. I expect you to be on it." Lowered in warning, his voice was ominous, but she ignored the authority in its tone and continued her retreat without a backward glance.

José rounded the settee and plunked himself down in the spot that Katy had vacated. "It is quite impossible, Captain."

Jason looked up, impaling him with that one eye. "I don't know what you mean, señor."

"It is impossible that Mary Kathleen leave here."

"Indeed?" Jason frowned. "And why is that, sir?"

"Well, she . . . she is too young, for one reason. Too young for marriage and too young to be exposed to the kind of men who are probably aboard your ship."

The captain's dark complexion colored a shade deeper. "And just what kind of men do you think are aboard my ship, sir?"

"We are both men, Captain." He smiled suggestively. "We both know what happens to men who haven't had a woman for a long time."

"I'm not sure I do." Jason's eyebrow cocked at an odd angle. "Why don't you enlighten me?"

José stiffened. "Come, now, Captain. You are playing games with me."

The Yankee shook his head, rubbed the back of his neck with his hand. "I do not play games, señor. I am being paid to perform a service, and although I can sympathize with your feelings, I think it only fair to tell you that if you do not allow the child to come with me now—"

"She is almost eighteen, Captain," Carolyn interrupted.

He seemed taken aback by this, but only for a moment. "Eighteen? She is so . . . small, I thought her much younger." He hesitated thoughtfully. "But as I was saying, if she does not accompany me now, her stepmother will only send someone else after her later. Pamela is quite adamant about having the girl brought to Yorktown. She seems to think that she has legal authority over the child . . . uh . . . girl," he corrected.

José crossed his arms. "Out of the question. She remains here

21

with us. And if you are worried about losing your purse, Captain, I will double any amount that Pamela promised you in order to keep my niece here."

Carolyn absorbed the shock of this statement with outward calm.

"I commend you for your persistence, señor, but as you know, that is not how a gentleman conducts business. I gave my word to Pamela Ryan that I would return her stepdaughter, and I mean to keep my word."

José brought himself to his feet. "There is no point in discussing the matter any further, Captain. Tomorrow you will leave without my niece. Now, I will show you to the door."

"Sherry, Captain MacAuley?" Carolyn could maintain her silence no longer. This tall, brawny sea captain might be the solution to her problem.

José shot his wife an angry look, which she ignored. "We have concluded our business, Carolyn."

"The captain is entitled to a glass of sherry for his trouble," she countered.

As one, husband and wife riveted their eyes on Jason for his answer.

The grooves that bisected his cheeks deepened. "I believe I will have that glass of sherry, señora. It has been a most trying day."

José nodded coldly. "You will pardon me if I do not join you. My wife will see you out later, Captain. Good evening."

The Yankee grinned at the sound of the man's fading footsteps. "I have already offended two members of your family, Mrs. Astruc. Are you not afraid I will do the same to you?"

"Not at all, Captain." She laughed. Rising, she walked to a side table and poured him a drink.

He accepted the glass from her and took a sip, then nodded favorably. "It's very good. From your husband's vineyard?"

She sat back down. "Of course! José cultivates the best everything—grapes, horses . . . women. But I did not ask you to stay to discuss my husband, Captain. Tell me about yourself. Where are you from?"

"A small area on the northeastern coast of Massachusetts called Frenchman Bay. I live on one of the islands in the bay. Mount Desert Island, specifically."

"And do you have . . . family there?"

He swirled the red-brown liquid around in his glass. "I am not married, Mrs. Astruc, if that is what you are referring to."

"Now I fear I have offended *you*, Captain." She laughed. "Forgive me for prying. Perhaps I should change the subject."

22

He did not object.

"Maybe I should try to explain about my niece. She is a very special person, Captain. When she was very young, she found my sister murdered, and I'm afraid she has never fully recovered from the shock. She suffers terrible nightmares, has suffered them for years, though she never mentions them." The woman stared into her glass. "After her mother's death, she didn't utter one word for over three years, and when she finally did start speaking, José and I created a shell around her. We thought only to protect her, but the shell became a prison, and now she wears it like a second skin."

As Jason brought his glass to his lips, Carolyn noted how his hand caressed the delicate crystal, how at ease he seemed with its fragility, as though he were accustomed to handling fine things and had tempered his rugged hand to gentleness. Unbidden, she felt herself quicken.

"I am undoubtedly boring you with my problems, Captain. Why don't we discuss your voyage. Will you be sailing directly back to Yorktown?"

"Not directly. From here we sail to Madeira to take on a cargo of wine; then we'll make passage to Bombay, Madras, and Calcutta."

"You're bound for the East Indies?" She was incredulous.

"Aye."

"Then exactly how long will it be until you *do* return to Virginia?"

The Yankee captain calculated rapidly. "I would say anywhere from eight months to a year."

"A year? You expect my niece to remain on your ship for an entire year? Unchaperoned?"

"I am well aware of the discomforts that a young girl will have to endure on a long sea voyage, madam. However, might I remind you that it was not I who thought up this bit of lunacy. I cannot alter my destination to please Pamela Ryan, or your niece, or you. I have already taken considerable risk by coming here in the first place. And as for the matter of your niece's being unchaperoned, she will be under my protection and I will look upon her as but another hogshead of wine."

Carolyn smiled. She doubted that the captain would very long look upon the girl and see a hogshead of wine. At that moment, she made an impulsive decision. Would it not be better to send Katy away from this place now, while there was still time? Surely Pamela Ryan was less threatening than José. And would it not be better to entrust her to the hands of a man who had vowed to see her safely home than to the unreliable hands of fate? Perhaps this

Yankee's seeming gentility might even leave the girl's attitude toward males in general, enabling her to accept the love that a man might nurture for her someday. Captain MacAuley seemed a man capable of miracles, and anything could happen in a year.

"You say you leave on the morrow's tide, Captain MacAuley?"

"Aye."

"Then I will see to it that my niece is prepared to leave with you."

His brows drew together. "A change of heart, madam?"

"If you will remember correctly, sir, it was my husband who spoke his disapproval. I never voiced my opinion in the matter."

"And you think your husband will concur with your decision?"

"My husband is a fool, Captain, and it matters little to me whether a fool agrees or disagrees with me."

"You are a brave woman, Mrs. Astruc."

"Nay, Captain. Only a little desperate." To his look of confusion she made no reply, but rather, seeing that his glass was empty, stood up. "Will you do us the honor of spending the night with us?"

"How can I decline such a tempting offer? Do you know how long it has been since I slept in a bed that did not pitch and roll with the rhythm of the sea?"

"And perhaps a hot bath?"

"Ah, lady! Throw a mellow cheroot in with that and I will be your servant for life."

"Follow me, Captain, and I'll show you to your room."

In her bedchamber Katy paced like a caged lion. She would not go. It was beyond her comprehension how her father had had the audacity to select a husband for her when he had ignored her existence for almost fifteen years. He had probably needed her as collateral in some business venture, and now Pamela was taking over where he had left off. Well, they could all go to the devil, because she was going nowhere.

She yanked the ribbon from her hair and threw it on the vanity, her hair parting naturally in the middle and falling in seductive waves around her face. Rather than call one of the maids to help her undress, she fumbled with the hooks on the back of her gown herself, ripping out several before she was able to wiggle out of it. Her chemise followed, and then came the arduous task of unwinding the roll of cotton cloth that bound her chest.

She had heard the stableboys talking one day—about her. And they were making lewd gestures with their hands, cupping them before their chests, and laughing loudly. Since that day she had hidden the object of their sport beneath a long remnant of material that she wound round her bosom until it was as flat as a child's. The encumbrance was far from comfortable, but if it meant that she would no longer be subjected to jeers and ridicule, she would continue to wear it.

As she unraveled the last yard of cotton, the breasts that had been so sorely constrained came free. Compared to the slightness of the rest of her body, her breasts were heavy, curving outward with absolute symmetry, and peaked with areolae of sensuous color like pools of claret.

Slipping into a gauzy nightgown, she stood at the balcony door. In the harbor the square-rigger lay at anchor, immersed in the shadows of night, its red and green side lights and mainmast lantern winking their presence like ugly eyes. She wrinkled her nose at the scene, then, after opening the glass-paned door a crack, turned toward her bed. Tomorrow afternoon the thing would be gone, and good riddance. Extinguishing her candle, she climbed beneath the covers. The moon was not yet up, so about her, all was blackness. She buried her head beneath her pillow and shivered, trying not to think about it.

She found herself in a long corridor, walking toward a door at the far end of the hall, her slippers making a soft pattering sound that echoed in the emptiness surrounding her. But it seemed that the more she walked, the farther away the door became. She quickened her pace to shorten the distance, and it was then that she became faintly aware of another sound in the narrow hall— the evenly paced sound of footsteps.

She stopped to listen more closely, not daring to turn around, and heard the thud of footsteps become louder and more rapid. And then, mixed with the pounding of footfalls, came a low moan which seemed to be calling her name, a voice coming not from behind her, but from the door before her.

"Mama?"

"Here, Katy! Where are you?"

"Mama!"

Hearing the footsteps almost upon her, she started running down the hall, trying to reach the safety of her mother. "Mama," she shrieked. "Mama!" Hot tears stained her cheeks. Beads of sweat pricked her forehead. The footsteps echoed. Louder. Faster. Their thuds boomed in her ears.

Faster, she screamed to herself. *Run faster.*

With her eyes blinded by sweat and tears and her heart pounding in her throat, she gained the door, lunged for the handle. Her wrist was manacled by a hand with a grip like iron. About to scream, she was struck by a second hand that clamped itself over her mouth and pinched her nostrils, bruising her lips and cutting off her breath.

She felt herself suffocating, dying, drifting into abysmal blackness.

Katy shot bolt upright in bed, a strangulated scream ringing in her throat. The room was dark save for a shaft of moonlight streaming across the floor. Her eyes swept round the room, desperately searching for familiar objects, and only when her hand touched the ivory charm at her throat did she realize that she was in her own room and the nightmare had ended.

She threw her covers off and hugged her legs to herself, pressing her forehead against her knees. When would it stop? When would the dream ever stop haunting her? How she hated the night and her body's need for sleep. How she loathed these nightly visitations of the footsteps, and the voice, and the man's hand across her face. Trembling, she wiped away thin rivulets of water that trickled down her neck, brushed her hand across her moist brow, feeling her hair spring into tiny ringlets around her face.

Getting up, she made her way across the floor and walked out onto the balcony, where the cool ocean breeze chilled the moisture on her flesh to frosty pinpricks. She leaned over the balustrade, burying her face in her hands. Aboard the *Elizabeth* a bell clanked a discordant note that diffused on broken wings into the night.

"It appears that we have been given adjoining rooms, Miss Ryan."

The girl spun around in the direction of the man's voice. Jason MacAuley leaned against the low railing, the stub of a cigar jammed between his teeth, its fiery tip glowing hotly.

"Forgive me for intruding, but I thought I heard something."

She stared in awe as he left the railing and strode toward her. Minus his neckcloth and jabot, his white linen shirt was opened to his waist, revealing a chest that was heavily muscled and matted with black hair. Beneath his shirt his shoulders were wide and thickened with powerful sinew, and even more overpowering than the aroma of his tobacco was the smell that clung to his body—of lightly scented soap, and warmth. As he stood towering above her, she became vividly aware of his commanding physical presence and leaned back against the balustrade.

"I heard a scream." He placed his forefinger beneath her chin and lifted her head to meet his gaze. "Yours?"

Katy brushed his hand from her face. "What are you doing here?"

"Your aunt was kind enough to offer me a soft bed for the night." He hooked his thumb into the waistband of his breeches. She observed his gesture, lending a passing glance to the lean tendons outlined beneath the dark flesh of his stomach. "Do you object?"

Her eyes lengthened to slits. "I find your very presence in this house offensive, Captain. I can only pray that the afternoon tide will arrive quickly so that your departure will be hastened by some small degree."

Jason threw his head back and bellowed with laughter. "And perhaps you could tell me how one so small has cultivated so sharp a tongue? I certainly hope your stepmother has not been expounding your quiet virtues to your future husband, Miss Ryan, for I am afraid he will be sorely disappointed."

She drew back her hand to lay it hard across his face at his mockery, but was thwarted as he caught her wrist in midair, wrapping his fingers so tightly about her that her hand numbed. She flinched at the sudden pain and let out a soft cry.

"You're hurting me, Captain." She squirmed in his grasp, glaring into the eye that had blackened like a storm cloud.

With his fingers still imprinting their mark upon her skin, he spoke to her, unsmilingly, a restrained edge to his voice. "I wouldn't try that again if I were you."

He released her hand with a jerk.

As she pulled her arm to her chest and rubbed the circulation back into her wrist and hand, he regarded her unbound hair. It framed her face like a sable hood and flowed sensuously over her shoulders, fanning itself over the swell of her breast. And at this observation his eye widened.

Holy Christ! How could she have hidden something like that?

The nightgown, though voluminous, dipped low enough to reveal a rise of pale flesh, and hung in such a way as to cause the cold peaks of her nipples to become clearly silhouetted against the buff-colored gauze, evoking tantalizing images of what lay beneath. How mistaken he had been in his earlier judgment of her. Quite unexpectedly he found himself responding to the woman who had been disguised in the child's body, suffering a pull on his vitals that reminded him of his continence in these past several weeks. He scowled, realizing that what the girl's uncle had intimated had not been so far from the truth after all. And the very fact that his own lusty reaction had been foretold by that slimy Spaniard made him angrier still. Thankful for the cloak of night to mask his condition, he drew deeply on his cigar.

A year? They expect me to be cooped up with this girl for twelve whole months without laying a finger on her?

He cleared his throat. "You never answered my question, Miss Ryan. Did you scream?"

"I was asleep, Captain. I have no idea what I do when I am so occupied."

"I will tell you, then. You scream. And quite loudly."

"Do you always make a habit of eavesdropping at bedchamber doors? If no one has been kind enough to inform you, 'tis a rude practice."

He gritted teeth that were white as snowdrops. She thought he would fling some terse rejoinder at her, but instead he reached out his hand toward her neck. She stiffened with tension as he set the back of his hand against her skin, balancing the ivory circlet at her throat atop two fingers.

"A wind-rose, lady? 'Tis a strange rendering. Have you somehow misplaced the rose?"

She paused, looking as if she had never before contemplated the whereabouts of the necklace's mate. "My mother used to wear the other half. I don't know what became of it after her death."

When the hand that lingered at the base of her throat made no attempt to move, she looked askance, trying to ignore the current that his touch sent through her body, for there was fire in his blood and she could feel its warmth.

"Do I make you nervous, Miss Ryan?" He grinned. Releasing the necklace, he ran the knuckle of his forefinger down the curve of her neck. "You will have to become accustomed to a man's touch, once you are married."

"Hardly, Captain. I have no intention of marrying any man." She quickly brushed past him.

The grooves reappeared in his cheeks as he looked over his shoulder at her. "We shall see, Miss Ryan." And as she closed the door behind her, she could not help but feel strangely chilled by the words.

After lighting a candle, she climbed back into bed, and though she would never admit it, the last thoughts she had before falling into a fitful sleep were to wonder how the captain had lost his eye and what he looked like without the patch.

At first light, after speaking to Carolyn Astruc, Jason MacAuley rowed out to the square-rigger *Elizabeth*. Carolyn was faced with a more difficult task, and as she stood outside her niece's bedchamber, she tried to decide what she would tell the girl. Her approach would have to be harsh. Katy would never leave willingly, and certainly not if she knew of her aunt's ill health, so Carolyn was going to lie, using words that would hurt both of them.

When there was no response to her knock, she opened the door and poked her head in. "Katy?"

The small lump in the middle of the bed remained inert. Carolyn closed the door behind her. "Katy."

Turtlelike, the girl's head emerged from beneath its shell of blankets. "Morning already?" She stifled a slow yawn.

"I have to talk to you, Katy." Carolyn seated herself on the corner of the bed, hating herself for what she was about to say. "I've decided that it would be best if you went with Captain MacAuley."

The sleepy green eyes flew open. Katy's lips parted, but she found no words to force between them.

"You are no longer a child, Katy, but for almost fifteen years I have coddled you, and cosseted you, and allowed you to do exactly as you please. Not once during that entire time have you said, 'Thank you, Aunt Carolyn.' If all children take and take and give nothing in return as you have, then perhaps my barrenness is not the catastrophe I once thought it. I have practically given you my soul, and frankly, I have nothing left to offer. I'm tired, and I don't want to be bothered with you any longer. That is why you will leave with Captain MacAuley today."

The girl shook her head, disbelieving. "You cannot mean it."

"Oh, yes, dear. I mean every word of it, and your uncle is quite in agreement with me," she lied. "The opportunity for you to leave is upon us, and we want you to take it. We want you to leave."

The assault drew fresh blood. Katy felt tears welling up in the corners of her eyes. Yet she was proud—too proud to display her hurt. "You would have me marry a man I have never seen?"

"No need to bother yourself about that, dear. When the gentleman discovers how utterly lacking you are in the domestic arts, I doubt that he will have you. I think everyone will be happy to let you grow into spinsterhood." *Oh, Katy, forgive me for saying such terrible things.*

Keeping her voice purposefully hard to deter her own tears, Carolyn stood up. "I will return in a short time to start packing your things. Find something else to occupy your time in the coming hours. You'd only be in the way here." She had to say that. Having Katy underfoot would remind her of the cruelty she had mouthed, and that would be unbearable.

"Get up, now. I have too much to do today to be indulgent with you."

The door closed quietly.

The girl's wound took root in the base of her throat and grew upward, strangling her vocal cords. The tears remained unshed. The breath she drew was hollow, and a throbbing knot began to vibrate in her throat as her aunt's words spun a tangled web in her mind.

I don't want to be bothered with you any longer.

The fearsome stallion that hurtled Mary Kathleen Ryan along in reckless flight from the house pounded the earth with hooves of iron. For endless miles she tore along the path that circuited the cliff's edge, burning the turf with her agony. The wind slammed into her face, scalding her cheeks and eyes, stinging, as her aunt's words had stung.

We want you to leave.

Biting her lip, she focused unblinkingly on the path before her, and when the horse began to lather, she slowed to a canter. In a spot far removed from the Astruc estate and the Yankee ship, she stopped, as breathless as her steed. She leaned forward across his neck, pressing her cheek to his mane, while from the corner of her eye a teardrop floated outward, staining her cheek and the horse's mane with unaccustomed moisture.

"I don't know *how* to say thank you," she whispered. "I don't even know how to tell Aunt Carolyn that I love her. And I *do* love her. . . ." Her early, shock-induced withdrawal had left her cold and aloof and she had never expressed the gentler emotions that were locked within her. She had thought there would be years to resolve her deep-seated terror, years to reshape her life. But the years had become minutes that, even now, eroded with the incoming tide. I probably deserve to be sent away, she thought, but the hurt and pain of this rejection seared her to the bone, leaving her as bereft and alone as the small child she had once been.

Long before the appointed time of departure, Katy was on the beach attempting to quell nerves and nausea and to simulate bravery. For the space of an hour she watched the great masted vessel, cursing it and the tide that was spilling into the cove, whitewashing the beach with frothy curls of seawater. At last, when the long expanse of beach had diminished to a narrow sandbar that defined the high-water mark, she saw two figures climb over the side of the *Elizabeth* and descend into a smaller ship's boat. The oars plunged through the water effortlessly, relentlessly. When the craft ran aground minutes later, Jason

MacAuley jumped over the gunwale and headed in Katy's direction, the stern line of his jaw bespeaking his foul temper.

He gestured as he stopped before her. "No baggage, Miss Ryan? Do you not think your present attire will become a trifle stale after a few months at sea?"

She looked up into his face, not knowing whether to focus on his good eye or the patch. "Captain MacAuley, may I reiterate my feelings about this voyage? I have no wish to go anywhere with you."

His burst of laughter rankled her and for a long moment she toyed with the idea of burying his beautifully polished boots in the sand.

"You seem to think that I am going to enjoy wet-nursing you for the next few months. You flatter yourself, girl. I am not looking forward to this voyage any more than you."

"If you expect it to be so distasteful, Captain, why did you agree to it in the first place?"

"For the money, Miss Ryan. Strictly for the money."

"Judas." Averting her gaze, she looked past him to the other man, who was still in the boat, and shivered to think that she would soon be surrounded by a whole shipload of these strange leering men.

"Tread lightly, Miss Ryan," he admonished. "It would be a shame for you to have to begin this venture on my bad side."

"Have you such a thing as a good side, Captain?"

He set his hands upon her shoulders and pulled her to her feet. "My patience has worn thin, Miss Ryan, so I will tell you this once only," he seethed. "When men aboard my ship disobey my commands, they are thrown into the brig. And that, I might add, is one of the more lenient punishments. If you expect to come aboard and undermine my authority with your insolence, then be forewarned. I can throw a woman into the brig as easily as I can a man."

"You would not dare!"

His eye was as black as a bottomless well. "Try me," he whispered softly.

She had thought it would be easy to be brave. Now she was not so sure. With his size and his strength and his threats, Jason MacAuley was frightening, and certainly no gentleman at all.

Movement at the brow of the cliff heralded the arrival of traveling chest and relatives. Carolyn Astruc pondered the discordant silence separating her niece and Jason MacAuley. When the Yankee struck out toward the ship's boat to direct the stowing of the chest, Carolyn's eyes trailed after him. He wore no outer coat today, only fawn-colored breeches and blousy white shirt, the breeches adhering to his lean flesh emphasizing his masculinity. A twinge of unease pricked her.

With the traveling chest secured, the captain returned and nodded toward the west. "It grows late, Mrs. Astruc, and I have a schedule to maintain."

Carolyn saw that the muscles in his jaw were so tense they were pulsating, and she felt a sudden fear that perhaps her decision had been too rash. Was this the same man she had entertained only last night? There was a ruthlessness about him today that had been missing yesterday. Could her assessment of the man have been that inaccurate? If she *was* wrong . . .

"Captain MacAuley." She squinted at him. "I am entrusting my only niece to your care. I hope I have your word that you will act in a gentlemanly manner toward her. I warn you, if I should ever hear differently—"

"Madam, should any misfortune befall Miss Ryan on our journey, I doubt there will be enough of my hide available to satisfy all who will want a piece of it. It appears my competence is in great doubt."

I think it is your competence I fear most, Captain. Turning and taking her niece's hand, she found the girl's fingers cold and reluctant. "There may come a day when you will be able to look back on me with kindness, Katy. I pray that hindsight will come easier to you than foresight has come to me."

Katy averted eyes whose greenness was underlaid with the depth of her anguish.

I don't want to go, Aunt Carolyn. Please, don't make me leave. With lips parted, she looked up—into the face of her uncle. José had not muttered an entire sentence since Carolyn had told him of her decision to send Katy away. He had not even tried to deny his wife's accusation that he desired the girl in a way that no man should desire his niece. His wife had threatened him, had vowed that she would leave him if he dared gainsay her. He would become a laughingstock, a man unable to hold onto the fair-skinned wife who had been a symbol of status for all these years. He had agreed, but he would not be denied his farewell.

Katy stiffened as his soft hands cupped her head. He leaned forward, bending his lips to her own. She tasted him then, the oily essence and stifling perfume of a man whose tongue was—

"Nooo!" she shrieked, pushing her uncle away. "Don't touch me!" She stumbled backward, her eyes wild with terror. Jason looked to her in alarm as she kept backing away. He had seen trapped animals with the same look in their eyes, but never a human.

32

"Katy!" Carolyn's voice pierced through the girl's sobs with tender authority. "No one is going to hurt you." She grappled for Katy's trembling hands, calming them within her own. "You're all right. You're fine. Hush now." When the sobs had diminished to whimpers and the green eyes had recaptured some of their former sanity, Carolyn placed a steadying arm around the girl's shoulders and guided her toward the waiting boat. The eyebrow crowning Jason's good eye slanted with curiosity. Was it just her uncle, or did she react like that to all men?

He wondered what her reaction would be if she ever discovered the truth about the man into whose temporary care she was being placed. Not that she would: he would see to that. And as for the people who already knew? Well . . . He flexed his long fingers. There were ways of dealing with them too.

From his full six feet, three inches, Jason stared down at the two women before him and in an unguarded moment heeded the extraordinary beauty of the younger. Katy rubbed a hand across her cheek, ventured a deep breath. "I'm sorry," she whispered to her aunt, not meeting the woman's eyes. "I can't . . ." The sentence culminated in a hopeless sigh and Katy shook her head. "I'm all right now."

"Miss Ryan?" Jason motioned her toward the boat and with an effortless motion lifted her over the gunwale and directed her to the stern thwart. When she was safely seated, the Yankee said something to her aunt, turned, and then he and the mate were pushing off, forcing Katy to seize the side of the boat against the backward lurch. The stern slid into the surf. The hull pitched crazily as the men clambered over the sides and took their places on the center thwarts to man the oars. As they came about, Katy was afforded a final view of the beach—the ragged seam where the boat's keel had ruptured the sand, the sinister figure of her uncle, her aunt, the cliffs, a swirl of earth, sand, sky, water . . . and then the open sea. She wiped a mist of salty drizzle from her cheeks, then threw her hood over her head, burying her face deep within the cowl. Her life here should have ended differently. She shivered and drew her cloak more tightly about her, hoping to diminish the bone-rattling cold that burrowed so deeply within her. She was so cold. So empty.

From the beach, Carolyn Astruc raised an unseen hand in farewell. *I love you, Katy. Someday you may come to realize just how much.* She did not waver when the blinding rays of the sun dimmed. The blackness was tolerable now. Katy was beyond José's reach. She was safe.

The massive hull of the *Elizabeth* sported a coat of dark gray paint that the sun had blistered and peeled like leprous flesh.

Below the waterline, the wood was painted black, though the fetid green algae that bred there left some doubt as to the original color. Katy forced herself to look away, a fist of nausea curdling in her throat. She watched the sway of main- and foremast pulleys being lowered, and after hooks were snugged into apertures at both bow and stern, realized that Jason MacAuley was patiently waiting attendance upon her.

"Are you quite ready to climb up, Miss Ryan? Or would you rather I attached a pulley to your hood and hoisted you up that way?"

With great distrust she eyed the narrow slats of the Jacob's ladder as she stumbled over to him. "You're green." He frowned, examining her face with his solitary left eye. "I hope this doesn't mean that I'll be playing nursemaid as well as wet nurse. C'mon, girl. Up you go."

Standing on the center thwart, she secured a handhold on the ladder and was about to jump over onto the first rung when the *Elizabeth* plunged into a trough, veered away, and Katy found herself being stretched like a human bridge over a widening gulf of ocean water.

"Oooohh!" As her fingers lost their grip on the ladder, she felt strong hands encircle her waist and yank her back and upward over a shoulder whose hardness nearly knocked the breath from her.

"You have much to learn about climbing Jacob's ladders, Miss Ryan," the Yankee rumbled. With an arm clamped tightly about her legs, he leaped onto the ladder and began an easy ascent. The girl cracked an eyelid to peek at the churning water below her and sank her fingers into the man's shirt, wondering what his reaction would be if he realized she was about to be sick all over him. In the next instant he bobbed her slightly and she screamed and jerked downward on his shirt for support. Jason grinned at her outburst, but the smirk disappeared when he heard a rending tear down his back. Katy stared dumbly at the two strips of bronzed flesh that were exposed beneath what moments earlier had been a shirt. Mortified, she let go of the tattered remnants and watched them flap behind the man like tails.

"Miss Ryan," he wheezed, feeling the tingling breath of the wind skid from shoulder blade to waist, "what have you done?"

Finding no other place to rest her hands, she latched on to the top of his breeches and pulled upward.

"Lady!" he shouted, but before she had an opportunity to discern the reason for his irritation, he gained the rail and vaulted over it, setting Katy none too gently on her feet. "Your touch is tender as a bull's," he commented as he craned his neck behind him to inspect the damage.

Once aright, she pushed disobedient strands of hair from her face but bit back a sharp retort when she discovered that she was the focal point of every pair of eyes on the main deck. The crew had been forewarned of the consequences should any man make unseemly overtures toward their new passenger, and each man had digested the warning respectfully, knowing that the captain did not mouth idle threats, but they had not been privy to the fact of the girl's extreme beauty, and could only gawk in astonishment. The abrupt cessation of activity seemed to freeze the moment in space and time, and during that brief lull Katy's eyes swept the deck, missing nothing. There was no escape from the eyes that stared at her.

"Clear the deck for running!" Jason bellowed. His command set in motion a tide of human flesh that swept the deck like waves. "Mr. Carrier!" At the sound of his name a barrel-chested man broke from the crowd and presented himself before his commanding officer. "Mr. Carrier, this is Miss Ryan. Please show her to her quarters."

"Aye, Cap'n." The man saluted. "Miss Ryan, if you'll follow me, please."

Jason stepped aside to let her pass, which she did without the slightest acknowledgment of his existence. But he was keenly aware of hers. Her fragrance still clung to his shirt, disrupting his thoughts. Ignoring the sensations that were surfacing against his will, he lent a practiced eye to the appointment of his ship.

Isaiah Carrier led Katy aft through an alleyway and threw open a door at the end of the passage. She preceded him into the cabin and examined her new surroundings with pleasant surprise. These were to be her quarters? Surely there was some mistake. Light filtered through the stern window to caress the tawny wood paneling with amber softness. In a far alcove a bunk was built into the bulwarks, a simple quilt tossed over the top and four drawers cut into its wooden base. Mid-cabin there presided a rectangular table flanked on either side by well-worn benches and at each end by shell-shaped swivel chairs on cast-iron pedestals, the whole bolted to the deck. Hanging from a beam above the table was a lyre-shaped oil lamp wrought in polished copper, and to either side of the bunk, brass candle sconces in gimbals were screwed to the wall, the gimbals allowing the candleholders to swing freely in rough seas and thus remain level. In the near-right corner a heavy armchair was bolted to the floor, while to the left of this, braced against the inner bulkhead, was a commode over which hung a small square mirror. A brass chamber pot rested to the side.

Katy could not mask the surprise in her voice. "Are you quite sure this is the right cabin?"

The sailor's brow puckered and he scratched his head as he looked about. "Aye."

"But 'tis so grand." She ventured farther into the room. "Who resides here normally?"

"Why, Captain MacAuley, ma'am."

"Indeed?" The corner of her mouth lifted slightly. Perhaps she had been too critical of the Yankee. After all, any man who was willing to relinquish such fine quarters to a passenger did not warrant her entire contempt. "And where will your captain be staying on our journey?"

Isaiah Carrier riveted wide eyes on the girl. "Uh . . ." Much discomfited, he paddled the air with his hand, but found no help for his dilemma. "Uh . . ."

Curious at his hesitation, Katy bent her gaze toward him, musing at the hand that stirred the air so aimlessly. "Do you not know?" she pursued.

From the deck they heard the deep tones of Jason's voice ring with the command "Heave short!" and the sailor took an automatic step backward. "They're startin' to weigh anchor, Miss Ryan," he stammered. "I'd . . . uh . . . I'd best see to my duties." He took another step backward.

"But—"

"Someone'll bring your trunk along presently. 'Scuse me now, ma'am." He tipped his head and retreated through the door, exhaling a long breath through his teeth. If the captain hadn't told the girl about the sleeping arrangements, *he* wasn't about to!

2

Draped over the chamber pot, Katy agonized over what further acrobatics the ship would undertake and threw up again. They had been at sea for three hours, and during that time she had watched shadows spill into every corner until a curtain of darkness enshrouded the whole cabin. In the gloom she heard the whine and cry of wooden planks, the painful creak of the oil lamp, and from the passageway the sound of footsteps as they approached the portal.

"Miss Ryan?" Jason's questioning voice flooded the compartment as his eye squinted against the darkness, seeking her tiny figure somewhere in the shadows.

"Miss Ryan?"

Daunted by the harshness in his voice, Katy wiped her mouth on the back of her hand and labored to the leather chair. Jason canted his head in the direction of the sound. Still unable to see her, he struck out on a path toward the bunk. "Why do you sit here in the dark?"

She made no reply as she listened to his fumbling about in the shadows, but was thankful when the cabin blossomed with a dim half-light that tinted everything a murky yellow. Walking around to the end of the table, Jason leaned against its edge and cocked a brow at the pale green figure curled up in the chair.

"Perhaps I shouldn't have bothered with the light. You look terrible."

Katy lolled her head against the winged back of the chair, her every word an effort. "For a man possessed of such limited visual acuity . . . your perceptions are truly astonishing, Captain."

The Yankee guffawed at her reply and touched a finger to the black leather that cloaked his eye. "Are you referring to this? Do not let the patch deceive you, Miss Ryan. I see better with one eye than most men see with two." Laughing still, he eased away from the table, and despite the rise and fall of the floor, made his way to the bunk with an unvarying step. Where she had torn it, his shirt was still ribboned. Assessing the damage over his shoulder once again, he let forth a disgusted grunt and yanked the garment over his head. She had seen a hint of the man's power the night before, but the reality far surpassed the hint. His naked back was broad, his spine arrow-straight and flanked by dark flesh that knotted and bunched with long muscles. When he turned around, her sallow complexion flamed red. She had never seen a man so naked before. In the instant before she dropped her eyes to study a knothole in the floor, she caught a glimpse of the extraordinary width of his shoulders and the thewy musculature of his arms. Her stomach executed a slow double somersault at the thought of his hands on her.

"You can look up now," he taunted after some minutes had passed. "I believe I am sufficiently clothed so as not to further offend your tender nature." When she heard him settling into the near swivel chair, she pried her eyes away from the knothole and stole a peek at him. He was dressed, but knowing now what lay beneath that linen shirt did not make her feel any more secure.

"Now, Miss Ryan, I think it time we had a little talk. There are certain rules you will be expected to follow as long as you are on board my ship. To start with, you will consider yourself confined to quarters for the duration of our voyage. You will be allowed on deck for fresh air only in the presence of Mr. Carrier or myself. As for matters of personal hygiene, I will have a kettle of hot water brought to you once a week for more thorough bathing, and I can see you have already found the chamber pot. Do you have any questions?"

Katy pressed her tongue to the backside of her teeth. "When do you secure the shackles around my wrists and ankles, Captain?"

"I'll pretend you didn't say that. Apparently your illness has not dulled your tongue, but if you're as seasick as you look, I suggest that you try getting something into your stomach. Dry biscuits and salt fish usually help."

"I cannot even think about food, much less eat any," she said through gritted teeth.

"Miss Ryan, there is something you should know about seasickness. If left untreated, it can be just as deadly as scurvy. Granted, your gums won't rot and your teeth won't fall out, but you'll get so dehydrated that your insides will shrivel like a dried sponge. Death usually occurs shortly after that."

Jason had not thought her able to move so fast, but as the ship plunged into the belly of a wave, she was out of her chair and bent over the chamber pot before he could draw another breath. At the sound of her violent retching he tore out of his own chair, for he had only meant to scare her, not make her sick again. He gathered her hair away from her face with one hand and made to lend support to her forehead with the other, but as he leaned over, she thrust her hand toward his face. He blinked at the eye-watering pain that sent a rush of blood streaming from his nostrils.

"What in the . . . ?"

"Don't you touch me," she choked as she staggered back, cowering against the bulkhead.

Jason tossed his head back and cupped his hand over his nose, but that did not stanch the profuse flow of blood from his nostrils. He withdrew a linen cloth from the commode and, once seated, pressed it firmly to the bridge of his nose.

"I was only trying to hold your head up! Next time you're sick, you can hold your own head. Just what did you think I was going to do?"

Silence.

He angled his head upward and peered at her from above the slope of his hand. "Did you hear me?"

Silence.

Suppressing an exasperated hiss, he threw his head back again. "Not talking? I can live with that, Miss Ryan. I find it becomes most women."

Her eyes flew to the door as a knock sounded.

"Come in!"

Burdened with the evening's provender, Holland Pray nearly dropped the whole tray when he saw the rag that the captain was holding to his face, for the cloth was so drenched with blood that the boy concluded the injury must be mortal.

"Cap'n! You're wounded! Don't fret, sir . . ."

By the time Jason had swiveled his chair around clockwise to see the boy, the lad had already slid the tray onto the table and was running back toward the portal.

". . . I'll fetch the cook to stitch you back up!"

"Holland!"

The boy halted stone still in his tracks and turned round slowly. "Sir?"

" 'Twas a nosebleed," the Yankee ground out humorlessly. "A common nosebleed."

"But . . . all that blood, sir. I thought—"

"You haven't met our distinguished guest, have you, lad?" Jason said, wanting to change the subject. He flung an arm out toward the larboard corner into which Katy had burrowed herself. "Holland Pray, meet Mary Kathleen Ryan. You'll see to Miss Ryan's needs as you see to mine, provided that her requests are reasonable."

"Yessir," the boy stammered.

"I doubt that she'll be much trouble." Jason slid the tray of food to the far end of the table and sat down. "She seems to have developed a particular fondness for that one corner."

"Yessir."

"That'll be all for now, Holland."

Before the Yankee captain began eating, he trained a stern look on the girl. "Do you intend to stand there for the remainder of the voyage?"

Katy inched back to the leather chair, deciding that he was infinitely more interested in his food than he was in her. She watched as he gulped his meal and drained his ale, slamming the mug onto the table. Suddenly he cocked his head, listening.

"There's Block Island turkey for you here," he said as he rose, indicating a plate of salt fish. "I suggest you try to eat some." Rounding the corner of the table, he stopped before her chair. "One more thing, Miss Ryan." She should have been prepared, but she wasn't. His hand lashed downward, encircling her wrist with such imposing strength that her fingers numbed instantly. Frozen with fear, she caught her breath and stared up into the hellish depths of his eye. "If you ever strike me again, I'll break your damn arm." Then, without another word, he turned his broad back on her and departed.

Sleep was slow in coming that night, and it seemed that she had just closed her eyes when she was startled awake by the clanging of the ship's bell. In the near-dark of the cabin she heard a closer and infinitely more threatening sound and rolled over to discover its source. "What are you doing in here?" she gasped.

From the opposite end of the compartment Jason MacAuley turned. In his hands was a tangled network of ropes. "You have not misplaced your tongue after all. I thought you might have lost it in the chamber pot." Deep, mocking grooves split his cheeks. "To answer your question, lady, I am preparing a hammock for myself. Shipmasters must sleep also."

She propped herself on an elbow, regarding him suspiciously. "Just where do you intend to set this hammock?"

He resumed the task of unraveling the lines as he answered, "In my cabin, of course."

Remembering what Isaiah Carrier had said, she shot upright. "But *this* is your cabin!"

"Good of you to realize that. There are certain benefits that accompany the title of ship's master. Having a separate cabin is one of them. Under extreme conditions, even that advantage must be foregone."

"Are you saying that you think you're going to sleep in here? With me?"

"Miss Ryan," he said calmly, "I am making an enormous concession by allowing you to share this cabin with me. The rest of the crew sleep in areas the size of dog kennels, so do not complain to me about your lack of space."

" 'Tis not space that concerns me, sir, but choice of a cabin mate. I have no intention of sleeping in the same room with you. If *you* have no intention of seeking other accommodations, *I* do." She tossed her legs over the side of the bunk and wiggled into her shoes.

"Unfortunately," he retorted, "there is no room in any other part of the ship for you, and *I* have no intention of abandoning my quarters. 'Tis enough that I have given up my bunk and my privacy."

"Then I give them both back to you, Captain." Straightening her skirt, she edged her way around the perimeter of the cabin to the portal.

" 'Tis nasty out there, Miss Ryan. I wouldn't venture on deck if I were you."

The alleyway was unlit, so she felt her way along the wall till she came to the heavy double doors that formed a bulkhead to the main deck. Yanking on the door handle, she staggered backward with its weight but escaped through the opening before it had a chance to slam shut again. The night was cool, the moon couched behind a cloud bank that obliterated its meager light, the air damp with the promise of rain. Before her the mainmast lantern bobbed precariously, deflecting light through bull's-eye glass onto the bucking deck. She backed against the bulkhead to steady herself, and nearly jumped out of her skin when the door flew open beside her.

"*Miss Ryan!*" Jason bellowed. Unable to see her since she was standing on his blind side, he lengthened his eye to a crack and peered out its tail end to improve his vision. Where in hell was she? He swung his big body around to the right and in the shadows espied the tiny apparition that had thus far eluded his detection. The line of his jaw became rigid.

"I thought you could see better with one eye than most men can see with two," she taunted.

"Miss Ryan," he said coolly, "you test my patience sorely."

"Will you show me to other accommodations, or will you not?"

A thread of moonlight pierced the cloud cover at just that moment, illuminating his face. What she saw in it was frightening. She could almost feel the heat of his anger. "If you insist. Follow me."

He removed a wooden grating from the deck floor, and after setting it to one side, motioned her to follow after him. The gaping hole of the companionway devoured him, and though she felt suddenly squeamish about doing so, she traced the footsteps that seemed to be leading her into perdition. Perdition indeed! As she descended into the belly of the ship, she swore that she could smell the rotting flesh and excrement of the damned. Pressing the back of her hand to her nostrils, she tried breathing through her mouth. Underfoot, the planking was black with a slick coat of mold that was likewise eating its way up the walls. Jason halted before a door and banged on it once with his fist.

"Holland! Open up!"

From behind the door there was a scuffling of feet and then the sound of a bolt being slid out of position. Wide-eyed and breathless, Holland stood before them. "Yessir?"

"You're bunking down in my cabin tonight. The lady has decided that she would prefer separate accommodation."

The boy's eyes registered such disbelief that Katy began to question the wisdom of her decision. The smell alone was enough to give her second thoughts.

"There's naught but a hammock strung up in here, Cap'n," the boy sputtered. "Are you sure Miss Ryan can manage—"

"The lady has made her demands quite clear. She'll manage." Stepping aside, Jason extended his hand toward the portal. "After you, Miss Ryan."

Looming shapes abounded within; as her eyes adjusted to the darkness, she realized that they were barrels and that the room was filled to capacity with them. Then somehow Jason was before her, leading her along a narrow passage that cut through the sea of hogsheads. At the end of the passage a pencil of flame from a single candle brightened a corner where a rope hammock was suspended.

"This is the spirits room," Jason began, making a sweeping movement with his arm. "These barrels contain our entire supply of ale and wine, so it's necessary to post someone in here to discourage thieves. Since Holland will be sleeping elsewhere tonight, the defense of the room will be in your hands, Miss Ryan."

Her nose twitched with the noxious fumes. She wanted to go back up to the mahogany-paneled cabin where there was a bed with a mattress and fresh air and where she wouldn't be in constant jeopardy of having the door broken down by some thirsty sailor. Instead she declared, "This will be fine." She did not see the corner of Jason's mouth lift wryly.

"Good! It pleases me to know that I've finally found something that meets with your approval. Holland!" The boy materialized out of nowhere. "Keep Miss Ryan company for a few minutes. I need to bring something down from my cabin."

When Jason had gone, the boy tucked in his lips and shifted nervously from foot to foot. Katy could only stare at the hammock.

"If you don't move around too much tonight, you shouldn't have any problem with the hammock, miss. Try to lie still in one position and you won't get dumped."

She tested the ropework gingerly. How encouraging. She wouldn't get dumped.

Jason reappeared minutes later, his arm wrapped around . . . Katy flushed. The chamber pot.

"I thought you might decide to get sick again." He set the vessel beside the hammock. "If someone breaks in, just bloody his nose like you did mine." When they had gone and she had bolted the door, she groped her way back to the hammock and with the utmost caution lowered herself onto the ropework. Lying flat on her back, her fingers clinging to either side of the hammock, she stared up at the wooden beams above her. Her eyes wandered across the ceiling rafters and down the wall, where a spiked candlestick was driven into a beam. The mellow light from the flame embraced the bulkhead with sinuous strokes, and as she watched, it flickered and then . . .

Blackness.

The candle had burned down to a stub and snuffed itself out, leaving Katy immersed in an inky void. There was undoubtedly more to fear from Captain MacAuley than from the darkness, but at the moment, that knowledge did little to ease her mind. Settling herself in for a long night, she capped her hand over her nostrils and listened to the waves thrashing against the hull, the wind, the scratching.

Scratching?

The noise sounded again somewhere in the cabin, and she lay paralyzed. More scratching. Or was it gnawing? And then she heard the tiny paws skitter across the floor. She swallowed slowly. More skittering. In another direction. Scratching. Squeaking. Things sounding like . . . rodents. She lifted her other hand to her throat. If she peered into the darkness, she knew she would see their beady eyes shining redly and their sharp little teeth poised to attack. She couldn't. She couldn't think about what was running around there in the dark. If she did, she would scream into tomorrow.

As the bell on the main deck struck eight times, marking the hour of midnight, Katy stared wide-eyed yet unseeing into the blackness. It had been a day that she would never want to relive. She wondered how she would ever survive the night.

*   *   *

"Miss Ryan? Miss Ryan, please open the door!" Holland rapped his knuckles against the portal. "You're to chow down in Captain MacAuley's quarters, and it's all ready. Miss Ryan?"

Katy groaned and inched a tension-stiff leg toward the edge of the hammock. "I'm coming," she muttered half to herself. She couldn't remember whether she had slept or not, but from the way her eyes felt, she would guess that she hadn't. Rolling her torso to the left, she was about to swing her other leg over the side when the hammock swung out beneath her.

Hearing a shriek followed by a resounding thud, Holland pounded more urgently. "Are you all right, Miss Ryan? What happened? Please let me in!"

After a stunned moment Katy raised herself up on her hands and shook the cobwebs from her head, then scowled up at the ropework that was looming almost invisibly above her.

"Miss Ryan! Let me in!"

"Just a minute!" she screamed.

She eventually found her way to the door, throwing it open to admit a sheepishly smiling Holland, and the nauseating stench of the bilge. Her hand automatically leaped to her nostrils.

"I'm sorry to disturb you, miss, but the captain said to wake you before your breakfast got any colder. That noise I heard . . ." He squinted at her, taking note of the bluish circles beneath her bloodshot eyes. "Did you fall or something?"

She compressed her lips. He knew well enough that she had fallen out of that godforsaken contraption, but she would not give him the satisfaction of hearing it from her own lips. "The candle in there has burned out. I would appreciate your replacing it before this evening."

"Yes, miss. Did you sleep well?"

The green of her eyes flashed, sending him back a full step, and she swept past him without speaking.

She could only pick at her breakfast and had just finished changing into a crisp black bombazine gown when Isaiah Carrier announced himself at the door. He explained that bad weather was setting in, "So if we don't take a turn about the deck now, we may not get another chance for a while, ma'am." On deck the wind screamed past her, bloating her skirt like a balloon and sending her hair streaming in four compass directions. She caught her hair with one hand and tried to bat down her skirt with the other, but the wind would not be denied its sport.

She allowed Isaiah to take her arm and direct her across the main deck, out of the direct path of the wind. As they walked, her green eyes roved the deck with lazy interest. Great lengths of anchor cable lay drying from fore to aft, making walking

44

hazardous. Several tars sat Indian-style on the deck, repairing eye splices with their tapered marlinspikes. Aft of the forecastle two men surrounded by a cloud of sailcloth were diligently forcing needles through the tattered canvas while at the same time trying to prevent the sail from blowing away. At the rail Katy grabbed onto a belaying pin for support and looked out over the rail to scan the horizon.

As the *Elizabeth* veered chaotically, a curl of foam licked Katy's face in a salty kiss. The sea was gaining momentum and Isaiah Carrier kept a wary eye on both it and his young ward. She was so tiny that it wouldn't take much of a jolt to pitch her headlong over the gunwale, and if that ever happened . . .

His insides began to quiver. "Miss Ryan, I think I'd better get you back inside. That gale is coming at us faster than I realized."

"But we just—"

"*Bear a hand*!" came the outcry behind them. They turned as one to witness the two canvas menders diving into the billowing sheet that the yardage had become. The men's slight bodies did little to anchor the flapping sail, and the whole thing looked like it was about to take flight.

"Holy . . . !"

Isaiah Carrier and a dozen other hands raced toward the wanton sail. Yelling graphic obscenities, they rolled the great sheet of linen up like a cigar and began retrieving their tools.

"You must forgive their language, Miss Ryan. They forget that there is a lady present." The deep tones of Jason MacAuley's voice rang out behind her and she turned away from the near-disaster to glance over her shoulder at him.

"No need to apologize, Captain. Their language is of little concern to me." Seeing that the sail was being hoisted onto shoulders and carried away, she returned to her original stance. Jason leaned with the small of his back pressed against the gunwale and ranged his eye intently from fore to aft and then aloft. He frowned at the vibrating yardarms. "Keep her on a tight bowline!" he shouted to the helmsman. Bracing elbows behind him on the rail, he studied the overhead rigging with a keen eye.

"So, Miss Ryan, how did you fare in the spirits room last night?" She could feel his eye on her, so she tilted her head to meet his gaze.

"Nothing bit me, if that's what you mean, Captain."

His lips pulled into a roguish smile. "I'm glad to hear that. Some of the men aren't so fortunate. Rats, you know. Can't seem to keep the lower decks free of them."

"Rats?" Her eyes paled. She had convinced herself they were mice—small, harmless mice.

"What did you think they were, Miss Ryan? Mice?"

Oh, how she loathed this priggish, egocentric man. "You could have told me what was down there."

Jason shook his head. "I'll not coddle you, lady. If you're going to make quarter-witted demands, you'll simply have to live with the consequences." He would not tell her that Holland had been posted outside her door all night, ready to call for help at the first sound of trouble.

"All in black today, I see," he needled. "Has someone died?"

"Nay, but if you would care to volunteer, I would have no objection."

His eye caressed her profile, the tendrils of hair gamboling in the wind, and he resisted the urge to protect her from the northeast trades with his body. Instead, he made a tsking sound that infuriated her. "I will attribute your ill temper this morning to your lack of sleep last night. At least I assume that those little blue pouches beneath your eyes mean that you didn't sleep." She pursed her lips crookedly. "You should stay away from black, Miss Ryan. It doesn't become you at all."

"Captain MacAuley," she seethed, "is your time of so little import that you can afford to waste it all by standing here and insulting me? Is there not someone else aboard who would appreciate your sarcasm more than I? Could you not just leave me alone?"

"But, Miss Ryan," he countered in amusement, " 'tis decidedly more pleasant to insult you than some gap-toothed shellback with Piccadilly weepers down to his navel."

She blinked vacuously. Whatever was the man blathering about? "If you were any kind of gentleman—"

"I have never espoused to gentlemanly status, Miss Ryan. I leave that to men who have softer hearts . . . and heads."

His laughter crackled in her ear. But the laughter ceased hastily when the whole ship began to shake. Katy threw her arms around the belaying pin as if the simple wooden peg could mean the difference between life and death, and stared at Jason.

"What was—?"

"Shhhh!" He held up a hand to silence her, yet his eye and the eyes of all the crew on deck were riveted to windward, where the edges of the sails were trying to buckle against the bowline. "Wind's veering," he spat. "*Fall off!*" At his command the helmsman spun the spokes of the wheel hard away from the wind. "Seven points on the larboard bow!" he shouted. As the rudder kicked into position, the prow heeled to larboard and the men dashed forward. "Ready the forebraces!" Both larboard and starboard watches manned the braces on deck, and when the order came to "Haul the yard!" they pivoted the yardarms to catch the wind on the new compass direction. With the wind nearly abeam the ship rode in the belly of the sea, rolling unmercifully with the waves. The men triced up the ends of the gear on the foredeck and were starting to make their way toward the mainmast when a hardy zephyr slammed against the starboard beam, and the ship keeled hard to larboard. Katy's scream sounded above everything as the rail rolled under, dumping the sea into her lap. Alert to their immediate danger, Jason looped an arm about her waist, and swinging her off her feet, held her fast against him until the deck leveled out. From the mayhem around the mainmast Isaiah Carrier emerged and rushed toward them.

"How long can we maintain this course, Cap'n? Sea gets any heavier, she'll set the whole main deck awash."

"We can still make some headway before we have to heave to," Jason yelled. "Keep her steady full, and if the wind backs more than four points, goose-wing the fore-topsail and muzzle everything else." Katy hung against him, her feet dangling just below his knees. She kicked weakly to indicate that she wanted to be put down, but the strong arm that girdled her did not relax.

"But what about Africa, sir?"

"We'll heave to before we hit it, Mr. Carrier."

"Aye, Cap'n." The first mate was not thoroughly convinced, but saluted anyway and headed back to direct the activity at the mainmast braces. Meanwhile Katy wiggled her arms out from beneath the confines of her cloak and tried to wedge her hand between the captain's forearm and her waist.

"Captain MacAuley," she grunted, "you may put me down now."

Even wet, she weighed no more than eiderdown, and holding her one-handed required as little effort as holding a rag doll. Yet having her body crushed to his was having a scintillating effect upon his loins—one that he was having a difficult time controlling. He didn't have to be asked twice to put her down.

"I suppose I should thank you," she sputtered as she pulled her sodden skirt away from her legs.

"I should think you'd be cursing me for not letting you drown," he gibed. "That would solve all your problems, would it not? A quick panacea."

"Ohhh," she hissed, "you are loathsome." Turning her back on his guffaws, she yanked the folds of her skirt away from her legs again and strutted off towards the quarterdeck, across the top of the drying anchor hawsers. Halfway across the deck she felt the cables begin to rotate under her feet, and Jason cringed as she windmilled her arms, tottered on one foot, then pitched forward on all fours, skidding to a grinding halt on her stomach.

"Oophfff!"

She could feel her dress and cloak up somewhere around her knees and turned her hands upward to find rope burns emblazoned across the heel of each palm. Wincing, she looked askance to find Jason, on one knee beside her.

"I think, Miss Ryan, that you are a disaster waiting to happen. Beautiful women are not supposed to be so clumsy. Well, are you hurt?" He touched a hand to her chin. She was surprised when his fingers came back bloody. "Rope burn on your chin. Anything else besides that and your hands?" He slid a concerned eye down the length of her and on an impulse lifted her leg. The skin from knee to ankle was broken and oozing blood. He shook his head. "Come on, my girl." He scooped her into his arms. "You're bleeding all over my anchor cables."

His strides were long and deliberate across the deck, and oblivious of the inquiring looks of a few crewmen, he threw the quarterdeck door open, made his way through the alleyway, and kicked open the door to his cabin. He held her over his bunk and seemed about to drop her, when he hesitated, turned, and dropped her into a swivel chair instead. "No sense in getting the bedclothes all wet." Her eyes followed him as he gathered various paraphernalia from the commode and a bottle of something from a drawer below his bunk. Ripping a square of linen into shreds, he uncorked the bottle, splashed some of the liquid onto a swatch of the material, and pressed it against her chin. "Here. Hold this up." Her eyes teared at the sudden stinging, but she blinked them away and did as she was told.

"What is that?" she asked, indicating the bottle.

"Brandy." Kneeling, he lifted her skirt and set her feet to rest on his thigh. Applying more brandy to the linen, he dabbed at her scraped shins. "Should have hired a nanny for you," he mumbled.

Despite his surly manner, he tended her bruises with gentle dexterity and didn't speak again until her skin had been wiped clean of the drizzling blood. "There. All done. Does that feel better?"

She nodded.

"Good. Now, let's have a look at your chin." Removing the compress from her face, he examined the abrasion carefully. She closed her eyes to avoid his close perusal. "Bleeding has stopped. Looks fine. What about your hands?" She held her palms up. Once again he shook his head. "I can't help but sympathize with the man who intends to take you to wife. God help the poor fellow." She soaked her burns in water, and after he patted her hands dry he doused the chafed skin with more brandy. She pondered his silent efficiency, and as he labored over her bruises, she regarded him with stealth, her gaze wandering obsessively to the patch over his right eye. What had happened? Was there an eye beneath that leather swatch, or was there an empty socket? Had he been blind since birth, or had he lost his sight by some act of nature . . . or man? She tried to imagine his face without the black cord slashed diagonally across it. He would be extraordinarily handsome, ruggedly good-looking. His face was craggy, his chin strong. The eye that was hidden was no doubt beautifully shaped and thickly lashed, like his good eye, the iris the same earthy brown. But she could not envision the whole face when only three-quarters of it was visible. Did he ever remove the patch? Did he sleep with it? Did he . . . ?

Jason looked up to find her staring. His eyebrow arched in surprise. "Have you discovered something intriguing about my face, Miss Ryan? My patch perhaps? Are you interested in how I came by it?"

Her cheeks stained brightly at his question. How could he be so adept at reading her mind? It was almost scary. She shook her head in denial.

"I will tell you anyway. A pirate gouged it out with his scimitar," he declared melodramatically, making a popping sound with his mouth that simulated the eye's excision. "And after he cut it out, he brandished it on the tip of his blade and threw it into the sea."

Her eyes froze open in disbelief. Surely he was joking.

"You doubt me, lady?" he accused. "Let me show you, then."

As he made to lift the patch, her hands shot out, stopping him. "Nay!" she choked. "I believe you! I have no wish to see."

"Are you sure?"

She nodded.

"Very well." He shrugged. He returned his paraphernalia to the proper niches. Had Katy found the temerity to look at him then, she would have smoldered to find his face animated with suppressed laughter.

"You'd better get out of that rig. Wet clothing causes saltwater boils, and I can guarantee you don't want anything to do with them." He walked to the door and turned. "You could do both of us a favor by curling up in my bunk and getting some shut-eye, Miss Ryan. That might be the only way to keep you from destroying yourself."

He left before she could think of a clever riposte. She wasn't as clumsy as he suggested, it was just that when she was out of her element, she became nervous, and when she was nervous, strange things seemed to happen to her. After fighting her way out of her gown, she draped both it and the cloth that bound her chest over the leather chair to dry, then, after donning a dry gown, crawled beneath a blanket and tried to convince herself that she wasn't as nauseated as she felt.

I would wager he has never even seen a pirate. Scimitar indeed.

By the time the wind reached a velocity of fifty knots and rain began pelting the deck with droplets that cut like shards of glass, the *Elizabeth* had heaved to, with only one corner of the foresail set, and the helm eased down, continually coming up, falling off, drifting to leeward. Thunder boomed within towering peaks of black clouds. Jagged streaks of lightning ripped through the celestial terrain like incandescent pitchforks, hissing, sizzling. Yet the *Elizabeth* remained secure, riding in harmony with the gale force of the wind, in the mandibles of thirty-foot waves that could snap her like straw.

Jason had returned to his cabin earlier for his oilskins and had paused to observe the unease with which Katy slept. She writhed back and forth, perspiring and moaning. The line of her face was distorted; her lips parted to emit a strange keening sound. Of what did she dream? What possible nightmare could torment her so? At the leather chair he handled the strip of cotton cloth in bemusement, its purpose eluding him until he remembered the generous endowment of breast he had witnessed that night on the balcony and her usual dearth of curves. So this was how she disguised her figure! But why would she want to do such a thing? He shook his head. He would not tell her that the material would never dry in this weather, would never dry until it had been rewashed in something other than seawater.

In the ensuing hours the legacy from the storm poured through the stern window in shades of gray and black, snuffing out the daylight. Pounding breakers clawed at the transom, seeking entry. Walls of green water thrashed across the quarterdeck. And Katy became violently sick—her illness growing apace with the storm. Day and night meshed, becoming one. Her world became shadow and sickness. She dozed on a perspiration-soaked pillow and woke to vomit the contents of her already empty stomach. The cabin was sour with the stench. The crockery from her last meal lay smashed on the floor. Like the crockery, Katy had tumbled out of the bunk and had lain prostrate on the floor until someone with strong arms had picked her up and tucked her firmly into the bunk. The hand he had set on her forehead had been deathly cold and wet. His voice had been soothing, though her head had been too thick with pain to comprehend his words. She didn't care. She hurt too much to care.

And she dreamed.

Of footsteps. Of running. Of a man who sat beside her, cradling her. A wet shadow who forced something to her lips. Too weak to struggle, she swallowed the salted water and spat it up again. His hand was cool on her burning face. She needed to escape the man, but his hand was so cool. She wanted to run. She couldn't. Her limbs were too feeble. His hand too cool. He was forcing the liquid into her mouth again, and she moaned for him to stop. He would kill her. He would drown her. She shook her head weakly. The water splashed down her neck, soaking her collar. The man's breath blew across her face in exasperation and then she was on her side and the cold hands were at her back, peeling the clothing from her body. She would have fought him if she had possessed the strength. She would have screamed. But she could do neither. It hurt too much.

Sometime during the second night of the storm a splintering crash jolted her into semiconsciousness. She heard terrified shouts, followed by an ungodly sound. Wood, ripping slowly apart, crashed downward in a snarl of lines, spars, and human flesh. On deck the shouts became cries, howls. The soft hairs on Katy's arms stood on end. They were sinking! She was going to die. But the thought held little meaning. If the only escape from her pain was death, she would welcome it. Her eyes slatted open. The cabin was dark, her vision bleary. The inside of her mouth tasted spoiled, acrid. From the alleyway she heard men's voices raised in alarm, and the heavy tramping of boots. Were they coming to rescue her? *No. Let me die. Let me be. Please.*

The door banged open before the rush of footsteps.

"Get him on the table! One of you light that lantern and hold it up so we can see something." It was Jason's voice, rising above the anguished moaning. Something heavy was slid onto the table.

"Where's that light?" Jason roared.

The blackness diminished, giving way to a hazy light that

stung Katy's eyes. She pressed her lids shut, flattening her sudden tears.

"Get those oilskins off him! He's bleeding somewhere."

She could hear their knives slashing through the slicker.

"Oh, Christ."

Someone began to retch violently.

"Dammit! Hold that lantern steady!" Jason barked.

"Oh, Christ."

"Get me a needle and some heavy thread. The lower right drawer of my bunk, Mr. Campbell. *Move!*"

Something was spilling steadily onto the floor. She cracked an eye again, caught a glimpse of the table and the cataract of blood that was pouring over its lip, and then the pain grew too great. For her, all again became blackness.

Jason took the needle from Campbell and bent over the injured man.

"It won't do any good, Cap'n!" Isaiah blurted out. Then, in a more quiet voice, "He's dead."

The ensuing silence was eerie. When Jason spoke again, his voice was bone-weary. "What of Walsh and Day?"

Isaiah shook his head.

"And their bodies?"

"Sea got to 'em first, Cap'n."

"Three men dead," Jason rasped. "Wasted." He handed the needle back to Campbell then spoke quietly to the first mate. "See to his body, Mr. Carrier. You know what to do."

"Aye, Cap'n."

Physically spent, Jason sank into the swivel chair while Isaiah Carrier directed the removal of the body. When the compartment had been cleared, the mate stood at the door. "Anything else, Cap'n?"

Jason stared at the runnels of blood filling the crevices in the table. "See if you can clear away some of that debris on deck before it does any more damage," he said vacantly. "I'll be out in a few minutes to help. But I need to rest—for a minute." He rubbed his eyes with a bloodied hand. "Only for a minute."

The oil lamp began to smoke, its smell intermingling with the sticky sweetness of blood and the sourness of bile. When Isaiah left, Jason doused the flame and in the dimness lowered his body back into the chair. His shoulders slumped forward and his head slid from his hands, to his forearms, to the table.

Spinning. Voices. Footsteps. Running. The blackness receded to gray, then to silver. A lusty breeze swirled about her head, expunging the dreadful odors of sickness and death. Katy opened her eyes halfway. Natural light sifted through her thick fringe of lashes to dazzle her with its brilliance. The ship rolled gently, the sea in abeyance. Outside, the sound of hammers and saws echoed in the silence.

Silence.

No thunder. No howling wind. The storm had ceased and they had remained afloat.

She opened her eyes wider, blinking, and saw the man standing at the commode, his naked back to her, his flesh rippling with fluid movements. Rinsing the excess lather from his face, he reached for a towel and turned as if by instinct.

"Are you finally awake?" The towel made a quick sweep of his face while Katy studied him. There was something different about him. Something about his face. Something . . .

Jason dropped the towel on the commode, then grabbed his eyepatch from where it hung on the mirror and adjusted it on his face as he strode toward her.

The patch! He had removed the patch. If only she could have seen.

"Have you rejoined the living?" he asked as he sat on the edge of the bunk.

Her tongue was thick and dry as cotton. She drew it across her equally dry lips, their soft pinkness cracked and blistered.

"Thirsty?" When she nodded, he fetched a mug of liquid, and after propping her up with extra blankets, brought the cup to her mouth. "This is water with a bit of lemon juice in it. Swish it around in your mouth, then spit it out. It'll get the stale taste out of your mouth." He watched as she did what she was bade, observing that she hardly had the strength to move the water from one side of her mouth to the other. When she was done with that, he brought her another mug. "Salted water," he explained. "Just take small sips. We don't want to shock your stomach." He held the cup.

Katy placed her hands over his, controlling the intervals at which she sipped. She should have been bothered by his partial nudity, by his nearness, she thought, but she wasn't. He looked too exhausted to entertain ideas about anything except sleep.

"There were a couple of times I wasn't sure you were going to make it," he said as he took the empty cup from her. "You banged your head up stoutly that one time you fell out of bed. Do you remember that?"

Her brows drew together in thought. "I thought I was . . . dreaming."

"Oh, you had your share of dreams, and they didn't seem at all pleasant."

"No." Images flashed in the recesses of her mind. Harsh light. Moans. More blood than she had ever seen. "They weren't pleasant." Hesitantly she scanned the cabin. The bench and floor by the table were red with the stain. The dream had been no dream at all. "That man!" She swallowed.

"I had hoped you might not have seen that."

"I . . . I heard . . . But I thought perhaps it was just a dream."

His eye looked distant, sad. "I wish it had only been a dream." He rubbed the back of his neck grimly. " 'Tis done. I would give him back his life were it in my power. But I am not God."

She could offer no reply, no solace. The depth of his emotion startled her. Could the man she had thought so callous actually experience sorrow? He rose and crossed the floor. Katy made a sudden observation.

"We're . . . standing still."

He peered out the stern window, his hands clasped behind his back, feet slightly apart. "Hardly standing, but you are correct. We're at anchor, and look to remain that way for several days to come. We sustained considerable damage in the storm."

"How considerable?"

He sat himself on the window seat and began to recite the litany to her. "We lost a section of the starboard gunwale, the ship's boat, forty feet of the foremast, and the topgallant sails of both main and mizzenmasts."

"But we're still afloat."

"Aye, Miss Ryan." He grinned. "We're still afloat. For a while at least. This storm isn't through with us yet, but we should be able to finish some of the major repairs before she slams into us again." Seeing her face fall at the news, he shook his head. "I'm sorry to have to greet you with such ill tidings. Maybe we can have you operating under full sail before the foul weather strikes again."

Discouraged, she drew a hand across her forehead. "I'll be happy if I can just keep this water down."

"I think the worst of your sickness is over. You should be able to retain some food now, but you may not like the menu."

One look at him told all. "Salt fish," she groaned. "When I'm better, I never want to *look* at another piece of fish."

He laughed then because she was so weak yet so defiant, so beautiful and so ridiculous. He needed to laugh to relieve the pressures of the last three days, to soothe his anguish. He had moved away from the bunk because there was another part of im that also needed to be relieved, and none but a woman could succor his craving. There was safety with distance, and with his resistance at such a low ebb, he would have to maintain as much distance between himself and Mary Kathleen Ryan as was humanly possible. He could not allow himself to forget that she was Pamela Ryan's stepdaughter. Matthew Ryan's daughter. She could not be touched.

The following day Jason carried Katy out to the main deck, and sitting her on the quarterdeck companionway, allowed her to watch the activities involved in piecing the *Elizabeth* back together. In the aftermath of the storm the clouds hung low, casting an olive-green hue on everything, and though the sun never penetrated the low ceiling and the air was heavy with moisture, the fresh sea breeze had a medicinal effect on Katy. By the third day she had regained much of her strength and by the fourth she was healthy enough to wonder at the trenchant glances Captain MacAuley directed at her when he thought she wasn't looking.

She could not fault his conduct. Since the storm he had been the epitome of graciousness and polite concern. He inquired about her welfare and saw that her needs were catered too. Yet other than that, he avoided her as if she were recovering from the plague rather than seasickness. His hammock was strung up in his cabin, so she knew that he was occupying the compartment at night, but he came after she was asleep and left before she awoke, giving her little to complain about.

As the wind veered on the fourth night, auguring the birth of another tempest, Jason sat angled in the window seat, his booted foot braced against the opposite wall. Through the mist of smoke from his cheroot he watched her. Her hand lay open on her pillow, her fingers curled like the petals of a flower. Her mantle of hair shrouded her with its silken tapestry. She was so soft. He had seen how soft when he had been forced to replace her wet gown. He would like to have touched her then, but she had been so sick. So helpless. Still, the memory blazed in his mind. *She is Matthew Ryan's daughter!* She tossed fitfully in her sleep. The black orb of his eye stalked her.

"Mama!"

"What is it, Katy? What's wrong?"

"Maaamaaa!"

The man had grabbed the ends of her hair and was winding them steadily around his hand. Her feet felt leaden. Her head was being forced backward, her neck stretched unnaturally. And he laughed. A hideous laugh. An unearthly laugh.

"Maaamaaa!"

"Katy!"

"*Noooo!*" Her hand lashed out. Finding his flesh, her fingers became talons. She dug deep furrows in the man, felt his skin rip beneath her nails. "Mama!"

"Katy!"

He was shaking her, hovering over her.

"Katy! Wake up!"

Balling her hand into a fist, she swung blindly and connected hard with his cheekbone. He swore viciously and swooped her into his arms as she screamed again. She struggled against the steely limbs that pinioned her, banged her head into his chest, tried to kick free of her imprisonment.

"You were dreaming, Katy. Open your eyes. *Look* at me!" He sat on the bed, crushing her to him. His voice was warm at her ear. "It was only a dream."

She cried in frustration at her bondage, but the man's last word somehow struck her consciousness. Her eyes flew open. Jason stared down at her, his eyepatch drawing her back to reality. She was not being strangled. She was . . . aboard the *Elizabeth*. Safe. Her ebullience at having escaped the horror drove all other fears from her mind. When she had stopped shrieking long enough for Jason to relax his grip on her, she threw her arms around his neck and clung gratefully. He cradled her head beneath his chin, rocked her back and forth in his arms.

"It's all right, Katy," he soothed. "You're with me. You're safe."

"He . . . he . . . he was going to kill me," she sobbed against his naked chest. "I *hate* him!"

He buried his lips in her hair, pressed a gentle kiss on the top of her head. "Who, love? Whom do you hate?"

"Hic. That man. He has no face, but I know who he is. 'Tis Seth Aldrich."

He recovered so quickly that the sudden break in his rocking was imperceptible. "Why do you say that?"

"He killed my . . . hic . . . mother, and he won't rest until he has . . . killed me, too."

" 'Tis nonsense," he reasoned. "Someone in a dream cannot hurt you."

Absently she brushed her fingers up and down the column of his neck. "Someday I will not wake up, and it will be because of him."

"Nay." His hand stroked her hair. She could feel his chest vibrate with his every heartbeat. "No harm will befall you as long as I am here."

Of a sudden she became keenly aware of the man who was caressing her and she stilled her hand. His flesh pulsed with restrained power. Where her cheek lay against the crisp hair on his chest he was warm, his scent heady. His bare arms girded her. *Entrapping her.* With a subtle movement he cupped his hand behind her head and with the plane of his thumb stroked her cheek. Wary now, she eased her hand from around his neck, but he seemed not to notice. He tilted her head back, the underlying crimson of his one eye beaconing his passion. He touched his lips to her forehead, traced a lingering kiss along the contour of her brow to her temple.

"Please don't," she breathed. As his mouth sought hers, she flattened her palm against his chest and tried to push herself away. A sticky wetness glazed her fingertips. Jerking her hand away from him, she squinted at the trace of blood staining her fingers. "You're bleeding!" She struggled upward.

" 'Tis nothing," he whispered against her ear.

She stared in awe at the bloody furrows etched across his chest. The tiny flame in the core of his eye reddened as his gaze dwelt on the softness of her flesh.

She is Pamela Ryan's stepdaughter.

Like watered silk her skin brushed his. She touched a weal that slashed down his breastbone, and winced at the damage she had wrought. "We need to stop the bleeding." He tried to hold her gently to him as she squirmed, but when her feet touched the floor, she slipped away from him like an ethereal spirit. His hands slid from her arms to her waist. Her hair trailed through his fingers as she moved away, and when the last strand of liquid obsidian cascaded over his fingertips, he stared at his empty hands, then leveled his one eye on her retreating figure.

She is Matthew Ryan's daughter.

Like a moth to fire he was drawn to her, stood and began to pace toward her.

She is a woman. Matthew Ryan be damned.

She heard his footsteps behind her as she sorted through squares of linen, and froze as she felt his hands on her shoulders, coaxing her upward. "Stand up," he whispered. When she did not move, he drew her to her feet. Stone still, she stood with her back to him. Gathering her hair in one of his hands, he draped its lustrous blackness over her shoulder and then his mouth was at the nape of her neck, burning. She grabbed the edge of the commode.

"Stop it," she choked.

"Katy."

"Stop!" With fists clenched for battle, she spun round.

Jason caught her hands midair. "You'll not raise your hand to me again, girl." His brown eye elongated, and within its dark sphere she read his intent and knew the terrifying reality of a man's passion. Her scream was cut short by the hard insistence of his mouth upon hers. He lifted her to him, imprisoning her within the strong band of his arms, forcing her head back with the pressure of his mouth. In futility she struggled against the man-beast whose body was rock hard, whose lips bruised and hurt her. Within her throat she made a strangulated sound that combined her fear and revulsion, but the man was made deaf by his own need and remained ignorant of her protest.

Please. I cannot stand to be . . . touched. Please! You are killing me!

"I want you, Katy," he murmured against her lips. His voice echoed inside her head and she could escape neither it nor him. "I won't hurt you."

Pleeeassse!

In her mind's eye she ran from him, and in seeking refuge she found a secret place deep inside her, a place where she had hidden years before and where her fright took her again. Miraculously the man ceased to exist. She was floating, weightless, blinded by golden reflections.

Jason did not question her passivity. His hands became anxious. Slipping one beneath the shoulder seam of her nightgown, he jerked his hand upward.

From far off Katy heard material being ripped. Her shoulder felt cool, as if water was rippling over it, and then a fiery wave swept across her skin. The man tasted the smoothness of her shoulder, and while his lips traveled downward over the swell of her flesh, his other hand split the seam across the opposite shoulder. The nightgown flapped down to her waist, where it was caught between their bodies.

Gently Jason gathered her into his arms. As he carried her to the bunk, his eye dwelt on the softly domed breasts whose existence she had disguised for so many years. The fire that kindled in his loins burgeoned into full arousal. He set her on the bed and only then did he notice her abnormal expression. The green eyes were unfocused, open wide, and unblinking, and she was still, so very still. Uneasy, he sat beside her on the bed, touched a hand to her cheek.

"Katy?"

In her mind the wind rustling through the leaves called her name. Strange how it sounded like a man's voice.

He cupped her chin and looked for some degree of coherence in her eyes. "Katy. Can you hear me?"

She smiled inwardly. There it was again. She liked this place, where even a summer's breeze bade her welcome.

"Dammit!" he agonized. "Answer me!" With hands that trembled, he tried to shake her into awareness.

She floated serenely, withstanding the turbulence that aggravated the water. Soon there would be calm again. Perhaps then she would be able to see beyond the sun's reflections.

3

"Sails off the larboard bow!"

In the gray light of morning Jason trained his glass on the distant ship and cursed beneath his breath.

"Can you make out the colors, Cap'n?" Isaiah Carrier slapped his arms and shuffled his feet in an attempt to keep warm.

With his scope riveted on the unknown ship's mainmast, Jason could see the foreign flag flapping in miniature—a montage of suns and stars emblazoned across a pale background. "Pirate," he spit. "She's a filthy pirate brig." Taking note of the ship's course, he handed the scope to the first mate. "She's heading straight for us."

In her cabin Katy rolled onto her back and rubbed a naked shoulder. Even in her drowsiness her contact with bare flesh smacked of something awry, and she shot upright, remembering. She clutched her nightgown to her breast. Her eyes fell upon the trail of blood smeared across the front of her gown, and silently she relived the horror of the previous night. Pressing the back of her hand to her lips, she endured a moment of physical sickness before she was overcome with outrage. For all his politeness and concern, Jason MacAuley was a lecher and deserved to have his other eye gouged out! How cunningly he had flaunted his sterling manners after the storm. The blackguard! Throwing back her covers, she peered at the washstand, remembered his lips at her neck, on her mouth. His arms had been banded around her and his voice had been warm at her face. She knew it had not stopped there, but her memory was hazy and she could not visualize a clear image of his violation. Nonetheless, he would be sorry.

Ridding herself of the blood-streaked lingerie out the stern window—the gauzy material reeking of Jason MacAuley—she sat stiffly in a swivel chair, slapping her hairbrush into her palm . . . and waiting. When he finally appeared at the portal, tall and imposing and seemingly invulnerable, she was ready for him.

"You!" she shrieked.

Both relieved and surprised to find that she was no longer catatonic, he blinked as her hairbrush skated over his shoulder, missing his head by the width of a hand and thunking into the door behind him.

"Whoring son of Satan! Bastard!" She was on her feet now, ransacking the contents of her trunk in search of a more potent weapon.

Catlike, Jason bent down and palmed the brush. "Your aim needs improvement, lady. You'll never kill me that way."

Finding a shoe, she hurled it across the room at him. "Killing would be too good for you. I think you should be gelded!" The other shoe followed, hitting everything except its intended target.

A half-smile affixed to his lips, he tossed a bold, lingering glance over her body. "Lusty wench. I don't think Pamela will be quite prepared for you."

"Get out!"

He shook his head and strode toward the table, where he set her hairbrush down. "I believe you dropped this."

Frantically she scanned the compartment for a weapon, but was greeted by objects either too big to throw or too small to inflict any real damage.

"About last night," he began abruptly. "I don't know what you remember, but—"

"I remember enough to know that you're the lowest form of beast aboard this ship. Compared to you, the rats in the bilge seem like august creatures!"

"Listen to me, Katy."

"I never gave you permission to call me that."

"My condolences. Now, kindly listen to me before it's too late."

" 'Tis already too late. I intend to leave this ship when the first opportunity presents itself, and if you try to stop me, I swear I'll wedge a steel blade between your ribs. I'll not remain here as a pawn for your perversions."

He smiled. "The opportunity to leave may present itself sooner than you would like, though you may have some objection to the means." He paused, calculating her reaction. "I see that I have finally captured your attention. Good. Two things, then. First, I apologize for my conduct last night. It was reprehensible. You have my word that it won't happen again. Second, there's an enemy ship bearing down on us, so you have your choice of packing your things and waiting to be rescued, or stowing away so you won't be found."

The green eyes became fearful. "What kind of enemy ship?"

"It looks to be pirate."

Her face paled. Jason continued. "At this point we're not exactly a treasure trove. We're without cargo, badly disabled, and carry no cannon. Frankly, my dear, the only item of any value aboard the whole ship is . . . you."

Feeling her knees buckle, she sagged onto the edge of the chest and stared at the floor. "What will they do to me if they find me?"

Had she been less than cooperative, he would have told her exactly what she could expect if captured, but seeing how the news had affected her, he softened his tack. "They'll not find you, Katy. Look here." She lifted her gaze and watched him move to the wall by the bunk and place his hand high on the paneling. Beneath the pressure he exerted, a narrow door swung open. " 'Tis neither wide nor deep," he said, "but then, neither are you. The master's most valuable possessions are usually hidden in here. Come over here and have a look at it. We don't have much time left."

Astounded by the existence of the false panel, she walked slowly over to it and peeked inside. It was longer than it was deep, and she felt suffocated just thinking about being trapped inside. It would be so dark. "Is there any way out from the inside?"

"Unfortunately, no. It was built to conceal goods, not people."

She looked skeptical. "What if the pirates should decide to imprison your crew and sink your ship? How would I get out?"

"You wouldn't. But that might be a more merciful alternative than what those barbarians would offer you." Without being explicit, he had explained much. She was suddenly overwhelmed by thoughts of the past.

"My mother once knew a man who had been captured by pirates," she said hypnotically. "I wish they had killed him."

Uncomfortable with her words, he cleared his throat. "Come on, Katy. Get inside." As he reached for her arm, she suffered a moment of panic and shied away from him.

"But my trunk! They'll know I'm here. They'll come looking for me!"

"The trunk merely contains garments that I have purchased for my wife. After all, what master would be foolish enough to transport a woman in such dangerous waters?"

"Your wife?"

"Aye." He nodded as he grasped her hand and coaxed her toward the secret door. "My wife."

The passage of time was impossible to mark, but it seemed an eternity. The closeness of the chamber was suffocating. Katy could feel her heart as if it were beating in her mouth. Its cadence drummed in her ears. What was happening? It was as she began to massage the stiffness from her neck that she heard the sound—a man's voice issuing forth profanities that could only have been learned in the worst hellholes of the world.

And the man's voice was Jason's.

She heard the footfalls almost instantly. Brisk. Deliberate. Heading abaft. Toward her. Pressing her body flat against the bulkhead, she bowed her head and listened as the interloper made his way to the cabin. Katy bit down on her lower lip. She heard the trunk being flung open, furniture banged, drawers dismantled and smashed. His footsteps crossed the floor and thudded to a halt before the wall. She could hear his hands brushing along the length of the mahogany, his nails scratching the tawny wood, and then tapping. He was tapping the paneling to discover which section was hollow! Just as she realized what was happening, an empty sound echoed back at him, and she let forth a scream as the door flew open.

With cutlass drawn, his scarlet robes flowing about him, the picaroon reached a dark hand into the cubicle for the girl, who beat at him with her fists. The fathomless black eyes that had grinned at so rare a find cooled at his prey's resistance. Growling maliciously, he stabbed his cutlass into the aperture, staying the weapon just short of her throat.

Katy's voice deserted her. She stared at the heathen's visage and knew that his soul was as black as his eyes. With a sardonic smile twisting his lips, he tossed his head toward the cabin door and snapped a command at her in his foreign tongue.

When she made no effort to move, he dragged her out of the compartment by her forearm and slung her carelessly over his shoulder. Kicking and screaming, he carried her from the cabin into the alleyway. Once on deck, he dropped her to her feet.

Quickly she snatched her skirt away from him and backed steadily in the opposite direction, bumping into a pirate who bellowed his laughter as she spun round to face him. The man was solidly built, his bare arms protruding from a sleeveless silk tunic, his hands resting securely on the hilt of the scimitar at his waist. Extending his hand, he tilted her chin up to him.

"Your wife, Captain?" Smoothing the sooty hairs of his Vandyke, he proceeded to make a slow circle about her, inspecting her up and down. He wound a strand of her hair around his forefinger and spoke in a mocking tone. "I think not. This one is a virgin. You see how she flinches at my touch? The dey will be pleased that Molkeydaur found him such a treasure."

Katy cringed not only from the pirate's nearness but also from his words. Desperately she bent her gaze outward, and in the colored haze of faces found Jason. On either side of him there stood a corsair, their hands like fetters around his arms, restraining him. Behind him stood another man whose blade was poised lengthwise across the Yankee's throat. The *Elizabeth*'s crew were corralled around the mainmast, their stances drab and weary in comparison to the freebooters', whose gaudy robes flapped in the breeze like plumage, whose scimitars were drawn in anticipation.

The man who had called himself Molkeydaur planted himself before her, commanding her attention. "By what name are you known?"

Cold terror turned the green of her eyes to marble. "M-Mary. Mary Kathleen."

"Mary Kathleen." He pronounced the name softly under his breath, then lifted two fingers to touch the corner of her eye. "Yes. It suits you well. And you, Captain!" He turned to face the Yankee. Jason's muscles tightened as the freebooter advanced toward him. "You have not only ruined your ship with your stupidity, you are about to lose your lovely passenger as well." He laughed. "Such ineptitude!"

"Call off your dogs and I'll show you how inept I am."

The pirate sobered. "Insolence does not become a man in your position, Captain. But how can I expect a man who has exercised such poor judgment with his ship to exercise good judgment where his fate is concerned?" He eyed the stump of the foremast. "I would think a man of your experience would have known to seek a port in the face of such a storm. A man truly at one with the sea can smell a tempest on the wind days before it strikes."

"Oh, I smelled something," Jason taunted, "but it wasn't till you climbed aboard that I realized what it was."

Across the sharp planes of the pirate's face there passed an expression of such malevolence that the man at Jason's back flexed his blade against the Yankee's Adam's apple.

"That makes twice, Captain. I have killed men for less."

Jason neither cowered nor blinked. With cold reserve the flawless line of his mouth slanted upward in silent mimicry of the man's threat, the pugnacity of his gaze proving him dauntless.

"You seem to have little regard for your own life, Captain. Perhaps you need to be reminded of your own mortality." Snapping his fingers high into the air, he barked a command that resulted in a pair of corsairs yanking a crewman from the knot of prisoners at the mainmast and shoving him to his knees. The Algerian whose blade was hovering at Jason's throat removed himself to the sailor's side. Throwing back his robes, he braced his feet wide and, two-handedly, raised his scimitar above the seaman's head. Katy's eyes widened in horror.

The corsair captain nodded, setting in motion the arms that wielded the mighty blade. Katy turned her back as the sibilant glimmer of steel hacked downward. Lifeless, the man's head rolled from his neck.

"You murdering bastard!" With a savage yell Jason rotated his body, tearing his arm from the grip of the man on his left and hammering his elbow into the man's midsection with such force that the freebooter reeled backward. "Slimy son of a bitch!" He moved so fast that the pirate on his right could make only a feeble attempt at unsheathing his blade before Jason's knee slammed into his groin, doubling him over. While the brigand choked on his agony, Jason joined his hands and swung his arms upward into the man's face. The pirate's nose shattered beneath the power of the blow, and a fountain of blood drenched his face as he fell to the deck. Jason pulled the scimitar from the man's sash.

He turned on Molkeydaur then, and Katy saw that there was something elemental in his rage—something primitive, and savage, and magnificent. The Algerian yanked his dagger from its scabbard, and as Jason advanced, spun round and wrenched Katy backward against his body. The girl shrieked as Molkeydaur wrapped his forearm across her throat and trained his dagger at her breast.

Jason and the Algerian locked eyes, each man taking the measure of the other, each man knowing by instinct that the other had killed before and would not hesitate to do so again.

"Do you value the girl's life, Captain?" The question was flung out as a challenge. Jason's eye narrowed as the pirate steadied the point of the dagger at Katy's heart. "The blade." Molkeydaur bent his head toward Jason's weapon. "Now."

The cords in Jason's neck strained with his anger. His knuckles went white around the hilt of the scimitar as the terror he saw paralyzing the girl's features curbed his berserk rage.

He dropped his scimitar to the deck.

A flurry of cloaks and cutlasses enveloped him. Molkeydaur cast the girl aside and in a half-dozen strides stood before Jason.

"Pig."

Jason's head snapped back as the pirate's hand slashed across his mouth.

"You will pay for your rashness, Captain. But nothing so simple as merely having your head lopped off." Impatient now, he clapped his hands and ground out a spate of unintelligible commands. Katy stood motionless as the marauders lashed the *Elizabeth*'s crew to the fife rail, then recoiled as the corpse of the headless seaman was dumped into the sea, the sound echoing with an impious splash. Molkeydaur clamped a hand around the girl's arm and herded her toward the gunwale. Jason was marched athwartship at the point of a cutlass.

"Your ship and crew will undoubtedly meet their end in the coming storm, Captain." The pirate chief gestured toward the cirrus clouds gathering above them. "Sad that you will not be here to witness their demise." He sneered in vicious anticipation. "Or they yours."

The man and the woman were taken aboard the pirate brig, and after the sails were trimmed on a tack that would allow the vessel to run before the storm, Katy learned the power of the pirate's words. They were dragged to the main deck, where Jason was stripped to the waist and bound to the mast, and while Molkeydaur stiffened his hand around Katy's neck, directing her attention toward the tableau that was unfolding before her, a stocky Algerian strutted toward the mainmast, a multithonged whip dangling from his dark hand.

"You will watch," the pirate chief decreed. "And you will see how brave your captain is when the cat dances upon his back. Begin!"

Then began the horror Katy would not have believed any human could watch, much less endure. As the stocky pirate drew back his arm, the ten tongues of leaded rawhide whistled in unison and slashed bloody seams across Jason's broad back. The shouts of encouragement from the onlookers were deafening as the process was repeated a second time, the thongs cleaving through flesh like a plow through snow. The air whistled. Blood splattered as the whip struck a third, fourth, and fifth time. With vicious talons the cat ripped and maimed, splitting Jason's skin. His body convulsed as the lash tore through exposed muscle, but he did not cry out. Again and again the whip engraved itself across his spine, and Katy stared, sickened yet mesmerized. The flesh that had once been bronzed and sinewy was crosshatched with ragged gashes that bled crimson, and still the whip sang.

"You're killing him!" she cried, sickened. She tried to turn her head away, but Molkeydaur would have none of it, levying obedience with the fingers he ground more deeply into her neck. So she watched the slaughter continue until it seemed that Jason had no more blood to spill. When her vision ran red with the spectacle of his mutilation, she fainted.

The brig ran before the storm for several hours before it was forced to heave to. Leaving Jason's unconscious body tied to the mast to rot, the brigands gathered below deck to enjoy the plunder from an earlier, more gainful raid on American shipping: rum that had been bound for Africa's slave coast. While the brig floundered in the churning seas, Molkeydaur drained mug after mug of the black brew, his thoughts lingering darkly on the girl locked in his cabin, his lust sharpened by the ribald needling from his crewmen, who intended to weather the storm in giddy delirium.

Katy sat on the pirate's bunk, her thoughts bent on Jason. Yesterday Jason MacAuley had been an adversary. Today, in the face of this greater peril, he was her only friend. Was he still alive? Had he been cut down and led to safety when the tempest struck, or was he still tied to the mast, there to await execution by the sea? As the brig vibrated against the foaming mountains of water that boomed across the deck, Katy's hopes began to dim for the man who, in certain death, had become her comrade.

The door blew open suddenly. In the shallow light of a gimbaled candle, Molkeydaur swayed in the portal, gripping the doorjamb with both hands. He leered stupidly at her, then grappled for the wall as the brig keeled abeam, catapulting him sideways. His lurching steps were testimony to his drunkenness, though Katy had no problem smelling the vapors from where she sat. He clung to the wall till the ship steadied itself, then inched himself slowly away from its protection and stood tottering in the middle of the cabin. A victim of the wind, his turban had become unraveled and drooped down over his ear and around his neck like a debilitated asp. Katy watched as he attempted to rid himself of its bothersome presence. Batting it as if it were alive, he accomplished little except to further entangle himself in its length. Frustrated, he began to fight in earnest to kill the thing, and only when the ship pitched both pirate and turban headlong against the bulkhead was the battle finally won. From where she sat Katy peered at the body of the brigand as he lay sprawled on the deck. On cat's feet she padded across the floor and ranged around him, half-expecting him to lunge at her. But he didn't move, save for the slow rise and fall of his chest.

Testing his shoulder with her toe, she jumped back, anticipating some reaction. When none came, she concluded that he was definitely unconscious and took a step closer, her gaze coming to rest on the dagger sheathed at his waist. She would kill him now and be done with it. Fumbling for possession of the weapon, she inhaled deeply, raised the dagger, then held it midair. Where should the weapon be pillowed? His heart? His throat? With waning resolve she inhaled again and squeezed the dagger more tightly. This was no time to be fainthearted. The man was a cutthroat, a scion of Lucifer. He had to be killed. But . . .

Her hand dropped to her side, anger at her cowardice welling within her. "I can't do it," she whispered. "I can't." And then the brig heaved to larboard again and Katy found herself crushed against the bulkhead, her thoughts racing toward any avenue of escape. *Jason. I have to find Jason.*

Leaving the pirate where he lay, she ran from the cabin. She pulled open the outer bulkhead door, and suffered a stinging blast of rain pellets in her face, accompanied by a gale of wind that blew her against the rail of the quarterdeck companionway. With her arms shielding her face, she slatted her eyes against the driving rain and peered through the downpour. Was he there? Squinting, her ears thick with the terrible keening of the wind, she pushed wet tangles of hair from her eyes and in a burst of lightning perceived the mainmast, and at its base, the figure of a man, lurid with his own blood.

Oh, Jason!

Heedless of the danger on deck, she plunged forward, the dagger still clenched in her fist. The wind tore at her flesh. The rain that fell in torrents intermingled with salt spray and bit into her, hurting her face and eyes. She staggered, hampered by the soggy weight of her skirt, and forced her feet to move, one before the other. Lightning ignited the sky. Thunder exploded like gunpowder. Off the starboard quarter a swell of foam and water rose ominously, sending Katy lunging for cover that was not there. Like an avalanche it broke across the deck, slamming her hard into the larboard gunwale, where it crushed her like a ton of earth. The taste of brine burned from her throat to her chest. Her hair was plastered to her face; her legs twined in the wet shroud of her skirt. But she had somehow managed to retain her grasp on the dagger. She crouched into the bulwark, away from the battering force of the wind and rain. Still shaky but too frightened to remain where she was, she focused on the mainmast, and rising on feet that tingled from the cold, stumbled feebly in that direction.

He looked dead. Not just unconscious. Dead. Where his skin was not ashen, it was tinged a cold blue from exposure. His head hung limply from his neck and lolled against the mast. She touched her hand to the lank hair that capped his head, then, choked with despair, lifted his head to confirm his demise. She felt a tremor ripple through her as his pain-ridden brown eye met her gaze. He was alive! Scrambling around the mast, she steadied her hand and sliced through the bonds at his wrists.

"I thought they had killed you!" she sobbed above the thunder.

He drew his hands to himself with ponderous effort. Already

the ropes had eroded his flesh, scoring his wrists in crimson. She bent down to him.

"You'll drown out here," he rasped, the reality of her presence not yet firm in his mind. Pain was reality. Deep, searing pain.

She cupped her hands to her mouth and spoke close to his ear. "We . . . have . . . to . . . leave . . . here!" His back glistened red.

His face contorted as consciousness and reason came flooding back. Shielding the girl with one of his arms, he struggled with thoughts that lacked substance. Everything lacked substance, except the consuming pain—and the girl who was searching his face so expectantly.

"What will we do?" Her words fell softly upon his face.

He bent his head against her cheek, the thought of having to move his body making him sick. "Where is Molkeydaur?"

"Drunk in his cabin! Unconscious!" She yelled to be heard above the roar.

Jason closed his eyes to the spiked raindrops being hurled at him and willed himself to a level of existence that transcended human feeling. Steeling himself, he straightened his back, his muscles screaming at the abuse. "You can't stay here, Katy," he choked.

"Neither can you! Just tell me what I'm to do!"

He would not tell her that there was little hope for escape. Even if they could cut loose one of the ship's boats, they would capsize once they hit the water. But was that not better than dying at the hands of these scum? Aye, if they were to die, they would do so proudly, not like thralls. "Listen to me," he began. "Go back to the cabin. Collect what you can find—candles, tinderbox, blankets. Wait for me there."

"Where will you be?"

His eyes strayed to the network of cables toiling with the weight of their burden. "I'm going to repay a debt," he said, venom in every word.

"You'll need this, then." She pressed the dagger into his hand. "Someone might try to stop you!"

"Nay," he shouted. "That bastard might wake up. Use it if he does."

She shook her head and closed his fingers over the hilt. "He's too drunk to wake up! You take it!"

Against his better judgment, he gambled that the pirate would not regain consciousness and reluctantly accepted the weapon. "I'll take you back," he said as he eased himself onto his feet.

Following his example, she clung to the mast and yelled into the wind, "I'll be all right! See to yourself!"

Gathering her courage she raced toward the shelter of the quarterdeck. In the dimness of the alleyway she leaned against the bulkhead for a moment, then staggered aft. In the pirate's cabin she found Molkeydaur's body sprawled where it had fallen. For a space she scanned the sparse appointment of the room and contemplated Jason's instructions. *Candles, blankets, tinderbox.* Her gaze passed over Molkeydaur and lighted on his turban. *And bandages. Jason will need bandages. Long strips of them.*

Loath to touch him, she knelt down, swallowing her disgust, and began to unwrap the length of satin from around him. That done, she stripped the blanket from his bunk and proceeded to ransack the lower drawers, tossing two candles and another blanket onto the floor. She did not hear the man crawling toward her, nor see the hand as it reached out to embrace her, but as she turned, he was suddenly upon her.

The galley was deserted. Like the rest of the crew, the cook had abandoned the forecastle to partake of the Yankee booty below deck. Jason scoured his domain, relieving the man of biscuits, a skin of wine, and a meat cleaver. After bundling the provender into a sack, he gripped the cleaver and headed out for the deck once again, turning his face away as a blast of wind and rain slammed into him. Wary of his footing, he edged along the forecastle toward the starboard bow, and upon reaching the gunwale, clung to the rail as he trudged toward the first row of belaying pins. Cables pulled and strained above him like a spider's web. Gritting his teeth with pain, he raised the cleaver. A tack line snapped and curled upward as he sank the blade into its width. Summoning all his strength, he hacked viciously at the next and the next, severing lines like a scythe through a field of grass. As he moved on to the mainmast and began to wield the cleaver into the running rigging, the foremast creaked with tension and began to quiver almost imperceptibly.

She did not recognize her scream as her own. The man struck swiftly, dragging her to the floor before she had a chance to thwart the attack, then rolled atop her, pinioning her beneath his weight. Her strident screams maddened the pirate. Enraged, he balled his hand into a fist and drove it into her skull just above her temple. Katy's head exploded with white light. When she blinked, she saw a double image of her attacker. Two men straddling her. Two mouths leering at her dazed expression. And then the humming transformed into laughter and the men were fumbling with their breeches and grunting like animals. She shook her head weakly. Four arms grabbed hold of her legs. She saw her skirt being thrown above her waist, heard her chemise rending apart. Groggily she lifted her arm to repel the assault, then cried aloud as the men dealt another dizzying blow to her face. The white light faded to gray. A high-pitched droning buzzed in her head. She felt a fleshy limpness against her thigh as her attacker wrestled with his liquor-induced impotence. Then a cry erupted from her throat that was haunting enough to make the man's flesh shrivel with sudden fear.

Jason slashed through the last backstay, then staggered toward the helm, where he clung exhausted. Before him, unbound rigging flagellated the mast, scourging the vibrating spires with savage fury. Jason stumbled down the quarterdeck companionway and lunged toward the door. There was a boat secured astern that a few swift chops would release into the water. If Katy could swim there might be a slim chance of escape, but he knew the sea too well to speculate on the odds.

The moment he entered the passageway he heard the horrible noise emanating from the far cabin, and he felt his blood run cold. *Katy!* Lumbering breathlessly toward the portal, he shoved it open with a shoulder. Unaware of the intrusion, the pirate slapped the girl again and again, angered by his impotence, crazed by the ungodly sounds that throbbed and gurgled in her throat. Jason saw . . . and his one eye blackened with demon wrath. His raging obscenities split the air as he drew back his arm and flung the cleaver, embedding it in the pirate's spine. Molkeydaur's howl of pain rang sweetly in Jason's ears. His eyes rolled back into his head as he died, slumping atop the girl, crushing her beneath him. Jason seized the man by his shoulders and wrenched him off Katy, then knelt helplessly beside her. Her face was marbled with blood where the pirate's fists had cudgeled her. Her thighs were inflamed with the man's unsuccessful attempt to enter her. And as Jason touched a gentle hand to her hair, she rolled away from him, whimpering and sobbing, her knees drawn to her chest.

"Sweet Jesus," he whispered guiltily, for it was he who had sent her back here. Stemming his emotions before they clouded his logic, he crooned softly in her ear as he lifted her, but she would not be comforted, her paroxysm only increasing as he swaddled her in a blanket. With the girl securely in his arms, he yanked the meat cleaver from Molkeydaur's back, and leaving the provisions behind, headed for the main deck. There was no longer any question of her ability to swim. He would have to find some other way of getting her off the ship if she were to survive. But what other way was there?

He stepped out onto the main deck and at the sound of cracking timber narrowed his eye at the foredeck. Even through the blinding rain Jason could see that the foremast was slanting abaft. His mouth dry, he scrambled up the companionway and looked frantically about him.

I can't save you, Katy! he screamed at himself. *I made you go back to the cabin, and now I can't save you!*

The ship rumbled as the foremast tore away from its base. The planks beneath his feet began to shake.

Christ! His eye fell dully on the fresh-water cask lashed to the bulwark, then back to the tiny girl in his arms. Water casks floated. If he were to empty it . . .

Like a giant domino the foremast toppled backward, crashing into the mainmast in its descent. Without further considering what he was doing, Jason set the girl down beside him and hatcheted through the ropes that bound the water cask to the rail; then, after prying the lid open with the edge of his cleaver, he emptied the remaining water from the cask. An eruption of splintering wood hastened his activity as the foremast veered to larboard and smashed through the quarterdeck. Jason grabbed Katy. Crazed, she tried to kick her way free of the blanket and his arms, and when he thrust her inside the barrel, her screams became so violent that he thought she would choke herself.

"Forgive me, Katy!" Jason yelled as she tried to climb out of the cask. Wincing, he doubled his fist and knocked her a solid blow on the jaw. She crumpled to the bottom of the barrel. The icy Atlantic poured into the gaping maw on the quarterdeck. Jason hammered the lid shut, and as the planking across the deck ripped away, he muscled the barrel onto the rail and heaved it over the side. The sea broke full force across the quarterdeck, clearing it of everything except the man who clung to the starboard rail. To his left the mainmast creaked. Beneath his feet, what had once been flooring was fragmenting and being devoured by the sea. He raced toward the ship's boat in the stern. The mainmast emitted a raucous grating sound, seesawed. Jason sliced through the cables that secured the boat to the davits. The boat torpedoed into the surf. Vaulting over the rail, he became airborne and then his body hit the water. The cry of agony that escaped his lips as the Atlantic purged his wounds carried eerily on the wind.

A breath of warmth skimmed her face and whispered softly against her cheeks and eyelids. Drowsily she tilted her face toward its radiance, the nearby sound of water impressing upon her mind that she was extremely thirsty. As she flicked her tongue around the inside of her mouth, a sudden ache intruded upon her repose and she flinched. She felt then not just one ache, but many. Her jaw. Her back. Her head. A haunting image jarred her memory. The pirate. A searing pain ricocheted through her vitals as testimony to what he had tried to do, and spreading her fingers across her face, she screamed into them.

"He's dead, Katy." A man's voice spoke beside her. Gently he tugged her hands away from her face. Blinded by the sun, she saw only the dark outline of Jason's face above her. Uncertain of what had transpired, she bolted upright and raked the horizon in every direction. Jason addressed the unasked question that worried her eyes. "They're all dead. The ship went down. All hands aboard. We're safe . . . for now."

Tears starred her eyes. Safe? She was safe? Nay. She was dead. Full of her own misery and unable to bear Jason's scrutiny, she turned away from him, and rolling up in a ball, buried her head beneath her arms.

"Do you want to know what happened?"

I was raped! Why did you not let me die?

"Katy?"

She shook her head vehemently. Tears glazed her cheeks.

"Are you in much pain?"

She didn't move.

"He hurt you badly. I know." The deep tones of his voice became a benediction. "I'm sorry."

She didn't want to hear that. Being sorry would change nothing. Being sorry wouldn't ease the pain.

"Would talking about it make you feel any better?"

She rubbed her hand across her nose and gave no indication that she had heard him.

Frustrated, haggard, and in pain himself, Jason lost his temper. "Do you think that you are the only one who has suffered?!" he blasted her. "Do you think I had an easy time keeping this boat afloat or retrieving the cask where you were hidden? I didn't! I had a hell of a time! And do you know why I did it? Not so I could sit here and have you turn your back on me! I should have let you float to Africa in that barrel!"

His words stung. She sat up abruptly to render an equally blistering obloquy, but the acute pain in her head diverted her attention and she only sputtered what had been foremost in her mind. "Why did you not let me die?"

Instantly contrite for his censure, he drew her into his arms and soothed her as she sobbed against his chest. "I didn't mean that, Katy. I'm sorry." Like an uncorked tap, her tears flowed, wetting her face and the hairs on his chest with indiscriminate equality. He caressed her hand within his and brought it to his lips, placing soft kisses across her cold fingertips. For long minutes he held her to him, offering understanding in his silence, comfort in his strength. She cried long and hard and deeply. Her body trembled with the intensity of her emotion, and in an attempt to calm her, he pressed his cheek against the crown of her head and folded her tightly within the circle of his arms, wanting to protect and love her.

"I thought I had lost you this morning. I looked for the cask at first light, but I couldn't see a trace of it, only debris and planking from the wreck. I thought I'd killed you, Katy. God, I thought you were dead." He touched his lips to her still-damp hair. "The oars in the boat washed away in the storm, so I broke off some of the planking from the wreckage and paddled around looking for anything that resembled a hogshead. I finally found you, but not before I added a good twenty years to my life." Smoothing her hair back from her face, he rocked her slowly, peacefully, and she was consoled and sought to ebb her tears. Sniffling, she sat aright, dragged the back of her hand across her eyes, and hiccuped.

"Why do you always hiccup?" he mused.

She stared at her hands and shrugged.

"Better now?"

She nodded.

"Do you hurt overly much?"

Again she nodded, still unable to look him straight in the face.

"If we tear off a strip of cloth from the bottom of your skirt, douse it in seawater, and press it to your face and thighs, it might aid the healing process. The salt will sting at first, but I think you'll feel better for it in the end." Her silence told him that this was not the source of her distress. "The pirate didn't . . ." He cleared his throat. "He didn't enter you, Katy." He saw her face suffuse with color at his words. "Sometimes when a man is besotted, he is unable to . . . to function as a man. The bastard hurt you, but he didn't rape you. Your virginity is still your own."

Suppressing the humiliation that seemed to choke her, she lifted her face to his. Red-rimmed and puffy, her eyes shone green with tears yet unspent, and for a moment Jason felt himself impaled by their astonishing intensity. She looked at his face for the first time then, and in her voice he heard her bewilderment.

"What has happened to you?" She raised a finger to touch the flawless right eye that had supposedly been gouged out, and traced the brow that sloped in an unblemished path toward his temple. His eyelid was thin-skinned and lashed with glossy black hairs that cast wispy shadows across his iris. The eye was finely shaped; in absolute symmetry with the opposite side of his face, with no imperfection to mar its comeliness.

"I lost my patch in the water," he explained. "I'm damn lucky 'tis all I lost."

"But . . . your eye!" She shifted her gaze from left to right, comparing the details of each eye. "There is nothing wrong with it. 'Tis perfect."

"Indeed?" He examined the socket with two fingers. "Feels better." He blinked, and at the expression of utter shock on her face, laughed. "Did you believe my story, Katy?" She pressed her teeth into her lower lip and merely stared. "I was hit by a snapped cable when we were making our crossing. Hurt like hell when I had to open my eye. So I slapped a patch across it for protection, and that seemed to help. I apologize if I have disillusioned you in any way, but I offered to remove the patch once. Remember?"

Aye, she remembered. "You play me for a fool, Jason MacAuley," she chafed, "but it pleases me that you are not blind." She set her thumb delicately on his eyelid and smoothed the flesh in awe. He looked as she had imagined he would. He was . . . beautiful.

A painful grimace tightened his features, and instinctively she pulled her hand away from him. "Have I . . . ?"

" 'Tis not you." He sucked in his breath. "My back continues to remind me of Molkeydaur."

Remembering then the horror he had undergone, she inched her way around to his side and gasped at the sight of the raw pulp that stretched from neck to waist. Suddenly overwhelmed with the fear that he would die, she still attempted to hide her fright. "I need to attend to this, Jason. We need bandages." Then she remembered. "Did you bring the provisions I found in the cabin?"

He shook his head. "When I found you, I . . . got too involved in other things to remember to bring them."

"Have we *no* provisions?" She scanned the small boat anxiously.

"None."

"No food? No water?" The dryness in her throat burgeoned at the thought.

"We have our lives, Katy. Last night I was not so sure I could salvage those."

She sank to the bottom of the boat, utterly devastated. "How long do we have?"

"That depends on how far off the normal trade routes we were blown. Someone might find us today or five days from now. There's no way of telling."

She held her hand to herself to prevent it from shaking. "And if someone should find us a week from now, would there be anything left of us to rescue?" His silence confirmed her suspicions. "I see." Training an eye on the horizon, she asked in a soft voice, "What will happen if we are rescued by pirates?"

"You need not worry about that. We will not set foot on another pirate brig. You have my word on that."

"But what can you do to prevent it?"

He sighed his exhaustion. *God help me, but I'll break your neck before allowing you to be subjected to that again.* "Don't ask me. Just know that I will take care of it." Reflexively he stretched his hands, and in their strength she discovered his meaning.

To divert her mind from the food and water she craved, she set about nursing their injuries. With Jason's assistance she tore her skirt away to the knees and used sections of the material to bathe both their wounds. She enjoined him to lie prostrate while she laid a long strip of wet muslin across his back; then she wet another square of cloth and in the privacy of the stern salved the areas of her violation. It stung, as Jason had said it would, but if she was inclined toward self-pity, she had only to observe his tolerance of his suffering. By sunset she had become inured to the pain and to the fact that, having escaped death once, she faced it yet again. But the terrible thirst—that was something she could not become accustomed to. They slept that night in the bottom of the boat, Jason on his stomach, Katy on her back, the one blanket that he had wrapped her in the night before covering them both. She had been reluctant to lie beside him, but found the darkness and the cold night air to be keen inducements.

Jason sensed her estrangement as she lay stiffly beside him. Turning his head, he perceived the rigidity of her profile, and resisting the urge to touch her, spoke lightly. "You're not asleep." It was more a statement than a question.

"Nay. I was thinking." In her mind she drew imaginary lines connecting the celestial dots that patterned the sky.

"Dare I ask about what?"

"About you, actually."

"You flatter me, lady."

When she blinked, all the lines she had drawn dissolved. "My thoughts were not very complimentary. I doubt that you would be flattered.''

"Try me.''

She hesitated. ''I was wondering if you would reconsider this foolhardy plan to take me to America and return me instead to Cádiz.''

"And how do you propose we arrive there? By swimming?''

"Do not make light of me!'' She turned onto her side and stared at the dark visage of the man beside her. ''You can tell my stepmother that I drowned. How would she ever know whether you spoke truth or not? I suppose I almost *did* drown, so you would not have to stretch the truth very far. Can you understand why I ask? I cannot go to America to be pawed . . . and . . . and . . . molested by a husband I have never seen. I would rather go back to a place where I am considered to be a worthless imposition. At least they would not force me to marry. Please, Jason?''

He digested what she told him quickly. Is that how Carolyn Astruc had convinced her niece to leave? By telling her that she was a worthless imposition? ''And what would you do in Cádiz? Evade your uncle for the rest of your life?''

"You presume too much!''

She rolled angrily onto her back. She *had* thought her uncle's conduct obscene, and was ashamed that Jason had noticed. A strained silence filled the void between them. When she could stand it no longer, she said, ''You have no intention of taking me back, do you?''

"Nay, lady. I cannot take you back.''

The tiny flecks of light above her blurred with unshed tears. ''What am I to you that you so want to destroy me?''

"I do not want to destroy you.''

"Yet you will. And for what? A fat purse of tainted money? What gives you the right?''

"Do not speak to me of rights, girl. I struck a bargain, and if I live long enough, I will see it met. A man gives his word and abides by it.''

"At the expense of another's welfare? Or are my wishes simply not important enough to consider?''

He cradled his head in the crook of his arm and rubbed his eyes with thumb and forefinger. ''You tire me with your blather.''

"I don't even know you!'' she objected. ''Who are you other than a previously one-eyed sea captain who may or may not be married? Who are you, Jason MacAuley? Where do you come from?''

"Shall I recite the entire bloodline or will immediate family suffice? My father died at sea many years ago. My mother lives on a small island in Frenchman Bay off the coast of Massachusetts. 'Tis where I reside when not at sea. My brother, Ian, resides in Virginia. The *Elizabeth* belongs to him.''

When he stopped, she waited for him to continue, but he didn't. '' 'Tis all?''

"What else would you have me tell you?" *The real reason why I am being forced to take you to your stepmother? That is something you must never learn.*

She snugged the blanket beneath her chin and turned her face, seeking his eyes in the dark. "Will you not consider my request?"

"I have told you my decision. Do not broach the matter again."

Stone-faced, she looked away. "Why did you even bother to save me?" she intoned. "I wish you had let me die."

In the morning she would not speak to him, but her anger did not extend so far that she refused to minister to his wounds. Wordlessly she cleansed the suppurating sores that had formed on his back, and tried not to inhale the putrid odor that was beginning to emanate from the inflamed flesh. His face and eyes burned with fever, but he said nothing of his distress. She remained in the stern the entire day, watching as he moaned and tossed fitfully in his sleep. The sun beat down on her, augmenting her already maddening thirst. Her tongue felt swollen. Her lips were dry and splitting. Around her, the cool wetness of ocean water lapped the sides of the boat and mocked her with its abundance. She trailed her hand in the surf for a time, then placed her wet palm across her mouth and grimaced at the taste. Her stomach churned and seethed at the lack of sustenance. Her limbs began to feel like sponges. Her head throbbed. On the horizon there was neither sail nor cloud, just a vast expanse of undrinkable ocean and imminent death.

The next day she could not muster the strength to drag herself into the stern. She lay beside Jason and every so often bathed the perspiration from his body and placed a cold compress on his forehead. His skin was like fire to the touch. She knew his back to be infected, but with no supplies there was little she could do for him. The sound of the water tormented her. She cursed it and cried at it, and when she felt Jason's hand on her shoulder, soothing her, she cried the more, because she did not want to be comforted by him. She wanted to hate him for ever appearing in her life, for not letting her drown, for refusing to take her back to Cádiz. She wanted to hate him because he was going to die and leave her all alone.

Sometime during the fourth day, when her tongue was so thick in her mouth that she thought she would choke on it, she pulled herself up to the gunwale, and cupping her hands, dipped them into the water. She had to have something to drink. She had to! Trembling with weakness, her fingers leaked most of what she had captured. By the time her hands reached her mouth, she had naught but a thimbleful to sip. She repeated the process, keeping her hands steady, but when she raised the miraculous liquid to her lips, a startling smack separated her hands and she found herself staring into Jason's clenched fist.

"It will kill you!" he raged in a gravelly voice. Barely conscious, he had propped himself on an elbow and inched his way over to her. His fevered eyes bored into her mercilessly. "Get away from there. You'll not die like that."

She tried to yank her arm away from him, but lacking the strength, fell into the bottom of the boat beside him. "I'll . . . I'll die anyway!" she wailed. "Please! I'm so thirsty."

"Nay!"

Pinioned to the floor by Jason's arm, she submitted to total despair and he was helpless to calm the deep racking sobs that beset her. Her body shook as she wept unceasingly.

"I will not let you kill yourself," he rasped in near-delirium. "I will not."

During the night a soft rain burst forth from the clouds to quench the thirst of the two asleep in the boat. Katy, awakened by watery darts slapping into her face, parted her blistered lips to receive the fluid and tasted with the rainwater the saltiness of blood draining into her mouth. Too enfeebled to move, she lay with her face open to the sky, drinking in the miserly gift it had bestowed upon her. Unable to lie on his back, Jason turned his face to the side and imbibed what he could that way, though it was very little. The rain that fell with such gentle insistence became his bane, for it flayed his butchered flesh like the tines of a pitchfork, and the excruciating pain became unbearable. Rain streamed across his face, yet only he knew that what set his face awash consisted of more than just raindrops.

On the fifth day he awoke with the sensation that he was drowning. Straining an eye open, he found two inches of water sloshing around in the bottom of the boat, and forgetting what had passed the night before, dreams and reality having mingled, he concluded that the boat had sprung a leak. Berserk with fever, he dragged himself out of the water to a kneeling position and studied the girl's pallid face with growing trepidation. With a hand that felt lifeless he sought out the pulse in her throat, and when a vibration flickered against his fingertips, he experienced an outpouring of relief that, for a moment, paralyzed him.

Don't fail me now, beloved. You must live.

Resorting to his seafaring instincts, he made a scoop with his hands and dumped a handful of water over the side, the pain of his movement cutting into his muscles and bringing tears to his eyes. He tossed out another handful and then another, and then the agony smothered him and he lunged for the gunwale to break his fall. Before his head hit the side, an image flashed before him, and when he slumped to the floor once again, unconscious, he still saw the great white sheets of canvas firmly imprinted on the back of his eyelids.

4

"Are they alive, Daniel?"

The man who had been addressed placed his ear against Katy's breast. "I think the man is dead, but I can hear a heartbeat here, faintly. We'd better get her back to the ship."

"But what are you going to do with him? We can't just leave him here. Can we?"

Daniel English rose with the girl's body limp in his arms. He stared down at the dead man. "No. I suppose not. Fergus would want to give him a decent burial. Let me get her into the boat. Then I'll help you with him. But by the bloody Virgin, I don't know if my stomach is strong enough to stand his stench."

Aboard the *Ugly Jane*, Fergus McFadden watched the skiff plod slowly through the water and slammed his fist against the rail. "By damn, Daniel, if you were rowing any slower, 'tis backward you'd be going," he muttered to himself.

When the smaller boat pulled alongside the square-rigger, Fergus sent two men scrambling down the ladder to assist his first mate, then paced before the rail while the bodies were carried aloft. Daniel jumped onto the deck, transferring the girl from his shoulder to his arms as he strode toward the captain.

"She's barely alive, sir. Where shall I put her?"

Fergus McFadden looked far down his nose at the black hair that veiled the child's features, then with a leathery finger parted the matted strands and regarded the bruised oval of her face. "Poor lass. Take her to your cabin, Daniel, and you bunk down with Snyder. What about the man?"

"I think he's dead, sir, but we thought you might want to say some proper words over him."

The captain looked askance at the half-clad body that was being placed facedown on the deck, and shook his head. "Aye," he whispered. "I'll see to it. You be getting the lass into a warm bed." When the young sailor had departed, Fergus took reluctant steps toward the body and bent on one knee beside it, the foulness from the decaying flesh of the man's back poisoning the air. " 'Tis a savage way to have to die. The poor wretch. Help me turn him over, and one of you be fetching some old canvas so we can stitch him up a fitting shroud." Respectfully three of them eased the body onto its back, and it was only then that the ship's master was afforded a clear view of the man's face.

"Jaysus! Jason!"

In the early-morning hours of the third day after her rescue, Katy was awakened by the clanging of a bell. She pried her eyes open, expecting to find the familiar trappings of the *Elizabeth*. What she found instead was a great bear of a man studying her face, apparently with as much shock as she herself was registering.

Defensively she clutched the blanket to her chin. Weak and distrustful, she studied the man. His pate and face were endowed with a lush abundance of silver hair through which darker strands were sparsely woven. His countenance was pleasant, his complexion florid. The eyes that beheld hers were wide and piercingly blue.

"Have you a name, lass?"

Though intact, she found her voice to be scratchy. "Mary Kathleen Ryan."

"There!" He laughed in a great booming voice, slapping his immense thigh. "I knew you to be Irish! Without even seeing the color of your eyes, I knew it!" When his laughter subsided, he wiped his eyes but continued to stare at her. "I apologize for staring, but 'tis uncanny how much you resemble . . ." The old man shook his head. "Yer eyes. The color is so much like hers, but that was many years ago and my memory is probably not serving me well. So tell me, Mary Kathleen Ryan, are you well enough to tell me what happened to you?"

She was unprepared for the question, and the vacant look that she leveled upon him told him as much.

"Perhaps 'tis a little too soon to be asking such questions," he conceded. "Later, mayhap, when you're feeling stronger."

Relieved, she nodded.

"Then I think I should be telling you a mite about where you are so you'll be more at ease. You're board the *Ugly Jane* and I'm her master, Fergus McFadden. We're nine weeks out of Bombay, and depending upon what kind of winds we can catch, we'll be making landfall in Boston sometime in early June or late May. Now, lass, can you at least be telling me where it is you were bound?"

She cleared the gravel from her throat. "Yorktown."

"Yorktown, you say?" The significance evolved slowly, yet once the connection was made, it hit him like a sledgehammer. Ryan? Yorktown? *Good God, Jason! What is it you were trying to do?*

Responding to the look of near-horror on the man's face, Katy hazarded a question. "Captain, there was a man with me—where is he?"

He blinked quickly and tried to look normal. "He's in my cabin. But I'll not mislead you, lass. He's a very sick man. Full of infection. I have a poultice on his back and hope that that will draw out some of the poison, but . . ." His voice faded, and he tried to assess her reaction. "A prayer or two might help more than my poultice."

"When might I see him?"

"Oh"—he scratched his bushy eyebrow—"I don't know if that's a good idea right now, lass. Wait until his condition improves a bit—yours too, for that matter. He's not a pretty sight, that one. What was it? A flogging?"

Katy nodded.

" 'Tis what I thought. And you, lass? Did the savages who did that to him hurt you other than the bruises on yer face?"

Absently she touched the hollow of her cheek. "Nay," she whispered. " 'Tis all." Yet the shame that surged through her blazed across her face. Fergus blanched at what he thought she was secreting from him, though he did not question her further.

"I'll have Daniel serve you up some victuals, and I'll rummage through the slop chest for a new rig for you, and maybe if you show improvement today, you might feel like taking a jaunt around the deck tomorrow. How does that sound?" He stood up, rising to his full six feet, five inches. "You be resting now. I'll look in on you later." He slouched down as he left the cabin, ducking his head to avoid the crosspiece, and when he had gone, Katy snuggled beneath the covers, her eyes dark in introspection.

His easy manner was not to be trusted. Yet what concerned her most was Jason, for her future hinged upon whether he lived or died. If he lived, he would undoubtedly find some way to drag her to Yorktown, but if he died . . .

If he died, who but she would know what his original intent had been? No one need learn of his bargain with Pamela or of the betrothal. No one need learn the true purpose of her voyage. If Jason died, she would be free—free to escape this impending marriage, free to return to Cádiz. She would tell Captain McFadden that . . . that . . . that she had been returning to Yorktown to claim her inheritance, but had decided to sign everything over to her stepmother and return to Cádiz. She would sign all the necessary papers in Boston and book passage to Cádiz from there. Yes. That sounded convincing. He would believe her.

But you have no money. How will you book passage on a ship or remain in Boston even one day without money?

She nibbled the knuckle of her forefinger. She couldn't allow herself to worry about that. Captain McFadden would be sympathetic to her plight. He would see that she was taken care of.

Satisfied, she burrowed into her pillow and breathed more easily.

But what if he doesn't die?

Her eyes flew open. If he didn't die, she would have to devise another plan. There had to be something she could do, and between now and the time they reached Boston, she intended to find out what. She really had no wish that he die, but it would certainly make her life less complicated if he did.

At precisely eight bells Daniel English, first mate, laden with the morning's fare of gruel and molasses, entered the cabin, making a seat for himself beside the bunk. Along with Fergus, he had attended to the girl for the past three days, and he still experienced an upheaval of resentment at the man or men who had inflicted such abuse upon her. She was so very tiny. How could anyone have raised his hand against her? In these past days the need to protect her had begun to consume him. Her vulnerability provided an outlet for the sensitive part of his nature kept hidden from others. In her helplessness, he found a source of strength for himself—a strength that he was hesitant to relinquish.

"Fergus said I should feed you your breakfast, Miss Ryan." Never having seen her eyes open, he peered at the light green irises in awe. "You have green eyes." He gaped. "I mean, I've never seen eyes that green before."

She colored at the sailor's observation, while he, noticing the tinge of pink blooming around her fading bruises, grinned at her improving condition.

"I'm glad you're feeling better. I wish I could say the same for the man across the way."

"You mean Jason."

"Aye. I don't see how he's lasted this long. I gave him up for dead the first day I found him."

She stared cross-eyed at the spoon of gruel hovering at the tip of her nose and squirmed backward. "I think I'm strong enough to feed myself, Mr. —"

"Just call me Daniel."

"And I'm Katy." Blushing, she gently wrested the spoon from his hand.

"But I was given specific orders to—"

"It's all right." She indicated that he should give her the bowl, but he shook his blond head.

"I think I'd better do what I was sent in here to do."

"Think you that I'll spill it? I am no bantling!"

A minute later, as he was scraping the mush off her blanket, she licked molasses from her forefinger and said quietly, "It slipped."

Laughing at the mishap, he rubbed the stain with a damp cloth, then sat back down and pondered the girl in fascination.

"I was nervous," she volunteered by way of explanation. "Catastrophes always seem to befall me when I'm nervous. Though Jason tells me 'tis merely that I'm clumsy."

It had preyed upon Daniel's mind that the girl might be bound in some inexorable way to the man Fergus had recognized as Jason MacAuley. "This Jason . . ." He addressed her shyly, "Is he . . . or are you . . ." His inability to phrase the question delicately confounded him. "Is he anything to you?"

"Aye." In that fleeting instant the fragile emotions that she had inspired in him shattered, and the hope he fostered of one day winning the girl was swept away.

"He is a thorn in my side."

"A thorn in your . . . ?" He smiled, hope returning. "Then would it be presumptuous of me to ask what you were doing with him?"

It surprised her with what ease she altered the truth. "My father died recently. Jason was taking me to Yorktown to settle my inheritance."

"And that's the only . . . the only connection between you?"

"What other kind of connection could there possibly be between us?"

"Well, a romantic connection."

"With Jason MacAuley? Not likely. I'd be more apt to fall in love with a toad."

He threw back his head in laughter, but sobered quickly. "I shouldn't laugh. He's lying close to death." Reaching out an awkward hand, he reassured her gently. "It must have been a terrible ordeal for you. I'm just thankful that you're alive and that it was us who found you."

Looking into the young man's face, the girl found an expression of such adoration there that she could not help but smile. He looked to be not much older than herself, and his complexion was so fair that she doubted it had ever sampled the bite of a razor. It was odd that she should feel so comfortable in his presence, that she could not sense in him the qualities that she had feared in so many others. He seemed shy to the point of timidity, and so gentle that she knew it would never occur to him to take advantage of her. Daniel English was . . . different.

Later that morning, in a tub of steaming seawater, she scrubbed the brine from her scalp and the memory of the pirate from her flesh. Fergus presented her with clothes from the slop chest—

boy's breeches, an oversize shirt, and a pair of droopy, mismatched hose—and though she was aghast at her new attire, Daniel lauded her appearance and provided her with a scarlet sash whose dual purpose it was to keep her shirt from falling off and her breeches from falling down. He could do little to improve the fit of her hose, so he simply admired the length of leg she exposed. He judged that she had lost a good deal of weight during her ordeal, but he was not oblivious of the natural fullness of her body. And he was bedazzled by the heavy mantle of hair that had become electrified with brushing, the freshly washed strands flying about her face like wisps of black smoke. By the time he left her to assume his watch that night, he was intoxicated with the thought of Mary Kathleen Ryan and completely, utterly, and unequivocally in love.

It was on the fourth day after her recovery that Fergus succumbed to her pleading and allowed her into the compartment across the way. The fetidness in Jason's cabin smacked her in the face like a foul wind. He was lying prostrate, a poultice of tar on his back, his face angled toward her. Where an unruly growth of beard had not sprouted, his face was sunken in and flushed with unhealthy color. Beneath his eyes an arc of cyanic blue discolored his flesh. Gingerly she touched his forehead. He was hot, so very hot, and deathly still.

"Smell it." Fergus sniffed. "The cabin reeks of his poison. Daniel takes one step in here and turns green. Weak stomach, that one." Placing his vast palm on the girl's shoulder, he guided her toward a chair. "It has been almost four days now, lass. Are you ready to tell me what happened?"

Having stretched the truth once, she found the second telling easier than she had anticipated. She related the story of the past two weeks, omitting any mention of her betrothal or the indignity she had suffered at the hands of the pirate chief. When she had finished the tale, Fergus leaned back in his chair and pulled thoughtfully on his beard.

"Damn barbarians." He slammed one massive fist against the cabin wall. "But what worries me most now, Mary Kathleen, is what *you* will do when we reach Boston if it . . . well, if it turns out badly for Jason?"

So touched was she by the man's honest concern that she lowered her eyes, unable to continue with the lie she had confected. "I . . . I thought . . ." She whipped the air with her hand. "So much has happened, I . . . I . . ."

"I understand, I understand," he quietened her. "Considering what you've been through, you're not so sure you even want to go to America. Is that right?"

Relieved that he had provided his own explanation, she nodded.

"In that case, there's only one alternative. You decide exactly where it is you want to be going, and once we reach Boston, I'll see that you get there. Maybe 'tis even back to Spain you'd want to go."

"You would help me to return to Cádiz if I desired it?" A mixture of shock and excitement left her breathless.

Fergus, still awed by her startling familiarity, could do naught but shrug the bulk of his shoulders and wonder how it was that she bore so strong a resemblance to a woman so long dead. "Of course, lass," he said, little knowing that he had just resolved the problem to which she had addressed four long days of worry.

With her return to Cádiz assured, Katy swallowed her bitterness toward Jason MacAuley. In truth, in the days that followed, she found herself being drawn with compelling frequency to his cabin. Daniel regarded her attendance upon the man as an indication of her sweet nature. He did not know that her daily vigil at the Yankee's bedside was undertaken as a form of penance for that time when she had admitted that her life would be less complicated if Jason would die, that in spite of her devoted nursing she believed he would die. She wanted to at least be able to take comfort in the fact that she had done everything in her power to ease his going.

But Jason MacAuley did not die. Even though his countenance was gnarled with pain and every breath rasped and rattled as if it were his last, he did not die. One bright April morning he opened his eyes, and Katy could only stare at him, her promise of freedom fading with his first word.

"Katy?"

He focused hazily on the two people who had rushed to his side the moment he stirred.

"Aye, she's been here the whole time," Fergus piped up as he placed a hand on the girl's shoulder, urging her to kneel down where Jason could see her. " 'Tis a lucky man you are to have such a beautiful woman worrying about you."

Aware of Katy's nearness, Jason opened his eyes once more, weakly, his dark gaze probing her with frightening intensity. He wondered at the paleness of her complexion and saw a thread of darker green suddenly tint the circumference of her irises in a look that he could not fathom. "Why?" His voice was whispered, grating. He could not understand why she had demonstrated any compassion toward him. He was the man who had forced her to leave her home, who had refused even to consider returning her there after the shipwreck. Could she actually care for him? She had haunted his dreams, and in those disjointed vignettes he had responded to her as a man, erotically, sensuously. Those remembered embraces warmed him now, for the girl was flesh and blood and but an arm's length away from him, making his fantasies not altogether impossible. He stretched his fingers toward her, beckoning for her hand, yearning to touch the girl who had made such passionate love to him in his dreams. For him nothing had changed except, perhaps, that he now wanted her more than ever. And it was not just lust. At one time it might have been. But not anymore.

Katy contemplated his long, well-shaped fingers, understanding his silent entreaty. Not knowing why she did so, she placed her cool hand within his grasp. His lips seemed to glue themselves together, so he could not speak what was in his eyes, but as far as Katy was concerned, he did not need to. The desire in those spheres of inky color was obvious to her.

"Why indeed!" Fergus grunted at the man's question. "You think the lass is a cold-blooded shrew?" Awareness of her true motives caused Katy to blush. "Let the girl's hand go now so she can run to the galley for some food for you."

But as she started to pry her hand away, Jason's grip tightened, and her frightened eyes riveted on the dark hand that, even in its weakened condition, held her fast. "Stay," he rasped. "Please." And his appeal was so pathetic that she might have considered it had Fergus not taken a step forward, clamped his hand around Jason's wrist, and exerted the needed pressure to wrest the girl's hand from the man's possession.

"I do this for your own good, Jason," the master of the *Ugly Jane* explained as Katy stood up. "Right now you need food more than you need a hand to hold. While the girl is gone, if you are so inclined, you can hold my hand." Ignoring the obscenity that the patient spit out, Fergus hastened the girl toward the portal. "You tell the cook that I want hot broth that's strong enough to float a marlinspike. And bring some lemon juice and water, too. I imagine his mouth must taste foul indeed."

It did not occur to her that she was being herded out of the room with undue haste. Fergus' genuine concern allowed little room for suspicion. Yet had she remained outside the door for a few moments after it had closed on her, she might have found the Irishman's first words to Jason MacAuley somewhat redoubtable.

"I've told the girl nothing, Jason. But you'd better start explaining to me exactly what it is you're doing, and pretty damn fast!"

After delivering Fergus' instructions to the cook, Katy meandered along the rail. She was thankful that Jason had recovered.

She really was. But she was not happy for herself. She did not want to be dragged to Yorktown. She did not want to be wed to a man who would do, in the name of marriage, the same things that Molkeydaur had tried to do. She felt a burning revulsion in her loins at the thought, and as if to ward off her fate, wound her arms about herself.

"Such a long face." Daniel's voice came from behind her. "Is something wrong?" She spun around, and as soon as he saw her face, he knew. "Is it Jason?" She nodded, then gasped as she felt herself being whipped into the boy's arms, her face being pressed with awkward tenderness against his chest. "My poor Katy. His passing must be a terrible shock to you. I'm so sorry. You must feel terrible after trying to nurse him back to health for so long. When did it happen?"

With her mouth flattened against his shirt, her reply came out garbled. Daniel, however, translated it into a comprehensible response and continued patting her head. "He was uncovered? When you went in? He must have been thrashing around when the end came, but what an abominable thing for you to see."

She rolled her eyes at his misinterpretation, then jerked her head loose from his viselike caress. "I said he has *re*covered," she emphasized.

The boy stiffened, searched her face, repeated the word silently, then set her from him. "Oh." Self-consciously he took a step away from her, then halted. "So if he has recovered, why are you sad?"

That did require some explanation, and she was unwilling to reveal to Daniel just how self-centered she was. But she had to gamble. Daniel's sympathies might be her only salvation. Sighing, she peered full measure into his face, little knowing that had she asked him to jump over the side of the ship at that moment, he would have complied without uttering a syllable of protest.

" 'Tis selfish of me, Daniel, but I am sad for myself. I did not want to accompany Jason to America. I did not want to leave Cádiz, but Jason was so insistent that he overwhelmed even my aunt and uncle. He has been promised a large purse if he returns me safely, and naturally holds my wishes of little consequence. Fergus told me that should something happen to Jason, he would allow me to return to Cádiz, but now that Jason is better, I must resign myself to doing what I have no wish to do."

To say that Daniel swelled visibly with righteous indignation would have been stating the case mildly. He fairly purpled with outrage and had to wrestle with his voice to keep it steady. "He *forced* you to go with him? The . . . the no-good scoundrel. The money-grubbing hack! And you! Nursing him back to life when

89

you knew full well what it could mean if he recovered!'' He bunched his hand into a fist, staring meaningfully at it, then at the quarterdeck. "Well, I know something that will delay his recovery by a few more days.'' His purpose unmistakable, he took a step in the direction of the cabin, and Katy, in sudden panic, reached out her hand to stop him. What if Jason blurted out the story of her betrothal? Daniel might be much too honorable to lend assistance to a woman who was the intended of another man.

"Nay!'' she finally spluttered as she grabbed the upper portion of his sleeve, yanking backward to deter him. Daniel heard the rending of material, and looking down, frowned at the bare shoulder that was now visible beneath the newly sundered seam. Katy snatched her hand from his arm. "I am truly cursed!'' she wailed, a chagrined expression coming over her face. "Why do I keep doing that? 'Tis the second shirt I have ruined! But do not fear. I shall mend it for you so well that you will never know it has been ripped.'' Her promise was not the good news it sounded, since she had never had occasion even to thread a needle before. Still, Daniel didn't know that, and the grin that he favored upon her suggested that he really didn't care.

"Now that you have successfully detained me,'' he said, "I want you to hear me out. Jason MacAuley may be twice my size, but he doesn't frighten me, and I won't have him frightening you, either. He is a mercenary of the vilest sort, and I swear to you that you'll not step off this ship with him. I swear it.''

"But what can you do?'' she prodded, unconvinced.

"I can do much, Katy. But I need do only one thing. Trust me.'' He would not pose the question to her now; he needed time to bolster his courage, for he had never asked anyone to marry him before.

Later that afternoon Fergus came to her cabin with a progress report on their patient, who, having been fed, shaved, and freshly bandaged, was now resting comfortably and seemed to be out of danger.

"He'll be needing more attention than I can give him now, though, lass, so if you could continue sitting with him, I'd be much beholden to you.''

Fergus could not have said anything that discomfited her more. Her obligation to Jason had ceased with his recovery. She wanted nothing more now than to avoid him. But how could she tell Fergus without sounding completely callous?

Attentive to her hesitation, the Irishman shot her a curious glance. "Do you have some objection to that, Mary Kathleen?''

"Objection?'' There was no way to explain it. No way at all.

"Nay, I have no objection," she lied. "I was just wondering . . ."—she eyed Daniel's shirt with a mixture of distaste and fear—"where I could find a needle and thread."

Even in his sleep Jason heard the strange scuffling. He cracked an eye, and when his pupil had adjusted to the light, focused on a diminutive figure whose round little rump was stuck precociously in the air, whose forearms were flush against the floor, and who, like a bloodhound, was crawling about the cabin muttering in disgust. When the creature rounded the table and struck out in the man's direction, he guessed its identity from the ebony tresses that swept the floor around it, and despite his persistent pain, gave out a hoarse guffaw that sent the girl springing to her feet.

"You must indeed be improving, that your voice rings with such levity." Her tone smacked of sarcasm, for it did not sit well that he should laugh at her.

When he had regained his self-control, he cleared his throat. His eyes ranged leisurely down the length of her, stopping at the sock that had bagged around her left ankle. "I must confess that in all my years at sea I have never seen a cabin boy who filled out a pair of breeches quite like that."

Unamused, she yanked up her sock. "You should not laugh at me."

"Where did you get that outlandish rig?"

"From Fergus. He dug it out of either a gurry bucket or the slop chest. I can't remember which one."

"I sincerely hope it was a slop chest. But that does not explain to me what you were doing crawling around the floor."

"Oh, that." Remembering her immediate dilemma, she returned her gaze to the floor. "I dropped a needle. Somewhere. I think it rolled over . . ." Tucking in her lip, she scanned the vicinity of her feet, then farther to her right, where a tiny glimmer of steel caught her eye. ". . . over there!" Plucking the needle from the floor, she carried it carefully to the chair where she had been working.

"What are you sewing?"

In answer she held up the shirt.

"Another item from the slop chest?"

"Nay. 'Tis Daniel's." She wet the end of the thread and rove it through the eye of the needle.

"Daniel?" he asked suspiciously.

"Daniel English. Fergus' first mate." Pressing the seams together, she aimed the needle and drove it through the material.

"Oh." He did not recognize the sensation that rippled through him as jealousy, but he did feel a tightening in his chest as the fellow's name flitted through his mind. Agitated with himself, he watched the movement of her hand as she stabbed the needle in and out, seemingly without pattern, and pondered the unconventional style with which she fashioned her stitches. "If that thing you are sewing wasn't dead before, I'm sure it is now."

Her lips formed around a painful Ω as her finger flew into her mouth. Sucking the bead of blood from her fingertip, she looked askance at him. "Why must you stare at me?!"

"What else do you suggest I stare at?"

"I don't care what you stare at as long as it isn't me." Having salved her finger with her tongue, she eased the injured digit out of her mouth. "I could tolerate you far better when you were unconscious."

"I'm sorry that my recovery is such a disappointment to you."

Unwilling to admit that fact to his face, she settled herself more comfortably into the chair, and making sure that her fingers were clear of the path of the slender weapon, took careful aim and jabbed the needle into the cloth. Silence ensued as Jason cushioned his face in his pillow. Now and again Katy stole a glance at his prostrate form, and recalling what Fergus had said about shaving him, wondered why he still sported a beard.

"I thought Fergus shaved you."

He turned his head toward her. "Trimmed. I've decided to keep the growth."

Their eyes joined for a moment before hers dropped to the work in her lap. She had not yet accustomed herself to the idea of his having two eyes. Now she had to accustom herself to the idea of a beard.

"Would you rather I cut it off?" he inquired.

She shrugged indifferently. " 'Tis no concern of mine what you do with your face."

"Does Daniel have a beard?"

She continued to ply her needle and answered him without looking up. "His skin is too smooth to grow such coarse stubble. He is very fair."

"You are most flattering, lady." Defensively he touched his hand to his face, patting the soft growth of hair. He was anxious to meet this fair-haired first mate whose shirt Katy was calmly mutilating. Where had she ever learned to sew like that? "You look well, Katy. Have you healed completely?"

Her hand froze for a moment before continuing its erratic motion. "Yes. Thank you."

"You still don't want to talk about it, do you?"

She shook her head and vented her spleen on the innocent garment in her lap. "I have told no one, I intend to tell no one, and I would hope you have the decency to do the same."

"Do you expect to tell Pamela of your . . . plight?"

Having worked the thread into a miserable tangle, she picked at the mess to separate the strands. "Nay, I will not tell her, for I have no intention of ever meeting Pamela Ryan."

"Indeed, lady?" He laughed.

"If you elect to continue the journey to Yorktown, 'tis your decision, but I shall not be traveling with you." Yanking impatiently on the thread, she exhaled a disgusted breath when the various loops choked into a thick knot.

The man's eyes elongated. Just what had Fergus been telling her? "We have discussed this before, Katy, and I regret to inform you that in my unconsciousness, my mind did not change. You will return to Yorktown—with me."

Not knowing what to do with the knot, she pretended it wasn't there and began to work around it. "Then you will have to drag me, because I refuse."

"An awkward solution at best," he taunted, "but it can be arranged."

And the very tone of his voice frightened her so much that she gazed up from her sewing to observe him. "Do you not owe me a debt of thanks for watching over you these many days?"

The corner of his eyebrow lifted slightly. "For that service I thank you. If you expected payment other than that, I fear you wasted both your time and your efforts." He was a master at disguising his emotions, and his stony countenance did not reveal the acute disappointment he felt at discovering the reason for her compassion. She had been concerned not about him but about how his gratitude could be manipulated for her own purpose.

"You freebooting cur!"

"Tread lightly, lady," he warned. "I am not so sick that I could not teach you to speak with a civil tongue."

" 'Tis the only way you know of dealing with people, is it not? Threatening them with physical violence. Well, nothing you can do could be any worse than what has already been done to me. Threaten me all you like: I will not be bartered like a common whore so that you might have your palm lined with coins."

'Tis not for the money that I do it, Katy. But you cannot know that. "You are my responsibility."

"I do not want to be your responsibility."

"That is unfortunate but unalterable."

"Nay, not unalterable. You are not immortal."

"If you had thought to kill me, lady, I fear the opportune moment has passed you by. But do not look so glum. Perhaps I'll die yet."

"You're too mean to die."

Before he could fire a rejoinder at her, a knock sounded at the door, and Jason, his face having become ugly at her comment, hurled a look at the portal that could have set it aflame. *"Come in!"* he bellowed. What walked into the cabin was a lean, tall, pink-and-white youth whose flaxen hair seemed to form a halo about his head. The youth's eyes wandered first to Katy, where they lingered with quiet passion, then to Jason, where they dwelt with barely concealed resentment. Jason regarded the boy glacially.

"I assume that this fair-haired, light-eyed, unstubbled cherub is the illustrious Daniel English. Am I correct?"

Katy saw Daniel's hand whiten as he balled it into a fist, and to prevent an untidy scene, she popped out of her chair and scurried to the boy's side, where she looped a hand around his arm. "How good of you to look in on us, Daniel," she said with exaggerated sweetness.

" 'Tis you I came to see," he answered her. His eyes locked with Jason's. "Not him. I've set your supper in your cabin, Katy. You'd better come and eat before it gets cold."

"God forbid that cold food should ever pass between Mary Kathleen Ryan's lips," Jason mocked.

The boy's pallid complexion suffused with blood. "You know, MacAuley, you're every bit the bastard that Katy said you were."

Katy winced and felt a flood of color crawl up her neck at Jason's slow and pointed perusal. "Did she, now?" he taunted. "And what else did Katy tell you? Did she inform you that when the moon is full, I feast on virgins, then toss their bones to the hounds?"

"How do you stand yourself?" the boy intoned. "I knew I should have left you out there for dead."

"So, we have two votes in favor of my immediate demise. That would certainly give you free access to the girl, wouldn't it, Mr. English?"

"Are you suggesting that my intentions are less than honorable, sir?"

"What do you think?"

"I am only interested in Katy's welfare, but I wouldn't expect a man like you to understand that."

Jason grinned. "From the way you've been ogling her, I'd venture that you're interested in a hell of a lot more than her welfare. And now, Mr. English, this conversation is starting to bore me, so I think it wise if you leave while you are still able to walk out the door.''

Sensing that Daniel was about to do something foolhardy, Katy jumped in front of him, blocking his path to the bunk. ''I think you'd better go, Daniel. Please. I'll join you in a minute. And, here . . .'' She thrust the shirt into his hands. ''Take this with you.'' He fumbled with the material that she had shoved at him, and when she stepped back and indicated the door, he quirked his brow as the shirt slid from his fingertips and floated back, magically, to where she stood, there to hang limply from her waist. Puzzled, she swatted at the shirt to detach it. When it continued to cling, she gathered it into her hands and gave a tug, and only then discovered that she had inadvertently sewn it to the loose end of her sash.

Jason, who had done an admirable job of suppressing his laughter until now, could contain himself no longer. Twin scowls were flung in his direction as he howled with glee. Katy tensed as Daniel snatched his knife from the lanyard at his waist; then she drew in a more normal breath when, after slicing through the threads that connected shirt to sash, he returned the weapon to its sheath.

''I'll wait for you in your cabin. The stench in here has not improved with his recovery.''

When Daniel had gone, Katy turned on Jason, fiery words dancing on the tip of her tongue. ''I think you delight in acting so scurrilously!''

His laughter ceased. His eyes hardened. ''Do not castigate *me*, madam! That young pup, for whom you have acquired so fond an affection, voiced the first insult. Would your sense of propriety have been less offended if I had turned the other cheek? Do not turn away from me when I am speaking to you! If you think that boy is your means to salvation, you are wrong, because I tell you this, Miss Mary Kathleen Ryan. You said it yourself. I'm too damn mean to die. I'm going to live, and when I'm completely well, I'm going to catch a packet to Virginia, and, by God, you're going to be on that ship with me if I have to chase you from here to hell and back. Do I make myself perfectly clear?''

She stared at him in a deadly rage.

''I assume from your silence that, once again, you are less than enamored with what I've had to say. Very well. But since Fergus sent you in here to serve a sick man, why don't you be a dutiful wench and pour me a cup of water. I find that defending myself leaves my throat parched.'' When she made no effort to do his bidding, he sighed. "Come now, Katy. If you remain in here much longer, your young friend might begin to imagine that something is going on between us."

Seething inwardly, she tromped to the table, where a pitcher of fresh water had been placed, filled a cup with the liquid, and returned to the bunk. "Your water," she said, holding the cup over his head. "I hope you drown on it."

Jason cursed her mightily as the contents of the mug splatted onto his head. Blindly he shot an arm out to grab her, but she was already halfway across the floor, and in a matter of seconds, out the door.

"Termagant!" he wailed. "You just wait till I get my hands on you!" When he heard the door on the opposite side of the alleyway slam shut, he rubbed his eyes dry and ruffled the water from his hair. She did the damnedest things! But knowing that in the end he would have his own way, he smiled a long, wicked smile.

No amount of persuasion on Fergus' behalf could convince Katy to set foot inside Jason's cabin again. She sometimes heard his voice as she passed by his cabin, but that was all. Daniel still bristled about his encounter with "that ruffian," as he now referred to the Yankee captain, but Katy found that the boy's irritability could be pacified with a smile. She did not ponder Daniel's extreme attentiveness during this time, nor wonder why his expression always seemed to be hedging on either ebullience or desolation. She did note that sometimes when there was a lull in their conversation, he would open his mouth expectantly, only to blush and clamp it shut again. Fearful of rejection, he had worded and reworded his proposal over and over again in his mind, but each time an opportunity had presented itself, the well-practiced phrases became jumbled and he had backed down. Having met Jason, the boy was more convinced than ever that his proposal of marriage was the only logical alternative. If he could only get the words out!

Toward the end of April Jason had mended sufficiently to warrant his taking short walks on deck. His legs were wobbly from having been so long abed, and at first he could not walk without assistance from Fergus. But as he regained his strength and the use of his limbs, the walks became more prolonged and more frequent. The gauzy bandages that entwined his torso soon disappeared; the suppleness returned to his gait. During the day, when the sun was high, he would strip to the waist and stretch out on the quarterdeck to bathe in the healing warmth of the sun's rays. With time a layer of healthy pink skin formed over the lacerations. Where deep wounds had been gouged out, there now ran cords of puckered flesh that muted but would never fully erase the pirate's atrocity.

He could not help but see Katy during his long hours on the quarterdeck, but not once was he afforded an opportunity to converse with her. She had become expert at avoiding him, a circumstance which did not hold true of her relationship with Daniel English, for she was with the boy constantly. It tormented him to see her obvious enchantment with Fergus' first mate, her willing laughter in his presence. He recalled the times he had shared with her in the past weeks; with him, her laughter had been rare. With two eyes now instead of one, he pursued the couple, missing not a single gesture or innuendo. The boy was fairer, perhaps more handsome, definitely younger. Was that what had captivated her? He detested the sensations that seeing her with another man had awakened in him. He was covetous of that boy's rapport with her, envious of their relationship, inordinately jealous that she exuded charm with Daniel, but not with him. He wondered what worse straits he would fall into when he delivered her into Pamela's hands, and he began to dwell on images of her in yet another man's arms in the marriage bed. His guilt grew apace with his illusions. He had thought himself immune to the weakness of such emotions. But he was wrong. The thought of losing Katy wrenched not only at his heart but also at his loins. He could not allow her to marry another when he wanted her for himself. And he did want her. He wanted her very much. So what her pleading had failed to accomplish, he decided to bring about with a simple plan of his own design. He would still return her to Yorktown, but he would assure her that she would not be coerced into marriage. He would see to that. Would she be less disdainful of him then? Would she laugh with him as she did with Daniel? Buoyed by what her reaction might be, he vowed to tell her of his decision the first chance he could get her alone.

Toward the end of the second week in May, Katy began to find herself unable to sleep. Rather than spend another night staring into the shadows, she donned shirt and breeches and padded barefoot out to the main deck. She found a niche in the lee of the ship, close to the cold metal shaft of a cannon, and boosting her elbows onto the rail, rested her chin in her hand and tilted her head up toward the luminous crescent of the new moon.

At the sound of footsteps she turned.

"I thought I heard your door close," Jason remarked. She attempted to sidestep him, but he placed an arm on either side of her, blocking her escape. "Nay," he snapped as she tried to duck beneath him. "I would speak with you." When it became evident that she could not wiggle from beneath the yoke his arms formed about her, she straightened. Her voice was accusatory.

"Have you been standing watch at your door waiting for me to come out?" Shirtless, his flesh gleamed palely, and she backed against the gunwale to avoid having to touch him.

"I couldn't sleep," he said softly.

" 'Tis no surprise. If I had your conscience, I wouldn't be able to sleep either. Is that why you are here?"

"I am here because I have a need to talk with you."

"I don't think there is anything you have to say that could possibly interest me. Please remove your arms—"

He shook his head slowly, his magnificent mane of black hair ruffling in the night breeze. "You will hear me out."

"I will scream."

"Think you the ubiquitous Mr. English will leap to your rescue?"

"Do you still intend to take me to Yorktown?"

"Aye, but—"

"Then we have nothing to discuss." As she made to scream, he clapped his hand over her mouth.

"I think not, lady."

"Mmmnhh!"

"For the past two weeks I have been watching that boy fawn over you, and it was enough to settle my mind about a few things." He ducked his head away from her fist. "Would you please stop that?!"

"Mmnhh!"

"You might be gratified to learn that I am not quite the scoundrel you take me for. I've decided that—" He hissed as she drove her knee into his thigh. Nettled by her perversity, he pulled her hard to him, glaring holes into the green eyes. "What must I do to make you listen to me?" Against his bare chest he felt the fullness of her unencumbered breasts and the hammering of his own heart in response. Desire for the girl pumped through him. Had he been less angry, he might have been able to ignore the provocative pressure of her body, but he *was* angry, his senses were piqued, and physical need replaced reason. He eased his hand from her mouth. She had time to utter a single half-hearted peep before he replaced the weight of his hand with that of his mouth. Enveloped by his massiveness, by rock-hard limbs and flesh that was ruggedly smooth and warm, she suffered a lightness of head as if he were sucking the very air from her lungs. His kiss was unhurried in its mastery, sensuous, unrestrained. She tasted the man's nature, his violence and passion, the warmth that emanated from the very core of him. She could not squirm. She could not breathe. She felt the press of his hand at the small of her back, then a rush of air as the tail of her shirt was jerked loose from her breeches. He savored the silken texture of her bare back as he traced a path up the long curve of her spine and felt her stiffen beneath his touch. Yet he could not release her. His need was too great. With one hand flattened against her spine and the other cradling her head, he lifted her against him, and kissing her deeply, lowered her to the deck, pinning her beneath him. Fire roared through her veins as his hand slid along her ribs, gathering within his gentle grasp the softly domed flesh that had yielded to gravity and spilled outward on either side of her chest. With thumb and forefinger he found the smooth claret bud at the crown of her breast and stroked it with delicate expertise until he felt the flesh peak and tighten, and then his hand moved downward, following the indentation of her rib cage toward the waistband of her breeches and the buttoned flap of his own.

"What in the hell are you doing, Jason?"

The Yankee captain opened his eyes to boots that had planted themselves directly before his face. He lifted his head to see the upper half of the man's body. That brief interlude of air was all Katy needed.

"Get him off me!" she shrieked at the shadow hovering above her.

Light and darkness contoured the stony slope of Fergus McFadden's face, and as Jason squelched the girl's screams in his hand, he saw the Irishman crook his thumb at him.

"Get up."

"This is none of your business," Jason panted, breathless.

"Yer on *my* ship. Whatever you do on these decks, be it eat, sleep, or piss, is my business. Now, get up."

Jason swore beneath his breath, released his hold on the girl, and got to his feet. He reached down for Katy, but she dodged his hand, struggled to her feet unassisted, then flattened her palm across his cheek with a resounding smack that stung her hand more than it did his cheek.

"You pandering—"

"Enough, lady," he warned, catching her wrist as she arced her hand toward his face again.

She winced at the constrainment and looked toward Fergus, who grabbed her other wrist and pulled her toward him.

"If you value your life, Jason, you'll unhand her."

Jason tugged her back toward him. "Get out of my way, Fergus."

"You'll not ask me to do anything in that tone."

"I'm not asking. I'm telling!"

"The hell you say!" Fergus boomed, yanking the girl back toward him. "Do you think you are so big that I could not knock you from one end of this ship to the other?"

"I intend to have her, Fergus, so you can do both of us a favor and just stop interfering!"

Not to be outdone, Fergus roared into the night, "Next time I catch you trying to molest the child, you'll be wearing your nose on the other side of that pretty face of yours. Now, let her go!"

As Katy tripped back in Fergus' direction, Jason lost his foothold just enough to allow her to pull him along with her toward the Irishman. Not waiting for the men to stretch her asunder again, she directed Jason's hand at Fergus' and with a burst of energy rapped the men's knuckles together. "Stop it!" she screamed. Both victims winced in unexpected pain, and surprised by the stridency in her voice, surrendered their handholds. "You . . ." Her head darted back and forth between them. "You . . .!" Choked with fury at their apparent disregard of her person, she clenched her fists and thrust them into the air. "Ohhhh!"

Two pairs of bewildered eyes watched her whirl around and race across the deck, leaving them to nurse their injuries and their pride. Jason blew a sibilant stream of air between his teeth, then, leaning against the cannon, rubbed his inflamed cheek. "How long has it been since you've had a woman, Fergus?"

Absently massaging his smarting knuckles, the Irishman joined his friend, camaraderie swiftly returning. "Longer than I would like to remember. But listen to me, Jason. Though your need may be great, you cannot be throwing the girl down and taking her like a common strumpet."

Emotional exhaustion had set in, and Jason's hand trailed to the nape of his neck, where he kneaded the tense sinews. "So what did you do in times gone by when your need was great?"

Fergus frowned in contemplation. In his lifetime he had loved only one woman, Jason's mother, Clare MacAuley. But since that love had never been returned, he had disciplined himself to be contented more with mental than with physical pleasure. But he remembered that there had been a time, long ago, when he had been of a different persuasion. "I took a lady once," he whispered. "It was in the autumn, by the side of a river. At the time I didn't even know her name." He chuckled lightly. "Funny. I had forgotten all about that."

"What happened?"

Fergus was slow to answer, for the memory had sparked an impossible notion that not even he could lend credence to. "I never saw her again," he said at last.

"Am I being obtuse, or is there a lesson to be learned here somewhere?"

Fergus' voice became stern. "No lesson. You know who you are. You know who she is. Can you afford an entanglement with the girl, knowing what the consequences might be?"

"I fear I already know the consequences," he said wistfully. "I'm in love with her."

Standing on the quarterdeck with Daniel next morning, Katy watched as he took measure of the other three-quarters of the deck. Daniel, at least, would never subject her to Jason's brand of attention. "Will you be master of your own ship on your next voyage, Daniel?"

"If I can find a Salem or Boston merchant who needs my services, I will be."

"And how difficult is that?"

"Fairly difficult." Taking her arm, he steered her toward the helm. "But Fergus has some connections. He might be able to help."

"Could you not be master of this ship on its next voyage?"

"Of the *Ugly*?" He shook his head, having a hard time envisioning anyone but Fergus McFadden as her master. "She's due to be overhauled down in Frenchman Bay after this voyage. Probably won't be seaworthy again till next spring or summer."

"Frenchman Bay? But . . . isn't that where Jason makes his home?"

"Yup. He and Captain McFadden are old friends. Didn't anyone tell you?"

"No." She frowned thoughtfully, wondering why Fergus had not mentioned it. "No one did."

"Well, I wouldn't be too concerned. It's amazing what some men forget." Gaining the helm, Daniel gestured to the steersman. "I'll relieve you for a while, Mr. Hewes." Stepping up onto the raised grating aft of the wheel, he secured his hands around the upper spokes, and when his bearings were correct, extended a hand to Katy.

The wheel was as tall as a man, so that even standing on the small platform Katy could not see over the rim. Daniel had sandwiched her between himself and the wheel, and at the feel of the boy's body behind her she suffered a twinge of unease. But his slightness of limb did not overpower her as Jason's massive-

101

ness had, so she was almost able to ignore his closeness. Experimentally she fastened her hands around the inner spokes and beneath her fingertips felt the power of the sea pulling the wheel to starboard. Looking up, she peered at Daniel's rigid forearms.

"Is this Fergus' only ship?"

"Oh, he has smaller ships—schooners and sloops. But they're used for the coastal trade mostly—lumber, fish, things like that."

"If Fergus were to offer you a ship for the coastal trade, would you refuse?"

"I think so. My ambition tends more toward the exotic." Except in women, he thought, where Irish was about as exotic as he wanted to get.

"Exactly how are you defining 'exotic'?"

He drew in a long, thoughtful breath. It was now or never. "Many merchants send ships to all parts of the world. Elias Derby and George Crowninshield are renowned for their trade with Canton, Joseph Teel and Samuel Ingersoll for the West Indies, and William Gray for his trade with Lisbon and . . . Cádiz."

The word sawed through her brain, obliterating every thought in its path. "Cádiz? There is a possibility that you might be commanding a ship to Cádiz?" She was thankful her back was to him, for she knew that her eyes had greened with avarice.

"Aye. There is a possibility. And if it comes to pass . . . I want you to come with me. As my wife."

Her sudden elation disintegrated. His wife? Of course she would go to Cádiz with him! But not as his wife. She didn't want to marry him. She didn't want to marry anyone. "Daniel," she hedged, "I—"

"I know you don't love me, Katy. I'm not so much the fool to think that. But . . . I'm in love with you. I've been in love with you from the first. And I want to marry you."

Oh, Daniel. Do not do this to yourself.

"If you were just a little fond of me, you might grow to love me with time. I can provide for you, and I'll protect you from men like Jason MacAuley."

At the mention of Jason's name her thoughts underwent a swift transformation, for it was, after all, Jason MacAuley who was the central problem in her life, not Daniel English. She was determined to do everything in her power to escape that hateful Yankee. What if she said yes to Daniel? Yes . . . with a provision attached. That they be married nowhere except Cádiz. Once they reached their destination, she would suddenly realize that they were quite incompatible and would have her aunt extend her deepest regrets to Daniel and send him on his way minus his would-be bride. Naturally he would be disappointed. *Nay*, she thought, projecting herself into the future, *he will hate me*. She would lose a friend, and that was a bitter brew to swallow.

But the alternative was even less palatable. She could not face what awaited her in Yorktown. As if by divine decree, her escape route had been charted and she intended to follow it. Her voice was demure when next she spoke, and in his restive state Daniel did not hear its undercurrent of deviousness.

"I'm so homesick that I fear I would make an unfit bride for any man, Daniel. I could not think of burdening you with a wife who missed her family so much that she cried all the time and made everyone around her miserable."

Encouraged that she had not refused him yet, Daniel allowed his mouth to start working before his brain did. "Well . . . I . . . I . . . if it means that much to you, we could . . ."—he grimaced as the words squirted between his teeth—"we could sail to Cádiz and get married there so you could be with your family." Though how, he wondered, am I going to maintain my composure in her presence for so many months?

Her eyebrows lifted at his easy solution, and a trace of a smile curled her lips. "But what happens if this Mr. William Gray has no positions available on any of his ships? What happens to me then?"

"Then . . . ." The boy's mind touched on bribery, kidnapping, and murder before arriving at the obvious solution. "My family lives in the Berkshires, in the far western part of Massachusetts. You can stay with them until a position comes available. They'd love to have you, Katy. And you'd be safe from everything way out there."

According to her mental calculations, that had been the last impediment. She would not have to worry about money if she stayed with Daniel's family. She would be well out of the way of Jason's clutches in an inland village. And she would have a means of transport back to Spain once Daniel was hired by William Gray. All she had to do was say she would marry this boy who had become her friend.

"All right, Daniel. I'll marry you."

"Would you say that again?" He faltered, not believing his ears.

"I said I would marry you."

"You will?" His voice squeaked in utter shock. "I mean, *you will*?" Removing one hand from the helm, he turned her around to face him and seeing the merry assent in her eyes, let go the wheel completely in his haste to smother his bride-to-be in a

103

bone-crushing hug. As the wheel spun out of control, the ship lurched sharply to starboard, and Fergus McFadden, who had just emerged onto the main deck, found himself being slammed into the bulkhead and watching in stunned horror as two men who were climbing the windward shrouds were hurled into the sea below.

"Luff up!" he screamed at the handful of crewmen who were picking their bodies up from the deck. As they scrambled toward the braces to set the mainsails aback, Fergus clambered up the quarterdeck companionway, and spying his first mate, splintered the air with a mighty roar. *"Daniel!"*

Looking above the spinning helm, Daniel blinked at the enraged face bearing down upon him and of a sudden realized that the wheel was no longer in his hands. Dropping his arms from around the girl, he lunged for the spokes, halting the wheel in its rotation at the same time that Fergus caught it.

"You numbskull! Are you trying to kill all of us?"

"You don't understand."

"I understand, all right. 'Tis a bit weak in the waterways you are!"

"Nay, Fergus. I was excited. Katy just agreed to—"

"Mr. Hewes!" Fergus screamed at the helmsman. "Take over here! And *you*, Mr. English . . ." He grabbed the boy by the scruff of his neck, and when Hewes had the wheel, stiff-armed him to the starboard rail. "You see those two men flailing about in the water, Daniel?"

"Yes sir, but—"

"Good." Seizing the boy by the neck and the seat of his pants, Fergus heaved him over the side, shouting after him, "You can keep them afloat till we get a boat out to them!" Not waiting for Daniel to hit the water, Fergus turned, grumbling and sputtering, toward the companionway and gestured for the boat to be unlashed from its cradle. Katy ran for the gunwale, peered down at the blond head bobbing in the surf. Behind her, footsteps approached, stopping beside her.

"A truly touching scene, lady," Jason mocked. "But considering your aversion to the masculine gender, I should think it would have been you who disposed of the swain."

"Hardly," she retorted, her gaze intent upon Daniel. "He asked me to marry him."

"Indeed?" The man's deep laughter rankled her. "From the mouths of babes. Well, mayhap this icy dip will cool his ardor."

"No need, Captain." Assured that Daniel could hold his own in the surf, she looked up at Jason, her eyes long and smug. "I said yes."

The sound of his laughter froze. His countenance mutated from blithe, to alarmed, to grim. "You what?"

Seeing that the boat was being lowered into the water, Katy stepped away from the gunwale. "You heard me correctly the first time. I'm going to marry him. And as for my stepmother, if you don't want to disappoint her, I suggest you find some doxy in Boston and pass her off as Mary Kathleen Ryan. 'Tis the only way you will receive your money."

"I suppose you did not bother to tell the boy that you are already engaged?"

"No. 'Tis your word against mine, and I think he would be more inclined to believe me."

He shook his head in hardened disbelief. "You'll do anything, won't you, Katy?"

Tossing him a haughty look, she made a wide detour around him and headed back for her cabin.

"Well, so will I, lady," he whispered after her. "So will I."

5

That night Katy lay rigidly between the covers, staring into the dark, hoping that the gentle roll of the ship would lull her into slumber, for the shock of what she had committed herself to would not allow her to rest. Amidst the creaks and groans of timber, she did not realize her own compartment door had opened until she heard the sound of footfalls closeby. The cabin ripened with drab yellow light. Jason tossed the tinderbox onto the table, and after bestowing a dark look on the girl, lowered himself into a chair.

"What do you want?" she hissed, her eyes straying nervously to her breeches and shirt at the bottom of the bunk.

Following her gaze, the man felt a smile pull at the corner of his lips. "Strange, you did not strike me as one given to sleeping in the buff, but then, I am discovering many strange things about you."

"I am sure you are not here to discuss my sleeping habits, Captain. Say what you have to say and then get out. Daniel would be most irate to find you here."

"Ah, yes. And we mustn't frazzle Daniel, must we?" Tenting his fingers, he touched them to his lips and tossed her a measured glare. "Mr. English was kind enough to blurt out the entire story of your future bliss to Fergus. You should be ashamed of yourself, Katy. Promising to marry that boy when you know damn well that when your feet touch Spanish soil you'll be off faster than a shot. Don't you think you should tell him?"

"I don't know what you're talking about." But inside, her stomach was churning into knots. He was doing it again. Reading her mind. But how could he know?

"You can appear so guileless when you want to, my dear. Is that the same look you fixed on the boy when you sucked him into your trap? Well, you forget. I am no innocent, and I know you far better than Daniel. You hate the idea of a man in bed with you so much that you wouldn't agree to any such proposal unless you had an ulterior motive looming behind those lovely green eyes of yours. It seems fairly obvious what the motive is. Daniel can provide convenient transport to Spain. You are postponing the wedding ceremony until you reach Cádiz, not because you want your family about you, but because you have no intention of marrying the lad in the first place, and once on your native soil, you think you'll be able to do as you please. Am I correct?''

How could he have dissected her plan so completely? It was like having her soul drawn and quartered. "You are not correct. You are crazy. Please leave.''

Ignoring her statement, he continued. "Do you love him?''

"Love . . . ?'' The question caught her off guard, for love had never figured into any of her suppositions. The word died in her throat. Admitting that she did love Daniel would be so preposterous that Jason would know she was lying. Admitting that she did not love him would only verify Jason's accusations. Dangling between the two, she swallowed audibly and began again. "I am fond of him.''

"Fond of him, lady? Are you so anxious to surrender your maidenhead to a boy who kindles no warmer emotion in you than fondness?''

"Considering my feelings toward other men, Captain, fondness is not so cool an emotion.''

"Sad. Had you been less mulish last night and listened to me, you wouldn't have found it necessary to hawk yourself like a streetmonger.''

"If my memory serves me correctly, had I been less mulish last night, I might have surrendered my maidenhead to you—for whom I bear no fondness at all. And I did not 'hawk' myself. I did not need to. Daniel is quite in love with me.''

To this Jason let forth a raucous guffaw. "But if he had been a little less enamored of you, lady, what then? Lucky for you that the lad is so simple. You were spared the drudgery of having to employ all your feminine charms to snare him.'' Her mouth opened and closed in rage, but Jason continued despite her. "Now I shall tell you what folly you have wrought with your ploy. Had you listened to me last night, you would have discovered that I have suffered a change of heart. Oh, I still intended to present you at Pamela's doorstep, but I had no intention of allowing her to peddle your innocence to some lecher. If she proved cooperative, you would have been free to do as you saw fit. If she were difficult, I would have taken you to my brother Ian's and dealt with Pamela myself. Either way, my dear, you would have been spared the atrocities of the marital bed which you now seem so impatient to sample. As I said before, 'tis sad you did not listen. It appears you have marketed yourself—for nothing.''

Her pupils dilated, devouring the green of her irises. What had she done?

"Speechless for once, I see. But don't fret. What you have done can be readily undone."

"How?" she asked quickly.

It was the one response she never should have made, for it conveyed to the man that his suspicions about her had been only too correct. He began to pace the floor, his hands clasped behind him. His shirt was untucked and bloused freely around his waist. His collar was open and slit to his breastbone, where the dark hairs of his chest curled thickly. In his stride he exuded a magnetism that commanded the attention of every nerve in her body.

"It appears, lady, that there are no sane limits to what you will do to avoid this confrontation with Pamela. And that frightens me, because if one of your harebrained schemes goes awry, God only knows what other half-witted plans you'll devise. You might end up as the latest recruit in a bordello somewhere. There seems to be only one way to save you. Since you have no aversion to binding yourself in holy wedlock to the first man who becomes infatuated with you, I have decided that you will not marry Daniel." He stopped then and raked her with a long, penetrating gaze. "You will marry me."

Incredulity flamed across her face. "*Marry* you? I don't even *like* you!"

"Your misfortune, my dear. It has been my misfortune to fall in love with you."

It took a moment to filter this into her comprehension, but a moment only. "If this is your solution, Captain, I regret to inform you that it is no solution at all. Thank you, but I prefer to take my chances with Daniel."

Weary of pacing, Jason seated himself on the edge of the bunk and grinned at the sudden motion of Katy's legs away from him. "Tell me, lady, in your grand scheme of things, did you ever stop to consider what effect your ultimate rejection will have on the tenderhearted Mr. English? I would hazard that he will be completely devastated."

She turned her face away from him, not wanting to hear.

"Does the truth offend you?"

"The truth does not offend me. *You* do."

"Come now, Katy. If you had a shred of decency left in you, you would want to spare the lad's feelings. And after all, do you not owe him a debt of gratitude for watching over you these many days?" She stiffened as he aped her own words of three weeks earlier. "You say he loves you. Is this how you will repay him?"

I have no wish to hurt him, but can you not see? I must!

"It appears to me that if you can still sit there and tell me that you're planning to use the boy as the scapegoat in your deception, you're no better than the people you have delighted in maligning for so long. No better than myself, and no better than Pamela Ryan."

Whether she wanted to believe him or not, she knew he spoke the truth, and it smarted.

Divining from the girl's expression that his accusations had cut to the marrow, he continued. "You needn't trouble yourself with telling Daniel anything. I'll tell him that we fell in love aboard the *Elizabeth*, that we had a divisive argument that left you vulnerable to his advances, but that we have since resolved our differences and are once more happily betrothed. If we curb his expectations before he has a chance to dwell on them, he should rebound from his disappointment in a few days."

Katy shook her head. "I will marry Daniel," she breathed. "So do not think that you can influence me by preying upon my sympathies."

"Ah, Katy. I had hoped it wouldn't have to come down to this."

She paused. "Down to what?" Something in his tone alarmed her.

"I wonder if Mr. English would be so enthusiastic about marrying you if he knew what you intended for him once you reach Cádiz?"

"You wouldn't!"

"Oh, I would, lady," he bluffed. "And I will. I told you that I love you. And I'll stop at nothing to have my way."

"Is that your idea of love? Threats and intimidations?"

"Mere inducements. Marrying me is the most logical solution to your dilemma. In fact, marrying me is the only solution to your dilemma because Daniel certainly won't want anything to do with you once he learns of your ruse, and, having met Pamela Ryan, I can guarantee you that marrying me will be far more pleasant than marrying anyone she might choose."

Katy's eyes roved the cabin in search of answers that were not there. Jason was right. Daniel would break their engagement if he discovered the truth, and she could not walk blindly into a marriage with her stepmother's lackey. Her throat constricted as the reality of the situation closed in about her. "You said that you had suffered a change of heart," she pleaded with him. "You said that you would protect me from Pamela and would

109

allow me to go free when we reached Yorktown. Can you still not do that, Jason? Please?"

"That was yesterday, lady. Today I am not feeling so solicitous."

Katy's voice thickened with her outrage. "How easy for you to compress my life into such a tidy bundle. You have thought of everything, haven't you?"

"Not everything."

"Nay? What else is there?"

His face softened. "I have not thought how to elicit a kind word from you. You respect Fergus. You are fond of Daniel. Is it beyond your capacity to utter an affectionate word for me? I tell you that I love you. Will marriage to me be such a mean choice?"

"Hold that choice against the fires of hell, Captain, then ask me which I prefer."

Beneath his facade of unruffled posture he flinched at her barbs. This little chit of a girl provoked him beyond reason. She insulted him as no other dared, defamed and vilified him when he spoke of his love for her. And as the fine thread of his composure became untethered, she continued with her imprecations, unimpeded.

"I do not like you, Jason. Are you deaf that you cannot hear me? Look at my lips, then." She enunciated the words with exaggerated slowness. "I . . . do . . . not . . . like . . . you."

With the pulse in his throat beating madly, he rose to his towering height and speared her with a look that evoked instant silence. "Do you think me a beast so low that I have no feelings?" Yanking up the sleeve of his shirt, he brandished his forearm before her. "Do I have scales for flesh that the wounds you inflict upon me will not bleed? Am I a creature so grotesque that you cannot accept the love I am offering?"

"You mistake love for lust. But either way, I have no wish to be pawed by you. I will fight you, Jason. I will fight you every time you come near me. You will discover that a union with me will bring you little joy. 'Tis a promise."

"You will marry me, Katy." It was a flat pronouncement. "And you will do so whether you like me or not. The ceremony will take place soon after we reach Yorktown. You will learn how a man tames a woman, lady. You will learn how to cull the thorns from your tongue so that naught will escape your lips but words of petal softness. I will instruct you with painstaking thoroughness," he charged, grinding air within his fist, "or, by God, I'll attain eternal damnation trying! 'Tis a promise also." Ravaged by her rejection, he tore his eyes away from her and

110

strode toward the table. "One more thing. I believe it is the custom for engaged couples to indulge in activities other than hissing at each other. From now on if you cannot be kind to me in public, you will at least be civil. For the sake of appearances we will be seen to take leisurely strolls on deck together, your arm in mine. We will act like lovers, Katy. Do not think to comport yourself otherwise." With that he extinguished the light.

"You can go to the devil!" she called after him, not quite understanding how her plan had failed so miserably.

Fergus stopped by the next day to say that scuttlebutt had it that congratulations were in order for her and that lucky black-hearted swab, an epithet he articulated with the greatest of affection. She nodded and negotiated her lips into a thin smile, yet her eyes remained conspicuously bereft, causing the Irishman to frown and then open his arms to the girl.

"I think those are not tears of joy I'm seein', Mary Kathleen. If you're opposed to the match, tell me. I can be a man of considerable persuasion if I've a mind to. Do not look so sad, lass. It grieves an old man to see the light snuffed from your eyes."

With the weight of misery and doubt pressing upon her, she walked into the inviting comfort of the Irishman's arms, and released a floodtide of emotion that surprised even Fergus with its intensity. She did not divulge the cause of her anguish. She knew that not even Fergus with his well-intended threats could improve her situation. Her tears soaked his shirt. Her subsequent hiccups became muffled in his chest. He soothed and consoled and stroked her lustrous mantle of hair with a hand that trembled slightly with memories of another era.

'Tis her hair, Mary Kathleen. 'Tis her hair exactly. How could I not know? I combed it for years, and years, and years.

Daniel did not stop by to extend his congratulations. Having thrown a punch at Jason after hearing the turn of events concerning Katy, he had been knocked to the floor and held there until the last details had been explained to him. Jason had apologized for the misunderstanding; Daniel had tried to bludgeon Jason to death with his head, and walked away from the fracas nursing a black eye and a heart filled with rancor. Katy did not see him for days. When she did, she was shocked not only by the purpling sphere around his eye but also by the disdain that had drawn his features into ugly distortion. Silently his eyes reflected the animosity that was eating away at him. Bitter disappointment etched itself across his lips, and in his own brand of rejection he turned his back on the man and woman who were seen so often now strolling leisurely across the deck arm in arm, speaking in hushed tones, like lovers.

Yet had Daniel studied the couple with a more discerning eye, he might have realized that only the man spoke in hushed tones, for the girl was too busy clenching her teeth to say even one word. Her reticence galled Jason, but he allowed it to continue until the day when, after a long speechless stroll, he escorted her back to her door, propelled her inside the cabin, slammed the door shut with his boot, and thrust her up against the portal, pressing his body into hers. There was no way to avoid his kiss. He locked her head within his hands and tilted her face to meet the hardness of his lips. His desire was heady brew for the girl to swallow. His urgency made her tremble. A whirling sensation took root in her head and spun outward, enveloping her in a warm dizziness that spread downward through her body. His mouth was hot and authoritative and assaulted gently. His tongue found and tamed hers with long liquid strokes. She was too shocked to struggle, too numbed to kick or scratch. His mouth became the focal point of her existence. Tasting. Bruising. Her lips felt distended. Her limbs felt oddly light. When he wrenched his lips away from her, she cried out at the separation. Marking the color in her cheeks, he impaled her with his eyes.

"If you cannot be congenial in public, lady, I will take it out in kind in private. I warn you not to goad me beyond endurance. I grow increasingly impatient to bed you and might one day forget my manners." That said, he released her and stormed from the compartment. She gasped, trying to catch her breath, and cursed herself for ever having tested his patience.

On the last day of May, Fergus began making noises about clam flats and pigsties, saying he could sniff them on the breeze. On June 2, when the boy in the crow's nest yelled, "Land ho!" Katy stood at the larboard rail, squinting at the skeletal irregularity they were calling land.

"We're about seven miles east of Wellfleet on the Cape." Jason came up behind her and gently smoothed his hands across her shoulders. "We'll heave to for the night rather than run the risk of navigating through the hazards in the bay. Tomorrow we sail into Boston harbor." With quiet eyes he studied the hairline band of indigo that paralleled the horizon. "It's a vast land out there, Katy. It's where our sons will be born, and our sons' sons."

His voice faded, yet his words continued ringing in her ears like a death knell: *Where our sons will be born where our sons will be born where our sons sons sons . . .*

Jason felt with some distress the cold tremors that began to rack her body. She was so tiny. So fragile. He wanted to love her, to pamper and coddle her. If only she would let him.

Boston. A city of hills and steeple churches, gabled houses and manicured brownstones, warehouses, countinghouses, retail stores, and taverns. As the *Ugly Jane* was towed alongside the granite quay know as Long Wharf, Katy stood at the starboard rail, unnerved by the anarchy in the dock area, where an animated hive of humanity pulsed around some invisible nucleus. Sailors with toothless grins and rolling gaits; merchants in broad-skirted coats, cutting a path through the rabble with the tips of their malacca canes; colored manservants in starched suits, wicker baskets swinging from their arms; frowsy females, high-bosomed and orange-headed; a sea of color and sound flowed with the tide. Dogs yapped at the feet of horses and sent chickens and geese on a merry chase through parted legs and broken crockery. Wagon wheels clattered through piles of dung and rotten produce, splattering filth and decay in every direction. As the *Ugly* was snugged up to the wharf and her great hawsers secured around the pilings, Katy stared out at the harbor. Naked masts rose like the trunks of defoliated trees, their barren yardarms forming stout branches. Vessels of every dimension and nationality glutted the bay. Below her, the water was a swill of green whose stench bore testimony to the offal that bobbed to the surface, companion to waves of seaweed, kelp, and algae.

Boston.

She pinched her nose and prayed for a shift in the wind.

Early that afternoon Jason stopped by Katy's cabin with an invitation. She could only laugh and point to her bare toes and breeches.

"You want me to wander around Boston with you? Like this?"

" 'Tis what I asked."

"How can I go anywhere dressed like this, Jason?"

"How can you forgo the luxury of dry land in favor of a cabin that you've been penned up in for six weeks?" Another possibility dawned on him. His countenance sobered. "Unless of course 'tis the company you're being asked to keep."

Her ambivalence prevented a ready response. She certainly had no wish to remain in this cabin any longer, but neither did she wish to become the object of ribald attention by parading around Boston dressed like a boy. While she attempted to decide which alternative was the least revolting, Jason, attributing her

113

reluctance to the reason he had suggested, squared his shoulders and strode toward the door.

"Stay here, then," he ground out in a deep, fire-eating voice. "But I would suggest that you have Fergus nail a bolt onto this door. The people who frequent the waterfront are not Boston's most august citizens, and a girl alone in an unlocked cabin is fair game for just about anything."

Perplexed by his sudden anger, she threw him a conciliatory look. "Can you not wait for my answer before storming out the door?"

"I thought it rather obvious what your answer was."

She crossed her arms. " 'Tis your most noteworthy flaw," she snapped. "You think."

"And yours, lady, is that you talk!" He tipped his head and departed.

"Hummph." Snubbing the space he had just vacated, she scuffed around the floor in irritation before plopping onto the bunk. "I had been about to say I would go with you!" she shouted into the emptiness. Bored and restive, she glared at the encroaching walls, realizing that she didn't want to remain in the cabin. Her eye fell on the unlocked door. What did Jason mean, that a girl alone in an unlocked cabin was fair game for just about anything? What was "anything"? Not wanting to find out, she grabbed her stockings and jammed her feet into them. She was not above swallowing her pride this once. After all, an afternoon with Jason would be far less perilous than waiting to be attacked by some derelict who might accidentally wander on deck.

Panting as she reached the rail, she spied the back of his head above the crowd and was about to yell to him when he turned sideways, showing his arm to be locked around the waist of a blond whose character was questionable even if her assets were not. Katy watched her sashay two fingers up the length of Jason's chest. He dropped his hand from her waist to give her buttocks a lusty squeeze, then leaned over to whisper in her ear. Katy gritted her teeth as the girl nodded her assent to whatever Jason had said. Well! He had certainly wasted no time in finding a companion.

Katy blew a stream of air upward to cool her face. Fine! Let someone else be victim to his rough kisses and suffocating embraces. Perhaps she would enjoy being held against a door while Jason's mouth blazed across . . .

An unsettling warmth crept into her eyes as she remembered that day in the cabin.

. . . while his tongue . . .

She blew more air upward into her face.

. . . while he fingered her cheeks and brushed his thumbs down the curve of her throat . . .

Smothering the sensations that were fighting their way into her consciousness, she watched Jason and his trollop fade into the background. The sight of him with that woman should have had no effect upon her. So why did she feel so hollow inside? Why did she feel so alone?

"He doesn't act much like a man who is about to be married, does he?"

She spun toward the voice behind her.

"But I could have told you that a long time ago," Daniel taunted. "I've seen his type before. What I don't understand is why you've decided to marry him, knowing what kind of man he really is."

"Daniel." She hoped the hollowness within her had not become evident in her face, "I . . . I . . ." She hesitated, stumbling over words in her mind. "I was going with him . . . he asked me to . . . but I couldn't very well walk the streets of Boston dressed as I am."

He bowed his head toward the quay. "So he found himself a substitute."

She averted her gaze. "It appears that way, doesn't it?"

"What is the matter with you?" Grabbing her arms, he pulled her to him. "You don't love him. You couldn't love him! You would have told me if you'd had an understanding with him. So why are you marrying him? Is he forcing you for some reason?"

Her eyes brimmed with tears as he shook her. Her mouth worked soundlessly.

"That's it, isn't it? He's forcing you! Why? Tell me why!"

"Daniel, you're hurting—"

"I love you!" he screamed into her face; then, hearing the harshness of his own voice, he dropped his hands and said more softly, "I love you. You said you'd be my wife, and I'm not going to give you up without a fight. Jason MacAuley can blacken my other eye and break every bone in my body if he wants to, but that won't discourage me. He has done something to you to make you change your mind, and I'm going to find out what."

"Let it alone, Daniel!" she cried. "You don't understand. There are things about me that you could never accept, things that would make you hate me. Just . . . just leave things the way they are," she sobbed. "And be thankful that Jason is taking me away from you. I will be his misery and not yours."

Bewilderment shaded the sensitive lines of his face. "What do you mean, 'things'? What kind of—?"

"Just leave me alone!" she screamed, slipping through the hands that he extended to her. "Go away and leave me alone!" He started after her as she ran from him but stopped when she fled down the companionway to her cabin.

"Katy!" Frustrated at his inability to reason with her, he drove his fist into his palm and cursed aloud. Women! There was just no talking to them. But he had to make a stand soon. MacAuley would be taking her to Virginia in the very near future, and Daniel had to assert himself before then. He would convince her that Jason MacAuley was no good for her. He had to.

It was well after midnight when she heard the footsteps. They did not surprise her. She had been expecting them, just as she had expected the knock at her bolted door and the voice that penetrated the stillness with sober authority.

"I know you're not asleep. Let me in. I have something for you." It was Jason's voice.

She walked to the door and whispered hoarsely, "Indeed, but I'll have none of what you have to offer. Remember? The waterfront is a dangerous place for young ladies, so they had best keep their doors bolted against all intruders. Good night."

There was a short pause before his voice sounded again. "Open the door before I break it down."

She slid the bolt across the door, as she had known she would in the end, then walked away from the place where he would enter. She might have to listen to him gloat about his night's conquest, but she didn't have to look at him. She heard the door open, his boots tread across the floor, and a muffled thud as of boxes falling on the table. Still she did not turn around.

"Well?" he demanded.

"Well what? Would you have me ask you how you spent your day? All right. How did you fare today, Jason? I saw your companion. Did you find her suitable to service your needs?"

She could feel the cabin swell with his presence, could imagine his eyes boring into the back of her head. "Let us hope that after we are married your performance will equal the wench's. And that day draws closer, lady. There is a packet ship leaving for Yorktown early tomorrow afternoon. We'll be on it. I'll call on you tomorrow morning to take you to breakfast. Be ready."

He left as quickly as he had come, and only when she heard the door close did she peek over her shoulder to make sure that he really had gone. It was then that she noticed the pile of boxes strewn over the table. She drew the bolt across the door again, just in case Jason was entertaining any idea of returning, then circled the table. Twitching her lips in indecision, she shook one of the parcels, then, unable to contain her curiosity, wiggled the cover off.

Green. Pale green. French lawn. Though she did not make the comparison, the color was the same stunning hue as her eyes. Shaking it out, she held it up to her and smoothed her hand down the skirt. It flowed like water and swished as she twirled around with it. The sleeves were puffed to the elbow, the bodice close-fitting with a low circular neck, the skirt softly gathered with a separate train attached at the high waist. In a matter of minutes the remaining packages were broken into and a profusion of femininity spread in disarray atop the table. White silk stockings. Garters. Linen chemises. Kid slippers. A silk nightgown. A violet muslin chemise gown that was drawn in around a low neckline and tied at the waist by a sash of purple silk. A hooded cloak worked in a heavy violet cotton with a lining that was fashioned in the same purple silk as her sash. She stared at the articles of intimate apparel and blushed at the thought of Jason's buying such things. Yet the materials were of the finest quality, soft and lacy, demonstrating not only Jason's impeccably good taste but also the fact that he was no novice when it came to the selection of feminine habiliments.

When he called for her at eight bells the next morning, the cargo was already in the process of being hauled up from the hold to the main deck, and the noise was deafening. Jason's mood this day had threatened to be sour, for he envisioned the entire time spent sparring with Katy, but when she opened the door for him, smiling, he blinked stupidly and gaped in wonder. She wore the green dress and like a porcelain figurine looked as if she might shatter if he touched her. She had parted her hair in the middle, then brushed the sides back and upward, gathering them at her crown with a green satin ribbon. The sourness within him disappeared, replaced by a smile that touched his lips, then his eyes. It appeared that yesterday had been worthwhile after all. The girl who had propositioned him on the quay had been about the same size as Katy, so he had paid her to accompany him while he attended to the business of providing a modest wardrobe for his bride-to-be. He had treated the young girl to dinner at one of the local taverns as an expression of his appreciation, only to find that she was anxious to say thank you in a more physical way than he had in mind. Throughout the meal he was repeatedly forced to remove her hand from beneath the table. He had been unable to understand why he had no desire to bed the girl. Gazing now upon the extraordinary beauty of Mary Kathleen Ryan, he knew why.

"Your hair is quite becoming like that, Katy," he managed to comment offhandedly, thinking that she would be exquisite even if she were bald.

"Thank you." Leaving him at the portal, she hastened to fetch her cloak, swinging it over her shoulders as she returned to him. "And thank you for all the lovely clothes. Wherever did you get the money?"

"Katy!" he reprimanded as he lifted her hair from beneath the covering of the cloak. "You should never ask a gentleman such a question."

"I thought we had already established that you are no gentleman." But she said it good-humoredly, so he only grinned and fanned the heavy length of her hair over her hood. "Truly, Jason. Tell me. I want to know."

"Do you allow a man no secrets at all?" When she shook her head, he laughed and scooted her from the cabin. "All right, then, if I am to be allowed no secrets, I obtained a small loan from Fergus."

"Aha! I thought as much. Well, you can be assured that I have every intention of repaying you when we reach Yorktown. I'm sure my stepmother will—"

"Lady." Catching up with her, he turned her around to face him. "A wife need not repay a husband for the necessities which it is the husband's duty to provide."

"You are not my husband, Jason."

"But I will be," he persisted in an undertone. "Have you not reconciled yourself to that fact yet?"

She dropped her eyes. "I don't want to talk about that today, Jason. I don't want to think about that today. Can we go now? I'm hungry."

Realizing the futility of pursuing the subject any further, he shook his head and let her go.

It was late in the morning when they returned from breakfast, Jason having stopped to purchase a small leather-bound chest for Katy's belongings. Her farewell to Fergus was a teary one, for she had grown fond of the burly Irishman and feared that, despite what he said, she would never see him again. He made much ado about seeing her when she eventually arrived on the island of Mount Desert, exacting a promise from her that she would tour the island with no one but him. She could not tell him that she was scheming to think of ways to avoid this marriage with Jason and that she did not intend to sail into

Frenchman Bay as Mrs. Jason MacAuley, did not intend to sail into Frenchman Bay at all.

Daniel was conspicuously absent, and Katy did not have to ask why. It was better this way. She had hurt him enough as it was. Standing on the deck of the packet ship with her worldly possessions at her feet and Jason at her side, she waved good-bye to Fergus. Had she believed in reincarnation, she would almost guess that in another lifetime, Fergus McFadden had been very dear to her.

On the morning of June 7 the packet anchored in Yorktown harbor and lowered her longboats so the passengers could be rowed to shore. Once on the mainland, Jason secured one arm around the sea chest, one arm around Katy, and plowed across the strand and up the grassy bank that fringed the green around which the village of Yorktown was situated. The way was lined with houses of impeccable charm—two-story brick houses with elaborately detailed cornices alternating with three-story mansions whose multiple dormers overlooked trimmed boxwoods and narrow brick walkways.

"Do you see anything that looks familiar?" Jason inquired.

The girl looked about her, recognizing nothing. "I find it difficult to believe that I ever lived here." On their approach toward an impressive brick mansion Katy looked up at the east wall, her eyes rounding with curiosity, for there was a hole the size of a cannonball puncturing the structure, and the massive chimney had crumbled to half its size. "What do you suppose happened there?"

"I imagine that was a result of the battle back in '81. You must have been about . . . what—three or four when Cornwallis went on his rampage? He destroyed much of the town in his final skirmish. That looks to be one of the many battle scars."

Katy's stomach bunched into grating knots. " 'Tis why my father sent me away," she said bitterly. "He told my aunt that he feared for my life in the coming battle. So he sent us to Savannah, and he was spared ever having to look at me again. How fortunate for him that General Cornwallis decided to make his stand at Yorktown. It made his rejection of me that much simpler." She choked down the lump in her throat, her exhaustion making her more vulnerable to emotions which she had resolved would never again hurt her. Jason, hearing the pain in the voice of the small child she once had been, tightened his arm around her as if, by so doing, he could eliminate her pain.

An hour later, after renting a buggy at the livery, they were traveling along a road that twisted through a primal forest of blue-green spruce. The fragrance from within the forest was quite the most refreshing scent Katy had inhaled for days. Leaning back in her seat, weary from four days and nights of sitting upright on a wooden bench in the packet's saloon, she considered what would befall her in a very short time. She was engaged to two men whom she had no wish to marry, and she was about to meet the woman whose greed had initiated the whole thing. How could her life have suffered such an ill turn in so short a time? How?

Seeing the apprehension etched across her features, Jason reached his arm around her rigid shoulders and snuggled her up to him. "We're almost there. I wish you could stop looking as if someone was about to eat you up. My brother and sister-in-law would never think of such a thing."

"Your brother?" She faltered.

"Aye. I'm taking you to Ian's for the night. Tomorrow will be time enough for you to meet Pamela. Besides, I'm anxious to find out if he has had any word from the *Elizabeth*. God only knows what happened to her after that second storm. In any case, I have much explaining to do."

She allowed his hand to remain where it was and leaned into him, resting her head against his shoulder, refusing to analyze the comfort she found there. His news eased the wrenching in her stomach a small degree, but she knew that the nervousness had not vanished. It would blossom anew tomorrow.

After a space Jason nosed the palfrey down a linear drive, bringing the buggy to a halt before a three-story red brick mansion whose finely clipped front lawn was resplendent with magnolia trees and exquisitely shaped hedges. The house itself was a masterpiece, combining black-shuttered windows, massive chimneys, and third-story dormers with a facile grace that exuded both warmth and tranquillity. After tying the horse up at the hitching post, Jason lifted Katy to the ground.

"If I know Ian, 'tis too fine a day for him to be cooped up inside. Why don't we walk around back and look for him there."

As they rounded the side of the house, Katy noticed two figures in the distance strolling arm in arm toward the main house, a small child skipping rings around them as they moved. The child suddenly stopped, tugged on her mother's skirt, pointed a tiny finger toward the house, then with a gentle prod from her mother, started running toward Jason.

"Uncle Jason, Uncle Jason!" Jason bent down on one knee and opened his arms to the small child, who, upon reaching him, flung her arms tightly around his neck and crushed her cheek to his. "Throw me up in the air like last time you were here, Uncle Jason." She laughed. "Please?"

Grinning, Jason stood upright, and catching his niece round her waist, tossed her high into the air while she kicked her feet and giggled excitedly. "Enough?" He guffawed. She nodded, and as she did so, he let go of her, scooping her up again as she plunged downward. She screamed in surprise and started giggling again.

"And now, young lady," he teased, "how about a big kiss for your uncle?"

Propped safely in his arms, she tilted her head toward his, then grabbed his beard in her tiny fist and pulled on it lightly. "You didn't have whiskers last time you visited us. There's no place to kiss your face now. It's all hairy." Her attention wandered to Katy, who was all but speechless at witnessing this side of Jason's nature. "Are you Uncle Jason's wife?"

Katy's eyes widened at the unexpected question, but it was Jason who supplied the answer. "Not yet. But she soon will be. Will you like that?"

She bobbed her tawny head and whispered none too quietly in her uncle's ear, "She's pretty."

"A fine eye you have, Rebecca. I agree most heartily."

"Jason?" Reaching the place where her brother-in-law stood, Elizabeth MacAuley let go her husband's hand and stretched to kiss Jason's cheek. "I don't know whether we are more delighted or surprised. We weren't expecting you for another eight to ten months. Dare I ask if all is well? And your companion . . ." She turned to Katy. "Surely this cannot be Mary Kathleen."

Jason crossed an uncomfortable glance with his brother as he spoke. "Elizabeth, Ian, I would like you to meet Mary Kathleen Ryan."

"And she's going to be Uncle Jason's wife," Rebecca piped up.

A fleeting look of concern darted across Elizabeth's face but disappeared before anyone could detect it. " 'Tis true?" she asked, looking between her brother-in-law and the girl with the extraordinary green eyes.

Jason nodded. "Aye, 'tis true."

Smiling, Elizabeth squeezed both the girl's hands and kissed her pale cheek. "Well, then, I am happy to welcome you not only into our home but also into our family. How in the world did you ever snare that old bachelor into giving up his solitary life? We gave up all hope for him long ago."

Katy directed a meaningful look at Jason. " 'Twas he who did the snaring."

Catching the look but not understanding its meaning, Elizabeth motioned to her husband. "Ian, can you offer your future sister-in-law no other greeting than to stand there gawking at her? Come, give her a kiss."

"It was not the girl I was gawking at," the man sputtered as he limped over to them, cane in hand. He nodded toward the small clothes that Jason had borrowed from Fergus and shook his head in comic disbelief. "I was gawking at *his* breeches. Damn if those aren't the ugliest knee breeches I've ever seen. They look like two gunnysacks. The tailor who made them was a crook if he made you pay for them." Attendant upon Katy now, his eyes reflected bemusement and perhaps a little awe. "It's not often that my wife encourages me to kiss a beautiful woman, and less often that my brother will stand by and allow me to do so. I had better take advantage of the opportunity before they both realize what I'm getting away with."

The kiss he placed on her cheek was painless, so she suffered through it with little import. Jason's brother looked to be his senior by a few years, the basis for this observation being that his features lent themselves more to mellowness than handsomeness. As rugged and tall as Jason, he carried more bulk through his girth so that as he leaned on his hickory cane for support, it seemed that the slender staff would splinter beneath his weight.

Noting the pallidness of Katy's complexion, he addressed his wife. "Our guest is looking a bit tired, Elizabeth. I think you had better take her inside and serve some refreshment."

Elizabeth took Katy's arm. "Ian is right. You must be exhausted after that long voyage. Come into the house with me. I'll wager you could do with a long nap about now." She motioned to Rebecca, who crawled reluctantly down from Jason's arms and chased after the two women as they strolled toward the house.

Ian hobbled to Jason's side. "Does she know?"

Jason shook his head.

"You're a damn fool, brother. Do you know what she'll do when she finds out?"

Jason looked toward the house as if he could see her slight figure through the solid brick walls. "She will find out after we are married. By then it will be too late for her to do anything."

Ian regarded his brother in disbelief. "When you fall, you fall hard. I only hope you know what you're doing." He paused. "I certainly didn't think she would be such a beauty. I suppose I must commend you for being able to keep your hands off her all this time. Not exactly what you were expecting, is she?"

Jason massaged the back of his neck. "Let's say she is a bit more than I was expecting."

"Well"—Ian slapped him on the back—"congratulations, I think. Now, suppose you tell me what the devil you're doing in Yorktown when you should be in Calcutta?"

"I assume that means you've had no word from the *Elizabeth*."

Ian's eyes turned to slate. "Tell me you're not going to tell me what I think you're going to tell me."

"Come on, Ian." Jason threw his long arm around his brother's shoulder. "A stiff drink will help you swallow what I have to tell you."

"Hell's fire, man! No amount of drink is going to help me if you're about to tell me that you've sunk my ship!" Jason's brother limped toward the house, trying to keep pace with the younger man's long stride. "And the least you can do is slow down for a cripple!"

Jason roared, "That will be the day, when Ian MacAuley is ever a cripple. By the way, has Pamela been by recently to invoke doom on our name?"

"No. And she's not likely to, either."

Frowning, Jason stopped to wait for his brother. "May I ask why?"

"Because she's dead."

"Dead?"

"Hanged herself about eight weeks ago."

6

"She is so young to have suffered so much misfortune—her mother, this terrible voyage." Folding her hands, Elizabeth MacAuley trained her eyes sternly upon husband and brother-in-law. "It was wrong to make any agreement with that awful Ryan woman, no matter what threats she held over our heads. That child upstairs has endured unspeakable atrocities, and for what?"

Ian tapped his cane on the floor and limped to the fireplace. "We had no other choice at the time, my dear, and we could not foresee what would happen." He heaved a great sigh and turned to Jason. "The girl is all right, isn't she, Jason? I mean, no one harmed her?"

Jason had not mentioned Katy's experience with Molkeydaur, and never expected to. "She's fine—exhausted and a little seasick, but fine."

"You see!" Ian gestured toward his wife. "These Irishwomen might look frail, but they're as strong as oxen. No need to fret about her."

Elizabeth pursed her lips in exasperation. "Someday you will learn that women and cattle cannot be thrown into the same class, Ian MacAuley. Now, since I cannot foresee my presence as coming to any avail, I will quietly depart and leave you gentlemen to your own resources."

She gathered her skirt together and stood up, extending her hand to Jason. "It really is marvelous having you here again. Let me know when I should start making plans for your wedding. It has been so long since we've had a large gathering at the house."

Jason lifted her hand to his mouth and kissed it softly. "Thank you for your kindness, Elizabeth. You can begin making preparations for the marriage immediately. In fact, the sooner the better. I find myself growing impatient to play the husbandly role."

"I can see why. She's beautiful." Turning her head, she arched one brow at her husband. "And you—I will discuss a few points with you later. Gentlemen . . ." She tipped her head and departed, the sweet scent of honeysuckle tingeing the air even after she had closed the door behind her.

Ian raked his hand through his hair, looking chagrined. "Well, I'll be crawling into a cold bed tonight, for sure."

"I doubt that one night of abstinence will do any harm to your male prowess," Jason needled.

"Abstinence? Who said anything about abstinence? I expect to hear a short lecture on my intemperate remarks concerning Katy, and after I make my humble apologies, I have every intention of partaking in a lusty romp beneath the covers. Abstinence?" he hooted. "That would be a helluva way to spend a night."

The grooves appeared in Jason's cheeks as he shook his head at his brother. "Are you telling me that that broken leg of yours hasn't slowed you down one bit?"

Ian's countenance became mischievous. "What I'm telling you is that this broken leg"—he slapped his thigh—"is the best thing that ever happened to me. For the past few months, when I should have been climbing the rigging of the *Elizabeth*, I've been watching my crops grow and seeing my daughter become more beautiful every day. And instead of being squeezed into a bunk half my size or riding the crest of a thirty-foot wave in the middle of a tropical squall, I retire into a large bed with fresh sheets and Elizabeth's body pressed against mine. I tell you, Jason, I didn't think I could ever be content with solid ground under my feet all the time, but I was mistaken. I'm a seaman, but I'm a man first, and that part of me wants to cling to the pleasures I've experienced these past few months—the lovemaking, the laughter. Besides"—he limped back to the sofa and sat down—"I want to see our next child born. I was at sea when Rebecca was born. I'll not miss the birth of what I hope will be a son. And if you had an ounce of sense, you'd settle down to a profitable land trade yourself after you're married."

Jason reflected on his brother's comments for a moment. "There's no end to what a good woman can do, is there? All right, Ian. I'll consider your arguments. But in the meantime"—he swung his calf across his knee and flicked a speck of dust from his boot—"suppose you tell me about Pamela."

"Messy business, that. Elizabeth is right, I'm afraid. We never should have made any deals with that woman. She spelled trouble from the beginning."

"Fine time to be telling me that."

"No one is blaming anyone for what happened, Jason. I'm only saying that about the time you were arriving in Cádiz, Pamela was stringing a noose around her neck, so it really wouldn't have made any difference whether Katy had decided to come back with you or not. No one knows why the woman committed suicide. It's all quite bizarre. And the estate is so far in debt that the commonwealth will undoubtedly confiscate every acre to pay her creditors. Even if Katy has been named beneficiary in the will, she has been left with nothing. She could never afford to pay off the debts, let alone maintain that place. And as for the money Pamela owed us for keeping our part of the bargain, you can well imagine the number of eyebrows that would be raised if I tried to squeeze that amount of money out of the estate. We've been had, brother. We've lost a ship, crew, cargo, and the purse that was promised us. Do you realize that one woman has nearly invoked economic disaster on us?''

"But we have her silence.''

"Is that any consolation?''

"It is.'' Jason's voice throbbed with restrained anger. "If the woman had not killed herself, I probably would have done it for her.'' His eyes became hard as he rubbed his hand across the leather of his boot. "What of Katy's fiancé?''

"Fiancé? What fiancé?''

"You mean there has been no mention of a fiancé waiting for her return?''

"Hell, no! It wasn't exactly a widely publicized fact that the girl was even coming back to the old homestead. If there *is* a fiancé, he's certainly keeping his identity a secret.'' Ian tapped his cane in front of him, his brows drawn together in confusion. "How'd you happen to find out about this in the first place?''

"That letter that Pamela gave me before I left. When Katy read the contents, I discovered that it was Pamela's plan to marry her off to some wealthy man around here. What I don't understand is why she didn't tell us the truth in the beginning. Doesn't seem as if it would have made that much difference, since she had us over a barrel anyway. Unless, of course, she deliberately didn't want us asking questions. I begin asking myself, 'Why?' ''

"Why, indeed.'' Ian grunted. "There's no one for her to marry from these parts. All the landowners are old men.'' He suddenly stopped, his mind dwelling upon this last statement. "That's it, isn't it? She was going to pander the girl to one of those drooling old men. Jesus!''

Jason nodded, a grim look on his face.

"There is one thing that still puzzles me, though,'' Ian complained. "If you knew the girl was going to be wedded to someone else, how is it that *you* ended up engaged to her?''

Jason threw his hands into the air, looking boyishly innocent. "Just lucky, I guess.''

"Sure, sure. Well, regardless of how it happened, it's a good thing that you two are going to be married. The girl would be stranded here without a cent or a roof over her head otherwise.

Not that she would be stranded for long, once people saw what she looks like. Might be persuaded to take her in myself—on a fatherly basis, of course.''

Jason smiled but his eyes remained apprehensive. He would probably have quite the time with Katy once he told her about Pamela's demise, but he had to tell her. And now that the threat from the woman no longer existed, the girl would undoubtedly try to back out of her agreement with him. But he would hear none of her excuses. He had made up his mind, and marry her he would, no matter how much of a fuss she created.

At six-thirty that evening, after Ian MacAuley had watched his brother pace continuously for thirty-two minutes, he finally lost patience. "Dammit, man, will you stop that confounded pacing before you wear a path in the floor?''

Jason regarded his brother for a brief moment, then continued pacing. "What could be keeping her so long?''

"Who?''

"Your wife!'' he bellowed. "She *is* checking to see what has detained Katy, is she not?''

He turned sharply and was caught completely unawares. Elizabeth stood in the doorway, contemplating him in amusement.

Ian motioned her into the room. "This brother of mine has been driving me crazy for nearly an hour, and save for your appearance, my love, we might have even come to blows. I have no idea where he gets his bad temper—it certainly isn't a *family* trait.'' Ian grinned archly before continuing. "So, what news of our lovely guest?''

Elizabeth seated herself beside her husband, then, unable to contain her mirth, began to laugh. "I fear the child is all but lost to us this evening. She's still asleep, and I haven't the heart to wake her. Sorry to disappoint you, Jason, but if she's that tired, we would do well to let her sleep. We can't have her yawning in the minister's face when we ride to the parsonage tomorrow. And I'm sure she wants to be alert to plan for her marriage ceremony.''

Jason cleared his throat with some effort. That would be the happy day, when Katy went to see a preacher about marrying him of her own accord. It seemed more realistic to accept the fact that he would probably have to drag her to the church by her hair when the time came.

"If you have no objections, Elizabeth, I'd prefer that you and I arrange the entire affair without Katy having to worry about anything. Why don't we simply . . . surprise her?''

A furtive glance passed between husband and wife before

127

Elizabeth smiled. " 'Tis your wedding, Jason. I'll do whatever you ask."

They dined and conversed till late in the night, and it was not until after the candles in the parlor were extinguished and Elizabeth and Ian had retired that Jason found his way to Katy's room. She was asleep, curled on her side, her nightgown gaping in front to tempt him with a view of cleavage that was awe-inspiring. Her cheeks were flushed, her lips soft and parted. He sat down in the chair beside the bed, listening to the quiet rhythm of her breathing. No nightmares tonight. But how long would it last? When would he hear her screaming that the man had almost caught her? That he was trying to kill her? And what would happen if one night the man did catch her? Could her life be so intertwined with this nightmare that if the dream murderer succeeded in a dream murder she would indeed cease to exist? She had suggested it herself. Could it be so? He shook his head at the absurdity of the idea, then braced his elbow on the arm of the chair, resting his jaw against his fist. How in hell was he supposed to battle an invisible enemy? He knew that if somehow he could remove the demon from her dreams, he could at least have a fair chance of gaining her affection. Most men lost their lovers to other men. He was losing his to an apparition.

He glanced up at her again and was amazed to find that her eyes were open and leveled drowsily upon him.

"Such a solemn face," she whispered.

He knelt at the side of the bed and folded her hand within his. "We missed you at dinner."

"Dinner?" Her eyes strayed to the window as if perceiving the darkness for the first time. "What time is it?"

"Past eleven."

"Eleven? At night?" She yawned and rubbed her eyes with her fist. "Ian and Elizabeth must think me a frightful guest."

"Aye." Interlocking fingers with her, he brushed his lips across her fingertips. "Frightful."

"Jason . . ." Now that she was awake, the reckoning that the morrow would bring preyed on her nerves. "If you must take me to my stepmother's tomorrow, could we go early in the morning? I don't think I could stand to wait until after . . ." The strange look in his eyes warned her that something was amiss.

"Katy, Pamela Ryan is dead."

The girl could not believe the words he spoke. She stared at him, dumbfounded. "Dead? Pamela is dead?"

"Ian informs me that the funeral took place several weeks ago. She is quite dead."

"How did she die?"

He hesitated, avoiding her eyes. "Suicide."

She said nothing for a long time, and when she did, her voice was almost inaudible. "I'm glad she's dead. I should be ashamed for feeling such a thing, but I'm not. I'm glad."

He searched her face, waiting for an outpouring of rage, a demand to know why he could not have foreseen this event happening, why he could not have let her remain in Cádiz as she had wanted. But he saw no rage, heard no demands.

"Have I shocked you?" she asked him, perceiving his bewilderment.

"I've seen too much in my lifetime ever to be shocked by anything you could say, lady . . . except . . . except perhaps when you told me the man who haunts your dreams might one day kill you. Can you not see that he has poisoned your mind with fear of all men? He has led you to imagine yourself as every man's victim, every man's prey. If we could wrest him from your dreams, give him a face, a name . . . Perhaps—"

"The man has never lacked an identity, Jason. 'Tis Seth Aldrich."

Jason bent his head, looking very tired. "Why him, Katy? If you have never seen his face, how can you be so positive?"

"How could it be anyone else? He was a murderer. He killed my mother. He was a vicious, jealous man who destroyed the things that had been denied him, so that no one else could enjoy them either. But what he destroyed was a human life, and for that I hope he is burning in hell."

"What do you remember about the day your mother died, Katy? What can you tell me that might have some significance?"

She shook her head. "I can't remember anything. I don't want to remember anything."

"But don't you see," he urged her, "you might have seen something that could explain your nightmares, your fear. Good God, you might have witnessed the whole thing and simply blotted it from your mind."

The green irises darkened. She looked away from him. "I can't remember, Jason. Please don't ask me to."

Though eaten up with anxiety, he bit his tongue and did not pursue the subject. He could bide his time, but eventually he would convince her to discuss the matter with him. Perhaps it would mean an end to her nightmares. Perhaps it would mean the beginning of his own.

Catching himself staring at the rise and fall of her breast, he rose to his feet. "I'd best leave now." Lamely he massaged the hand that had joined hers. "I'll be in the next room should you need anything during the night. Don't be afraid to call out. Sleep well," he whispered, then started toward the door, a cold bath utmost in his mind.

With sad eyes the girl watched him move away from her. Loneliness had always been so much a part of her existence that she had considered it a natural state. But that assumption had been incorrect. The time she had shared with Fergus and even Daniel had been bountiful with laughter and friendship. Maybe she need not be lonely, if she could humble herself to admit that she needed companionship. But *she* had to take the first step. Jason could fill the darkness with his presence—if she asked him to.

"Jason?"

He turned toward her.

"Would you think me bold if I asked you to stay with me a little longer . . . just until I fall asleep?" She could have sworn that his first reaction was a grimace, but catching the subsequent glow in his eyes, she concluded that it had only been her imagination.

"Very bold, lady," he replied from the portal, but as he retraced his steps to her bed, he shrugged. "But I have a peculiar weakness for bold women. I'll sit with you as long as you like." Which could never be long enough as far as he was concerned, he thought. Lowering himself into the chair he had just vacated, he slung his calf across his knee and watched as she yawned, stretched, rearranged her blankets, and finally nestled into her pillows.

When she heard him move, she opened her eyes to find him tugging at her blankets.

"Lady," he said as he pulled the blanket up over the swell of her breast, tucking it beneath her chin, "I am neither priest nor monk. I pray you remember that and keep that blanket where it is." Perhaps, he thought, if he closed his eyes, the aching in his loins would disappear.

He was certain that he had dozed for only a few minutes, but when he opened his eyes again the morning sun was streaming in through the windows and Katy's bed was empty. Where the devil was she? And how had she escaped without his hearing her?

He ran his hand through his hair and brushed the wrinkles from his shirt as he sprinted down the stairs. He entered the dining room, half-expecting Katy's face to be smiling up at him, but found only Ian, elbows on the table, staring pensively into the contents of a teacup. Looking up when Jason appeared, the older man grinned widely. "Before you start frothing at the mouth, the lovely Miss Ryan broke her fast about two hours ago, and that's the last that any of us have seen of her.''

"Two hours ago! How did she—?''

"—creep past you without your knowing it?'' Ian chuckled to himself. "Well, we found her roaming around in the wee hours of the morning . . . said she was hungry . . . so we fed her and listened to her tell us about how you fell asleep in her room last night. Then she asked if she could take one of the stable horses and ride along the river. So Elizabeth rounded up some properly small riding clothes, helped her dress in the bedchamber which *you* were supposed to have occupied, then sent her on her way down the old bridle path by the river. A fetching sight on a horse, she is. I wouldn't worry about her, Jason. She knows what she's doing, but that's not going to stop you from chasing out after her, is it?''

Jason was halfway out the door before Ian finished his question, and galloping by the edge of the York River in less than ten minutes, his dark eyes narrowed against the glaring reflection from the water's surface. He was worried that Katy might try to find her father's estate by herself. That could bring disaster. He intended that she should visit the plantation—it might serve as the catalyst to unlock her memory. But he could not allow her there by herself. There was no way to predict what she might remember, but whatever it was, he wanted to be there. Someone would have to pick up the pieces.

He had ridden several miles before he caught sight of a chestnut horse grazing in the distance. Slowing to a trot, he spied Katy perched atop a rock that overlooked a bend in the river, her legs drawn up to her chest, her chin cushioned on her knees.

She turned at the sound of hooves and watched Jason dismount and leave the gray stallion by her chestnut before taking long strides in her direction. He had not bothered to change his clothes from last night, and they indeed looked like he had slept in them. It was odd to see him so rumpled—Jason, who was usually so fastidious about his person.

"Good morrow, lady,'' he offered lightly. He propped his foot atop the rock and leaned over, his forearms braced casually across his thigh. Patches of wetness stained his breeches and shirt; his forehead glistened with sweat. In his shadow she found herself feeling very small and defenseless.

"You've been riding hard this morning,'' she observed. "I hope not on my account. But you surprise me with your equestrian ability. I had always thought that seamen were supposed to be awkward around horseflesh.''

"Most seamen are. Like myself, they are more comfortable with either a ship or a woman beneath them."

She rolled her eyes at his jest. "Indeed."

The corner of Jason's mouth curled upward. "Now, am I to understand that this early-morning ride indicates that you are completely rested?"

She nodded and looked down at a wildflower she was twirling between her palms. "I needed to think about what you told me last night." Pausing, she plucked a petal from the flower. "I have arrived at some decisions."

Jason regarded her intently. "Go on, Katy. I'm listening."

"Well, it has suddenly occurred to me that I could be a very wealthy heiress. With my father and Pamela both dead, I can no longer be forced into the marriage they arranged. I'm free to manage affairs as I see fit, and I think I would like to accept some responsibility and prove to myself that I can operate my father's plantation just as well as he did. You probably think I'm being absurd, but it's very important to me."

His eyes did not betray his knowledge of the futility of her proposal. "If I remember correctly, you were extremely anxious to return to Spain."

"I was," she explained thoughtfully, "but the situation has changed. I have nothing to run away from anymore, and I find the serenity here most appealing. Think you"—she tilted her head up, questioning him with a spirited gleam in her eye—"that Elizabeth and Ian would help me? There is so much that I'll need assistance with. I shall have to hire servants, and field hands, and I don't know the first thing about growing tobacco."

Jason looked out over the water while he bandied words about in his head. He had two options open to him: he could tell her the story Ian had told him and squelch all her newfound enthusiasm; or he could let her think that the estate still belonged to her and he could purchase it in the meantime while letting her proceed with all her plans. Why not? He could afford it, Ian could oversee operations when they went to Mount Desert. It might be a good business investment. He should have thought of the idea before.

"All right, Katy," he agreed, turning back toward her. "It can be arranged. We'll move in after the wedding, and when we go up north, Ian can take charge of things."

Her face suddenly went white. "I was under the impression there would be no wedding."

"And why would you think that?"

"Pamela's death has changed everything. There is no longer any reason for you to marry me."

132

He regarded her darkly. 'Twas what he had feared. "Not everything has changed, lady. I am still in love with you. That's reason enough."

"Nay!" she choked, throwing her flower to the ground. "I . . . I cannot. I will not be forced into a marriage with a man whom I care nothing about."

"You seemed to have a different opinion last night."

"I didn't know what I wanted last night."

"But this morning you do?"

"Yes," she defended. "And marrying you is not high on my list." She failed to notice the anger seeping into his eyes as she continued her tirade. "From the beginning, I did not want to come to this place, but you forced me. When I asked to return to Cádiz, you gainsaid me. When I would have entered into a union with Daniel, you told me nay. Now, when I would remain here to live in peace and create a life for myself, you tell me that I may not exist except as your wife. You are such a fool! Do you know why I sat with you while you were recovering from your wounds? Not from concern. I feared that if you recovered you would fulfill your promise to Pamela, so I wished you dead. But I could not have your death on my conscience. I nursed you, not out of concern, but out of guilt! Are you anxious to marry a woman who has placed so little value on your life?" Rising to her feet, she stepped down from the rock. "I think you have more pride than that. I'm going back to the house now. I'll have my belongings packed and will be ready to leave by noon. I trust that Ian and Elizabeth will be kind enough to see me to my father's estate. You need not accompany me back. I believe I can find my own way."

The fleshy wings of his nostrils distended with anger as she swept past him. His lungs burned with the air he sucked into them. The little bitch! The unfeeling, callous little bitch! His fury cauterized the piercing sting of her words. He balled his hands into tight fists. Had he once been so lunatic as to think her a delicate creature? Nay, she was a python! How witless he had been to think that her attitude had changed! He remembered the strangeness in her eyes the day his fever had broken. What he had ascribed as loving concern had apparently been disappointment that he was alive! She was a parasite. Always taking and never giving in return. She would have hurt Daniel in order to secure passage back to Spain. Last night she had been receptive to him out of some warped need of her own, and he had been fool enough to allow himself to be manipulated. His chest expanded ominously. He would not make it that easy for her. So she wanted to seek sanctuary in her father's house, did she? That could be arranged. By God, he was just angry enough to show her what awaited her at her father's house!

He shot out after her, matching every one of her strides with three of his own. She gathered the chestnut's reins in her hand and reached for the pommel, only to be intercepted by a hand much larger than her own. Nettled, she slanted her brows at the hands binding her wrist and forearm.

"Take your hands off me."

"Be thankful that my hands are where they are and not fanned across your backside where you deserve them. Now, be good enough to step away from the horse." When she responded by staring defiantly into his face, he pulled her toward him, slapped the chestnut into motion with a whooping "Heyahh!" then struck out toward the gray, dragging the girl behind him.

"Let . . . . me . . . . go!" she shrieked, beating at him with her free hand and digging her heels into the earth to hinder any forward motion. When her raging at him did not halt his step, she kicked her legs out from beneath her and burrowed her backside into the soft earth. Her action stopped him only momentarily. She screamed as he came at her, and thrashed at his arms as he yanked her up from the ground and tucked her beneath his arm. When they gained the stallion, Jason swung her high onto the saddle, then hoisted himself up behind her, bracing his arms around her before she had a chance to scamper down the other side.

"Since your independence is so important to you, lady, I have decided to give you a preview of what to expect from your inheritance. And if you wish your head to remain where it is," he snarled, "I would not scream again."

She was bruised and breathless when Jason reined the palfrey down an oak-lined drive, but she did not have to see the rambling mansion in the distance to know where they were.

In the far recesses of her mind there flickered a specter from childhood—a blur of white, of elegance and order, of Doric columns and polished glass. What she saw when Jason lowered her to the ground shattered the image. An outgrowth of vegetation grew tall and ragged about the columned mansion. The whitewash was weathered and graying. Windows were broken. She stared in stunned silence as Jason dismounted and tethered the horse. The house looked like it had been deserted not for weeks, but for years. Jason came up behind her.

"Your inheritance, madam. Go ahead in. 'Tis what you wanted."

Her resolve fled as quickly as it had appeared. If ever a house looked haunted, it was this house. Opening that door would be like opening the portal to hell. She would be walking into a past that she had struck from her memory, resurrecting the ghosts who had been born within those walls. Puddles of perspiration dripped down her sides. She had decided to undertake the business of her family's plantation, and she still intended to do that. No matter that the decision had been much easier when she had not seen the house.

With chills banging a tattoo up and down her spine, she climbed slowly to the veranda. Avoiding the ornately carved double doors, she walked to the panel of leaded glass framing the entryway, and with the heel of her palm rubbed a circle of dirt away and pressed her forehead to the glass.

Shadows. And within the shapeless shadows, the central staircase, a relic from the past rising like a phoenix to live again in her mind. Hearing Jason mount the stairs behind her, she caught her breath and snapped her head back from the vision.

"Have you decided to enter through the window, or could you be induced to use the door?"

She would not tell him that she felt too much the coward to do either. Taking reluctant steps toward him, she focused on the door handle he was indicating with his outstretched hand.

"Open it!" He forced her hand around the handle; then, with his thumb atop hers, he depressed the bronze tongue.

Locked.

She exhaled a quick, relieved breath. " 'Tis locked. I'll come back some other time."

He laughed gruffly. "Think you the door is more likely to be open later?" Motioning her aside, he raised his foot, and like a battering ram drove the heel of his boot hard into the portal. With a rattling of wood and hinges the door flew open. Jason bowed at the waist and directed her over the threshold. "After you, lady."

Her eyes shifted to the dark maw and paled with her inner turmoil.

"Lady . . . ?" Her hesitation provoked him. "Your inheritance awaits you." Grasping her hand, he propelled her gently into the foyer. "I would have you see what you have chosen above me."

The house seemed to suck her into its depths, and like a frightened child she stood statue-still and suffered its inspection. High above her a chandelier creaked on a gentle zephyr. A host of ancestors whose mirthless countenances had been set to canvas lined the walls, leveling their vacant eyes upon her. The echo of Jason's boots sounded as he walked around her, past the dead, unblinking eyes and the door to the adjoining corridor. At the stairs he stopped and turned to face her.

"Acquaint yourself with your lover, madam!" he bellowed. "Note the color of his hair." He flung a hand toward the silver cobwebs dangling from the sconces and chandelier. "The texture of his skin." She followed the direction of his gaze toward the parlor, where the once exquisite silk rug had frayed and tattered along the edges. "The delicacy of his scent." He inhaled deeply of the musty dampness. "Think you he will embrace you more warmly than I at night? Will you be more receptive to the whisperings from these walls than you are to my words? Walk around, lady! Explore the chambers where you romped as a child. Look beneath the beds and the shrouds that cover the furniture. Look for the ghosts that have turned you into a cold, inhuman puppet."

Her eyes kept pace with him as he trod back and forth across the place where she might have found her mother. There was no body, no blood, but she sensed something. A presence? Could there be a lingering presence in this room? And if not in this room, then in another? She looked away from Jason for a moment. There *was* something here. Tangible or intangible, she could feel it. But where? Her eyes darted to the doors in the east and west walls. She knew what lay behind them. Narrow, linear corridors that led to—

The word burst whitely in her mind.

Corridor. Narrow corridor. A door at the end of the corridor. She shook her head as if to expunge the tableau. Footsteps. Rapid footsteps. Running.

Her face went white, her eyes wide, and she swayed where she stood. Jason grabbed her shoulders and shook her. "Remember, damn you! Don't blot it out! Remember the faces. Remember what you saw. Tell me what ghosts have caused you to hate me so much. Tell me!"

"I . . . I can't!" she screamed at him. "I don't remem—"

"You do remember!" he shouted. " 'Tis in your eyes. Look at the room, Katy." He spun her around to face the staircase. "It all started here. What happened that day? Think, girl. Think!"

"*Sssstop*! I can't re—"

From the silence of the parlor a great whooshing sound split the air and reverberated through every chamber in the house. Katy covered her ears, trying to still the noise that vibrated in her eardrums, and when the sound rang out again, echoing nearer, she pinched her eyes shut and screamed a scream of pure terror. Not waiting for the noise to erupt again, Jason raced into the parlor. Finding nothing out of order, he slowly stalked the room.

What in the hell? From the corner of his eye a fluttering shadow swooped upward, wings clacking. Jason pivoted around as it landed on the mantel.

"Pigeon," Jason muttered to himself. "A damn pigeon." Shaking his head, he walked back to the hall. "It was just a . . ."

The hall was empty.

"Katy?" He was not so superstitious as to think that the house had swallowed her, so that left only one possibility. He ran out onto the porch and found her scrambling onto the stallion's back. "What are you doing?" he yelled at her.

Seated rather unsteadily in the saddle, she peered over the gray's head to the reins that she had been in too great a hurry to untether from the hitching post. Jason walked up beside her. He sidled an amused glance at the hitching post. "It appears you have forgotten something, lady. In future, when trying to escape from ghosts, do remember to unleash the horse."

"Untether him, Jason," she panted, her eyes fixed on the mansion as if expecting the nameless horror within to come flying out at her. "We have to get away from here."

"We?"

"You can remain if you like. I'm leaving."

Jason loosed the reins, brandishing them in his hand. "Not without these, you're not. Now, slide off the horse. I want you to see the ghost."

Her eyes widened at his suggestion. "I'll not set foot in that house again until it has been scrubbed and aired and exorcised of all its spirits."

"Indeed, lady?" The horse pranced skittishly as Jason continued to restrain him. "Were you not going to make this your permanent residence as of noon today?"

She ignored the question. "Please give me the reins."

"You did not answer my question."

"Nor will I!"

He wrapped the reins tightly about his hand. "Then here you remain until you do." At the sound of distant rumbling he turned his head and frowned at the sight of a buggy rattling down the drive toward them. "Now what?" he hissed.

The carriage drew to a halt in a whirlwind of dust that settled on a finely garbed gentleman who was flailing his handkerchief like a white flag of truce. Spitting and coughing, the man whipped off his spectacles, and as he began to polish the dust from them, spoke. "M-might I inquire what you are d-doing here, sir?"

Jason stared at the old gentleman, confused as to why the man was addressing his question to the horse.

"C-come, come, sir. Have you a t-tongue in your head?" The old fellow squinted at the long-faced giant in front of him, thinking him to be quite the biggest man he had ever seen, and quite the ugliest.

"If *I* might inquire, sir," Jason asked in a deep voice that bespoke his irritation, "who are *you*?"

The old man stopped rubbing his glasses and elongated his eyes to tiny cracks. Why did the giant's voice sound like it was coming from somewhere else? "I, sir, am Ma-Madison Bane." Curling the wire bows around his ears, he peered through the squares of glass. "And who might . . . ? Oh, m-my." His eyes darted from the stallion's face to Jason's. "I . . . I was t-talking to your horse, wasn't I? You m-must forgive me, Mr. . . . ?"

"MacAuley." Jason smiled acidly. "Jason MacAuley."

"Ja-Jason MacAu . . . !" Behind his spectacles Madison Bane's eyes splintered with light. "You're the m-man! You're the man Pamela told me about. You were to bring . . ." He scratched the fringe of white hair that banded his head. "W-what was the girl's name? Well, it escapes me at the moment."

Katy perused the plump, pink-cheeked gentleman with wary interest. Was this the man to whom she had been promised? How could her father have considered such a match? The man had to be at least sixty!

"The girl's name, Mr. Bane, is Mary Kathleen." Jason bowed his head toward Katy.

Madison pushed his spectacles up the length of his nose. "Th-this is Pamela's stepdaughter?" He regarded the black-haired creature atop the horse and wondered if closer inspection would prove her even more lovely than she appeared from a distance. "W-well, this *is* splendid!"

It was then that Jason's thoughts became consonant with Katy's. "Have you reason to be particularly interested in Miss Ryan's arrival, sir?"

"Particularly interested?" He appeared to think for a moment. "I am m-merely delighted that the young lady has arrived without incident. My par-par-particular interest is with you, Captain." Katy slumped with relief. Jason stiffened. "I have something to deliver to you. Before her death P-Pamela entrusted something of yours to me and s-specified that I should give it to no one but you. Since you are here now, I w-would like to give it to you."

Jason looked doubtful. "I think it rather unlikely that Pamela Ryan could have had anything of mine in her possession."

Madison bobbed his head delightedly. "N-not so, not so. The

item has been in my k-keeping for several weeks now, and P-Pamala assured me it belonged to you. If I did not have b-business in town, I would take you back to the p-plantation right now and deliver it into your hands, but a previous appointment prevents that. Perhaps you and M-Miss Ryan would consent to dine with me this evening so I m-might transfer this item to its rightful owner."

Unwilling that Katy be privy to anything the old man might reveal, Jason shook his head. "I might be available this evening, Mr. Bane, but Miss Ryan—"

"Would not think of declining your invitation," she said hurriedly. Since the old man's interest lay not with her, but with Jason, she felt not only relief but also curiosity as to what this bumbling fellow had in his possession and why mention of it was making Jason so nervous. "We should both be delighted to dine with you this evening. What time should we be expected?"

"S-seven will be fine," he stammered, not understanding why the man suddenly looked so angry. "Well, n-now that that's settled, I suppose I should see about getting to my appointment on t-time. What good fortune that I decided to s-stop by today. S-seven o'clock, then." For a brief moment Madison searched the grounds, then scratched the crown of his bald head. "You have only one h-horse. Did you both c-come here on only one horse?"

"Mine bolted," Katy explained, hoping to give the old man the impression that she was in need of transportation back to the MacAuley plantation.

"B-bolted? Well, isn't that strange? Might I offer you c-conveyance back to where you are staying, Miss Ryan? I can assure you that my b-buggy will be far more comfortable than that gigantic b-beast you're sitting on."

"I am afraid Miss Ryan and I still have unfinished business to . . ." Hearing movement behind him, Jason looked over his shoulder to find the saddle empty and Katy scurrying toward the buggy.

"I would be happy to ride back with you, Mr. Bane," she said as she clambered into the vehicle beside him, a smug smile playing over her lips.

Reins in hand, Jason led the gray alongside the buggy. "An amusing way to delay the confrontation, lady. But make no mistake. It will come."

At six-fifteen, accompanied by the maid and Elizabeth, Katy paraded downstairs in a cloud of green French lawn. Her waist-length black hair was coiffed in a dozen springy curls atop her

139

head, yet her high coloring and dancing eyes belied her demure appearance, for she was still bristling over the tidings that Elizabeth had let slip that afternoon. She intended to render a few choice words to Jason MacAuley on the subject of this marriage he was planning to surprise her with.

From where he stood leaning against the doorjamb of the front portal, Jason watched her descend, his eyes drawn to the one long curl that caressed the flesh from the curve of her throat to her breast—flesh he had oft yearned to fondle. Pushing off from his backrest, he strode across the floor and met her at the base of the staircase.

"If this is the reason I was denied entry to your room all afternoon, I must admit that it was well worth the wait." Regardless of how irritated he was with the girl, he could not disavow her beauty, nor ignore the fact that the sight of her set fire to his blood.

"I'm sure the ride over to Madison's will allow you enough time to discuss whatever you thought was so important this afternoon," Elizabeth said to her brother-in-law.

Jason frowned. He had been so angry with the little chit that he had had every intention of describing to her in graphic detail what a pauper she had become. She did not deserve to be treated with special favor, certainly not by him, but his heart softened as she looked up at him with those green eyes of hers. He decided to postpone the telling until they were on their way back from Madison's. There was no sense in ruining what chances they had of spending a pleasant evening, though he had his doubts about just how pleasant a night with a stuttering dandiprat would be.

"You are right, of course, Elizabeth," Jason conceded as he removed Katy's cloak from the maid and snugged it around the girl's shoulders. "I will have a captive audience on the way to Mr. Bane's, won't I?"

Polite discourse ended when their buggy pulled out onto the road.

"Just what did you mean by telling Elizabeth that she should speak to the minister about performing a marriage between us this Saturday?" Katy fumed.

"I did not specify the day, but Saturday is as good a time as any, I suppose."

"Jason! I have already told you that—"

"Do not waste your breath, my love. I am resigned that we shall enjoy ourselves this evening. I refuse to allow myself to be drawn into any verbal jousts with you. Just sit there quietly and enjoy the scenery."

"Think you I can be placated so easily?"

In response Jason drew rein, halting the buggy by the roadside. Around them grassy banks abounded, and it was to these that he summoned her attention. "Have you ever made love in the grass, lady?" He laughed at the look of wide-eyed horror in her face. "I take it not. Then let me warn you, with the way you look this eve, I could be easily tempted to lesson you in the act now, and seek out a preacher to seal the vows later. So I caution you again, sit there quietly and enjoy the scenery, lest your much-touted virginity become a relic of the past." The passionate intensity in his eyes affirmed that he spoke truth, so rather than rack his tolerance, she flung her hood over her head, burying her face deep within its shadow, and sat quietly, glaring at the scenery.

After greeting his guests Madison Bane led them into his parlor. "I m-must apologize if I seem a bit unsettled," he explained to the two people as they seated themselves. "I have not entertained since Pa-Pamela died, and I believe I have become a bit stiff in the joints about s-social etiquette. And I fear that I am s-suffering from a dearth of domestic help. There is not much in the house that cannot be t-tended to by Mahalia and Samson. My needs are really quite s-small nowadays."

Responding to the trace of melancholy in the old gentleman's voice, Katy fingered the ivory petals at her throat and looked about her at the faded grandness of the room. "Your house is magnificent, Mr. Bane," she said kindly. "Do you spend most of your time here or do you ride about your tobacco fields overseeing the activities there?"

"Oh, no, no, gracious n-no. I stopped planting tobacco years ago. Keeping all those records was so t-tedious. I simply didn't want to bother with it anymore. Besides, I had accumulated s-so much money by that time that the idea of collecting any m-more became quite a boring prospect. That is where I differed from your f-father, Miss Ryan. He was a most ambitious man. R-right up until he died."

"Did you know him well?" Katy asked.

"N-no, no. Not well. I conducted business with Matthew once m-many years ago, but he was not one to socialize a great deal. Kept m-much to himself, you know. After his death, P-Pamela was quite miserable, so she became friendly with me. Can you imagine? Me! N-no one has bothered with me for years. I must admit, it was delightful. She was a f-fine woman. A fine woman. I wish she had m-mentioned this preposterous idea of suicide to me. There was no sense in it. No sense at all." He shook his head at the needless loss of life. "When I learned of her death, I was quite convinced that she had d-done it because of her financial situation. Fine friend that she was to me, I m-must admit that Pamela was exceedingly improvident with your father's profits. In the two years following his d-death, she managed to deplete her resources to a state of bankruptcy.''

The word shocked Katy: it was one she had not expected to hear. ''Bankruptcy?''

''Oh, yes, d-dear. P-poor Pamela owed money to everyone.'' Noticing that the girl had suddenly turned gray, Madison leaned toward her. ''Oh, m-my dear, I have upset you. Are you going to have an attack of v-vapors? Shall I fetch the salts?''

She waved him back into his chair. ''I'll be fine in a moment, Mr. Bane. I am just taken aback by your news. No one mentioned this to me before,'' she declared, raising an eyebrow in Jason's direction.

''Oh, M-Miss Ryan, you must forgive me. I thought you already knew! How st-stupid of me. Of course, I have not spoken with the solicitors who handled Pamela's affairs, but I f-fear that they will only confirm what I suspect. I am so sorry, my dear.'' When her color did not improve, he stood up. ''You're terribly pale. I would be much relieved if you would consent to eat now. I'll run ahead to see that everything is prepared. C-Captain MacAuley can escort you into the dining room as soon as your color returns.'' Shaking his head and mumbling to himself, he hastened from the room. Katy lengthened her eyes accusingly at the man beside her.

''You knew all the time, didn't you?''

''I tried to tell you, but you were too preoccupied with ghosts this morning to listen to me. I would have told you this afternoon, but you were too busy confecting those ungodly little curls to let me in.''

She snapped her head away from him. ''You knew all the time,'' she repeated. ''You knew . . .'' Then she remembered. ''But you said this morning that we could live on my family's estate! Oh, what a brazen liar you are.''

''Nay, Katy.'' He shook his head. ''This morning I would have bought the estate for you out of my own pocket. I had no wish to dampen your dreams. But having discovered your true feelings about me, I have dispensed with the idea. You inspire no consideration from me, cruel as that may seem, my love.''

Disappointment flooded her face. She had nothing! No wealth. No home. Nothing! Even from the grave, Pamela Ryan continued to torment her. Could the woman not have left her at least enough money to buy passage back across the Atlantic? Nay. She groped about in her mind for an alternative, but the thoughts would not take form. She had nowhere to go, save with Jason. She owned nothing, not even the clothes on her back. Jason owned those too. Jason, Jason, Jason! Was there no escaping him?

"Did you think that your having money would make a difference, Katy? Do you still doubt the sincerity of my word? I intend to marry you, and I will not be swayed from my purpose. Now, if your color has returned sufficiently, shall we proceed into the dining room? I do believe the old boy's stutter is improving. Mayhap he just needs to become accustomed to our faces."

"Mr. Bane might become accustomed to your face, Captain." She rose to her feet. "I never will." Whipping her skirt around, she headed toward the hall, while Jason's low laughter trailed hauntingly behind her.

The dining room was immense and sported an elegant black walnut table that spanned two-thirds of the existing space. Katy watched Madison worry over the exact placement of china and utensils, and when he had straightened the linen for the final time and lighted the candelabra, she stepped into the room. He smiled as he ambled over to her.

"Ah, my dear, you're l-looking better already, but . . ." He squinted, searching into the hall behind her. "Where is Captain MacAuley?" She was spared having to answer when the old man spotted his guest at the far end of the corridor. "Oh, splendid! There he is now. Well, shall we be seated?"

The three sat crowded together at one end of the long table, Madison at the head while Katy and Jason sat opposite each other. The old man elevated his wineglass in a toast. "To the future! May it not be spoiled by memories of the past." Over the rim of her goblet Katy noticed that once again Jason's countenance had a look of unease, and she wondered what cryptic message had been present in the toast that could produce such a reaction.

"I suppose you are curious about why I asked you here, C-Captain." Madison dabbed his mouth dry with his napkin. "You must understand that it is not often that I am entrusted with a position of such responsibility, so naturally, I am a trifle nervous. And I was not at all sure how to present your little trinket to you, but I b-believe I have affected a most ingenious method of presentation." He pointed to a covered dish to Jason's left. "G-go ahead, Captain. Remove the cover."

Following his host's instructions, Jason pondered the significance of the bed of lettuce he was staring at, but urged on by Madison, discovered something hidden within the frothy green leaves. He hefted a leather pouch into his hand, loosed the drawstrings, then, after peering at the contents, settled a questioning look upon Madison. "There's gold in here. I never left any gold with Pamela Ryan."

Madison, whose color had heightened considerably, clapped his hands in delight. " 'Tis your payment, Captain!"

Jason stared at the man.

"Your payment from Pamela! I understood her to say that for the services you rendered by returning Miss Ryan to Virginia, you were to receive a handsome sum of money. For some reason she decided to commit the whole amount to my care and gave me explicit instructions that if anything happened to her, I should deliver full payment to you and no one else. And you see what a fortunate happenstance that was, Captain, for something did indeed happen to her. Had it not been for her foresight, you would be a much poorer man right now."

Katy glowered at the sack of coins. "So your thirty pieces of silver have finally found their way into your hands. How quaint."

Madison bobbed his head. "Not silver, my dear. G-gold."

"I believe Miss Ryan was attempting a play on words," Jason explained to his host, who muttered an "Of course, of course," as if he had realized that all along. "What the lady has failed to realize is that I have yet to receive any proof that she is worth the value of a single coin of silver *or* gold. And I certainly have had no indication that she is worth all the trouble she has caused me."

"Caused *you*!" she shrieked.

Thinking that the conversation was getting out of hand, Madison tapped his spoon against his glass. "M-my good people. I did not mean to create such a stir with the little spectacle I arranged. Please. P-please," he calmed them. "You mustn't take my theatrics so seriously."

Katy unclawed her fingers from around the arms of her chair and sat back. Jason drained the contents from his glass in one long gulp and loosened his cravat.

"Th-there. Now, if you are both settled, I shall ring for the first course."

Halfway through the soup course, Bane deemed it safe to resume civilized conversation. "T-tell me, Miss Ryan, how was your journey across the Atlantic? I have never made such a voyage myself, but I should think it would be most intolerable for a woman."

"It was," she agreed. "I believe a person has to be insane to want to spend his life being tossed around on some smelly wooden boat."

"We refer to them as ships, lady," Jason interjected coolly.

"Ships. Boats. What matter? They all smell."

Jason poured himself another drink.

Madison chuckled. "You do not hold the sea in very high esteem, M-Miss Ryan. Has the captain been remiss in convincing you of its value? After all, he does boast a most impressive lineage of seafaring relatives."

Katy's attitude remained impassive. "The captain informed me that his father was killed at sea. I hardly consider that an incentive to follow in the man's footsteps, and certainly nothing to boast of."

"Killed at sea?" Madison set his spoon down and regarded the man whose glass had become frozen at his lips. "Killed at sea, Captain?" he asked humorously. "Wh-which father was that?"

"You've said enough, Bane," Jason rasped.

Katy looked puzzled. "What do you mean, which father was that?"

"I cannot believe that the captain did not tell you how his father really died. P-poor child, they have most assuredly kept you in the dark, haven't they?"

"Bane!"

"Did he not t-tell you that if things had gone as planned, you two might have been brother and sister?"

Katy looked from man to man in complete bewilderment. "I have no idea what you are talking about."

"Your m-mother was engaged to Jason's father. If his father had returned from his last voyage when he should have, your p-parents would have been married and the two of you would have been siblings."

The girl shook her head. "I know of no man named MacAuley to whom my mother was betrothed. The only man to have that honor, besides my father, was Seth Aldrich."

"W-well, who do you think Jason's father was?"

From the direction of the kitchen there came a thunderous crash followed by a loud wail. Madison popped out of his chair. "Oh, L-Lord, I hope that wasn't Mahalia with our next course. Excuse me for a m-moment, would you?"

Like a caterpillar shrouded in a cocoon, Katy sat transfixed in silent disbelief. With effort she elevated her eyes to the man opposite her and beheld him as if for the first time. Lesser men would have been cowed by that stare.

"I would have told you," he whispered. "I just didn't think this the time."

Her eyes did not leave the stranger's face, but lingered there, assessing the individual features that comprised his visage. The eyes were too perfectly shaped, the nose too fine, the hair too black. Were they Seth Aldrich's eyes? Had that nose, that hair, descended from a murderer's visage? Was she looking into the very face of Seth Aldrich? Why had she never suspected a thing? "You." Her voice erupted in a hiss.

Jason rubbed his hand across his eyes. "If you will not fly off into a rage, I will try to explain."

"You? Explain? Do you think me dim-witted enough to listen to any more of your lies? Tell me true, Jason, for I would hear it from your own lips. Was Seth Aldrich your sire?"

His eyes flickered painfully. "Aye."

"My God," she breathed. "Fleeing the father, I have run into the arms of the son."

"I would hardly classify what you've been doing as running into my arms."

"You have been playing me the fool all these weeks! You and your bogus name and family. I suppose Fergus was aware of the truth all along. Was that why he never mentioned the fact that he knew you?"

Jason nodded. "Fergus is an old friend of the family. He is well-acquainted with our family history."

"Which family history?" she spit. "The real one or the abbreviated version you gave me? And who is this woman in Frenchman Bay? Is she another product of your vivid imagination, or have you somehow acquired two mothers?"

There was a certain flinty hardness in the gaze he directed at her—a hardness which had not been there before. "My natural mother died giving birth to me. Ian and I were raised by my father's sister, Clare. She's the only mother I ever knew, so 'tis how I refer to her."

"And the name MacAuley? Whose invention was that?"

"The name was no invention, lady," he corrected, becoming more defensive. "After my father's death, we sold the plantation here and Clare moved back to the family house in Frenchman Bay. A man named MacAuley had been hired years before to maintain the house and manage business while my father resided in the South, so when she resettled, she married him. Ian and I adopted the name after we learned that shipping firms were less than anxious to hire ship masters whose ancestry was tainted with scandal. It seemed that Aldrich was not a welcome name among ships of the line."

"You paint the story very prettily, Captain. One could almost be led to believe that it was *you* who suffered the injury."

"Lest you should forget, Katy, Matthew Ryan splattered my

father's brains from one end of our stable to the other. Think you I should have cause to rejoice about that?''

"The difference here, sir, is that Seth Aldrich deserved everything he had coming to him.''

His face suffused with red anger. "If you were a man, I would kill you for that.''

She returned his look contemptuously. "What matter that I be male or female? It obviously made little difference to your father." His chair banged to the floor, and like an avenging angel he rounded the table and was upon her, yanking her to her feet. His hands pressed cruelly into her upper arms.

"My father was not a killer of women. But it is all very easy for you, isn't it? You have the whole story worked out in that narrow little mind of yours, and you haven't the capacity to conceive that you could be wrong. You are so mired in self-pity that you cannot see beyond the tip of your nose. Well, you are not the only one who suffered a loss. You are not the only one who bleeds when wounded or cries when hurt. I was sixteen when my father was murdered, and my tears were very real. But I had to cry in isolated corners because I was at sea when I learned of it, and weeping men are an embarrassment to those around them. I could not wear my heart on my sleeve as you did, and I could not claim injury as you did, because my father was the accused. I knew he could not have committed such a deed, but I had no proof. I could defend neither his honor nor his name. But not so with you, Katy. You might have been there to witness the whole thing. You could prove his innocence if you wanted to.''

"Were I to remember that day, Captain, your father's guilt would only be reaffirmed. He was a butcher and he died a butcher's death. Nothing will change that. Now, get your hands off me. The thought of being touched by you is more repugnant than the thought of being sullied by that filthy pirate." She cried out softly as his fingers tightened around her flesh.

"Lady, you have mouthed the last of your insults.''

"Oh, m-my word, what is going on here?" Madison stammered from the doorway.

Jason speared him with an icy stare. "Keep out of this, Bane. You've said enough already.''

As Katy struggled to be free of her captor, Madison moved closer. "You are a g-guest in my house, Captain MacAuley, and I do not permit g-guests to manhandle other g-guests. This is really quite preposterous, sir. Please unhand the girl and return to your s-seat.''

"I think not. The lady and I are leaving.''

"Oh, no—the lady is not leaving," she contradicted him. "At least she is not leaving with you!"

"That's what she thinks." Grabbing her around the waist, he hoisted her across his shoulder in a flutter of screams and petticoats.

"N-not so fast, Captain."

Jason looked toward the portal, where a man of Polyphemian proportions had suddenly appeared. His face was wide, his nose broad and flat, and the eyes that he leveled upon Jason were black as inkwells. In height Jason estimated the man to be about six inches taller than himself, but in body weight he guessed the black man to outweigh him by seventy-five to one hundred pounds. The man was shirtless save for a buckskin vest that in no way concealed the heavy musculature of his arms and chest, the rippling knots of sinew that bespoke the power of ten men.

"This is S-Samson, Captain. If you do not release M-Miss Ryan, I fear that it will be necessary for him to become a trifle more p-personal."

"You tell your thrall to get out of my way," Jason advised.

Ever chivalrous, Madison shook his head. "The lady has expressed a w-wish that you should leave without her. Be g-good enough to do so, sir."

"Has the lady also mentioned that we are to be married in four days' time?"

"Why . . . n-no. She didn't mention that. Married? Well, my g-goodness, isn't that delightful! I am so glad to hear that you t-two young people can put all that messy business behind you and p-patch up the differences between your families. How very romantic. Th-this definitely calls for a celebration. Why don't you set the girl aright now, C-Captain. She must be g-getting quite dizzy."

"I'll celebrate nothing!" Katy ranted. "I never said I would marry him!"

Madison scooted his glasses up his nose. "It appears we have a s-slight disagreement here."

Jason dropped the girl to her feet and flung an arm toward the old man. "Tell him!"

"Tell him what?"

"The truth!"

"He is lying to you! I never said—"

"You little shrew!" he raged at her. "I should—"

"Oh, dear, s-stop this instant!" Madison pleaded, but to no avail. Seeing the demented anger in the Yankee's eyes and fearing that he would do harm to the girl, Madison gestured for Samson to intervene. The black man took a great lumbering stride toward his prey. Jason's gaze fell to the hands the slave was flexing into mighty fists. Instinctively he shoved Katy toward Madison, then planted his feet firmly apart to await his attacker. Samson struck with the force of a grizzly, his arm smashing out at Jason's face but catching only air as the Yankee ducked easily below the muscular limb. Growling something unintelligible, the giant spun around and straightened up to set his fist upon the man who had eluded him, but as he did so, Jason clubbed his own hands together and swung them into the slave's midsection, striking with an impact so powerful as to cause the black to clutch his stomach in agony. While he was still doubled over, Jason delivered another smashing blow across the back of his thick neck. The giant's knees buckled. His massive frame crashed to the floor like a felled oak. Katy covered her mouth to stifle a cry and did not even notice Madison slip his hand beneath his coat to extract a small flint-lock pistol that he directed steadily at Jason's head.

"This is qu-quite enough, Captain MacAuley. Please gather yourself together and remove your odious p-presence from my home."

Jason wiped his brow on the sleeve of his coat, then suddenly realized what the old gent had aimed at his head. His eyes blackened. "I intend to leave, Bane, but not without everything I came with." He trained those black eyes on Katy. Madison reached out a hand and pulled the girl close beside him.

"I think you will l-leave alone, sir. Miss Ryan will remain here with me. And do not try to be heroic, C-Captain. My gun is loaded and primed and I would have no c-compunction about blowing your head off to protect the lady's virtue. Now, p-please leave before I am forced to do something that I w-would rather not do in the presence of a lady."

Scowling darkly, Jason fixed his gaze upon Katy. "Are you coming?"

She shook her head and backed behind Madison, who now brandished his weapon with increased bravado. "I would suggest that you leave before S-Samson regains consciousness, Captain. He has never been s-struck down before, and I warrant he will awaken in a m-most foul temper, perhaps beyond my control."

Jason raked the two people before him with calculating eyes, the muscles in his jaw working angrily. "Aye, I'll leave," he swore, spitting out each word with disdain. "But you have not seen the last of me. No one has ever deprived me of what is rightfully mine." His eyes narrowed at Katy. "And no one is about to." He turned on his heel, and as he passed the table, glimpsed the pouch of coins which he had placed by his dish.

Muttering a vivid obscenity, he swept the pouch into his fist, turned, and hurled it across the room. Katy screamed and ducked as it passed over her head and smashed into the wall above the mantel, spraying coins about the room. He stormed out, leaving the air echoing with the last vestiges of his fury. Madison coughed from the dryness in his throat but found the soundness of mind to take Katy's trembling hand into his own and pat it reassuringly.

"There is no need to fear, my d-dear. I shan't invite him here again."

Madison put a guest room at Katy's disposal, and having no other recourse, she accepted his hospitality. But that night she was not able to sleep, for each time she heard a floorboard creak or a window rattle, she cast a terrified glance about, half-expecting Jason to have materialized in her bedchamber. His last words still haunted her, as did the tale he had told. Jason MacAuley. Jason Aldrich. What a cool liar he was. What a fool she had been. And because she was hurt and shocked and so deeply deceived, she cried until her tears turned to racking sobs.

Late in the morning of the following day, Madison rode into Williamsburg to discuss Katy's economic situation with the estate's solicitors. After explaining that he was acting for her, he sat for two hours listening to a report so dreary as to make the downpour outside seem like sunshine. When he returned to his plantation later that afternoon, he stared up at Katy's bedchamber and wished that he had never made the acquaintance of Pamela Ryan.

Katy was wearing a rut in the floor with her pacing when Mahalia summoned her to the parlor. She followed the black woman downstairs and found Madison nervously pouring tea when she entered the room.

"You're here. G-good. Won't you please join me in a cup of t-tea? There is such a chill in the air today."

As she moved closer toward him, he crimped his eyes at her from over the top of his wire-rims. "Oh, my d-dear, you've been crying." He seated her on the love seat and handed her a cup of tea. "Perhaps this will m-make you feel better."

Sitting in the chair opposite her, he wrung his baby-soft hands in his lap and let his head sag forward from his shoulders. "I fear that much of your m-misery is all my fault. If I had never mentioned the captain's father, you w-wouldn't be so dispirited today. Why, at this very minute you might be sitting with the Ma-MacAuleys, discussing wedding plans, rather than—"

"I had no intention of marrying the man, Mr. Bane, so I seriously doubt that I would be discussing wedding plans."

"Oh, yes. That's right. But nonetheless," he persisted, "I f-feel responsible. Once I start a story, my dear, I find it very difficult to s-stop, and the account of the captain's father was just s-so fascinating that I could not help myself. But that is not the immediate p-problem." Leaning back in his chair, he removed his spectacles and buffed them with his handkerchief. "I have dismal news from Williamsburg, my dear. It was as I suspected. The estate is in c-complete bankruptcy. There is not so much as a p-penny to salvage from the remains. I'm sorry."

"So am I, Mr. Bane." She sighed. "So am I."

"You must not allow yourself to feel stranded, though, dear. I'll h-help in any way I can. And . . . Oh! I almost forgot!" After settling his glasses back on his face, he reached inside his waistcoat and withdrew a missive which he handed to her. "This was waiting for you at the l-law office. It arrived three weeks ago, but since there was no one to receive it at your f-father's home, the post delivered it to Williamsburg. G-good news, I hope."

Katy stared at the vellum. The curly, flamboyant script was unmistakable. It was her uncle's. Stricken with a deep sense of foreboding, she broke the seal and unfolded the letter. The vellum fluttered in her hand as the ink translated itself into words.

"Are the t-tidings that calamitous, my dear?" Madison asked, having watched her face gray as she read the news.

She extended the parchment to her host. A thick lump bulged in her throat. "My aunt," she choked out. "She's . . . dead."

"Your aunt? The one in S-Spain? Oh, child, that *is* dreadful news. How terrible for you. How terrible for her! Poor woman." He traced a finger along the letter, lip-reading each word. "It says here that your uncle wants you back with him. Well, my dear, it appears you no longer have to be concerned about your future. Your uncle proposes to take good care of you."

Katy's mind had not yet caught up with Madison's conversation. Her gaze became vacuous, her voice ethereal. "I did not know she was sick. She never said anything. She should have told me. I never would have left."

"You're v-very kind, dear. Had you stayed, I'm sure you would have been a great comfort to your uncle."

Madison's last statement somehow penetrated her torpor. Had she stayed, she would have been left alone with her uncle. There would have been no Aunt Carolyn to protect her. She would have been at his mercy—and all alone. The implication left her cold. "She knew," Katy breathed, suddenly enlightened. "She knew she was dying. And she knew that if she told me, I would refuse to leave. 'Tis why she had to say all those awful things. She had to make me want to leave!" Somewhat bewildered, Madison scratched his head. "Don't you see, Mr. Bane? She *did* love me. She loved me so much that she sent me away when the opportunity arose. I was too selfish to understand. I never said thank you. I never told her what she meant to me." Katy bent her head. "Now she'll never know."

"S-surely you can tell your uncle."

"I can't go back there, Mr. Bane. Not now."

"You c-can't?"

"I fear what my uncle would try to do. The way he used to look at me . . . touch me . . . I can't."

Madison rattled a finger in his ear in an attempt to unclog his hearing. "Your uncle? But, my dear, he is the only family you have left! If you d-don't go back to Spain, what will you do?"

This persistent change in her fortunes was beginning to border on the ridiculous. Engaged to Daniel. Not engaged. Engaged to Jason. Not engaged. Affluent heiress. Penurious vagabond. What matter that she devise plan after plan? She was foiled at every turn anyway. Perhaps she should just do nothing and wait to see what happened. "What will I do, Mr. Bane? I think . . ." She pondered the cup and saucer she had set on the table. "I think I shall finish my tea."

"N-no, no, dear. I don't mean this very minute. I mean after you finish your t-tea."

She shook her head. "I don't know."

"Then I had best provide some s-solution."

While Katy sipped tea, Madison paced before the hearth, mumbling, scratching, and shaking his head. Three cups of tea and a full twenty minutes later, the old gentleman reclaimed his seat. "I believe I have it, but I'm afraid you may think me daft, not just forgetful and a little nearsighted. Perhaps I should p-preface this with something." After perusing his fingers for long moments, he looked up. "Miss Ryan, I am referred to as an eccentric recluse b-by many people in the vicinity. Now, that may be t-true, but I am a recluse by my own choosing. There are so m-many sniveling popinjays roving about that I find I much prefer my own company, and I d-deem that quite sane. But it can become a prodigious bore. I have told you before that I am extremely wealthy, and if the truth be known, there is n-no one with whom I can share my riches. When I die, all this d-dies with me." He indicated the room around him with a sweep of his hand. "I have neither wife nor children, and a p-person does not bequeath a fortune to his slaves. You see, m-my dear, I am quite at the mercy of fate, as you are. And it has occurred to me that w-we might glean mutual benefit from an association of sorts. For you, a life of comfort, uncontested affluence, and f-freedom from the lewd proposals that a lady in your impecunious state may fall victim to. For me, an existence that could be m-marked with laughter and vitality in the years that I have left." He fumbled with his spectacles in self-conscious awkwardness. "What I am asking, M-Miss Ryan, is that you consent to be my w-wife."

Her empty cup tottered in her hand, and she quickly set it down. *Not again!*

"Oh, g-goodness, please don't look so alarmed. I suppose I'd best qu-qualify my proposal. Not a real marriage, my dear. Not the kind you would have had with Captain MacAuley. G-goodness, no. There would be no question about my exercising h-husbandly rights. Gracious!" He bobbed his head in amusement. "I am simply too old for that sort of physical activity. The marriage would be in name only."

"Mr. Bane . . ." She hesitated. "Your offer is most generous, but how can you suggest such a thing? You don't even know me."

"W-well enough, dear. Well enough. By the time you reach m-my age, you can determine much about a person with a single glance."

Unable to think clearly, she bit down on her lip and probed Madison's face. "Mr. Bane, I have been beleaguered by proposals of marriage since leaving Spain, and in truth, I hold as little fondness for the idea now as I did then. I have found the majority of men to be an ill-bred, unreliable lot, and though I have no reason to dispute your word, it is fixed in my mind that I have no guarantee you would not try to hoodwink me. If one day you should decide to exert your marital rights, what would prevent you from doing so, or me from having to play the part of the subservient wife? It is in the vows. I would be legally bound to you."

"Then we will strike it out of the vows! And furthermore, we will draw up a c-contract. Yes, yes. Splendid. A contract. And in it we will specify that should I ever attempt to impose myself upon you physically, should I break the contract, my estate will be y-yours. We will write up the transaction and h-have a copy delivered to my solicitors. They will have power of attorney over the entire affair."

"One point, Mr. Bane," she objected. "How do you know that one day I might not tire of the charade and give false testimony to your solicitors in order to secure your estate for myself in advance?''

Madison did not show the slightest hint that he had been shocked by the question. "I don't." He shrugged. "That is a risk I must take, just as there is a risk you m-must take. I think, my dear, that the odds are evenly matched."

She nodded in agreement. "So they are." Her body felt drained. She was so tired of manipulating events to ensure her survival that she just didn't care anymore. Here was someone who was offering her wealth and security in return for a little companionship. Here was someone who would provide for her, care for her, and she would be asked to do nothing except exist. Its simplicity was absurd but incontrovertible.

"All right, Mr. Bane," she said with words reminiscent of the ones she had spoken to Daniel weeks earlier. "I'll marry you."

By the next day, Thursday, the weather had cleared sufficiently for Madison to take the buggy into town to deliver one very odd contract to his solicitor and to speak to the minister about performing a marriage ceremony on Saturday next.

Katy spent the morning exploring the house, and by noontime wandered out to the garden. She strolled beside a row of hedges, inattentive to sight or sound, but when she felt a sudden coolness, she paused, and focusing downward, found herself to be standing in the shadow of a human form. The shadow of a man. She froze.

Jason.

She whirled around, a scream forming in her throat, only to die there when she saw the color of the man. "Samson." She clutched her hand to her throat. "You about scared me witless. I thought you were . . ." She sucked in a calming breath. "I thought you were someone else." The giant looked upon her mutely, his eyes dull. "You are very cat-footed. From where did you come that I did not hear you?" Like a clay statue he remained as he was, his lips motionless, his eyes unmoving. The man's unresponsiveness making her nervous, Katy took a step backward. "Uh, I'm going to sit down over there," she said, pointing to a stone bench beneath a dogwood tree. "I'll let you get back to whatever you were doing. Excuse me." In her anxiousness to be away from the slave, her feet sprouted wings. Seating herself on the bench, she looked back to find him hunkered down, clippers in hand, snipping mangy growth from the hedges. The chill that she had felt in his shadow persisted. Was he lack-witted that he could not answer her? And if he was lack-witted, was he dangerous as well? She stared at the width of the man's back. She had never seen a more gargantuan person in all her life. She had thought Fergus and Jason to be men of extraordinary stature, but this man . . .

At the thought of Jason, she stole a glance around her again. Come Saturday she would be rid of him for good. No longer would she be the object of his jibes or his bawdy affections. She would be safe from the hands that she remembered banded so cruelly around her arms. From the body whose hardness had pressed into hers so often. From the lips that had found hers that day in the cabin and lingered with such intensity, with such authority. She shook her head and with an unconscious movement rubbed her cheek, which, of a sudden, had blazed red. *He is Seth Aldrich's son!* she reminded herself. *Do not think to pine over what can never be.* Yet the memory of his kiss tarried long in her mind. It had not been unpleasant. Nay. Not at all.

With her musings spinning off in random directions, she had been sitting for quite some time before she heard Mahalia calling out to her.

"Miz Kate, chile . . . ." The woman gestured to her from the French doors. "Miz 'Lizabeth is waitin' to see you, and she come all by herself, she did." Mahalia shook her head in blatant disapproval. "Drivin' buggies is men's work. Don't know why a fine lady like Miz 'Lizabeth has got to drive her own buggy."

Following close at the servant's heels, Katy arrived at the parlor quite out of breath and apprehensive. A meeting with Jason's sister-in-law was something she had not reckoned with, and she could think of no good that would come of such an encounter. When she saw the distraught lines of the woman's face, she knew that she was in for trouble.

"Elizabeth, what a pleasant surprise," she said, but her voice faltered, communicating her apprehension.

Elizabeth managed a weak smile as she fanned her face with the rim of her bonnet. "A surprise, yes. But I have no idea how pleasant it will be."

Katy seated herself and indicated that her guest should do the same.

"You're looking well, Katy," the older woman commented after a brief pause. "Mr. Bane is treating you well?"

Katy nodded.

"Good. I'm glad to hear it." Another pause. Elizabeth fumbled with the ribbons of her bonnet. "I have only a few things to say to you. I won't take up much of your time."

Katy squirmed uncomfortably and sat in dejected silence as Elizabeth began talking.

"We have had quite the time with Jason since Tuesday. He came back in such a rage, and since then has been poisoning himself with liquor. He has refused to tell us what happened here, but I can well imagine. You have learned who he is, have you not?''

Katy bowed her head once in affirmation.

''The truth would have been better coming from Jason's own lips. Ian told him as much. But he feared he would lose you if even a hint of the truth became known.'' Elizabeth's eyes softened. ''He loves you, Katy. More deeply than you realize.''

Finding her tongue, Katy wound it around a sharp barb. ''What Jason MacAuley knows of love can be fitted on the head of a pin.''

''I think not,'' the woman chided. ''He never told you why he agreed to bring you back from Spain, did he?''

Katy's eyes flamed as she recalled the reason. ''He mentioned a fat purse which my stepmother promised him. He was gracious enough to fling it against the wall after the soup course on Tuesday.''

Elizabeth continued as if she had not heard the last remark. ''He consented to return you here, Katy, because Pamela Ryan threatened to expose all of us if he did not.''

Some of the fire died in the girl's eyes.

''It would have mattered little to Jason if the woman had publicly denounced him. His ties are in New England now. But the story is different for Ian and me. I met Ian several years ago when he was involved in the coastal trade. He was buying tobacco from my father and shipping it to Northern ports. When our relationship looked to be getting serious, he told me the truth about everything, and like you, Katy, I was shocked. But I loved him too much to reject him for something his father did. I married him and we vowed never to reveal the truth to anyone else, not even my father. When my father died, the plantation passed into my hands, mine and Ian's. We are respected here, Katy. We have friends, and the beginnings of a family, and much to look forward to. Can you imagine what would happen if the truth about Ian surfaced now? Can you imagine the gossip and degradation? People around here do not forget. Oh, they might cease to mention something for a while, but they never forget. Jason loved us enough to want to spare us that fate. He loved us enough to allow himself to be blackmailed by Pamela Ryan. And he fell in love with you knowing that you would come to detest him if you discovered the truth about him. He has been a man tormented with love and guilt since your journey began. Don't abandon him, Katy. Come back with me before he drinks himself to death. Let whatever is in the past remain in the past.''

156

Katy poked at the folds of her skirt, feeling ashamed and trite in Elizabeth's presence. "I can't," she whispered. "I am too close to the past, Elizabeth. I still have nightmares about Seth Aldrich. I cannot barter myself to his son."

Elizabeth fanned herself with her wide-brimmed bonnet again. "If you could only see him! He is so besotted with drink that he has become quite unreasonable. He is now threatening to catch the packet that leaves on Saturday's tide so that he may be rid of us all. He frightens me, Katy. I have never seen him like this before. Will you not reconsider? Just talk with him." She searched the girl's face gently. "Do you not love him even a little? Have you forgotten that you were to be married?"

"I did not consent to the marriage, Elizabeth. Jason commanded it."

That disclosure left the woman in stunned speechlessness. "He commanded it?" she repeated. "You never gave your consent? Why did you not tell me this before?"

"You were being so kind to me that I . . . I couldn't."

She shook her head. "So you do not love him."

"Nay." *But he kissed me once, Elizabeth. And if I could recapture that feeling . . . But it was a fleeting thing. It blossomed like a rosebud and then died. Nay, I do not love him.*

"Then there is no reason for me to remain here any longer." Yet she seemed hesitant to depart. "May I ask how long you expect to remain with Mr. Bane?"

"Forever." Katy's voice barely reached the level of a whisper. "Mr. Bane and I are to be married come Saturday."

Elizabeth's face contorted with shock. "You can't be serious!" But the somber look in Katy's eyes told her otherwise. "Child! The man is old enough to be your grandfather."

"He is kind and honest."

"Kindness and honesty will not put babes in your belly."

"That is a sacrifice I must learn to accept."

"You need not make any sacrifice. You tell me that you don't love my brother-in-law. But can you tell me that you *do* love this tottering old man whom you have known for the better part of two days? Would it not be better to marry the man whose very existence hinges upon whether you accept or reject him?"

Having no recourse, Katy folded her hands together and answered quietly, "I shall marry Mr. Bane on Saturday. It will be a very small affair; I regret that I cannot invite you and Ian, Elizabeth. Please try to understand. I must do what I think best."

"And you must live with your decision. Oh, Katy, I don't

know if you realize what you are doing. Is there nothing I can say that will make you change your mind?''

The girl attempted a smile. ''Elizabeth, I sound unkind and I don't mean to, but nothing you can say will influence the decision I have made. And please, do not think that my choice in any way reflects my feelings about you and Ian. You are warm, wonderful people and I appreciate everything you have done for me. I simply cannot oblige you by marrying Jason.''

''I suppose it was brazen of me to suggest it in the first place, but I feel accountable for your welfare. It is partly my fault that you are here. Had I been less concerned with the MacAuley reputation, you would still be safe in Cádiz with your relatives.''

I would be with my uncle and not at all safe. She frowned. Considered from that point of view, she could not fault Jason, for indeed, he had done her a service. ''It is no one's fault, Elizabeth. I shall be content here, and neighbor to you.''

Elizabeth nodded, and finding no other words to speak, settled her bonnet on her head and tied the ribbons beneath her chin. ''Do not be a stranger to us,'' she said as she stood up. ''And I wish you every happiness. I mean that.'' Awkwardly she squeezed the girl's hand. ''I did not bring your belongings with me. 'Twas silly, but I was so convinced that you would return with me that I saw no need. I presume too much, I know. I shall gather up what you brought with you and have it sent over here. You must be anxious for a change of clothing.''

Katy shrugged. '' 'Tis of no great consequence. I have survived on much less for longer periods of time. Thank you for coming, Elizabeth.''

Elizabeth favored Katy with a warm hug and quietly took her leave. Katy stared after her, and when the front door clicked shut, she sat down again and tried to remember the reasons why she had agreed to marry Madison Bane.

Madison returned later that afternoon bursting with high-spirited banter about the Reverend Overfelt's reaction to the impending marriage of one of the area's oldest bachelors. He found Katy sitting alone in the parlor, and, too excited to notice her abstraction, proceeded to relate in prolonged alliteration the good reverend's suspicions about a woman who would agree to marry such an old man. His chatter continued through dinner that evening and compensated for Katy's pronounced withdrawal, a circumstance which left him extremely uneasy. She made her excuses early and retired to her bedchamber immediately after dinner, leaving Madison to wonder if perhaps he *was* the fool that the Reverend Overfelt had implied he was.

Katy's melancholy lasted into the next day, at which point

Madison Bane felt compelled to speak what was on his mind. He found her on the stone bench beneath the dogwood in the garden, her eyes veiled and resting on Samson, who was laboring over yet another row of hedges.

"We had a w-wet spring," Madison said as he sat down beside her. "The shrubs become so unruly when we have an abundance of rain that Samson rarely has time for anything except t-trimming."

"But he must enjoy it. There is so much solitude here."

"He enjoys the solitude. I don't know if you will find it quite so enchanting after you have b-been exposed to it for several years."

A flag of alarm rippled through the girl's brain. She studied the old man's face. "That is a leading statement, Mr. Bane."

He nodded. "It was meant to be, my dear. I just wanted you to know that I w-would understand if you decided to reconsider about tomorrow."

"Reconsider? Why would I want to do that?"

"Did you think I hadn't noticed? You have been so lachrymose since yesterday that I would almost guess you are in mourning for Captain MacAuley." As she opened her mouth to reply, he shook his head. "Let me finish first before I forget what I was going to say. You did not utter an entire s-sentence last night at dinner or this morning at breakfast. I believe our pact stated that you would be my s-social companion, not my silent companion." He paused for breath. "Now, I m-might be nearsighted, my dear, but I am not blind. Despite his lack of morals, Captain MacAuley is a handsome scoundrel and you are a stunning young woman. It only s-seems natural that the two of you would be attracted to each other. I therefore would be most understanding if you should have a sudden change of sentiment. Mayhap you r-really are in love with the captain but are not fully aware of your feelings." He snapped his mouth shut and awaited her reaction, which found its way to her lips forthwith.

"Bosh." True, she *had* undergone a change of sentiment, but not in the way Madison implied. Elizabeth's explanation of why Jason had agreed to become Pamela Ryan's pawn made her realize that she had judged him too harshly in one respect. He was not the Judas mercenary she had accused him of being. He had been adamant about taking her to Virginia, not out of greed, but out of a sense of duty to Ian and Elizabeth. She had defamed him unjustly and branded him with names he did not deserve, and she was sorry. But her heart remained unmoved in another respect. She could never bind herself to the scion of Seth Aldrich. "My heart remains steadfast in its purpose, Mr. Bane. If you will still have me, I would like to see this thing done tomorrow. I apologize for my reserve of late. I have been brooding over a guilty conscience."

"My dear child, how can someone of your scant years p-possibly have a guilty conscience?"

"Oh, Mr. Bane, I have said some wicked things. At the time, I thought they were true, but now I know better."

"So you have gained wisdom along with a g-guilt-ridden conscience," he temporized. "I would venture that a fair trade. I have known many men who acquired the bane of the latter without the boon of the former." When she did not smile at what he had considered a very clever postulation, he became serious. "Are you sure you d-don't want to speak to Captain MacAuley one last time before tomorrow?"

"Nay, he haunts me enough now without having to see him in the flesh. Elizabeth told me yesterday that he will be leaving on a packet ship tomorrow. Perhaps when he is gone I will feel more relaxed. But until then I fear he is foolhardy enough to try to make good his threat."

Madison's body shook with laughter. "N-not likely, my dear, but I almost wish he would try." Katy's questioning glance prompted him to continue. "Samson has been posted outside your bedchamber at night, you see, and he is eager to have at the captain again. He was shamefully humiliated by the episode the other night, and I predict that s-should they meet again, the captain will not be so fortunate as to escape unscathed."

Katy's regard was drawn outside herself toward the slave. "He would not have to strain himself overly much to deal anyone a lethal blow. I did not think it possible that a man could grow to so tremendous a size."

"Physically, I've never seen his equal, though there are probably a m-multitude more like him back in Africa. That's where he came from, you know. Africa. I've heard t-tell that he was a king among his own tribesmen."

"A king?" Katy did not take issue with Madison's assertion, for in the slave's countenance and bearing there was a quality that lent itself more to majesty than servitude. "Did he tell you this?"

"Heavens, no, child. Samson couldn't tell me anything if he w-wanted to. The man has no tongue. Had it cut out of his head some time ago."

Katy recoiled, sickened by the profound cruelty of such an act. Madison patted her hand. "You mustn't pity him. What he lacks in verbal ability he quite m-makes up for in size. A man of his stature can afford to be a man of few w-words. And we have devised an ingenious system of communication." He wiggled the fingers of his left hand in demonstration. "It's really q-quite simple. I trust you will find it so when I teach you. We'll s-start next week, not that there is any great hurry. After all, we have all the t-time in the world."

In the serenity of the garden, where honeybees toiled amid the lush greenery and where magnolia leaves rustled in the breeze, his words assumed a deeper meaning, for indeed, the hand of time seemed to have stopped completely.

The hour was late when they retired that evening. Katy donned the voluminous night shift whose use Mahalia had volunteered, then after dousing her candles, crawled into bed.

She was urged awake not by a raucous sound, but by a dull creaking that gnawed at her subconscious until it roused her into full wakefulness. She lay for a moment on her side, wide eyes peering into the darkness, nerves prickling on end, her ears pounding thickly with the all-pervading silence.

Something scraped against the floor.

She shot up in bed and stared into the blackness. "Madison?" The silence swirled about her until she thought she would go mad from its deafening tones. From the corner of her eye she noted the curtain catch the breeze and swell plumply around the open window.

Her throat contracted.

The window had been closed when she went to bed.

Her eyes darted around the room in search of the presence which she knew to be hidden somewhere in the shadows. "Madison?" she pleaded, crying out more loudly this time. As she lost control of her composure and opened her mouth to evoke a scream, a monstrously black figure rose from the side of the bed and clamped its massive claw across her face, smothering her scream in its overpowering embrace until she reeled backward into a haven of unconsciousness.

7

Her head throbbed behind her eyes as she drifted slowly back to awareness. Forcing her eyelids open, she frowned at the all-encompassing blackness, and only when she heard the man's voice did she realize what had happened. She was flung over his shoulder while he hammered his fist against a door, each pounding blow sending violent currents through her aching head.

"Open up, blast it!" Jason raged. "I haven't got all night. Dammit! How long am I expected to stand out here?" He smashed his palm repeatedly against the door until the sound of footsteps came trailing out to them. The door was whipped open by a lean little man whose spindly legs trembled visibly beneath his dressing gown. He lifted his candle toward the tall figure blocking the entrance.

" 'Tis a strange hour for a man to come knocking, sir." He held the flame closer to Jason, trying to distinguish his features.

As Jason secured his grasp more tightly around the legs that dangled over his shoulder, the stocking-capped little man gaped in alarm. "Is that a body you have there, sir?"

"Aye, and 'tis wedding her I would be, if you will find your Bible and shay shome words over us."

Jason's last words jarred Katy into full consciousness. "Wedding?" She beat at his back with forehead and fists. "I would exchange vows with the devil himself before I would ever consent to marry you . . . you swine, abductor of women! Now, put me down!"

Deep grooves appeared in Jason's cheeks as he grinned beneath her harsh invectives. "Ah! There's the wee one now. Mind your language, Mary Kathleen. We don't want to shock the good minishter here."

The Reverend Nathaniel Temple looked doubtful.

"Put me down, you lecher!"

" 'Tis really not so complicated as it looks, Reverend," Jason slurred, the world around him starting to spin ever so slowly. "If you would be good enough to show us into your houshe so we might be done with the formalities. . . . My ship leaves on the tide, and I need not impressh upon you the importance of my being aboard."

The reverend hesitated, then stared at Jason indecisively. "This is highly irregular, sir."

Katy squirmed atop Jason's shoulder. "You will never get away with this, Jason!" she screamed, kicking her feet to be free of their imprisonment. "You can kidnap me, but you will never be able to put words in my mouth. Now, set me loose!"

"There's a very shimple explanation for all of this," Jason offered, aware that the minister was becoming progressively more skeptical. "Shall we move inshide?" And without waiting for an answer, he swept past the minister and into the hallway, then reached back and pulled the man along beside him. "Where do you want us?"

Overwhelmed by Jason's manner and the authority in his voice, and choosing to ignore the drunken diction of his speech, the reverend directed them to the parlor, and after lighting the tapers, bade them enter. "You'll need a witness if the ceremony is to be legal," he continued as he started for the hall again. "I'll wake my wife, and then you may enlighten me with your simple explanation."

Jason watched him disappear; then, thinking to hasten the man's footsteps, he called after him, "I urge you to hurry, Reverend. My time grows short!" He turned back into the small parlor, rumbling with hoarse laughter.

"You have the sense of a jackass, Jason MacAuley!" She squirmed and twisted against his hard limbs. "Now, put . . . me . . . down!"

"What," he chortled, "so that you may flee from me like a greashed pig once your feet touch the floor? Nay, my love. I have yet to become *that* much of a jackass." He staggered slightly as he paced about the room.

Katy sank her teeth into her lower lip. He had cast a deaf ear to her screams, but perhaps he would choose not to ignore a plea that struck closer to home. "Have a care, Jason. If you do not soon place me aright, I shall swoon again, and I doubt if I would be easily revived. 'Twould be a pity if you missed your ship."

He paused for a moment, contemplating this possibility; then, just as swiftly, he walked to the nearest chair, grabbed Katy around her waist, and as he wedged his long limbs into the delicate piece of furniture, swung her down onto his lap. Bracketing his arms around her shoulders, he drew her tightly against him.

"Just what do you hope to accomplish by this masquerade?" she demanded.

When he turned his face toward her, she spied the pattern of

163

thin red veins staining his eyes, and as he opened his mouth to speak, she recoiled, for he reeked of stale whiskey and tobacco.

"We made a bargain, my shultry little vixen, and I intend to see it met."

She glared at him in disgust. "You're drunk."

"Nay, madam. I am *shtinking* drunk, and will get even drunker if the mood strikes me, though now that more lusty entertainment awaits me, I may decide to decline any further libation for the promise of much shweeter nectar." He pressed his bearded lips to her ear. She twisted her head away from him. "Dammit, woman," he bellowed, *"Sit still!"*

"How did you get into my room?"

Undaunted, Jason again sought her with his lips. She ducked below his advance and craned her neck to the side, presenting the back of her head for his eager caress.

"Plucky little thing, aren't you?"

"How did you get into my room?" she repeated.

Jason drew a long, exasperated breath. "If you musht know, I climbed a tree, jumped onto the roof, and crept in through your window. But I had one helluva time getting back down again." His eyes crossed dizzily, remembering. "The ground kept moving on me. 'Tis a wonder we're both here now."

"I would rather be dead."

"Now, now, my love," he reproved, guiding his eyes down the mantle of black hair that flowed over her cloak. "No need to act as if you had been sho greatly maligned. I am merely laying claim to that which was promised me."

"I promised you nothing."

"We made a bargain."

"*You* made the bargain," she corrected.

"And you will abide by it. I told you one night long ago aboard the *Ugly Jane* that I would wed you when we arrived in Virginia. We are *in* Virginia, Mary Kathleen, and I am a man of my word."

She turned her face back toward his, her eyes narrowed with determination. "Your word will be worth nothing when Madison finds out what you have done. I should hate to see your handsome face when Samson finishes with it. He has acquired an exceptionally strong dislike for Yankee sea captains—one in particular."

Jason threw his head back in a burst of laughter. "I can't imagine why! But I thank you for the warning. I shall be sure to keep my eyes peeled for the black giant. And if I happen upon him, I must remember to have him extend my apologies to Mr. Bane for absconding with his houshe guest. If I had waited one day longer, I suppose I would be apologizing for absconding with his wife." He rocked his head from side to side drunkenly. "Katy, Katy. When are you going to stop offering yourself in marriage to adolescents and old men? I grow weary of reshcuing you."

His eyes traveled to the front of her cloak, which had separated, exposing the nightgown beneath. Removing one hand from her shoulder, he seized a fistful of the gown and stretched it out before her. "Am I to assume that this was Mahalia's contribution to your troussheau?" He clucked in distaste and pressed the material to her abdomen, feeling the warmth of her flesh beneath. His thumb stroked back and forth, tracing a semicircle below her breasts, and then, aware that this simple motion had whetted his appetite, he lifted his hand toward her breast.

From the hall came the brusque shuffling of feet. Jason averted his gaze to the door to find the minister scudding into the room, obviously in a huff. Swearing under his breath, Jason stayed his hand and met the reverend's agitated glare.

"I cannot please everyone," the minister stammered as he plodded to his desk in displeasure. "My wife will be down presently. She does not voice the enthusiasm for my vocation that I would hope for—at least not at this hour of the morning she doesn't." Removing his Bible from the desktop, he turned to Jason and frowned at what appeared to be a most loving embrace between man and woman. "It appears that your bride's attitude has softened within the past few minutes. Why don't we get started? If you would be so kind as to step over here . . . ?"

"My attitude has *not* softened," Katy contradicted him. "Nor will it ever soften! I will have nothing to do with—"

Jason clamped his hand over her mouth, squelching her protests. "You musht forgive Mary Kathleen, Reverend," he quipped, trying to omit the slur from his speech. "She had her heart set on a large church wedding, and now that I have been called away, she musht appease herself with an inelegant ceremony, the very thought of which is an affront to her every sensibility." He shook his head in feigned dismay. "Needless to shay, she is rather piqued with me."

With growing uncertainty the minister regarded the contortions the man was forced to execute in order to muffle the girl's shouts and fetter her thrashing legs. "The lady appears so distressed, sir. Could you not postpone the marriage till you return?"

" 'Tis quite impossible," he grunted as Katy threw herself against him. "I am a sea captain, Reverend, and when next I shet shail, I should be gone anywhere from eight months to a year. By the time I returned here to wed my bride, the babe would have already been born a bashtard, and I am much too proud a man to allow that to happen. My son will bear the name of his father."

The minister's jaw dropped open. "The lady is with child?"

"Aye, though she will refuse to admit the fact if you ask her."

Katy fairly turned purple at his lie. Her eyes brightened with outrage and frustration as she gnawed at the hand pressed across her mouth.

"Considering what you have just told me, Captain, I think it imperative that the ceremony be performed without delay. I would not want to be the cause of your child's being born illegitimately. Again, if you and your bride would stand in front of me . . . 'Tis customary to marry a couple in an upright position."

As the minister indicated the place where they should stand, Jason grinned and made to rise, but not before Katy found the fleshy part of his palm with her teeth.

Swearing fiercely, Jason tore his hand away from the girl's mouth and shook it in the air, taking note of the ugly red marks engraved on his palm.

Katy wasted no time in verbalizing her protests. "He fills you with lies," she screamed at the minister. "I do not carry his child, nor shall I ever!"

Nathaniel Temple stared at the girl with a singular bewildered expression. This entire evening was fast becoming one which he would like to forget. "Are you telling me that you are *not* with child?"

"That is exactly what I am telling you, sir."

Jason laughed. "I told you she would deny the fact if questioned. She is ashamed of that which I gave her, and was reluctant to inform even me of her condition. She is not likely to divulge her humiliation to a complete shtranger."

"Oh!" She turned angry eyes on the minister. "Can you not see he is drunk?"

"Aye," Jason retorted, "but just drunk enough to do what I musht do, and I did not snatch my bride from her bed merely to sit here all night." He rose abruptly, scooping Katy up into his arms, and carried her to where the minister stood. He set her down firmly beside him, his hand braced around her upper arm, his tall frame towering above her.

"Let's get this over with, Reverend. I am anxious to return my bride to her family before they discover she is missing."

Katy clawed at his hand, trying to loosen the fingers from

around her arm. Jason grinned down at her, tiny laugh lines wrinkling the corners of his eyes. " 'Tis useless, my love."

Nathaniel Temple looked from one to the other, then to the doorway where the corpulent figure of his wife stood surveying the scene, her ruffled night bonnet framing her bulldog face. "I'm glad you finally decided to join us, Mrs. Temple." The reverend sighed with relief.

With his wife at his side, Reverend Temple opened his book to a ragged page that was marked by a purple satin ribbon and began reading. "Dearly beloved, we are gathered together in the eyes of God to join this man and this woman in the bonds of holy matrimony." As he spoke the words, he looked up at the bride and groom, only to find Jason's eyebrow arched rather disapprovingly at him. He swallowed and inhaled a nervous breath of air, then closed his book. "Since you are so pressed for time, perhaps we can overlook some of the preliminary dialogue, Captain." Taking a deep breath, he began again. "Do you, Captain . . . uh . . . ?"

"MacAuley."

"Do you, Captain MacAuley, take Miss . . . ?"

"Ryan," Jason interjected.

". . . take Miss Ryan to be your lawful wedded wife as long as you both shall live?"

"I do."

The reverend nodded. "And do you, Miss Ryan, take Captain MacAuley to be your lawful wedded husband as long as you both shall live?"

"Nay, I will not take him to be my husband! Nor will I *ever* take him to be my husband."

The minister's coarse brows drew together awkwardly. This had never happened to him before. Surely she didn't mean it.

"Think of the baby, sweet," Jason argued.

"I carry no man's baby!"

"You're working yourself into a frenzy, Mary Kathleen, and that's not good for a woman in your condition."

"I am not in any condition!"

Nathaniel Temple scratched the top of his stocking cap. It was obvious they were getting nowhere, and, indelicate as it might be, there seemed only one solution.

"Miss Ryan," he stated hesitantly, "you can see that I am in a quandary over what to do, so if you can assure me truthfully that you are still . . ." He coughed in embarrassment. ". . . that a man has never known you, in the biblical sense, I may see fit to stop this ceremony right now."

Katy stared at the minister with wide eyes. "I . . . I . . ."

She lowered her head, feeling the color rise to her cheeks remembering Molkeydaur's assault. Despite Jason's assurances, in her heart she still felt ashamed, as though the pirate had achieved the ultimate violation.

Nathaniel Temple regarded the lithe figure of the girl, then peeped at the bulky frame of his spouse. The girl's silence could mean only one thing. He just hoped that she would not be too angry with him for what he was about to do. She looked so fair and gentle. Surely she would be a most loving wife to the captain once her temper cooled—lucky man. "Very well, then. I will continue the ceremony," he said.

Jason smiled, a sly look in his eyes. "Under the circumstances, Reverend, would it not be possible to marry us without Katy's verbal assent? After all, the marriage is for the good of all concerned, and I'm sure that once the babe is born, Mary Kathleen's anger will subside and she will thank you for your cool logic and firm resolution in seeing this thing done tonight."

The reverend considered Jason's proposal skeptically. "I have never done anything like this before, but . . ." He chanced another view of the sour expression on his wife's face and quickly made up his mind. "In light of the circumstances, I can see your point, so"—he raced to finish—"by the power vested in me, I now pronounce you man and wife. You may kiss the bride."

Katy's mouth fell open. "You cannot do this! I have not said yes."

"A small matter, my love," Jason said. "Now, be a good wife and give me a kiss."

She threw him a scathing look. "I'd rather kiss the backside of a—"

Her last word became lost in the hand that Jason quickly placed over her mouth.

"Reverend, see that papers attesting to the marriage are drawn up and given to my brother, Ian. He will make sure I receive them."

"And now for your trouble, sir . . ." With the hand that was not muzzling his wife, Jason reached beneath his coat, extracted several banknotes, and pressed them into the minister's hand. "Small payment for the service you have rendered this night. If it's a boy, we'll name him after you." Hesitantly he removed his hand from Katy's mouth. "Will you come with me quietly, madam?"

She stood firm, her bare feet planted solidly on the floor.

"As you wish," Jason said, then swept her into his arms and

back over his shoulder in one sturdy movement, her bare feet kicking in protest even as he carried her out into the night.

The first traces of dawn were illuminating the eastern sky as Jason lowered Katy to the sand of Yorktown beach. He eyed a lone skiff at the water's edge, then slapped his bride's hand away from the handkerchief he had been forced to tie over her mouth.

A sailor leaning against the skiff nodded to Jason as he dismounted. "Cutting this one a bit close, mate," the tar ventured in a raspy drawl. "Was goin' to give you another minute before I took off without you, and if we don't get our tails out to that ship, the cap'n's goin' to weigh anchor without the lot of us."

"Come along, lady," Jason growled. She held her cloak up with one hand and with the other fumbled again with the knot in the handkerchief. Unsuccessful in her attempt to loosen the gag, she found herself being swung into the stern of the tiny boat and pressed firmly down onto the seat.

She could feel Jason's breath warm upon her cheek as he spoke into her ear. "I would warn you either to keep your hands off the gag or prepare yourself for a paddling which you will not soon forget."

Her eyes cursed him, but he quickly disappeared behind her, set his horse free, then, aided by the sailor, pushed the skiff into the waters of Chesapeake Bay. Both men sat side by side on the center thwart, each powering an oar through the black water, each leveling his gaze upon the nymphlike creature who sat like a stone statue on the stern seat. The sailor ran his tongue over his lips and lowered his bushy brows over eyes that squinted to catch a better view of their young companion.

"How long you aimin' to keep her tied up like that, mate?"

Jason eyed her as she gathered her cloak to herself, hoping to shield herself from the penetrating stares of the men before her.

"I'm paying you to row me out to that ship, not to ask questions," Jason cautioned.

"Sure, sure, bucko, but she's too pretty a little thing to be all bound up like that. I could think of uses for those lips other than being wrapped around a damn hanky."

Jason regarded the man icily. "Do you have all your teeth, sailor?" There was a strange, forbidding quality to his voice.

The man held his oar in check midair as he tossed Jason a queer look. "What in hell's my teeth got to do with anything?"

"Because, *bucko*, the lady is my wife, and if you so much as look cross-eyed at her again, I'll shove my fist down your throat so fast that you'll be spitting out teeth for a week. Now, if you have any other comments to make, I suggest you swallow them.

My patience has reached the point where it could be said to be nonexistent.''

Their cabin aboard the schooner was appointed with a minimum of luxury—a narrow bunk in the corner, one straight-backed chair, a washstand that was bolted to the floor, and an oil lamp in gimbals. Beside the washstand was a small sea chest which Katy recognized as the one Jason had purchased for her in Boston. He must have packed up her belongings, or rather, what was left of them, and had them brought aboard ahead of time. Well, he had apparently thought of everything.

"What do you think of it, love?" Jason queried as he dragged his heavy coat off, tossing it over the back of the chair.

She glared at him.

"You could at least be a little appreciative, Katy. I had to pay an arm and a leg for these accommodations." He pulled his shirt over his head, his hirsute virility bared shamelessly before her. He was of the earth, lean and powerful, his arms corded with sinew, his shoulders broad and heavy. He was fire and lust. She was ice. And as he moved with leonine grace about the room, she began to realize just what might be expected of Mrs. Jason MacAuley, and she trembled at the thought.

Jason seated himself on the edge of the bunk, yanked his boots off and dropped them to the floor. He leaned back on his elbows, his faced framed by his massive shoulders, and regarded her curiously. "If you think you can control that vicious tongue of yours, I will loose your gag."

Her eyes flickered, but she made no move toward him.

"I can see I will be expected to do everything for myself for a while." Removing his long limbs from the bed, he ventured over to her, a slightly unbalanced swagger to his step. Placing his hand on her shoulders, he turned her around and plucked at the knot until it came free, then, with longing, slid his hands down the length of her glossy hair, winding several dark tendrils around his fingers. He drew her rigid back to him, pressed a warm kiss on the top of her head.

"Is it not time you honored your husband with a proper kiss?" he breathed.

She could not move. Anger and fear paralyzed her body as well as her mind.

"You are my wife now, Mary Kathleen."

Slowly he turned her around to face him, his eyes pools of black fire. "It is my right." He could not comprehend the look she cast upon him, but since she was not spewing obscenities at him, he assumed she had accustomed herself to the situation and was merely accepting the inevitable. Encouraged, he unfastened

170

the hook of her cloak, letting it drop to the floor in a heap about her feet. When still she did not protest, he slipped the wide-necked nightgown over her slim shoulders, allowing it to join the cloak.

At first neither moved, she frozen with terror, he dwelling upon the swell of her breast, the roundness of her hips, then lower, until his arousal reached its peak and he drew her against his chest, stroking her hair down the soft curve of her naked back. She felt his heart pounding against her face, felt the coarse black hair that matted his chest pressing roughly against her. He was so warm. So hot with his lust. So deceitful. He had tricked her, lied to her, deceived her. And she would never let him forget it. His hands moved upward, cradling her head in his palms, stroking her cheeks with his thumbs. Tilting her head back, he brushed his mouth against her pursed lips, then, blinded by his craving, set his mouth upon hers, striving to elicit from her some human response.

Wood. She was like wood.

With his tongue he sought to gain entry into the chamber that she had closed to him, but was unable to penetrate her tightly compressed lips. He raised his head and scowled his displeasure. Her blistering look was not lost upon him.

"Do you find me so distasteful, lady?"

In answer she untucked her lips and spat full in his face.

Reflexively Jason blinked, then with deliberate slowness straightened and wiped his forearm across his face.

"Had I never expressed my distaste for you, I could almost feel sorry for you, but I could not make my feelings any clearer than I did this evening, and you still refused to listen. You have brought this upon yourself, Jason. You and your lies. I will never be wife to you, and if you ever try to touch me again, I swear I'll kill myself."

He twisted his mouth to one side in a rather comic expression and started to laugh. "You should have been an actress, Katy!" Turning suddenly, he strode toward the bunk. "And put your damn clothes on before you begin to imagine that I could actually enjoy making love to you." He rubbed his hands together, his flesh still burning from the memory of her touch. This mood of hers could not last forever. But he did not know how much longer he could wait before he would be forced to claim his rights, with or without her consent. As she slid the gown up over her shoulders, she turned, accidentally profiling her breast for Jason's perusal. He gritted his teeth and swore under his breath.

"Do whatever you like for the next few hours so long as it is within the confines of these four walls. As for myself, I shall be sleeping off the effects of two days of drink.'' He sat down on the bunk. ''I'm a bit unsteady from all the liquor I consumed to forget about you. Enjoy yourself, Mrs. MacAuley.'' Turning his long body toward the wall, he buried his head beneath the pillow, trying to blot out the violent ringing in his brain. No more whiskey, he vowed—no matter what he was trying to forget.

Katy snatched her cloak off the floor, still smarting from his mockery. If he found her so undesirable, why did he marry her? She had tried to hurt him, and what did he do? He laughed at her. Find *her* undesirable, did he? Laugh at her, would he? Well, she would never give him the chance to laugh again.

Deciding that the floor was the only suitable place to sleep, she flung Jason's greatcoat onto the deck and curled up in its warmth, covering herself with her cloak. She viewed the muscled body stretched out on the bunk and hurled invisible daggers at the whip-torn back whose jagged welts had become neatly camouflaged beneath flesh that had healed and bronzed in the sun. He was truly a brute! Yet she recalled, somewhat reluctantly, that when she had been pressed against his naked chest, there was an instant when her fear had been overcome by another sensation—a not altogether unpleasant sensation. She snuggled beneath her cloak. But that was ridiculous. The only sensation that Jason MacAuley could possibly evoke in her was disgust. She must have been imagining that other feeling—whatever it had been. She closed her eyes and tried to recapture the sleep she had lost that night.

She awoke to the familiar lunge of a ship on the open sea, and while Jason still slept, changed into the violet gown that was in the chest. Unable to find her shoes among her belongings, she cast a fervid glance at Jason's reclining figure. If he was so insistent on kidnapping her, the least he could have done was remember to bring her shoes! You wouldn't catch *him* running around a wooden ship in his bare feet as *she* was expected to do. She slammed the cover of the chest down in exasperation; then, feeling the oppressive weight of her ill fortune pressing upon her, she grabbed her cloak and headed for the main deck.

The wind was hauling abeam, whining and whistling through buntlines and clew lines. Above her, like billowing circus tents, the sheets of canvas flapped, anxious to be free. Katy drew alongside the rail just aft of the forecastle. In the path of the advancing ship, the sea churned a white froth. Her face moist with spindrift, she inhaled great drafts of the salt air, and despite her inner turmoil, she smiled, for standing here, touched by the sun and the spray and the wind, she seemed to feel a certain peace settle about her.

Hypnotized by the rushing water below her, she lent a thought to Clare MacAuley and what the woman would think of her. Would she be loath to live under the same roof with a Ryan? With the daughter of the man responsible for her brother's death? The thought pricked her mind like a bur, for never before had she stopped to consider anyone else's feelings about the tragic events of the past. She could see now that Jason had been right that night at Madison's. There *were* two sides to the story, but she had been so mired in self-pity these past years that she had elected to see only one narrow viewpoint—her own. She had lost her mother, but other people had been deprived of loved ones also, a sister of her brother, two young boys of their father. She could only hope that through the years the MacAuleys had been more forgiving than she had been. And their task had been complicated by having to overcome shame, gossip, and even blackmail. The very idea of what her stepmother had tried to do soured her stomach. It was no wonder Jason had been so cold when she first met him. The reputation of his brother rested upon *her* being returned safely to Pamela. And she certainly had not made his undertaking any easier.

A strange swirling motion toward the bow caught her eye, and she leaned farther over the rail for a clearer view. Before she knew what was happening, the vessel listed sharply to larboard and a wall of water broke across the gunwale, setting the deck awash. Katy lunged for the rail, gasped as it hit her hard in the midsection, then felt herself being dragged over the side by the sheer force of the sea.

Waking in alarm to find Katy missing, Jason had hurried painfully into his shirt, for even the iron pendulum smashing his head from ear to ear could not dull the sudden dread that her absence foreboded. He emerged from the companionway just as the ship began its ominous roll to larboard. Out of habit he stood fast against the steep incline of the deck and looked toward the bow, where he saw a cloaked figure draped over the rail as if ready to plunge into the ocean's depths.

He sucked in his breath.

Katy! Her threat had not been in jest! She *was* going to kill herself!

He reached her just as the wall of water pounded across the deck. As she choked on the brine that flooded her mouth and nostrils and felt her tenuous grip on the rail give way, he caught her by the waist and pulled her to him. Sputtering and gasping for air, she fell into his arms, knowing that if he had not arrived at that very moment, she would be sinking to the floor of the icy Atlantic right now.

"Jason . . ." she coughed, but when the waters ebbed and the ship righted itself again, he held her away from him, his eyes assaulting her with inflexible sternness. Without speaking a word, he swung her around in front of him and pushed her across the deck before his long, angry strides. With her dress plastered tightly around her legs she stumbled down the companionway, but Jason did not break his pace. He threw the cabin door open and slammed it behind them.

"What is it you try to do, Katy! Make a widower of me before I play the part of the groom? Do I treat you so miserably that you find it preferable to feed your flesh to the sharks rather than endure my company?"

She stared at him in awe as she wiped wet strands of hair from her face. "Think you I did this on purpose?"

"Have you not threatened as much?" he shouted. "I would put nothing past you!"

"Oh," she seethed, "you are a fine one to talk! You, who cannot even entertain one lucid thought without a bottle of whiskey in your hand."

He continued as if she had said nothing. "Have I not warned you before to avoid standing by the rail? Do you take my advice so lightly that you are wont to disregard it whenever it so pleases you?"

She compressed her lips and glared at him.

"Answer me, wife!"

" 'He that is slow to wrath is of great understanding: but he that is hasty of spirit exalteth folly.' Proverbs, chapter fourteen, verse twenty-nine."

"Do not preach to me, Katy. It does not sit well with my mood."

"I have found *nothing* that sits well with your mood!"

His eyes darkened, a nerve in his jaw pulsed angrily. " 'A foolish woman is clamorous: she is simple, and knoweth nothing.' Proverbs, chapter nine, verse thirteen. If need be, I will tie you to the bunk to prevent you from doing harm to yourself. But heed me well, for I shall not tell you a second time. Do not venture near the gunwale again. Do you understand?"

Stony silence.

"You will learn to obey me, lady. You will become a proper New England wife and you will discover the meaning of the word 'obedience.' "

"I think not, *husband*," she said, emphasizing the last word with mock affection.

"There will come a day when you speak that word with a different inflection in your voice.'

Storming across the cabin, he flung open the portal, then turned and thrust a finger at his young bride. "I warn you not to venture out this door, or so help me, wife, you'll wish you had succeeded in throwing yourself overboard."

For the next four days she saw no one but the sailor who brought her meals to her. By the time the schooner moored alongside the quay in Boston harbor at dawn on June 16, Katy was suffering so badly from ennui that when Jason came for her, she was cloaked, sitting atop her traveling chest, and sporting a dimpled smile that unmanned him.

Warily he regarded her and then the cabin. "Excuse me. I must have the wrong cabin. The face is familiar, but I don't recognize the smile."

"Do not tease me, Jason. I have remained cooped up in this . . . this stall much too long to even laugh about my seclusion. May we please disembark? Now? If I have to stare at these walls for another minute, I shall become a blabbering idiot. I do not even care that my dress is damp and my feet are bare. There is no one in Boston I would care to impress."

He took her hand and drew her up from the chest. "Come along, then. Fergus' ship is still in port. If he plans to depart shortly, perhaps I can convince him to make room for two more passengers." Jason hefted the sea chest beneath one arm, then guided Katy through the door and out onto the deck.

In minutes she was racing along the waterfront beside her husband, matching his every stride with two of her own, so intent on watching out for piles of rotten produce that she only vaguely heard what Jason said to her.

"Pardon me?" Her face contorted in disgust as she side-stepped a clump of horse dung.

"I said mackerel sky. Probably rain tomorrow."

"Oh." Feeling a slimy substance squirt up between her toes, she stopped mid-stride, lifted her hem, and winced one-eyed at what she had just graced with the imprint of her foot. "Oh, Lord. Jason!" She had to run to catch up with him, and when she gained his side, her breath was coming in pants. "Had you noticed . . . that . . . I do not have wings?"

"I am well aware of the fact, Katy. Why do you think I am walking so slowly?"

"Slowly! I daresay if you kept up this pace, you would arrive back in Virginia before the next packet! Now, where exactly did you see Fergus' ship?"

Jason stopped and regarded the girl strangely. "Look around,

175

lady. Surely you can recognize the ship that was home to you for so many weeks.''

She studied the spearlike masts in the harbor for a moment, then shrugged her shoulders. "I fear they all look the same to me.''

" 'Tis pure blasphemy for a sea captain's wife to make such an admission.''

"Would you prefer that I lie?''

"I would prefer that you learn to distinguish one ship from the other, and if you do, then perhaps I will refrain from telling Fergus that you failed to recognize his pride and joy while standing right before it.''

Katy looked past her husband to the black hulk moored at the end of the quay. "The *Ugly*?'' she asked weakly.

Jason nodded.

"Oh.'' She shot a cursory glance about the harbor again before lifting her gaze to meet her husband's. "Well, they still look the same to me.''

Sticking his tongue in his cheek, Jason turned on his heel and struck out toward the ship, and Katy, refusing to be abandoned for even a minute amid the suspicious-looking characters nearby, scurried after him like a lost puppy.

"Do not appear to be in such a hurry.'' He grinned as they climbed the plank onto the deck. "People will be under the misconception that you are my mistress, not my wife.''

The deck of the *Ugly Jane* was deserted save for great lengths of cable stretched athwartship. Jason set the chest by the rail, then cautioned the girl with a mischievous glint in his brown eyes. "Wait here for me. I am sure the last thing Fergus expects at this hour of the morning is a lady caller, and I doubt that he is dressed for the occasion.''

"But I would like to surprise him, Jason.''

"Aye. You would probably surprise him by tripping over one of those ropes and breaking your leg.''

Lifting her chin proudly, she looked away from him. "You, sir, are frightfully unkind.''

"I, lady, am frightfully honest,'' he mocked; then, placing his forefinger beneath her chin, he turned her face toward his. "Do as I ask. I shall be only a moment.''

She watched him disappear into the alleyway beneath the quarterdeck, only to return several minutes later sporting a doleful expression.

"He doesn't have room for us?'' Katy asked.

"Oh, he has plenty of room.'' He rubbed the back of his neck as he always did when confused. "The only problem is, he and

176

Daniel are wandering somewhere around the city trying to find buyers for his next shipment of timber, and the lad in the cabin says they expect to remain here for quite some time yet."

Katy grimaced. "So we must remain here indefinitely?" She had already decided that she was not particularly fond of Boston.

"Not likely. We'll have to consult the schedule at the harbormaster's office to see when the next packet leaves for Frenchman Bay." Jason hefted the sea chest under his arm once again and motioned her toward the plank. "It's just down the harbor a bit. Probably no more than a mile's walk."

Katy wiggled her cold toes. That was exactly what she had been dreading. "Has it slipped your mind that I have no shoes and the ground is littered with garbage and . . . and other unmentionables?" Jason followed close behind her as she maneuvered her way back across the gangplank. He stopped on the quay to stare down at the grubby little toes that stuck out from beneath her gown.

"It has not slipped my mind."

"Well, would it have been so difficult for you to kidnap my shoes also?"

"If you had not been so blasted stubborn, there would have been no need to kidnap anything."

"*Me* stubborn! Did you expect me to leap into your arms after what Madison told me about you that night?"

He motioned for her to follow him and took several long steps in silence before answering her. "I have no wish to argue with you, Mary Kathleen."

"I would wager you'd not forget your *own* shoes," she muttered, falling into stride once more with her husband's pace.

They had not been walking more than five minutes when a voice called out behind them, "Jason! Jason MacAuley!"

He turned about to find a man running toward them, his arms waving in an arc above his head. Jason kept staring till his eyes registered recognition.

"Well, I'll be damned."

Dropping the sea chest to the ground as the man reached them, he welcomed the stranger with a firm clap on the shoulders.

"Obediah! What the devil are you doing in Boston?"

"I could be asking the same of yourself. You're supposed to be somewhere off the coast of Calcutta or Bombay, not carousing around Boston with a pretty young girl hanging on your arm!" He winked at Katy admiringly, then broke out in good-natured laughter. "You always had an eye for the women, Jason, and it seems that your eyesight is improving with age. Tell me, though, where is your ship?"

"That, my friend, is your guess as well as mine."

Obediah looked puzzled. "You don't know where your ship is? Are you serious?" Jason's expression told him he was. "Good God, man. How did you lose something that big?"

" 'Tis a long story, Obed, and nothing that I am proud of, but the telling will have to wait for another time, because at the moment we're heading for the harbormaster's to find a schedule for packets back to the island."

Obediah's ears perked up. "Back to the island, you say? And when might you want to be going?"

"As soon as possible."

"Would within the next half-hour be too late?"

"You're on your way back now?"

"Aye. And I have a fat wager with Lemuel Brown that I can sail the distance between here and Mount Desert before the sun sets on the same day. Believe me, I can use the extra crewman!" Removing his thrum cap, he crumpled it in both hands. "Now, what do I have to do to earn an introduction to this lovely bit of fluff? My boys will be angry that you found her first, Jason, but I can see the lot of you were not shopping in the same part of town."

Jason's eyes glinted humorously. "I can assure you we were not. Obediah Breed, I would like you to meet Mary Kathleen MacAuley . . . my wife."

Obediah tipped his head to Katy, then, hearing Jason's last word, looked up at him, his jaw nearly dropping to his chest. "Your wife?"

Jason clasped his hands possessively around her shoulders and drew her to him.

"You're sure to set the women's tongues a-wagging back home. The island's most eligible bachelor married." He shook his head slowly. "What will Mrs. Meacham say?"

"Congratulations, I hope, which is more than I've heard from you, Obed."

"Of course congratulations! I'm merely a little stunned by your news. No one expected you to come back with a wife."

Glancing at the ever-lightening sky, Obediah quickly fixed his cap atop his head. "We'll have enough time for conversation later, Jason, but right now we'd best be thinking about getting under sail. If we leave directly and fly every inch of canvas that we have, chances are we'll win that bet."

Jason picked the sea chest up from the ground and shoved it into Obediah's arms. "You can do me a great service by settling Katy in. I have a small matter to attend to elsewhere, but it shouldn't take more than ten minutes. I trust you will not leave without me.''

"If you're not back in twenty minutes, you can be damn sure I'll leave without you. And then you can imagine the time I would have explaining your bride to my Abigail.''

Jason laughed at the thought before he left them, falling into the long strides that so characterized his gait, retracing the path from which they had just come.

"One knows better than to ask Jason what he is about where his business is concerned," Obediah reflected, "but I do wonder what he is up to.''

Katy strained her eyes after her husband till his dark head was no longer visible, then turned to Obediah. "He's probably going to leave a message for Fergus that we have gone on ahead of him.''

"You know Fergus?''

"Yes, I know him.'' Her voice faltered as she realized that this admission could serve as the doorway for a multitude of questions which she was not prepared to answer.

"Well, that old goat! And to think I didn't believe him.''

Katy looked confused.

"Oh, he has told me for years that he knows every beautiful woman this side of the equator. Now I'm apt to believe him.''

Katy let a sigh of relief escape softly below her breath as she followed Obediah down the quay toward his ship.

8

In the pink glow of sunset the island rose in mountainous peaks above the surf and freshened the wind with the scent of balsam. As Katy stood at the rail, hopelessly drenched in salt spray, Jason came up behind her and lowered his hands to her shoulders. Despite the chills that racked her body, she found herself growing warm from his touch even beneath her damp cloak.

"I have been neglecting you, Katy. You're trembling."

She sneezed, and Jason removed his waistcoat, snugging it around her. Embracing her within his crossed arms, he pressed her close to him, allowing the contentment which flooded his body at the sight of his home to purge his thoughts of the doubts which had beset him since his marriage. If he had permitted her to marry Madison, she would have withered in the old man's solitary company. Jason could not abide that. She was yet a frightened bird. He would indulge her with supreme patience, ply her with gentle words, and wait for her wounds to heal, and then surely she would accept the love which he nurtured so silently within him.

They moored the schooner in Cromwell Harbor where a fourth Breed son met them with a buckboard. Sandwiched between Obediah and Jason on the front seat, Katy was kept warm by the heat radiating from the two men, but their proximity did nothing to alleviate the sneezing that was occurring at more frequent intervals. Following the carriage path that bordered the shoreline, with only the buckboard lantern to light their way, they rumbled through shallow pockets of fog and primeval forests where the aroma of cedar and pine overwhelmed even the smell of the sea. After forty-five minutes Obediah rattled down the narrow drive that led to Oak Hill Cliff. He stopped before the shadow of a massive house.

Jason jumped to the ground. "You're a good friend, Obediah." He drew Katy off the seat and into his arms. "I will find some way to repay you."

"Aw, go on with you," Breed clucked; then, over his shoulder: "Abram! Tobias! Carry Captain MacAuley's sea chest to the house for him. If you had eyes in your head, you could see that his hands are full!" As the two boys scrambled out of the back,

Obediah continued. " 'Twas my pleasure, Jason. And I don't mind telling you that I feel a little smug knowing some island gossip before Marian Pettyface. It will grate on her nerves to discover that I met your bride before she did!"

"You are becoming a shrew, Obediah." Jason laughed. Katy nuzzled her head into the crook of her husband's neck. She was exhausted and perfectly content to relax against Jason's hard warmth, little knowing what lusty message her simple gesture had relayed to him, for with her lips nearly touching his throat, and her fingers brushing idly across his earlobe, and her sweet scent perfuming the air, he suffered a constriction in his loins that cut short his laughter. He cleared his throat self-consciously. "Should Lemuel Brown raise any doubts about the credibility of your voyage today, send him to me and I will erase all doubt from his mind."

Obediah noticed the husky tone that had crept into his friend's voice, but attributed it to weariness. "You can be sure I will, Jason. He may question the facts if it's me doing the telling, but he would think it gospel if the words came from your mouth."

Katy rubbed her nose again, wondering at the esteem so easily afforded her husband by his friends. He was obviously a man of high regard within the realm of this island.

"Take your bride inside before she catches more cold, Jason. I fear 'tis she who has suffered most from my folly today. Mrs. Meacham will surely be none too pleased with me for allowing such a thing to happen."

"Are you sure you would not like to step inside with us, Obed? I should enjoy seeing you parry the thrusts of Hannah's tongue."

"Another time perhaps," he returned palely, having no wish to fence with the MacAuley housekeeper this eve. As the boys piled back into the vehicle, Obediah snapped the reins, waved his farewell, and guided the buckboard back along the drive. The lantern bobbed on its perch, illuminating the darkness like a giant firefly. When the rickety wagon wheels dulled to a whisper, Jason sauntered toward the imposing structure before them, his reluctance to unhand his wife slowing his steps.

"He is a nice man," Katy said. She felt his body stiffen.

"Have you a particular interest in him, that you wish to mention it?"

"I have a particular interest in no man, and in you only that I might escape from you someday."

He brushed his lips across her hair. "You cling prettily for a woman so bent on escape."

Jerking her head up, she saw the truth in his words and began to kick her feet in protest. "If I cling, 'tis your fault. Had you remembered my shoes—"

"Enough prattle about your shoes, Katy. The subject has worn thin."

Having climbed the three steps to the porch, he set her down and sounded the brass knocker.

"Need you knock to gain entry to your own home?" She wandered closer to the house, running her hand along its cool rough surface. The wall was hewn from stone.

"As far as my family is concerned, I am still in the East Indies. Would you have me barge in on them unannounced and have them think I'm an apparition come to visit them from the dead? I am well acquainted with you Irish and your superstitions."

Katy followed the lay of the house to the end of the porch, and finding no warmth emanating from the cold granite, turned around to seek reassurance from the tall shadow of her husband. The door suddenly opened inward, casting a long shaft of golden light across his body, and as she saw him lift his hand in greeting, she heard the satiny voice of a yet unseen female and saw his countenance elevate in delight.

"Jason? Oh, I prayed thy journey would be a short one. I have missed thee sorely!"

Digesting the mawkish salutation, Katy felt a grin tug at the corners of her mouth, but when the owner of the voice stepped from the portal to throw slender arms around Jason's neck with such possessive familiarity, she quickly suppressed any thought of smiling. Was this Hannah?

The woman was of a height with Jason, and though her face was buried in the angle of his neck and shoulder, Katy discerned that the lustrous brown hair and lithe body did not belong to any matronly housekeeper. Within her a tide of foreign emotion swelled and quickened her pulsebeat.

In the girl's steadfast embrace, Jason's customary ease abandoned him, and finding no neutral quarter upon which to rest his hands, he spread them, palms up, in a pleading gesture before him. Katy twisted her pursed lips to one side, frowning.

"Hast been away too long this time, Jason." The girl's airy voice whispered against his throat. "Hast been forever." Tossing her head back, she looked up into his face. "Thy beard hides thy handsomeness, but I would have thee back safely, bearded or no. Oh," she crooned, "how I have missed thee."

With that, the girl fanned her fingers through Jason's hair and lifted her mouth to his, favoring him with a smoldering kiss that left no doubt as to her passionate nature or the object of her desire.

Katy's eyebrows shot up in an angry slant while Jason attempted to disengage himself from the discomfiting embrace.

"Desire!" The word was half-mumbled and half-choked as he fumbled with the slender fingers entwined about his neck, putting the girl away from himself. He straightened his coat and coughed in embarrassment. "Your affection is gratifying, but, I fear, misplaced."

She sought the meaning of his words through his eyes, but failing that, was about to question his cool reception when she heard a sneeze close by. Whirling her head around, she caught sight of a fey-looking girl fringed in darkness, a girl to whom Jason extended his hand, beckoning her presence beside him.

"I do not return alone."

Katy smarted beneath that other's scrutiny as she took her place beside Jason. Caressing the back of his wife's neck in his large hand, he made the introduction. "This is Mary Kathleen. Katy. My wife."

The taller girl's beautiful face withered, her proud features contorting with shock, then horror. "Thy wife?" Disbelief stained her cheeks a vivid red.

"Aye," he returned. "Katy, this is Desire Meacham, Hannah's daughter."

Katy mumbled some unintelligible comment that was completely lost on Desire Meacham, who was thinking only of how she had demeaned herself, how she had laid bare her soul before this waif. And Desire Meacham was not accustomed to abasing herself before anyone. Assuming a haughty demeanor to disguise her injured pride, she curtsied stiffly, and averting her eyes, spoke flippantly into the air.

"Thee need not stand here in the cold, Captain. 'Tis thy house." With a swish of her skirt she retreated through the doorway.

Jason rubbed his neck, hating the awkwardness of the situation; then, after lifting the sea chest under his arm, he guided Katy into the front hall.

In the pale glow of candlelight, Desire Meacham was breathtaking. Her henna-brown tresses were long and straight, her eyes so darkly brown they were opaque, her unblemished complexion cast with an olive tint. Her hands were delicately molded, soft and long-fingered, her nails finely manicured till their shape formed perfect ovals. On one finger she wore a ring of crude design—a square of yellowed whale's tooth whose face was etched with the fine lines of a sailing ship. It was a homely piece, yet on Desire Meacham's hand it attained much nobler status, for the girl flaunted it as if it were a stone of great worth.

Exceptionally tall for a woman, she carried herself with a willowy elegance and grace that at this moment made Katy feel very small and dumpy and angry that her appearance was such a disheveled mess. Sneezing into the back of her hand, she cursed that even her hair was tangled into hundreds of damp windblown strings.

"Thy wife is ill, Captain?" Desire's gaze dropped to Katy's bare feet. "Mayhap thee should clothe her feet in something other than their skin."

Katy curled her toes as if to hide them from the creature's view. Jason scowled at this further reference to the absence of his wife's shoes; then, bracing his boot atop the sea chest, he leaned his forearm casually across his thigh and regarded the housekeeper's daughter. "Am I to hear not even a word of congratulation from you, Desire? I had hoped you would be pleased."

Inwardly Desire Meacham seethed at the ugly chit who had stolen the man whom *she* had expected to snare into marriage. "Congratulations," came her terse reply. "I shall fetch my mother to welcome thee." She spun her regal form around to find her mother bearing down upon her from the opposite end of the hall.

"My ears are playing tricks on me," Hannah Meacham sputtered at her daughter. "I thought I heard . . ." As she approached the foyer, its occupants came into view and she halted mid-stride. "I knew there could not be two voices such as yours in the world," she spouted at Jason. "What in the devil are you doing here when you should be halfway around the world?"

Jason bellowed with laughter as he regarded the woman. "What would you have me do, Hannah? Depart again just as I arrive? 'Tis sad fare for a weary man."

She tucked a stray lock of gray hair into the bun at the nape of her neck and straightened her apron. Like Desire, she was tall, yet hefty in the places where her daughter was slim. "A body never knows what to expect from you next, Jason MacAuley. Look at you! Sporting a face full of hair like some heathen pirate." She shook her head in disapproval while Katy endured a bone-crushing chill at the analogy. "And who is this you have with you?"

"My wife." He gestured offhandedly.

Hannah's jaw fell slack. "Your what?"

"Do I speak a foreign tongue of a sudden that none of you can understand me? I say 'my wife'; you say 'your what?' What is it about the word that confuses you? Wife, spouse, mate, bride—are none of the meanings clear?"

Hannah observed the girl pointedly. "God Almighty! From what cradle did you steal the child?"

Katy's eyes flared like Chinese fireworks.

"Hannah," Jason warned, " 'tis of my wife you speak. Tread lightly."

"Will you at least tell us where you found her? I am curious how you acquired a wife mid-ocean."

"I made a side trip to Spain."

"A Spaniard?" she shrieked. "A papist?" Hannah Meacham was of Protestant French-Irish descent and brooked no opposition to her insular views of either religion or nationality.

"She is Irish, Hannah. Her name is Mary Kathleen."

"Well"—the woman seemed appeased—"at least you have not taken leave of all your senses. Irish, you say?" She ran a finger along her jaw. "Can she talk?"

Jason laughed aloud. "When she's of a mind, she can talk the feathers off a bird."

Katy tapped her foot impatiently at their discussion of her.

"She looks as helpless as spilled beans on a dresser. But mayhap not too helpless. She has already plucked the feathers off one strutting peacock." The housekeeper cocked a brow at Jason, who missed neither the jibe nor the look.

"Well met, Hannah," he conceded. "But if you are through with your interrogation, I would beg your leave for this feather-less cock to strut to his bedchamber, where he might indulge himself with a hot bath, a warm meal, and . . ."—he leveled sooty eyes on Katy—"a soft wife."

Katy's back stiffened at the passionate resonance in his voice, and Desire, who had yet to relieve Jason's bride of her scathing perusal, mused curiously at the gesture.

"If you will excuse us, ladies . . ." Jason hefted the chest atop his shoulder and jaunted halfway up the stairs before turning to stare down at the immobile figure of his wife. "Are you coming?"

Like an obedient pup she lifted her gown in preparation to ascend the stairs, only to drop it again at the sound of Hannah's voice.

"No shoes?" the woman chided, directing her attention at the man on the stairway. "If you cannot keep a wife any better than that, Jason MacAuley, you don't deserve to have one. You be seeing about getting her proper shoes before she catches her death."

Within the depth of his eyes a spark ignited and burned hotly. "For where she goes tonight, she needs no shoes," he intoned, leaving no doubt as to his meaning.

185

Unnerved by her husband's comment and eager to escape the cold stares of the two Meacham women, Katy dashed up the stairs. From where he stood, however, Jason perceived her folly, for she had failed to lift the hem of her dress, and predictably, on the sixth step, caught her toe, prostrating herself the length of the stairs. Desire's astonished giggle rang in his ears as he strode down to his wife, pulling her aright.

"Tomorrow I pay a visit to the cobbler, madam," he said in exasperation. "But do you not think that if you held your skirts above your feet, like so"—he stuffed a section of her skirt into her hands—"that you could avert such catastrophes?" With his hand planted firmly in the middle of her back, he steered her over the stairs, while Hannah, muttering to herself, scurried toward the kitchen.

"Riley! A fire in Captain MacAuley's bedchamber. 'Tis himself who is home—and with a wife, if you please!"

Desire wended a path back to the kitchen more slowly, a wry twist affixing itself to her beautiful mouth.

After Jason lit several tapers, the bedchamber bloomed with an amber light that reflected off stark white walls and a highly polished parquet floor. At one end of the room stood a huge four-poster canopy bed, its heavy curtains and quilt patterned in dark blue and white, a design repeated in the draperies that hung at the balcony doors and in the upholstery of the furnishings before the white marble fireplace. The pelt of a giant black bear covered the floor before the hearth, his opaque eyes fixed dully upon a tall Oriental screen in the far corner of the room. To the right of the fireplace a bookcase extended from floor to ceiling, its shelves glutted with volumes bound in richly colored leather.

Rubbing her nose self-consciously, Katy looked about the room for a doorway which would connect with an adjoining chamber.

"Have you lost something, Katy?" Jason opened a drawer of the tallboy and removed several items.

"I . . . I was looking for the door to my bedchamber."

" 'Tis behind you."

She looked over her shoulder at the door through which they had just come, then back to Jason. "Is it not fashionable for a husband and wife to maintain separate sleeping accommodations?"

"Fashionable for whom? A man does not beget sons by sleeping alone."

"And you are just conceited enough to want dozens, I suppose." She sneezed again, her stomach churning nervously.

Jason arched a dark brow at her and tossed her a handkerchief. "Have you a wish not to share my bed?"

"You are well acquainted with my feelings on that topic," she flung at him.

He ate up the distance between them in several short strides and stood inflexibly before her. "You will sleep in this room, in that bed, with me," he ground out. "And now you know *my* feelings on the topic."

"Has Desire Meacham shared that bed with you? She impressed me as a most willing bedmate. I'm sorry if my presence stifled your response, but I had no idea—"

"You have said enough, lady." He walked away, controlling his temper with great effort. When he spoke again, his voice was low and tense. "The girl is guilty of nothing more than being a trifle demonstrative. She means naught to me. She has never shared my bed and never will." Katy's skin prickled as his eyes found hers, dwelling there with purpose. "I save that honor for you."

Tucking his shirt more neatly into his breeches, he regarded her solitary figure in the middle of the room and smiled to himself. She was jealous! Despite her rantings and her threats and her vows of revenge, she was jealous! *Ah, wench, I have found the chink in your armor. Beware.* Encouraged, he hid the lightness of his mood behind a stern face.

"I suspect Riley will be up shortly to kindle a fire. Try your best to be cordial, Katy. He is a gentle sort of person and not overly comfortable in the presence of women, though Lord knows why, having spent so many years in the same house with four of them. In the meantime, I leave you to offer my greetings to Clare."

Katy looked doubtful. "What will you tell her . . . about me?"

"What would you have me tell her?"

Removing her cloak from her shoulders, she draped it over her forearm and stared at it thoughtfully, smoothing out the material with her fingertips. "Will she hate me?"

"Why would she hate you?"

"For what my father did," she whispered.

He wanted to go to her then, so small and alone did she seem, but surmising that she would be no more receptive of him now than she had ever been, he held fast and answered softly, "Do you hate *her* for what you think *my* father did?"

"She had naught to do with that, Jason."

"Aye. And neither did I." The thrust of his words found tender flesh. "She will not persecute you unjustly, Katy. She understands that we cannot, any of us, be held liable for the deeds of another. Indeed, I hope she will come to know and love you for yourself. You will find that, unlike the rest of my family, *she* is not a tyrant.''

''I never accused you of being a tyrant.''

''Nay. Only a son of satan, abductor of women, and deceitful liar. I wonder if tyrant would not be better?''

He left her standing where she was, his insinuations making her feel very awkward, regretting the words she had spoken so often in anger.

By the time she had struggled out of her dress and slipped into Jason's robe, there came the sound of voices in the hall, followed by a timid knock at the door. What she found upon answering the summons was not only a small thin-shouldered man bent over a kettle of water but also a young girl, auburn-haired and round-eyed, a bumper crop of freckles splattered across her face. Instinctively Katy sensed that within this girl she would discover the warmth that she had found lacking in Hannah and Desire, and in glad relief she smiled at the girl, who curtsied in reply.

''Welcome, mistress! My mother has asked that I assist with thy bath.''

''Mrs. Meacham has two daughters?''

''Aye.'' The girl laughed. ''An ugly duckling and a swan. The duckling stands before thee—Mercy Meacham.'' She bobbed. ''I believe 'twas the swan who met thee at the door. And this is Riley Sprague.'' She elbowed the man beside her, who gazed downward, enchanted by the tips of his boots.

''May we come in?''

''Oh! Of course!'' Katy stepped aside.

While Riley lugged the heavy kettle to the hearth, Mercy flew to the corner to drag a wooden tub out from behind the Oriental screen and push it the length of the floor to the kettle. Beneath Riley's swift labors the logs in the hearth were soon ablaze. Turning from this, he poured the kettle of cold water into the tub, and, as Mercy scuttled about gathering soap and towels, started back toward the door, kettle in hand.

''Art fetching more water, Riley?'' the girl called after his back.

''Eayh.''

''Hot, now, mind thee!''

The door closed silently behind him.

Katy chuckled at the man's extreme reticence, then punctuated her laughter with a loud sneeze that drew Mercy's complete attention.

"Hast a cold, mistress? Come stand by the fire," she insisted, herding Katy in that direction. " 'Tis a sorry welcome for thee—the beginnings of a cold and bad weather on the morrow." Katy curled up on the bearskin, marking the girl's comment on the weather with curiosity.

"I will have my mother brew thee something for thy cold, mistress," she chattered on. Spying the sea chest, she unbound the strappings and flung it open. "Is it not wonderful?"

Katy blinked in absolute confusion. "Is what not wonderful?"

Suspending one of Jason's shirts in the air by its shoulders, Mercy blushed faintly. "To be married to such a man as the captain! He is so frightfully handsome. Desire will never forgive thee, but do not be disturbed by that." She dropped the shirt to the floor before rummaging through the chest for another. "My sister's head has been inflated with grand illusions for quite some time. She should not have nurtured false hopes of marrying the master of the house. 'Tis one of the pitfalls of being beautiful. One begins to imagine that one can aspire to heights that no common serving wench should even think about."

"Well . . ."—Katy plucked at the coarse fur on the animal's hide, remembering Desire's arms about her husband's neck—"she *is* beautiful."

"Aye. But she is well aware of the fact, mistress, and I think that makes one less lovely."

Arms akimbo, the girl peered at the garments piled about her feet, mostly Jason's, and frowned into the empty chest. "Hast more trunks arriving later, mistress?"

Katy thought back to her trunk of clothing aboard the *Elizabeth* and reluctantly shook her head.

"Hast nothing more? One dress and the rest undergarments?" She held up a lacy chemise to illustrate her observation. "I know not where the captain expects to take thee dressed only in these. And 'tis true thou hast no shoes?"

Feeling a slow red crawl up her neck, Katy scratched the warmth uncomfortably. "Jason mentioned that he would visit the cobbler tomorrow."

"A bride without shoes," Mercy twittered. "One would almost think the captain had snatched thee from thy bed!"

Hannah Meacham's younger daughter was forced to beat stoutly on her new mistress's back before Katy could overcome the fit of coughing that had suddenly beset her. "Swallowed . . . wrong," she gasped out. But Mercy still wondered at the color that dyed the girl's cheeks.

Riley arrived presently with hot water, and after dumping his burden, was hastily shooed from the room so the ladies could attend to the bath. Katy remained submerged till her fingertips puckered their disapproval, then toweled dry, slipped into Jason's robe, and sat on the rug before the hearth combing out her hair and laughing lightly at Mercy's humorous anecdotes.

The door to the chamber opened. Jason entered, preoccupied with some thought that glazed his eyes with worry, and only when he became aware of the stifling silence did he look up to find the two women staring at him.

"Mercy! How good it is to see you." The lines of his face softened as he beheld the lanky fifteen-year-old, who popped up from the floor and curtsied a brisk greeting.

"Captain! Thy beard!" She laughed. "It likens thee to some great woolly beast. Doth wish to hide thy beauty from thy wife?"

"Nay." He spoke distractedly, lingering on the gentle face of his bride. "I would hide nothing from her."

Sensing the emotions behind the man's words, Mercy experienced a sudden romantic thrill for what would transpire in the room this eventide and grinned rather lopsidedly at the ceiling. "Will thou be wanting to bathe before supper, Captain, or shall we bring thy meal up directly?" She comprehended her error when he muttered a vague "Aye," leaving her to wrestle with the problem of deciphering to which end of her query he had said yea. As he strode toward the hearth, loosening his shirt, Mercy gathered the dirty laundry in her arms and hastened toward the portal, turning to see his shirt sail into a chair. " 'Tis gratifying to have thee home again, Captain. I hope thy stay will be prolonged now that thou hast a further incentive to keep thee here. Thy wife will surely charm the entire island with her loveliness." Smiling, she bobbed again and disappeared into the hall.

Alert to his wife's wary scrutiny, Jason shed his boots and stretched his long body beside her on the pelt. With his head cushioned in his palm, he stared somberly into the crackling flames. After a while his hand found its way to her knee, and there he let it remain, not fondling or caressing, but simply touching, without passion, as though the reality of her presence would help ease his sorrow.

As Katy regarded him in his abstraction, she tried to envision the man as others saw him. Aside from the awe that his physical magnificence inspired, she knew that his other qualities likewise affected his colleagues. His resoluteness, which she had dubbed cussedness, was seen by others as a sign of strength and determination. While she had found him overbearing, sarcastic, and underhanded, others witnessed these same characteristics and called him protective, witty, and resourceful. He was respected by the island folk, lusted after by its women, and held in great affection by his family. Could she have misjudged the man so completely? She watched the pulse beat steadily in his neck, then slid her eyes along the bare flesh that stretched tautly over muscled biceps and forearms. She had thought him insensitive and emotionless, but saw now his vulnerability as he experienced a sorrow which dulled the light in his eyes and weighed even his massive shoulders down with its burden.

Distressed by the intensity of his mood, she set her brush in her lap and hesitantly placed her hand upon his. "Is it your mother who causes the deep furrows in your brow?" she asked softly.

He neither spoke nor moved, but continued to stare deep into the fire while the tongues of flame cast their sinuous shadows across his face. The silence became overpowering.

"She is dying."

Katy flinched.

"Each time I go away, I hope that when I return she will be able to greet me at the door, standing tall and proud as she once was. I am a fool to be distracted by such dreams, but reality is sometimes difficult to swallow. She is dying, and there is nothing I can do." He squeezed her knee as if in anger, then lifted his eyes to hers, piercing her with a gaze she could not meet. A single tear slid from the corner of his eye, and Katy's fright was suddenly transformed into a warmer emotion. Leaning over, she brushed the tear away with her thumb, stroking his cheek gently as she did so. Yet she grappled for words. His fits of rage she could counter. His outpouring of grief found her at a loss.

"I am sorry, Jason," she finally offered, all profound thought having escaped her.

"They know not what the disease is," he continued quietly. "In the beginning, only her hands shook, but now her limbs have become stiff, so that she can no longer walk. Her flesh sags from the weight she has lost. She speaks of regaining her health now that I am back to watch over her, but it will never come to pass. There is death in the room."

Caressing his neck with her fingertips, Katy searched his face as he spoke.

"She is anxious to meet you, Katy. When you are feeling better, I will take you to her. I only hope that you will not be disgusted or sickened by her condition. 'Tis not a pleasant sight."

"Do you think me that shallow, husband?"

Within the blackness of Jason's eyes she saw a new light kindle as he removed her hand from his neck and pressed it to his lips. "Nay. But you have been hurt enough by death. I have no wish to injure you further."

"Your lack of faith does me more hurt, Jason. I will befriend Clare MacAuley if she will have me, not shun her because she nears the end of her life."

Linking his fingers with hers, he considered the bond thoughtfully. "It appears you have acquired the wisdom I lack. I am not sorry I brought you here, Katy. You will be good for this house"—he lifted his eyes to hers, holding her gaze to his own—"and for me."

That his eyes smoldered with passion was obvious as he reached out for the ends of her hair and wound them around his hand, drawing her slowly to him. Yet she could not hide the apprehension that welled up inside her, and he, feeling desire stir, saw with frustration the fear on her freshly washed face.

Kneeling only inches away from her husband, Katy placed her hands flat against his chest to steady herself and to prevent herself from being drawn any farther into his embrace. "Your supper will be brought up at any moment," she said breathlessly, feeling his heart pound beneath her fingertips. "Should you not attend to that before you . . . before. . . .?"

Unable to withstand his penetrating stare any longer, she dropped her eyes to the floor.

"Before I what, love?"

"I . . . I do not know."

He slid his hand around her neck and rested his thumb in the hollow of her throat. "I love you, Mary Kathleen MacAuley," he whispered.

She kept her eyes averted as conflicting emotions surged within her. In a moment Jason removed his hand and stood up, his tall shadow hovering silently above her. When he moved away, she slipped back to her place before the hearth, and picking up her brush from where it had fallen off her lap, started pulling it warily through the long strands of hair which, moments earlier, had bound her to her husband. She could not think when he spoke to her so softly, touched her with such tenderness. Fixing her gaze upon the ripples of heat that smote the air, she saw him in her mind as a man much different from the insolent sea captain who had arrived in Spain, and yet . . .

"Katy?"

As if newly awakened from a dream, she turned her head, and just as quickly turned away, her cheeks flaming. On the backside of her eyelids the image of her husband's unabashed nakedness burned deep, while in her chest a fluttery upheaval rendered her breathless.

"Look at me, Katy."

Clutching her hairbrush to herself, she exhaled a nervous breath but did not move.

"I said, look at me."

The compelling insistence of his voice tore through her paralysis, and slowly she eased her face upward to dwell upon his naked splendor. He stood with his feet braced unashamedly apart, his legs long and straight and hardened with sinew. She blanched at the fullness of his arousal, and as he discerned the cause of her anxiety and drew her eyes upward to his own, she heeded the muscled flatness beneath his rib cage, the expansive chest dark with hair, the bulk and width of his shoulders, and she quickened at his extraordinary perfection.

"Come here, Katy," he commanded softly.

Spoken by him, her name was elevated to a caress. She felt every nerve in her body pulse with its own separate heartbeat as he held her transfixed in the consuming power of his stare. He beckoned to her with outstretched hand, and unable to resist that silent command, she unfolded her legs and walked slowly toward him. With dark, brooding eyes he watched her advance, and when she stood before him, he cupped her face in his strong hands and smiled down at her.

"I would have thee now, wife."

With one hand he loosed the tie at her waist and drew the robe aside, exposing her nakedness to his full view.

"Nay!" she cried, and would have fled had he not caught her wrists, anchoring her to the spot. "I cannot play whore to you!"

"You are not my whore!" The fleshy wings of his nose flared his impatience as he curbed her struggles with a firm hand. "You are my wife!"

"If you take me to your bed, I will be no better than whore," she screamed, shaking her head back and forth as if that simple motion would free her. "I do not love you! I cannot love you!"

Remembering his earlier resolve of gentleness and patience, he sighed in vexation and pulled her to him, feeling her bare flesh tremble against his long limbs. Unknowingly, her body touched his in places that no woman had fondled for months, and this, coupled with the fact that he wanted her so badly, fanned his frustration.

"All right, Katy," he soothed, closing his eyes against the pain of his decision and sucking in his breath as he endured the pressure of her breasts against him, the softness of her loins crushed to his thighs. "I will not force you, but hear me well." At his words, he felt her body ease, and he tilted her head so he could regard her face. He pressed his thumbs lightly against her lips and outlined their delicate plane as he spoke. "You are wife to me, legally bound, and you will not deny me what is my right to take. I give you three months to accustom yourself to your new status. At the end of that time we will be man and wife in all things—with or without your consent."

Her green eyes flickered at this final decree, but he cut short any adverse reaction with a savage kiss. His lips retraced where his thumbs had explored, searing, consuming, bruising her with his desire, and within the iron circle of his arms she was suddenly powerless, surrounded by his smooth flesh and dizzy with the heady scent of his virility. His mouth was hard and insistent, and when it moved across her cheek, burning a path to her throat, she became aware of her own lips, raw and tingling and suffused with blood.

"There are many ways to content a man, my love," he whispered against her mouth. "And there is one that would give me great pleasure." He placed her hands flat against the hollow beneath his ribs, and as he started to guide her palms down the length of his nakedness, a foot thudded against the door. Katy gasped and pushed him away. Jason reached out to regain his wife, but she had already stumbled backward and was fast drawing the robe about her. The thud sounded again. Muttering a string of obscenities, he clenched his fists and glared at the offensive portal. "Who is it?" he spat.

After a pause, Desire's voice floated in to them. "I have thy supper, Captain."

Looking as though he had just been doused with a bucket of ice water, Jason eyed the room in a desperate search for some means to conceal his condition, and spying the wooden tub, took three long strides toward it.

"Come in!" he bellowed as he sank waist-deep in water.

Desire entered the chamber sensing that her interruption had come at a most inopportune moment for the two people. The air was charged with tension and as she set the tray down by the settee, she was cognizant of Katy's animated blush and the muscle in Jason's jaw pulsing furiously, and she smiled at her well-timed arrival. She cast an admiring glance at Jason's rugged torso, and seeing the soap in a dish on the floor, arched an elegant eyebrow at him.

"Hast forgotten something, Captain?" Ignoring Katy's presence, she sashayed to the tub, picked up the cake of soap, and held it over the bathwater, balancing it on the tip of her fingers. "Is it not customary to bathe with the soap *in* the water?"

Katy narrowed her eyes at the intruder's leisurely appraisal of her husband's nudity and bristled her indignation. She would scratch the hussy's eyes out! Jason was full wed, yet this . . . this trollop was lusting after him like she was a bitch in heat and he was a prize stud. As her blush deepened a hue, she saw the bar of soap slip from Desire's fingers and plop into the water in the vicinity of Jason's lap.

"Oh! How clumsy of me!" And as if to correct her mistake, the wench plunged her hand deep into the bathwater to retrieve the elusive cake of soap.

Jason stabbed at Desire's hand and pulled it stiffly from the water. "The soap," he instructed, "may remain where it is. "You"—he bowed his head toward the door—"may leave, and there will be no need for you to disturb us any more this evening."

Desire looked from Jason to Katy; then, lifting her chin proudly, she flicked the water from her hand. "Very well." With a final leer at Jason, she turned about and marched from the room.

Jason grabbed the soap from the bottom of the tub and started scrubbing his upper body with a vengeance, as if by erasing the feel of his wife from his flesh he could diminish his ardor. When he noticed her still gaping at the closed door, he shook his head and motioned her toward the tray. "Eat your supper, Katy. There is no sense in our both eating cold food."

"Cold? If she looked at our food the same way she looks at you, we will be lucky if our soup has not evaporated. Cold indeed!"

She seated herself before the low table and started to consume the chicken broth, her eyes flitting now and again to the movements of her husband in the small tub. After sipping the tea provided her, she held the cup up. "What is this, Jason? It tastes . . . strange."

"Probably some of Hannah's catnip tea. She swears that one pot will cure any cold in twenty-four hours. So be a good patient and drink all of it."

For the next fifteen minutes, while Jason reclined his head against the back of the tub, Katy swallowed cup after cup of Hannah's brew, till the pot stood empty and tiny beads of perspiration began to dapple her forehead.

"How is this tea supposed to cure one's cold?" she asked as she wiped her sleeve across her brow. She felt like the burning bush of biblical lore.

Jason turned his head lazily; then, seeing the rosy tint to her complexion, he laughed. "It makes you perspire, my love, and the sweat cleanses your body of fever and other such ailments. And since you appear to be cooperating so well with nature, I would suggest that you get in bed and cover up before you catch a chill."

As she walked toward the highboy for her nightgown, she stopped to stretch and yawn. "Does this tea also render one uncontrollably sleepy?" She turned her head toward Jason to find him staring at her with that darkly intense expression that always stripped her of her composure.

"You're beautiful with a clean face and damp hair," he mused, his eyes touching every part of her. "The tea should ensure you a long, uninterrupted sleep tonight," which, he thought, was probably more than he could say for himself. "Sleep well, Katy."

She donned her nightgown behind the Oriental screen, then dashed across the cold floor and crawled into bed. Once settled amid the heavy quilts and goose-feather pillows, she started to doze, but through the feathery thickness of her lashes she saw Jason step from the tub and dry himself quickly. With his tall silhouette bathed in golden firelight, he resembled no mere mortal, and she was once again arrested by his magnificence.

She would have prolonged her clandestine observation, but involuntarily her eyes fell shut and she descended into the deep womb of sleep.

9

She startled awake to gaze into the canopy above her head, realizing where she was only when she turned her face and found a rumpled pillow beside her. Jason had obviously slept with her last night, but she had been unaware of his presence. She smiled to herself, thinking that if all nights could be spent thus, she would not object to calling him husband. As she propped herself on her elbows, she noticed him standing before the balcony doors, his hands clasped behind his head, his bare back etched with fine lines of muscle. The morning had brought with it storm clouds and gusting winds, and Jason appeared to be hypnotized by the raindrops that splattered against the windowpanes. From a distance she could hear the roar of the surf as it crashed into the granite cliffs, and she suddenly realized that the weather was as foul as Mercy had predicted.

To announce her awakening, she sneezed loudly. His reverie interrupted, Jason turned.

"Good morrow, Katy. I was beginning to wonder if you would ever wake up." The grooves in his cheeks deepened. "I might even venture to assume that sharing my bed agrees with you."

He walked toward her and sat on the edge of the bed. "How are you feeling?" He felt her forehead, then pinched her chin and lifted her face upward, assessing the glassiness in her eyes with concern. "You have a fever."

"But I feel fine," she objected.

"You would not feel fine for long if you got up. I want you to spend the rest of the day in bed. I have some affairs to attend to in town and will probably be gone a good part of the day, but I'll send someone up to keep you company in my absence."

Her mouth curved down at the thought that she would be subjected to Desire's scrutiny all afternoon. "But, Jason—"

Silencing her with a finger across her lips, he drew her into his arms and brushed her hair away from her face. As her cheek pressed against his warm chest, she could almost hear the blood pounding through his veins.

"I do not expect to return home tonight to find that you have disobeyed me, Katy. One day in bed may be all the medicine you need.''

"I thought you said that Hannah's catnip tea would be all the medicine I would need?''

The line of his mouth reflected the laughter in his eyes. "Is that what I said?''

"Oh, you cad. Move aside, I want to get up.'' She pushed against his chest but found herself shoved gently back into her pillows and girded on either side by her husband's arms.

"If you refuse to heed my advice, lady, I will find it necessary to resort to methods other than words to make you obey.''

As his eyes traveled to the thin silk bodice of her nightgown, she ascertained his meaning and withdrew her resistance.

"All right. I shall remain abed, but I will not like it.''

With a devilish grin he leaned over and placed a warm kiss at the base of her throat. "Good wife.''

Removing himself from her side with great reluctance, he dug a shirt out of the highboy and pulled it over his head. "I'll have Riley keep an eye on the fire for you today. The house gets drafty as a cave when it rains.'' As if Jason's order had been obeyed before he could speak it, there came a knock on the door. Katy heard the clink of china and the rustle of a skirt, and even before she heard the silky voice, she guessed the identity of the caller.

"Good morning, Jason,'' Desire greeted him. Katy sucked on the inside of her cheek as the woman stepped into the room, breakfast tray in hand. "This is for thy wife. Mother will serve thee in the dining room.''

Jason lifted a dark brow. "Is there any reason why I should not be served breakfast with my wife?''

"Why, no,'' she replied, innocence creeping into her long eyes, "but Mother indicated that she had business to discuss with thee and had no wish to bore thy wife with matters that would little concern her. And if thy wife were still indisposed, it would be better for her to remain abed. But if this does not agree with thee, Captain, I could—''

"Nay.'' Jason motioned her toward the bed. "Once does no harm, but in the future I should like to partake of my meals with Katy, be it in our chambers or downstairs.''

He stood by the commode at the head of the bed while Desire set the breakfast tray across Katy's lap. As she bent over, her lush strands of hair fell forward, caping her beautiful face, and the full bodice of her gown gaped wide, affording an unhampered view of breasts with rosy nipples. Katy rolled her eyes heavenward at the girl's wanton display, realizing that the pose was deliberate, and expecting to find Jason's reaction in accord with her own, she looked askance at her husband, to find him leering at the fleshy spectacle with the attentiveness and awe of a schoolboy in a bordello.

Lips pursed, Katy glared at the food before her. The strumpet!

Desire straightened and pushed her hair behind her shoulders. "Shall I plump thy pillows, mistress?"

Katy looked into the darker eyes without blinking. "Must you bend over for that also?"

Smiling coyly, Desire flashed one lovely dimple. "I'll return for thy tray later." She curtsied to Jason. "Captain."

Gathering the previous night's dishes from the table before the settee, she carried herself with an elegance of movement toward the door and disappeared.

Katy leveled her eyes on the door, shooting green daggers through it. "Jezebel."

"Katy!"

She turned on him with fire in her eyes. "Do not 'Katy' me!" she raved, noticing that the lips that had been curled in appreciation moments earlier had drawn taut, and his dark complexion was even darker. "She preens before you like some . . . some . . . cow swinging capacious udders, and you do nothing but gawk in pleasure! Tell me, did she acquire the name Desire before or after she acquired breasts?"

Not waiting for his reply, she spilled milk onto her gruel and slapped her spoon into the mixture. "Your breakfast is probably waiting for you downstairs. You had better go."

"I can see our morning is off to another fine start."

Despite the inclement weather, the day passed quickly and not so unpleasantly as she had anticipated. Her fever disappeared by early afternoon, at which point Mercy dragged a bolt of dull gray cotton into the room and proceeded to cut out the pattern for a gown for her. The girl apologized for not having a more flattering material available but explained that Jason took them to Boston once a year for yard goods and supplies and they were not planning to go till next month, so they were at the end of everything— especially pretty material.

Mercy sewed in the same manner that she talked—swiftly and enthusiastically—so that by the time the supper tray had been cleared away, the only things left to be sewn were the collar, cuffs, and hem. Excusing herself after supper to prepare Mrs. MacAuley for bed, she returned an hour later with warm milk and a stocking that bulged with odd shapes. Katy accepted the milk, smiling. "Am I to be put to bed already?"

"Aye. Hast need to regain thy strength. Captain MacAuley says thou art exhausted from thy long voyage and require much sleep."

"He hasn't returned yet?"

Mercy laughed. " 'Tis more than likely that he and my mother are alerting the townfolk of thy existence, if Obediah Breed hast not done so already. I expect we will be flooded with visitors hoping to catch a glimpse of thee in the days to come. Everyone will want to meet the captain's bride and to speculate on what the captain saw in thee that he failed to see in any other woman. He was a man much sought after, mistress. News of his marriage will be quite a shock to the island's maidens."

As Katy drained the glass, Mercy held up the stocking. "Mother left this in the pantry with instructions that I should give it to thee before retiring. 'Tis supposed to prevent thy cold from going to thy chest."

Katy made a moue with her mouth as a strong odor assailed her nostrils. "Mercy"—she cringed—"what do you have in there?"

"Salt pork and onions."

"And you want me to eat them?"

"Nay!" Mercy giggled. "Dost sleep with the stocking around thy neck, and the fumes prevent thy chest from filling up with mucus."

Katy squinted at the stocking doubtfully before shaking her head. "I think not."

"Oh, but thou must!" the girl pleaded. "Mother expects her instructions to be followed to the letter. She left thee in my care, and she will expect thee to be better by tomorrow. Please, mistress? Please?"

Closing her eyes, Katy sighed in exasperation. "All right, all right. I will spare you your mother's ire, but I begin to question my sanity for allowing you to do this to me."

Relieved, Mercy wrapped the stocking around Katy's neck, then, after extinguishing the candles and promising to have her gown ready for the next day, she left the room.

Katy tossed, turned, and punched pillows for a while before falling asleep, only to be awakened hours later by the steady thud of boots in the hall. The door to the bedchamber opened and closed again. She heard Jason's footsteps tread softly about the room, heard the brush of material as he slipped out of his clothes. Lying on her side with her back facing him, she feigned sleep as he climbed into the bed beside her. He slid low beneath the covers, but after a few quiet moments sat upright. She could sense his movements as his eyes peered through the darkness, searching among the shadows.

And he was sniffing.

"Katy?"

She bit her lip but did not turn over. "Yes?"

"What is that smell?"

"Onions," she mumbled.

He considered this before replying. "Why does our bed smell like onions?"

" 'Tis not the bed. 'Tis another of Hannah's cures for what she thinks ails me."

"I know of no medicine made with onions," he argued.

"Then perhaps you can tell me why I am wearing this disgusting thing!" She sat up and threw her hair back, indicating the stocking around her neck.

Jason frowned. "What in the hell is that?" Grabbing one end, he pulled it into his hands and brought it to his nose, then exhaled a loud breath. In the next instant he threw off the covers, stalked naked across the room, and flung the stocking out the balcony door.

"Jason!"

"My love, your fever has broken, has it not?" He climbed back into bed.

"Well, yes, but . . ."

"So there is no need to smother yourself in onions. The cure has already taken place. I will speak to Hannah in the morning about her new method of curing colds. Now, go to sleep."

He leaned back into the pillows and stretched his arms behind his head. Katy watched the firelight kiss the hollows of his face. Sinking back into her own pillows, she tucked the quilt under her chin. "Did you have a pleasant time paddling about in the rain today?"

"Pleasant?" He shrugged his heavy shoulders. " 'Twas necessary. There was much that demanded my attention after so many months abroad—my ships, my cargoes, my crops."

"Ships?" she asked, suddenly curious, for it had never occurred to her that Jason was anything more than a sea captain. "You own ships?"

He flung a forearm across his tired eyes. "Aye."

Rising on an elbow, she marked the rise and fall of her husband's chest and smiled subtly. "Are you wealthy, Jason?"

His silence pricked her. "Go to sleep," he persisted.

"Well, are you?"

She found herself staring up into his lambent eyes from the

bottom of the mattress. His breath blew warm across her face. "Would it stimulate your interest in me any more if I were?" he asked harshly. She caught her breath as he lowered his eyes to lips that were warm and moist in the deep red shadows of the bedchamber. "I tell you to sleep for your own good, Katy, because there is another way I would expend my energy this night."

His kiss was slow and thorough and singed her flesh like fire. His hands were firm yet gentle, caressing her face, winding through her hair. As he pressed her deeper into the down-filled mattress, she felt a tingling in her breasts that spread to her loins, rooting there, pulsing, aching. Shocked by the naked length of the man, pinned beneath his crushing weight, she could do naught but breathe, and even that with difficulty. Without warning, his body tensed and he strained upward, striking a menacing pose above her before rolling over on his side.

"Henceforth, when I say sleep, you will do well to heed my advice," he said over his shoulder, cursing the day he had ever promised not to touch her for three months. With his blood roiling in his veins, he tossed off his blankets and thought of cold mountain streams and icicles.

Katy stared at his back dumbly, and when her breathing had returned to normal, she crawled to the far side of the bed, away from the man whose touch had imbued her with sensations she could neither understand nor quell.

It was not until the next morning, when Jason escorted her to breakfast, that Katy caught her first glimpse of the interior of the huge stone mansion. The rooms of the first floor were numerous, and like Jason's bedchamber, were decorated simply yet tastefully, from the darkly polished floors to the stenciled walls and decidedly feminine furnishings. He treated her to a short tour of the parlor and library before ushering her into the dining room, where Hannah's sturdy figure was bustling around the table. The housekeeper looked up as the two approached.

"A good morning to you, Captain, missus. Breakfast is almost ready, so sit yourselves down and I'll be right with you. You're looking slick as an eel this morning, missus. I'd say a day in bed did you a whole world of good, wouldn't you?" Without waiting for an answer, she turned and shuffled toward the kitchen, disappearing behind the door.

Jason laughed as he directed Katy toward a chair at one end of the long table. "Hannah is so accustomed to giving orders that she carries on entire conversations with herself without even realizing it, but it's simply her way. Don't feel slighted if you can never squeeze a word in edgewise. She does it to everyone."

Within the next several minutes Katy discovered that breakfast at the MacAuley house consisted of the entire household's sharing the morning meal at the same table, minus one of the Meacham women, who served the meals on a daily rotating basis, then ate by herself in the kitchen. Noticing Mercy's absence from the table, Katy concluded it must be the girl's turn to serve and was proved correct when she swooped through the door with a tray of food.

Mercy made her way around the table, and stopping at Katy's side, brightened visibly. "I woke early this morning to finish thy dress, mistress. I'll bring it up to thee after breakfast if that is convenient. I do hope it fits."

For the duration of the meal Katy listened to Hannah discuss economics with Jason, informing him of the transactions that had transpired in his absence and of the investments she hoped they could make in the coming months. She elaborated on the present trade price of cod, the expected yield from their crops, the competitive price at which they should sell ice this winter, and the approximate board feet of lumber stacked at the mill awaiting the bite of the saw. It soon became appparent that Hannah Meacham served not only as housekeeper but also, in Jason's absence, as chief decision maker and protector of the family fortune, endowed with the freedom to spend, save, or invest as she saw fit. And if the intensity with which Jason was listening to her was any indication, Hannah Meacham did not make many wrong decisions.

As Mercy freshened the teacups, however, Jason, remembering his episode with Katy the night before, changed the subject. Tenting his fingers before him, he leaned his elbows on the table and peered at Hannah rather humorously. "Now, Mrs. Meacham, suppose you tell me of this cold remedy you have invented which requires a sack of onions to be wound about my wife's neck."

Hannah regarded him as if he had gone daft. " 'Tis speaking in riddles, you are. What sack of onions?"

"The one that is catching a breath of fresh air outside my balcony door."

Hannah squinted her eyes. " 'Twas a bottle of whiskey I left in the pantry, with a note for Mercy to give the missus a warm glass mixed with honey before she went to sleep. Are you telling me the whiskey turned into a sack of onions? I have used that remedy in the past, for sure, but I have more sense than to use it on a new bride, especially one who's sleeping with you! Mercy!" she shouted toward the kitchen. "Come here!"

While Mercy tried to explain what had happened the day before, Katy glanced across the table to find Desire nervously sipping tea, her eyes held purposefully downcast.

"Well, those onions didn't just roll out of the bin and stuff themselves in that sock!" Hannah scolded her younger daughter. "Were you trying to play a trick on the lass?"

Suddenly enlightened, Katy returned her gaze to the elder daughter, realizing why she seemed so uneasy, and Desire, sensing that her indiscretion was about to be revealed, conveniently choked on a mouthful of tea and ran gasping from the room—Katy's accusing eyes nipping at her heels.

"Land sakes, what's wrong with her? Mercy, go see to your sister. There's no help for her in the kitchen. And, Riley, if you're through, there's wood to be chopped in the back. I've got to see about Clare's bath, and the morning is not getting any younger. There'll be time enough to solve mysteries later. You'll be excusing me, Captain."

Jason rose as Hannah removed herself from the table. Katy's eyes still flamed at the kitchen door. So it had been Desire who created that little diversion. Wouldn't she be delighted to learn that Jason needed no extra incentives to keep his distance? Having a wife who broke out in a cold sweat every time he attempted to touch her was more than enough to cool any man's ardor. But last night, she temporized, last night had been different. There had been no fear, only a feeling like the breathless upheaval she had experienced when she had first seen him naked, and then there had been something more—something unspeakable in her nether regions. . . .

"Katy?"

She looked up to find the room deserted save for Jason, who stood beside her.

"Are you all right?"

"Oh." She looked around quickly before sliding out from behind the table. "I didn't hear everyone leave."

Concerned, Jason tested her forehead. "Are you sure your fever hasn't returned?"

"I'm sure." She shrugged away from him. "I feel fine. I was merely thinking."

"Ah, what manner woman have I taken to wife? One who is not only beautiful but who can think as well! A dangerous combination indeed!"

"Firebrand," she scoffed.

"Mind your tongue, wife. I intend to have you meet Clare this morning, and I will not have you in a spiteful mood."

A ready knot formed in the pit of her stomach, and as she realized she must face the inevitable, her eyes held both fear and apprehension. "When this morning?"

"After I tend to a few things outside. Mercy will be up in a few minutes with your new dress, so take your time and I'll return for you in a bit. And try to relax, Katy." He smiled. "You look like I have just sentenced you to death. My mother is *not* an ogre."

As she climbed the staircase to her bedchamber, however, she was not at all sure what to expect, and even less anxious to find out.

Mercy arrived shortly, the gray cotton dress draped across her arms. "I must apologize for my conduct of last night, mistress," she stammered. "I hope dost not think I would do such a thing apurpose, as Mother suggested. I truly thought—"

"I know," Katy soothed. "It was a jest, but not of your devising. 'Tis forgotten. Little harm done."

In its finished state the dress was a lesson in simplicity, long-sleeved and high-collared, with a row of tiny buttons forming the closure from neck to waistline. It was cinched tightly at the waist, and much to Katy's dismay, at the bosom as well. The reflection that peeped back at her from the mirror resembled the Katy of old—raven-haired, green-eyed, and flat-chested.

Mercy eyed her handiwork critically. "I fear that I have sorely misjudged thy figure," she lamented. "The dress was cut to my dimensions, leaving scant room for one so well endowed." With a discerning eye she poked at the dress seams here and there, and finally shrugged helplessly. "It will be a major undertaking, mistress. A few seams could be ripped out, darts added, but I suspect I have ruined thy gown. We will both have to ply needle and thread to salvage it."

"We?" Katy asked self-consciously.

For a long moment Mercy said nothing. She had thought this young mistress unaffected by her new status, but perhaps she had been wrong. Why should the captain's wife work a needle when others were available to do it for her? Disappointed, she shrugged her thin shoulders and tried to make light of the situation. "I should not have made such a request, mistress. 'Tis not thy place to demean thyself with such banalities. I will alter the dress myself."

Katy shook her head, perceiving that the girl had misjudged her hesitation. "You misunderstand me, Mercy. It is not that I *will* not assist you. It is that"—and this last came out as a whisper—"I do not know how."

Mercy's surprise knew no bounds. "Canst not . . . sew?"

Katy shook her head.

"How can one clothe one's self without sewing?"

This time it was Katy's turn to shrug. "My uncle had gowns sewn for me."

"Thy uncle must have been extremely wealthy, mistress. Someday I should like to own a gown made in one of the shops in Boston, but I will not hold my breath." She laughed, her spirits restored. "If thou wouldst not take offense at being instructed by one such as myself, I could show thee a fancy stitch or two. 'Twould be a start."

Katy nodded her agreement. "I should like nothing better."

"First"—Mercy lifted Katy's skirt and pondered the still-bare toes—"I think I should fetch thee some footwear. A pair of my shoes will suffice until the cobbler finishes with thine, though mine may prove a trifle large. I'll rummage about my room to see what I can find." As she dropped Katy's skirt, her eyes wandered to the mantle of black hair. " 'Tis so lovely," she said, touching the flowing tresses, "and of a color with the captain's. I had thought that none other could possess hair black as his. 'Tis almost as if thee were of the same seed." Removing her hand, she stuffed it into the pocket of her apron and smiled awkwardly into the green eyes. "Do not go away."

When the girl had gone, Katy peered into the mirror again. With a white cap atop her head, she would cut a figure to rival that of any Puritan—saintly, innocent, flatter than a flounder. With Desire flaunting her assets with such verve, it seemed important now that Katy rise to the occasion and demonstrate that she was just as much woman as that other. Profiling herself in the looking glass, she ran her hands over her nonexistent breasts and bemoaned their loss.

As she reached up to unloop the buttons at her throat, she heard a rhythmic thudding from beyond the house—a dull, hollow thumping that echoed, and dimmed, and echoed again. Undoubtedly it was Riley chopping wood, but, curious, she threw open the balcony doors and walked out into the morning. Tempered by a northeast wind, the breeze was fair and teased the ends of her hair with inquiring fingers. In the aftermath of yesterday's storm the sky was freshly washed with blue, cloudless, serene. Below her, fifty yards of manicured lawn stretched to a ridge of granite boulders at the lip of the precipice. To her left a stand of oak and evergreen hid the tall shadow of the livestock barn, and in the distance she heard the muffled growl of the surf. Setting a hand upon the balustrade, she dropped her gaze to find, not Riley, but Jason, standing before a stack of wood, stripped to the waist, wielding a double-bitted ax above his head. As he swung the iron blade into the log at his feet, she watched in fascination as the muscles in his back thickened, then spread down and across his flesh. His blows fell with vigor, lacerating the wood until the log was clove in two, and as he bent down to throw each section into another pile, Katy savored his powerful movements, the lusty strokes that knotted and bunched his muscles.

And she became confused. She wanted to reach out, to touch him, to speak his name. An aching sense of possession twined itself about her. Was she so hypocritical that she could willfully deny him her affection, yet chafe at the thought of someone else in his arms?

Yes. She spurned him but wanted no one else to have him.

She was jealous! It was a feeling so new and so alien that it left her light-headed, and she ground her nails into the railing for support. With a word from her, all could be set aright, though, and she could lay claim to that which, at this moment, she wanted to possess more than anything else in her life. But could she? If Jason used her as a man used a woman, would her childhood scars fade, or would they open anew?

There was only one way to find out. Lips parted, she was bolstering her courage to call to him when she noticed a movement from the house, and shifting her gaze, likewise held her tongue. Desire crossed the green as if she owned the very earth upon which she trod. Draped in a fluff of pale pink, her long hair barely ruffled by the wind, she gained the spot where Jason stood, and as he poised the ax above his head once again, she set her hands upon his back, startling him. He snapped his head around, staying the ax on its downward swing.

"I did not mean to frighten thee." She blinked innocently.

Jason sank the blade into the log before answering. "Have a care, woman," his voice rang, "unless you fancy spending the rest of your days with a split skull."

She blanched at the reprisal, but being in a magnanimous mood from the beauty of the morning and his vigorous exercise, Jason wound a hand behind her neck and thought to soften his words. "More's the pity." He grinned. "I would hate to see such a lovely face mutilated."

Warming to the man, she rubbed her cheek against his rugged forearm. "I love thee, Jason."

Anticipating the bend of the conversation, Jason tried to inject some humor into the moment. "The young are always plagued with dreams of love. I vow you would not find me so fanciful if

you were constantly subjected to my irascible moods. Ask Katy."
He laughed. "There are times when she thinks me the devil
incarnate, and tells me so!" He would have removed his hand
then, but she held it to her.

"That bantling," she hissed.

"Two years younger than yourself." He spoke evenly, masking a more dangerous tone. "Hardly a bantling."

"Jason, I have seen the way she looks at thee! I saw the way
she cringed that first night when thou led her to thy chamber.
Canst tell me that she has satisfied thy lust? She can barely get out
of her own way, much less content a man such as thyself. Didst
marry her as a jest?"

His grip was like steel as he pulled her closer to him. His eyes
were savage. "What say you, lady?" he growled.

"I love thee." She leaned into him, undaunted. "I have
always loved thee. And I do not believe thou canst actually love
this gamine-faced child thou hast taken to wife."

"You missay what is mine," he warned. "That gamine-faced
child bears my name. Remember that."

Her hand found its way to his breastbone and there gently
stroked the coils of dark hair. "Hast forgotten the way thou
kissed me before thy last departure, Jason?"

The hand roving his chest was distracting. Her hair whipped
his nakedness like silken tongues. He had forgotten, but now the
memory came whirling back to him—the lips, the eagerness, so
easy to . . . Damn her! "I am married, lady. You would be wise
to seek your fortune in some other quarter."

"Where? I want *thee*, Jason. I care not that thou hast recited
feckless words to bind the waif to thyself. Keep her as a dalli-
ance if it pleases thee, but do not reject me. I can live with thy
wife, but not with thy rejection. I will be mistress to thee, Jason.
I will content thee as no other can." He started as he felt the
pressure of her hand at his groin. "I crave thee, and thou cannot
tell me thou dost not share my lust."

"Dammit, woman!" He wrenched her grasp from his groin,
only to have his hand pulled to her breast, where she held it fast.

"Thy wife need not know of thy infidelity, Jason. We can be
discreet. Love me," she purred against his neck. "Love me."

Coherent thought eluded him. She was too close, his senses
too raw. His blood slowed, thickened, steamed through his
veins. Her lips smiled a wanton invitation as she drew his face
downward, fusing their mouths, finding his tongue. Caution and
resistance fled, and he crushed her against him.

Far behind and above them a gray-clad figure stepped back

from the balustrade. Their words had been inaudible, but their actions had spoken more loudly than words. She turned rigidly, green eyes cold as a hard rain. The hand that flung open the balcony door was white-knuckled and trembled with rage. *He deceives me still.*

In his sensate world of fantasy, Jason willed the woman in his arms to be Katy, her lips hungry for his own, her sharp nails digging into his back. But Katy's nails were short-clipped and didn't scratch, and her body was smaller, softer, gentler, like a feather, not like . . .

Damn! What am I doing?

He tore his mouth away from the woman and held her forcibly away from him. His breathing was ragged, and he saw that the perspiration from his torso had impressed her bodice with dark stains. "Get away from me," he panted.

"But, Jason . . ." The girl laughed nervously, taking a step toward him.

He deterred her with a raised hand. "Nay! My body would yield to the temptation. But my mind will not. Get from my sight, girl. I will not humiliate my wife by sowing my seed among the household help."

"Household help!" Her eyes flashed at the slur. "I tell thee this, Jason MacAuley. Sow thy seed with thy child bride, if thou can. But I will wait for thee. And eventually"—her lips curled in guile—"thou will seek that which I offer." Haughty and sensuous, she turned her back on him and proceeded toward the kitchen door.

Muttering a few choice invectives, Jason grabbed his ax and sliced through the log at his feet in one powerful motion, snapping it like a twig.

Women!

The one he wanted would have nothing to do with him. The one he wanted nothing to do with would have him drop his breeches anyplace. Damn!

He severed another log in his fury.

And he! He was so hot after the one that the slightest contact with the other reduced him to nothing more than a bull on the scent. Could he not even control the urgings of his own body? By the end of three months, every inhabitant of the island would begin to wonder if the bulge in his breeches was a permanent fixture, as he was beginning to wonder!

The iron blade hissed through the air. An observer might think the man not a man at all, but the god Thor hurling lightning bolts to earth. Swearing under his breath, he flung the firewood onto the pile, then turned to stare at the balcony off his bedchamber. He needed to cool down. Perhaps he could convince Katy to ride to the cove with him. He could cool his ardor in the icy Atlantic surf, they could talk, be alone—entirely alone. And given the idyllic backdrop of this island paradise, who knew what would happen?

With his spirits lifted considerably, he cradled the ax against his shoulder and strode toward the house with a light step, thankful that Katy had not witnessed his earlier escapade. How would he ever explain that to his wife?

10

Mercy had come and gone, sent away by a distracted Katy, who professed a sudden headache. When Jason's footsteps sounded in the hall, Katy was alone, seated before the dresser mirror.

He had not taken long with his whore. Perhaps they were so adept at coupling that they did not require great amounts of time to service each other. She called to mind his words about Desire: "Miss Meacham has never shared my bed." Hah! Lies! All lies! She tried to ease the tight constriction in her throat. Her breath came in deep, trembling sobs. Could he not have waited the three months? Were his words of love simply that—words?

So, he wanted both wife and mistress. Well, he wouldn't have them. Not if she had anything to say about it. The worm. The filthy lecher. "Contemptible" was too kind a word for him.

The door opened.

Through the mirror she watched Jason pace leisurely across the floor, tossing his linen shirt on the bed as he passed. Coming up behind her, he set his hands on her shoulders and immediately felt her body tense beneath his touch. She stared at the reflection of his well-shaped fingers in the glass, saying nothing.

"I see you have donned your new apparel," he ventured, sensing that something was awry. "Stand up so I can look at you." As he eased her from the seat, she wondered at the mellowness of his voice. Fornication had undoubtedly turned his tongue to silk.

Drawing her away from the dresser, he stood her in one spot, then stroked his beard intently, walking in a full circle around her.

She clenched her teeth. "You gaze upon me as though I were horseflesh," she flung at him. " 'Tis demeaning," She walked away from him toward the fireplace.

"Forgive me, my love. I was merely pondering the where-abouts of your breasts. I thought we had gotten rid of that cotton binding you used to wear long ago." The levity in his voice irked her. "Their disappearance will not be permanent, I trust?"

For me, no, she thought. For you, yes. But rather than verbalize her thoughts, she ignored his statement and spoke to the mantel. "If you intend to introduce me to your mother this morning, you had best think about getting the formalities over with. I have other plans for this afternoon.''

He quirked a dark eyebrow at her. ''I didn't realize you had such a busy schedule.''

''Apparently there are many things you didn't realize.''

He studied her a long moment before crossing to the tallboy to retrieve a clean shirt, cursing to himself. Things were not going as he had anticipated.

''I had hoped to take you riding with me this afternoon, Katy.'' His voice held a note of expectation as he pulled a lawn shirt over his head. ''Several of our ships are in port, and I thought to let you glimpse this ostentatious display of wealth while at the same time allowing the village folk to catch their first glimpse of you. I promised Abigail Breed that I'd bring you by to meet her, and then I thought we could stop at Newport Cove and—''

''I think not.'' She bit off his sentence. ''Fergus said he would conduct me on a tour of the island when he returned. I would prefer to wait for him.''

Jason's eyes darkened at her response, but masking his irritation beneath a cool exterior, he pressed his tongue against his teeth and answered her with an air of indifference. ''Very well. Never let it be said that I forced my presence where it was not wanted.''

She turned on him then, her eyes dancing. ''Since you are being so liberal with your considerations this morning, husband, perhaps you would grant me another small request.''

She did not see the firm set of his jaw as he leveled his gaze upon her. ''Pray continue, madam.''

Pacing slowly before the hearth, she hugged her arms to herself as if to ward off a chill, and directed her conversation to the floor. ''*You* might think that sharing the same bedchamber is charming. *I* do not. In fact, I find it stifling.''

''Stifling! You have spent a grand total of one whole day in this room. How could you possibly find anything about it stifling?''

''Perhaps I should be more specific. I find your presence stifling. I want to move to another room.''

''The hell you will,'' he retorted in a low voice. ''I made known my feelings on that subject two days ago, and I have not deigned to change my mind. It appears, madam, that you are simply stuck with me, unappealing as that may be to your delicate senses.'' Taking measured steps to the balcony doors, he peered out, arms folded, feet braced apart, contemplating this latest rejection. Her moods changed more quickly than the tides!

''There must be more than a half-dozen bedchambers in this

house," he heard her voice from across the room. "It seems ludicrous that I should be forced to occupy this one when most of the others are empty."

He snapped his head around, his eyes narrowing to slits. "You have denied me every part of yourself. Would you deny me this also?"

She wanted to scream at him, to tell him that he would have been denied nothing had he but waited a little longer. Could he not sense that she had been changing ever so slightly? But what had he done? Gone off to rut with the first piece of womanflesh that wiggled her rump in front of him. If it was his purpose to humiliate her, he had succeeded, and she was not likely to forget it for a long, long time.

"You should not have kidnapped me and you should not have forced this marriage upon me. If you are denied anything, 'tis your own fault. 'Twould be better for both of us if you had left me in Yorktown. I do not like playing the pawn in your perverted schemes."

He flinched inwardly, but his face did not reflect the sting. Balling his hand into a fist, he strode to the table beside the sofa and poured himself a glass of brandy. Swirling the liquid in the stemmed crystal, he stared almost hypnotically at its deep yellow reflection and spoke as if to himself.

" 'Tis said that if a fine wine is stored in a cellar and not touched by human hands for many years, its taste will be sweet as honey when it is finally consumed. But if that same wine is exposed to the air for any length of time, it will be bitter when it is brought to human lips. It will turn to vinegar."

He slowly looked toward her, his visage ominous. "You have become like that second cask of wine, Katy—sour, like vinegar. So sour that I want to spit so that I can cleanse my mouth of your taste." Bringing the glass to his mouth, he downed the contents in one gulp, then looked back to her. "You think me base. Perhaps. But not so base that I cannot make a few minor concessions. If you require more privacy, I can arrange to spend as little time as possible within these hallowed walls. You can dress, undress, bathe,—all without fear of being intruded upon. I grant you your privacy, but when night falls, madam, you will be in that bed with me."

As her lips parted to object, he thrust the glass at her contemptuously. "One more word from you and you'll wish you'd never learned to talk!"

Her lips clamped shut.

"Hear me out, wife, and hear me well. I have not laid one finger upon you, yet it seems that you grow more intolerant of me each day. I have vowed myself to abstinence for three months, but at the end of that time I expect to experience fully the pleasures of the marital bed, and your performance had better be worth the wait. Until then you can have your damn sanctimonious privacy, but cherish the days, because when they elapse, I will not be so generous with my considerations."

He stormed to the door and held it open for her. "My mother is waiting for you." He looked not at her, but beyond her, and she knew by the dullness in his eyes that she had hurt him. But it gave her no joy.

Clare MacAuley was dying. She lay propped up on pillows in her bed, her bony face framed by wisps of white hair, her bloodless flesh caved in below her cheekbones, her eyes lidded with sagging flaps of flesh. And all about the room was the underlying odor of urine, human decay, and death. Katy stopped as she passed through the door and caught her breath, wanting to bolt in the opposite direction. She couldn't go through with it. But as she took one step backward, she felt Jason's hand around her arm, quashing any ideas she might have of escape.

Sensing her revulsion, he led her to a chair beside the bed and sat her down. He had warned her that reality was not a pretty sight, but at this moment he had no desire to shelter her from the harsh truth of life . . . and death. Releasing her arm, he took a step toward the bed, and leaning over, kissed the transparent skin of his mother's forehead.

She smiled up at him. "Jason." Her voice was soft and low as a whisper. "I must have dozed off."

" 'Tis early, I know, but I brought someone by to visit." Jason patted the clawlike hand she extended to him. "This is Katy, Mother. I'm going to leave the two of you alone so you can become better acquainted."

Katy flashed him a pleading look. "You will not stay?"

His eyes were cold with anger as he turned toward her. "Nay, I will not." And his voice had lost all the warmth that coated the words he had spoken to his mother. She stared after him as he left the room.

"You must have had a quarrel," Clare mused after a few moments of silence. "All newlyweds have quarrels."

Katy turned her head toward the cadaverous figure on the bed and tried to swallow her fright. She looked headlong into eyes that held her steadily within their serene gaze, and as she clasped her hands together for security, she felt her palms become moist with sweat. How could the woman seem so tranquil when her body was deteriorating like this?

"Do I frighten you, Katy?"

A coldness washed over the girl. "No, ma'am, I—"

Clare shook her head knowingly. "Don't try to hide it. Let there be no secrets between us. I frighten people who have known me for years. Lately they have just stopped coming. And those people are my friends! I can imagine what the sight of these pathetic bones must do to you."

Ashamed, Katy bent her head low. "I wasn't expecting you to . . . I didn't think you would . . ." Hearing a low chuckle from the bed, she looked up.

"Would it help if I put a sack over my head?"

At this Katy laughed, and the air which had been so thick with tension suddenly cleared and she breathed more easily.

"You must find all this newness rather formidable—new surroundings, a new house, a new husband, and Hannah—Hannah is always formidable. I can't blame you for being overwhelmed. But it's not these things that you find the most distressing, is it?"

Katy shook her head.

"You think I'm going to hate you. It's all right," she reassured the incredulous green eyes. "I know. Jason told me. Would it help you to know that when I discovered whom he had married, I was afraid of the same thing?"

"You were? Truly?"

"Indeed I was. But then I reasoned that if you bore any ill feelings toward our family, you wouldn't have married Jason."

Taking note of the fact that Jason had obviously not explained the truth about how they had come to marry, Katy began hesitantly, "What happened between our two families was terrible. It must have been dreadful for you. I heard that my father . . ."

". . . blew Seth's head off," Clare breathed. "I found him, you know. I still have dreams . . ."

"You have dreams, too?"

"Aye. Not so bad as they used to be, maybe because I don't remember dreams like I used to." Clare MacAuley leveled curious eyes on her daughter-in-law. "Do you still think that Jason's father was responsible for your mother's death?"

Katy toyed with her fingers. "I used to. . . . I'm not so sure anymore."

"You were so young when it happened. An experience like that could have scarred you for life, but I'm relieved to find out that you've grown up to be a normal young woman."

Katy managed a wan smile. If only that were so.

"Seth loved your mother more than himself, more than his sons. He never could have done anything to harm her, no matter how angry he might have been. He was not a murderer, Katy, and he never would have done anything to disrupt the life of the child who should have been his.''

Katy flinched. Madison Bane had said the same thing. Jason should have been her brother, not her husband. It sent chills creeping up her spine.

"You must believe me." Clare's voice wavered as she reached her grotesque hand out for Katy's. "My brother was not malicious. Someone else committed that abomination. Not Seth. He couldn't have.''

Katy squeezed the misshapen hand gently. "Then who? Who else would have any reason to want my mother dead?"

"I don't know," Clare wheezed. "I just don't know. Perhaps you hold the key to the mystery locked somewhere in your memory."

" 'Tis exactly what Jason said. He tried to make me remember, but I couldn't. All I remember is the blood. I can't bring myself to . . . to even think about it."

After a long silence Clare picked up the threads of the conversation. "Why don't we talk about something less painful? Tell me about your voyage on the *Ugly Jane*. Is Fergus as cantankerous a master as I've heard tell?"

Thankful for the opportunity to change the subject, Katy simulated composure and proceeded to relate puckish tales of Fergus McFadden and the *Ugly Jane*. Clare chuckled at Katy's stories, but when the woman's head sagged against her pillows, she realized that it was time to terminate the conversation. "I have tired you out, Mrs. MacAuley," she apologized. "I should leave you alone now." And as if lending support to her decision, the door clicked open and Hannah appeared, sleeves rolled up to her elbows.

"Not to be disturbing you, Mrs. MacAuley, but would you mind if we saw to your morning constitutional now so I can commence boiling down the lye? I'll not be caught low on soap again this year."

"You work too hard, Hannah."

" 'Tis only what has to be done, and no one is going to do it for me." Hannah remained steadfast by the door until Clare nodded her assent.

"I suppose we might as well get it over with."

Thoroughly confused, Katy watched Hannah carry the chamber pot to the side of the bed and stand anxiously behind it, her hands positioned on her wide hips.

Looking from one woman to the next and deducing what a constitutional was, Katy ejected herself from the side of the bed. "I really should leave now and let you have some privacy."

"You'll come back, though?" Clare inquired.

"I intend to come back so much that you'll probably want to send me back to Yorktown."

Hannah's brows shot up like half-moons over her eyes. "Yorktown?" she sniffed. "Captain MacAuley said the lass was from Spain."

"Not originally," Clare offered. "Katy is Kathryn Ryan's daughter."

Hannah's features congealed into a mask that dissembled deeper sentiment. " 'Tis a Ryan you are? The captain did not mention that." As Katy stood back, the housekeeper drew back the covers from the bed. The putrid stench of rotting flesh hit her full in the face, and she made a conscious effort not to raise her hand to her nostrils.

" 'Twas your father who did away with Captain Aldrich, was it?" Hannah asked as she straightened Clare's nightgown.

Sensing her daughter-in-law's disquiet at the question, Clare hushed the housekeeper. "That is all forgotten, Hannah. Let sleeping dogs lie. Matthew Ryan is dead, and as far as I am concerned, so is any memory of him."

But Katy wondered at the housekeeper's question. Had there been venom in the woman's voice, or had she merely imagined it? Perhaps everyone was not as forgiving as Clare MacAuley.

As Katy stepped out of the bathtub later that evening, she found her thoughts dwelling on Jason's mother. Clare—who had shared an experience similar to Katy's. Clare—who was likewise disturbed by nightmares. And somehow, knowing that someone else's life had been permanently affected by the incident made her own experience seem less dreadful. But what if Clare were correct in suggesting that Katy could prove Seth Aldrich's innocence or guilt? Was it not her responsibility to try to recall the details of her mother's death? But how could she? How could she, when the very mention of it terrified her so?

Donning her nightgown, she climbed between the cool sheets and curled into a fetal position. When last she had seen Jason, he was in the library with Riley, cigar in mouth, brandy in hand, having a game of chess. He had not even raised his head when she passed the room.

With the sound of waves rumbling in her ears, she slept—to dream of footsteps and running and laughter . . . and suffocation. She awoke to a high shrill sound vibrating throughout the room and nearly lost her breath as a large hand clapped down hard over her mouth. In her frenzy she kicked off her covers and clawed at the hand and shoulders of the man above her.

"Katy! Wake up!"

As the horror of her dream floated into obscurity, she recognized Jason's shadowy features above her, and, still gasping deeply, stayed her hands and fell back into her pillow.

"If I remove my hand, will you stop screaming?"

She nodded her head, and as she did so, felt his hand drop away. He was panting almost as hard as she was, and while he leaned over to light the candle at the side of the bed, she pushed her hair away from her forehead and took a deep, steadying breath. Jason turned back to her.

"Do you want to talk about it?"

"What good would that do?" She was surprised to find her voice trembling.

"It won't do *me* a damn bit of good, but I'm not the one having the nightmares, am I?"

"It was only a bad dream. I'm sorry if I awakened you."

"Oh, you didn't awaken me. You only added to the crop of scars I sustained last time you had a 'bad dream.' It seems more and more apparent that sleeping with you could become a very dangerous occupation."

"Well, I can remedy that situation to both our satisfactions, I believe." Grabbing her pillow, she flung her legs over the side of the bed and was about to get up when Jason caught her arm.

"Just where do you think you're going?"

Looking back at him over her shoulder, she regarded his face and cursed the lips that had molded themselves to Desire's. "I intend to sleep on the sofa." She traced her eyes along his forearm to the hand that he had wrapped around her elbow. "Now, kindly let me go. I would not want to further involve you in the perils of my personal battles."

"They would not be personal battles if you would allow me to help you."

"I do not need your help."

She heard his breath escape sharply from between his teeth. "I would say you need someone's help if you persist in waking up every night screaming like a God-blessed Fury!"

"'Tis not every night. You exaggerate."

"If you could see yourself writhing back and forth in utter—"

"I have told you, I do not want your help!" she cut him off. "Not tonight, nor tomorrow, nor any day after that. And if you cannot understand that, Captain, I suggest you have your hearing attended to. Now, let me go."

She had not expected him to release her so easily, but release her he did, narrowing his brown eyes at her as he did so. "Get back into bed."

218

"I told you I was going to sleep on—"

"I said get back into bed!" he shouted. "It makes no sense for both of us to leave."

She eyed him curiously as he threw off his covers and swung his long legs over the side of the bed. Snatching his robe from the floor, he flung it over his shoulders.

"Where are you going?"

He stood and tied the belt around his waist before turning to face her. The look he cast upon her was not pleasant. "Should I conclude from the tone of your voice that you would rather I stayed here?"

She did not reply.

"No matter. Since you refuse help, I see no reason why we should both have to contend with your insomnia. Personally, I could use some sleep."

He strode to the door, but before leaving, frowned darkly at her. "It appears you have won, lady. I'll be sleeping in the bedchamber next door from now on. I'm sure you will be able to confect some plausible explanation for this sudden arrangement for the benefit of the rest of the household. You may even lock the door if you feel it necessary, though I assure you I shan't break the door down if I hear you scream again."

She wanted to heave something at the door as he closed it behind him, but spying nothing nearby, settled for slamming her fist into the mattress.

Fine! And good riddance. Now Desire could steal into his room anytime of night and fornicate to her heart's content. She hoped there was a fire some night right when they were in the middle of—

She slammed her fist into the mattress again and flung herself back into her pillows. It made no difference. She didn't care what they did.

So why did she feel so miserable?

The sun did not appear the next day, and as Katy changed quickly into the gray cotton gown, she wondered how much colder the room would be during the winter. With cold air nibbling at her toes, she made her way to the dining room, where she ate a quiet breakfast with Mercy. And whether from the dismalness of the day or her lack of sleep the night before, she found herself suffering from the megrims when she returned to her bedchamber.

She also found something she had not counted on.

Jason.

As she entered the room, he turned away from the highboy, a stack of neatly folded shirts in his hands. "Ah, Mrs. MacAuley, how good of you to trouble yourself to bid me a good morning, though a damnably black and stormy morning it is.''

She stood with her hand on the open door, watching him remove clothing from the drawers. After a few moments of silence, however, he stopped what he was doing and shook his head at her, the slightest trace of a grin curling his lips. ''Why do you hover by the door? 'Tis your room. Come in.''

Not being able to think of an excuse to leave the premises, she closed the door quietly behind her and wandered over to the bed, where she busied herself with the details of making up the disheveled blankets.

Jason proceeded to empty out his drawers. ''I trust you slept well after I left you last night?''

She shrugged her shoulders. She had not slept at all.

''Should I interpret your silence to mean yea or nay?'' He trained a fleeting look upon her. ''Considering the way you look this morning, I would think nay.''

Her brows lifted petulantly. ''And what is wrong with the way I look this morning?''

''The circles beneath your eyes, my dear. They're the color of your dress. Perhaps you should think about taking a nap later on. Not much else to do on a day like this.''

She looked to the balcony, where rain was beating a rapid tattoo against the rough stone. In the distance, lightning flashed, purpling the sky.

''And what will you do?'' she hedged.

She heard him laugh. ''I thought that was fairly obvious. I shall move my odious belongings into the next room so that you might wallow in your solitude without fear of interruption from me. That should cheer you considerably, or would you rather I simply moved out of the house? That can be arranged also.''

Her face brightened with feigned expectancy. ''Oh?''

But reacting to her gesture, he scowled, his flippant mood disappearing completely. ''You *would* like that, wouldn't you?'' Throwing the last few items of clothing atop the growing stack, he snatched everything up into his arms and skewered his bride with a withering glance. ''I begin to realize the folly of this marriage more each day. It seems that perhaps I *have* made a mistake. Now the question remains: what will we do about it?''

He looked weary as he strode to the door. ''I will have to think about this, Katy. If I am forced to hold you here against your will, then what we have will never be a marriage. 'Twould be better to dissolve the bonds now.''

A booming roll of thunder ushered Jason from the room. Katy

sat down. Without laying a hand on her, he had just knocked the wind from her lungs.

During the course of the next two weeks summer gradually descended upon the island, dappling the fields with clusters of bluets and wild iris. Within the dark spruce forests, purple violets and fern fiddleheads sprang up, while in the peat bogs there grew the tiny cranberry, huckleberry, baked-appleberry, and purplish-rose rhodora that spread its color like a delicate mist over the earth.

But Katy saw none of these things, for her hours became consumed with domestic chores whose acquaintance she had escaped for eighteen years. She served as Mercy's apprentice in the kitchen, engaging in minor culinary tasks, and learned how to properly collect the ashes that Hannah would leach with rainwater and boil down with hog's fat to produce soap. Her true ability, however, manifested itself in a place where the other members of the household were infrequent visitors—the barn. After she had snooped around Riley Sprague's domain for several days, the man finally waved a stiff brush before her face, which indicated that she should make herself useful, so naturally, she did—rubbing down the horses and milking the cows, two tasks which she could perform tirelessly and efficiently.

She saw Jason rarely during this time, for on days when he did not rise before dawn to fish porgy in the deep water off the outlying islands, he disappeared into the forest to cut timber or to the western side of the island to inspect his crops. The townsfolk thought it odd that he did not devote more time to his new wife, yet the good people of Cromwell Harbor so decried idleness and soppy romanticism that the captain's lack of self-indulgence soon came to be known as his most admirable virtue. No one but Jason knew what drove him to the brink of exhaustion each day. No one knew that if he allowed himself to think of his wife's rejection, he would go mad. So he cluttered his waking hours with activity in the hopes of forgetting the woman who caused him so much hurt and frustration.

If the calluses on Katy's hands were an indication of the work she had been doing, then Riley's asking her to handle the milking one afternoon while he saw to an ailing horse the other side of the island was a measure of the man's confidence in her ability. Humming to herself, her dress pulled up to her thighs, she squirted the thin white liquid into the bucket between her feet and wondered why she had created such a fuss about not wanting to tour the island till Fergus returned. It seemed that by the time he decided to sail back into Cromwell Harbor, summer would be over and she would have missed all its beauty. She would like to have absconded with the stallion Asticou to explore on her own, but she reminded herself that she *had* given her word to Fergus, so she would have to forgo any sightseeing until she next saw the Irishman.

Bosh!

As she forced milk down the cow's teat with four curled fingers, she heard the clop of horses hooves behind her and smiled inwardly at how proud Riley would be of her efficient work. Without turning around, she called back to him, "You are home early, Riley! Have you cured the poor beast already?"

He did not answer immediately, but she could hear him go through the motions of unlatching the gate, leading the horse into the stall, unsaddling him, then relatching the gate and aiming his footsteps in her direction. All without a word. Typical Riley Sprague.

Yet the footsteps sounded almost too heavy to be Riley's. They sounded more like . . .

"My dear Mrs. MacAuley! Your talents will never cease to amaze me."

. . . Jason's.

Startled, she overshot the bucket and squirted a stream of milk across her bare foot. As the liquid drizzled down between her toes, she looked up into the tanned face of her husband.

"And just where is Riley that you are forced to do a man's job by yourself?" He was leaning casually against one of the support beams, his shirt open to the waist, his thumbs hooked into the waistband of his breeches. His beard was trimmed close to his face and the angles that rendered his features so exquisite were darkened by the sun to a coppery color. Beneath his dark brows his eyes were warm and sensuous and fixed curiously upon her. She wanted to yank her skirt down over her knees to hide herself from his rakish perusal, but she refused to allow him to see how much his presence unnerved her.

"Riley was called away to the other side of the island— something about a sick horse." She concentrated on the cow before her rather than the man. "And 'tis not a man's job. I can handle the eight very well by myself, thank you."

Jason's eyes slid down her shapely leg, from thigh to calf, and stopping at her foot, he observed the milky runnels that patterned her skin, and sniggered in some amusement. "So you can handle the eight very well by yourself, eh?"

Peeking up at him and seeing the source of his mirth, she

curled her toes beneath her foot. "That," she emphasized self-righteously, "was an accident. You frightened me, so I missed."

Jason watched her work with more than a casual gleam in his eye. He had barely seen her for the past two weeks, ever since the night he had moved into the adjoining bedchamber, and in that time she had become more beautiful than he had ever seen her. Her skin glowed like warm apricots, her eyes were a clear, vivid green, and her hair shone with such deep highlights that it looked polished. The life here was definitely agreeing with her—but it was a life that excluded him, and the fact that she was not only surviving, but actually thriving without him, pricked his ego more than a little. As he settled his gaze once again on her bare thighs, he felt the muscle below his eye begin to twitch, and he cursed to himself.

"Shall I carry that bucket back to the house for you, Katy?"

"I have carried two pails back already. I think I can manage this. 'Tis not full." Sitting upright on the stool, she arched her back to relieve her cramped muscles, not realizing what an enticing spectacle she was creating for her husband. "Will you be dining with us tonight?" she asked shyly. "Mercy and I have prepared a special dessert." She dragged the bucket out from beneath the cow.

"I'm afraid I've made other plans for this evening." His tone was soft, apologetic.

"You're home so early, I thought—"

"I only came back to change my clothes. One of my ships is fresh back from Canton, so I wanted to wine and dine its captain in the tavern this evening. He's been gone for sixteen months and I suspect has many a tale to tell. I'm anxious to discover what treasures he has brought back with him."

"Can you not bring this man home to dine with us? 'Twould be more comfortable than a dim tavern."

Jason hesitated for a moment. "We're only going to discuss business, Katy. I had no wish to bore you."

"Oh." But the reality was that her husband no longer sought her out, and that fact left her strangely bereft.

Sensing a hint of disappointment in his wife's voice, Jason regarded her, somewhat bemused. "Would you rather I bring Elisha here?"

"Elisha?"

"Elisha Hastings—my ship's master."

"Oh." Immersed in self-pity, she shook her head. "Nay. I probably *would* be bored. I hope you spend a pleasant evening at the tavern." Forcing a smile as she stood up, she wiped her hands self-consciously on her apron. "I'll, uh . . . I'll give your dessert to Riley. I never would have thought it, but he has an insatiable sweet tooth.''

"I don't have to go tonight, love." He extended his hand to her. "I could stay home with you. You need only say the word."

In her pride she ignored his hand. " 'Tis not necessary.''

An awkward silence lengthened between husband and wife. Jason pushed off from the support beam and came to stand before his young bride. "We have barely spoken for two weeks and haven't even seen each other for the past few days. Would you not have me spend *some* time with you, lady?"

Reluctantly she looked up into the man's face, and as she did so, he cupped her chin in his hand and kissed her. A languid warmth coursed through her body as her mind became filled with his presence—and his presence only. "Have you not missed me even a little?" he whispered against her cheek.

She wiggled out of his embrace and stumbled backward. "I am content with the way things are, Jason. I require nothing more."

Jason's temples pulsed as silence again spread between them. She was being as unrelenting as ever. Why did she always withdraw from him? Why did she refuse his attentions? Indeed, why did she prefer everyone else's company to his own? And why did that fact aggravate him so much?

"Well"—his deep voice filled the void between them—"since my services seem to be an unwanted commodity, there is no sense in my trying to peddle them any longer. Be about your chores, Katy, and I'll be about entertaining Elisha in town, and perhaps if you're lucky, you won't have to look at me for another two weeks."

"Jason, I—"

He held up his hand, cutting off her sentence. "No more, my dear. At least allow me to tramp back to the house with the remnants of an ego. 'Tis not an unreasonable request from a man who makes no other demands of you." He tipped his head— "Madam . . ."—then strode past her, walking till he had rounded the corner of the barn. How could he have explained to her the reason why he did not invite Elisha Hastings to dine at the house? Elisha—the good-looking rogue who could charm the most stalwart of virgins into bed. Elisha—who was always seeking out fresh bait. Elisha—whom Jason did not trust within five miles of any woman, much less his wife. It was for Elisha's own well-being that Jason had not invited him. He hated to think what he would do to the man if he made any amorous advances toward Katy. By damn, if *he* was not allowed such privileges, no one else would be either!

224

In the barn Katy stared dejectedly at the milk she had just collected, touched the back of her hand to her lips. The gap was widening between them, and though that should have pleased her, it did not. In the past weeks she had developed a particular affection for the things of this island—for Mercy, and Clare, and these animals. And though she would not admit that she bore any great affection for her husband, she could not deny that she had missed his company. How could she be so hypocritical? Why did she find his attendance upon her so irritating, yet when he ignored her, why did she feel so dispirited? It did not follow reason! She had lain awake nights listening for the soft-pedal sounds of Desire's voice emanating from Jason's bedchamber, but she had heard nothing. Had he mended his ways with the tart? Little good it would do Katy if he had. She had done nothing to endear herself to her husband, and now that he was treating her as she had treated him, she was discovering that being shunned was not a pleasant experience at all.

Grabbing the bucket, she returned along the pine-needled path that separated house from barn and was about to cross the lawn when she caught her toe on a protruding tree root and yelped as the earth rose up to meet her. She rattled every tooth in her head when her chin impacted with solid ground. Spread-eagled on her face, she boosted herself onto her hands, then eased herself into a sitting position and clutched her injured foot. To her left the milk bucket was resting oddly on its side, and the milk . . .

Feeling a moistness beneath her dress, she tested the ground on which she sat and grimaced.

She was sitting in it.

Hearing a door slam, she looked up to find Hannah trudging across the lawn toward her.

"What in the blue blazes are you about, girl?" the housekeeper ranted as she came to a sudden halt before her. "Do you not know enough to ask for help when you can't carry something by yourself?"

"I thought I could manage everything by myself."

"Well, you were wrong." Hannah glanced at the overturned bucket. "If you were in the house acting like a respectable lady, this wouldn't have happened."

"I'm sorry."

"Sorry! Sorry isn't going to provide any more milk for us. Bah! Never heard tell of a Ryan who knew any more than Adam's off-ox anyway. 'Tis all alike you are. Don't know why the captain couldn't marry his own kind instead of importing a Ryan to the island."

The truth that had been hidden behind Hannah's eyes for the

past two weeks had finally surfaced, and Katy found its sting far more painful than the one in her foot. Ryan was a hated name and Katy would not be forgiven for bearing it.

"And look at you—your dress. You're sopping wet with milk." Hannah sighed and shook her head. "Get yourself back to the house, Mary Kathleen Ryan, before you cause more trouble."

"*MacAuley*," Katy retorted. "Mary Kathleen *MacAuley*."

Pulling her skirt down over her legs, she pulled herself up from the ground, and refusing to meet Hannah's gaze, straightened her back and limped painfully across the lawn, leaving the housekeeper and her harsh imprecations behind.

11

Returning from Cromwell Harbor late that night, Jason found his way to the foot of the central staircase by the flame of a single wall sconce. He chuckled at the memory of Elisha Hastings' falling asleep on him and wondered whether it was the liquor the man had consumed or Jason's company that had put the lead in his eyes. In the shadowed light his gaze wandered to the second floor, stopping at the portal to his wife's bedchamber. He had not sought her room for two weeks now, but had his feet possessed a mind of their own, he would have liked to vault up the stairs now to claim that which was his right to take. And so thinking, he placed one booted foot on the first riser, then after a moment retreated.

Damn.

He braced his forearms across the newel post, bowed his head against their support. For a fortnight he had pretended she did not exist, but she had continued to haunt him. He saw the curl of her hair in the clouds, the water; the green of her eyes in the lush coastal meadows; the texture of her skin in the silkiness of the very shirts he wore. Today he had seen her, touched her. Today she very much existed and her reality made him ache with the pain of the promise he had made.

The sound of the clock chiming the half-hour accompanied him as he climbed the stairs to the hollow stillness of his bedchamber.

By ten o'clock the next morning Katy was up to her elbows in cod—slicing, decapitating, and eviscerating. Hannah had left for town much earlier with Riley, leaving the household duties to the three girls, and since Mercy had said that Katy could either wash clothes with her and Desire outside or salt cod by herself in the kitchen, Katy decided that the latter would be more to her liking. Anything would be more tolerable than having to be subjected to a dose of Desire's sarcasm.

Earlier she had fed Clare MacAuley, and Mercy had bathed her. Jason was up with her now. As she layered the cod in the bottom of the hogshead and spread coarse salt over them, she wondered why he had changed his routine this morning. Why was he staying close to the house rather than venturing off as was his custom?

Jason.

Remembering his kiss of the day before, she bit her lip and tried to concentrate on what she was doing. It was at this point that she looked out the window to find Mercy scrubbing clothes by herself, and it was also at this point that she became curious as to where Desire might be, since she was not where she should have been.

With Jason?

Scolding herself for having such a suspicious mind, she returned to the table and set another dozen fish before her on the chopping block, but just as she finished slicing the first one, she put her knife down and listened.

Someone at the door?

From the hall the noise sounded again—knuckles rapping loudly against the front door. Katy regarded her blood-encrusted hands with disdain. Desire had to be somewhere in the house. Perhaps she would answer it. But as the knocks persisted a third, fourth, and finally a fifth time, she realized that no one was going to answer the door—except her. Wiping her hands on her apron, she tucked a stray wisp of hair behind her ear and scurried down the hall. When the door lay open before her, a big, strapping man confronted her, his light brown hair caught at the nape of his neck, his gray eyes smiling down at her with a jauntiness that marked him as a rake. For some reason the sight of him made her blush, and he, surprised by her reaction, laughed heartily.

"You're a bonny one, aren't you? Good morning! Would the master of the house be about?"

"He would."

The man, who was clad in loose shirt and tight breeches, bore himself proudly and prompted Katy to wonder if there was any man on this island under six feet tall. When he spoke, the tiny lines that scored the outside corners of his eyes crimped in amusement.

"Would you mind fetching him for me, lass, and putting these in a vase of water for your mistress?" From behind his back he removed a bouquet of wildflowers and handed them to her. "If I had known of your existence, I would have picked some for you also."

Gathering the flowers into her hands, she smiled inwardly. He thought she was a new household servant! But before she had a chance to correct him, he was down on one knee, looking up at her eyes with profound interest. "Green. They're green as the

228

water off the Bermudas. Forgive me for staring, little one, but eyes that green are a rarity. Beautiful.'' His smile was dazzling, and it widened as he studied the perfect oval of her face. ''Beautiful.''

She blinked at the windburned face before her, but feeling the color crawl up her neck and into her cheeks, she dropped her gaze to the lavender irises.

''Who should I say is calling?''

''Elisha Hastings,'' he said, stretching to his full six-feet-one. ''Captain Elisha Hastings.''

Ah, she thought, the man whom Jason had refused to invite to dinner last night. ''If you would be so good as to follow me to the library, Captain, I'll inform Captain MacAuley that you are here.'' Turning, she led the way through the hall, completely unaware of Elisha's discreet perusal.

He liked what he saw—tiny waist, hips small but well-rounded, hair lustrous and black as any Oriental's. She wore it coiled in braids at her ears, but he wondered what it would look like flowing down her back or fanned across a pillow. He considered her embarrassment of a few moments earlier and grinned widely. She blushed like a virgin, and he found himself wanting to be the man who gave her something to blush about. How could Jason have run off to get married when he had this sweet little tart right beneath his own roof?

Leaving the man to browse in the library, Katy returned through the hall and was about to ascend the staircase when Desire suddenly materialized at the top of the stairs. Instinctively, each stopped and eyed the other, but it was Katy who spoke first.

''Did you not hear someone at the door?''

''I heard.''

''And you chose to ignore it?''

''I was occupied elsewhere.''

If the words which each spoke had taken form, they would have frozen midair.

''Occupied with what?''

Desire lifted her finely shaped brows in defiance. ''Ask thy husband, mistress. 'Twas his bidding I was about.''

Tightening her grip around the stem of the flowers till her fingers paled white with rage, Katy absorbed Desire's lively intimations with a well-bred grace. ''I will repeat my question. With what were you occupied?''

Desire's eyes danced with a smugness that caused Katy to bristle like a porcupine. ''If it is of such great import to thee, I was changing the sheets on thy husband's bed. But thou wouldst not know of such things, would thee? Having such an aversion to beds—at least his bed. 'Tis sad, thy having to sleep all by thyself at night, mistress. Mayhap thy smell reminded more people than myself of thy preoccupation with cows."

Katy's cheeks flamed blood-red, and if she had had something more lethal than a bouquet of flowers in her hand, she would surely have flung it at the wench. When she finally found her voice, it was gravelly with anger. "Tell Captain MacAuley that he has a guest awaiting him in the library. I assume you know where he is. You seem to make a point of knowing everyone else's business."

Spinning around, Katy returned to the kitchen and jammed the flowers into a glass vase. Taking up her knife again, she glared at the multitude of brown eyes set before her, then began hewing away with a vengeance undue the helpless carcass of a dead fish whose eyes had the misfortune of being the same color as those of Desire Meacham.

Upon reaching the library, Jason was surprised to find Elisha pacing back and forth as if a brisk northwest wind were blowing at his heels. Jason laughed aloud at the frenetic picture which his otherwise calm ship's master presented. "One day back and already anxious to return to sea, Elisha?"

As Jason's deep basso sounded, Elisha turned to greet him, but it was clear from the intensity of his light eyes that his mind was on a matter other than the sea.

"Jason!" Taking three long strides toward his employer, he gripped Jason's hand in his own powerful one and clapped him firmly on the shoulder with the other. " 'Tis a miracle you are still speaking to me after my rudeness last night. I blame it on the fact that the floor was not rocking beneath me to keep me awake."

"Why not tell me the truth?" Jason reproved. "You found my conversation dull."

"What, and ruin all my chances of another run to the Orient? I am a more clever liar than that, my friend!"

Jason tossed his head back and rumbled with laughter, then directed the young captain to a chair. "So, Elisha, what brings you here this morning? Certainly not more dull conversation."

Lacing his fingers together, Elisha stared at them foolishly, not knowing how to broach the subject. After a long pause, he abandoned all hope of etiquette. "Who is she?" he spurted.

Jason's brows drew together. "Who is who?"

"That gorgeous female!"

"I live with an entire household of females. To which do you refer?"

"The beautiful one—with the eyes. The one who blushes so prettily."

Jason looked perplexed.

"Good God, man, do you live among so many beautiful women that you cannot distinguish one from the other? The girl who told you that I was here—who is she?"

If Elisha had not displayed such a painful expression, Jason would have laughed. Instead, he merely looked stunned. "You mean Desire?"

"If she is the one who fetched you, then she is the one I mean. Tell me she is not married."

"She is not."

"Promised?"

Jason shook his head. "She is our housekeeper's daughter—one of our serving girls. As far as I know, she is promised to no man. But . . ." He hesitated. "She has cast designs upon a man she cannot have."

Elisha looked thoughtful. "What ails the man, that he can ignore such beauty?"

"The man is married."

"Ah! The lout. What was his game? Did he try to lure the girl into his bed with cunning words and deceit, and then, when she refused, did he marry some fish-faced maiden to spite her? For indeed, Jason, she does not look the type to fall into bed with a man unless he were her husband, legally bound. She probably fell in love with the knave and he was too much the bastard to marry beneath his station. Poor lass."

Jason's eyes widened as if he had been slapped in the face. He had not encouraged the girl! 'Twas *she* who was supplying the cunning words. "Elisha," he began, trying to sort out words in his mind, "Desire does not understand that this man married because he truly loves another woman. When she realizes how hopeless—"

"I cannot imagine it!" Elisha thundered, slapping his hands on his knees.

"What?"

"I cannot imagine a man marrying another woman once he had seen that lovely creature. The man must be blind as well as stupid!"

Grinding his teeth at the misguided insult, Jason continued, "As I was saying, once she realizes how hopeless it is to continue her pursuit of m . . . uh . . . of this fellow, I think she may be more amenable to receiving suitors."

Within the dark crannies of his mind, Jason was formulating a plan. If Elisha was as smitten with Desire as he claimed, then a major portion of Jason's problems might be solved. If Desire could be safely wedded and bedded, she would no longer be interested in flaunting herself before him, and he could devote his time to wooing his wife rather than running away from the help. "What would be your intentions toward the girl, Elisha?"

"To marry her, of course! Today, tomorrow, name the time!"

"I cannot name the time, but if Desire cottons to you, we can hope that *she* will—and with my blessings. Why not sup with us tonight, and you may gaze upon her the entire evening. And, Elisha, I cannot impress upon you enough the need to be . . . forceful with her. It might even serve your purpose best if you overwhelmed her—swept her entirely off her feet so that she would not have a chance to think about this other man." A devilish light flickered in Jason's eye. "In fact, I have an idea, but I'll not discuss it here. Come down to the ship with me—you may show me your chinaware and silks, and I shall instruct you on the vulnerable points of Mistress Meacham."

Both men rose and started through the hall, but as he reached the front door, Jason stopped and scratched his head. "You never did tell me the purpose of your visit this morning, Elisha."

"Oh." It was difficult to tell whether the young man's face mirrored guilt or chagrin. "My purpose was well-intended but self-serving." He hesitated briefly before continuing, and as he did, Jason conceded that Elisha and Desire would make a handsome couple, both gifted with striking good looks. "I was curious to meet the wife that no one has met. 'Tis rumored she is exquisitely beautiful, so I could not understand why you would want to hide her." Elisha shrugged his bulky shoulders. "I decided to find out for myself. And I still have not met her, have I?"

"Tonight will be soon enough. Then you may judge her beauty for yourself."

"I fear that after my encounter with this lovely sylph today, all other females will appear as dogs in comparison. I can conceive of no one being more beautiful, or enchanting, or innocent."

As Jason smiled, one of his eyebrows slanted upward at an odd angle. "If Desire is a star that glows in the night, then Katy is the moon that lights the entire sky. Hold fast your opinion of the rest of womankind till you have met my bride."

"Come in!" Katy managed a muffled reply to the knock on her door even though she was struggling for air beneath numerous folds of violet muslin that were caught around her head while she punched her fists this way and that in search of the two elusive armholes.

She heard Mercy before she saw her—a shuffling of footsteps and then a shrill giggle that spread into an uproarious laugh—but Katy had lost patience with the situation for the moment. "Don't stand there laughing like a ninny. Help me!"

For a brief moment she felt the material being twisted around her body, then grunted as it was tugged firmly over her head. Expelling a deep hiss, she blew a strand of hair away from her face and sucked in her breath as Mercy tied the sash for her.

"The dress was not meant to be washed so many times, mistress. One more dunking and I would almost guarantee that the threads will disintegrate. 'Tis time we thought about preparing a new wardrobe for thee."

"Wardrobe! What? So that I might ruin more gowns with my clumsiness? If I were not hindered by hems, mayhap I would be able to walk a straight line without falling on my face!"

Mercy, little knowing that Katy was still smarting from her encounter with Desire on the stairs, frowned. 'Twas not like her mistress to become riled so easily. Perhaps she was just tired. "I . . . I came to tell thee that we are having a guest for dinner tonight."

"A guest? Indeed? Are you not worried that my smell will offend them?"

Mercy's eyes grew wide. "Thy smell, mistress? Is something wrong with thy smell?"

Seeing the girl's troubled look, Katy relented. "I'm sorry for snapping. I'm angry and you're the first person I have found to vent my wrath upon. My words are as empty as my head." Taking the girl's hand, she squeezed it with affection. "Now, who is this guest who honors our table tonight?"

Her composure restored, Mercy smiled. "Captain MacAuley has brought home with him Captain Elisha Hastings, mistress. Captain Hastings has just returned from the Orient and is a most attractive man by any standards. Thy husband has asked thee to join them in the library for drinks."

Katy smiled, remembering the handsome face given so easily to laughter. Elisha Hastings. She pondered what his reaction would be when he discovered he had mistaken the mistress for the maid, her mood improving at the thought of playing out the farce.

"Shall I tell the captain to expect thee presently?" Mercy contemplated the mischievous gleam in Katy's eye with concern. 'Twas a most bawdy expression she was displaying this evening, not at all the sublime countenance of a lady.

233

"Yes, tell him . . ." She paused, then bit her bottom lip. "Nay, tell him nothing. I will tell him myself."

Completely confused, Mercy curtsied and took her leave. As she descended the stairs, lines of worry creased her forehead. She had been allowing her mistress to work too hard, and it was beginning to take its toll. Tomorrow she would forbid her to lift a finger around the house, and mayhap, after a day of rest, she would return to normal.

Meanwhile Katy had run to the mirror, dragged a brush through her freshly washed hair, pinched her cheeks and bitten her lips till both were highly colored, and tweaked her nose at her reflection. She probably *had* resembled a serving wench this morning, with blood splattered over her apron, but tonight no one could accuse her of the same. After checking her appearance once more, she doused the candles around the room and made her way swiftly to the library.

"An elephant!" Jason's voice swelled with laughter. "Are you sure you were not doing your looking through the bottom of an empty whiskey bottle?"

"God's truth, Jason. I let a number of the crew off in Salem harbor and I'll be damned if there wasn't an elephant plodding about on the wharf. It appears he had flung his mahout off his back, nearly killing the poor man, so his keepers tried to tame him by feeding him bread and hay. The beast became so docile that he began lifting morsels of bread from spectators' pockets! Then, when he was presented with a bottle of port, he yanked the cork off with his trunk and began pouring the brew down his gullet as if he had once nursed on it! Jacob Croninshield had just brought him back from the East Indies and 'tis rumored he got ten thousand dollars for the animal right there on the dock. Now, I ask you, what in the bloody hell would anyone want with an elephant in Massachusetts?" Elisha slammed his hand down on the arm of the chair for effect while Jason wiped the tears from his own eyes.

" 'Tis good that you decided not to bring an elephant back with you, Elisha, for I am well enough pleased with your present selection of cargo. The next question, of course, is when will you be ready to go back?"

Seated at an angle where the hall was readily visible to him, Elisha cast a sidelong glance at the portal, willing Desire to appear. "This morning"—he returned his attention to Jason, whose chair was facing the hearth—"I would have told you that I would be ready to round the Horn again in, say, a fortnight. Now, I am not so sure. You're a new bridegroom yourself,

Jason. How does the thought of abandoning female flesh for as long as two years sit with you?"

Before he had the chance to answer, Jason heard the faint rustle of skirts, and if that alone had not indicated Desire's arrival, the fact that Elisha had jumped out of his seat eager as a bridegroom would have.

"I have been counting the minutes till I could gaze upon you again, my lovely green-eyed sprite. And now that I have you within my sight, I will be heartily opposed to ever letting you out of it again."

Jason suppressed a guffaw as Elisha disappeared in the direction of the door, presumably to "sweep Desire off her feet." In a minute he would make the proper introductions. Leaning back in his chair, he drew thoughtfully on his cheroot. Something that Elisha said had pricked his mind . . .

Green-eyed sprite.

Desire's eyes were not green; they were brown. The only person with green eyes in the entire house was . . . He mashed his cheroot into the ashtray beside him. *Katy!*

He bounded from the chair, whipped around in one fluid motion, and felt his blood begin to boil with mad jealousy at the scene before him, for Elisha had locked Katy in a passionate embrace, bending her over his arm, kissing her long and deeply, and with her arms thrown around Elisha's neck, it seemed to Jason that she was making no protest at all at the indiscretion.

Jason was not aware that the attack had taken Katy so much by surprise that she had been too numb to struggle and had only thrown her arms around the man's neck as a reflex action to prevent herself from falling over backward. In fact, Jason was aware of nothing except that Elisha Hastings was caressing *his* wife in a way that had been denied him since he had first met her, and the fact that she was tendering no resistance to a complete stranger, whereas she would have fought *him* pitchfork and barn shovel, enraged him even further.

With blood in his eyes, he stormed across the floor and laid a restraining hand upon Elisha, who, feeling fingers bite into his shoulder, eased his lips away from the softness of the girl, only to look up into the face of a man he did not recognize, nor care to know.

"I see you have already made my wife's acquaintance, Elisha." Jason's voice was stony, his eyes dark and threatening, and Elisha Hastings, who had battled hurricanes off the coast of Africa and quelled more than one argument with a single blow of his fist, suddenly feared for his life.

"Your . . . wife?"

"Aye, my wife. And I will not tell you a second time to take your hands off her."

In almost as much shock as Katy, Elisha slowly detached his arms from around her waist and stepped back, trusting that there would be safety with distance.

"How . . . I . . . dammit, Jason, how was I to know this is your wife? 'Tis the same girl who answered the door and said she would fetch you. The same girl whom you declared to be your serving wench, Desire."

Jason leveled a dangerous look upon his bride. "Obviously not the same girl." His eyes demanded explanation from her, but Elisha's utter consternation as he slapped the heel of his palm against his forehead diverted her attention.

"All the scheming, the wheedling, all the elaborate plans we have made . . . *for your wife!*" The last three words caught in Elisha's throat and emerged more as groans than as parts of speech, and only then did Katy understand completely what had transpired.

As she pondered the ridiculous imbroglio, a smile flitted across her face, and she began to laugh—not hysterically, but quietly, savoring the jest. Jason glared at her, cursing her laughter with a chilly silence, and as she tried to conceal her mirth, her ragged emotions began to pour themselves out in the form of unconstrained giggles, and she could do naught but laugh more loudly at the face that was black as a thundercloud. Unable to control her giddiness, she threw herself into the nearest chair and bent over, holding her sides so they would not burst. Tears streamed over her cheeks and into her mouth, ran off the tip of her nose and down her chin.

Then she started hiccuping . . . and she could stop neither the laughter, nor the tears, nor the hiccups. She thought she would surely die—if not from laughter, then from Jason's evil stare.

Elisha, having recovered sufficiently from the shock of having almost molested his employer's wife and confident that Jason had calmed down enough so as not to pose any immediate threat to his person, regarded Katy MacAuley's blithe manner with awe and then with amusement. Damned if the whole thing wasn't funny! Catching her mood, he let out a hardy roar, then a series of snorts and guffaws that far surpassed Katy's in volume, and together they filled the room with their hilarious noises.

"Oh, Jason . . . hic . . ." She gulped a mouthful of air and wiped the dew from her eyes at the same time. "Do you not see what . . . hic . . . happened? I answered the door but sent Desire to tell you that . . . hic . . . Captain Hastings was here to see you. The joke is on you, husband . . . hic . . . I fear you almost

236

made arrangements to provide me with a . . . hic . . . second spouse.''

Jason did not smile. Seeing his wife so docile in the arms of another man had left a taste of bile in his mouth and a pox upon his good humor. ''I do not find your jocularity entertaining. In fact, I find it quite offensive. We have a guest, lady. Be gracious enough to mind your behavior in his presence.''

His words had the same effect that a pail of ice water thrown in her face would have had. ''How would I know how to behave in the presence of guests, when you bring them home so rarely?''

Elisha was beside her in a moment, raising her hand to his lips. ''Madam, if I had a wife as comely as yourself within my home, I would never bring another man home for fear that he would steal her away from me, as I almost succeeded in doing with you this evening.''

''I warrant that my husband would never have allowed that, Elisha. See how he is still nettled by the kiss which you gave me?''

Jason flung both people a murderous look, but more so at Elisha for pawing his wife's hand with such obvious delight. His eyes seemed to spill over with blood again. ''If I were nettled, lady, you would not be sitting there so calmly now.''

''Pray tell, what would I be doing?''

Elisha shifted uneasily, fearing the turn that the conversation had taken, and he was therefore greatly relieved when a young girl appeared at the door to announce that dinner was ready. Taking matters in his own hands, Elisha guided Katy from her chair, securing her arm within his. ''My passion has left me famished. Lead me to the dining table, that I might partake of pleasures other than the flesh, for indeed, my lovely Katy, knowing I have lost you, I must drown my sorrow in something. It might as well be food.''

Katy chuckled at his theatrics as she led him through the door beneath Jason's unrelenting glare.

Had it not been for Elisha's charming wit, dinner would have been disastrous, for Jason was as dour as a miser and the three Meacham women, ever proper in the company of strangers, would not speak unless spoken to first. Katy, however, compensated for the dearth of conversation by chatting enthusiastically between small bites of food and large gulps of wine, and, seated beside Elisha, persistently plied him with questions of every type—questions which he twisted around into tales of adventure and feats of courage, making himself sound almost invincible. Of course she knew that half of what he told was fabrication, but that did not lessen her enjoyment. She liked this man whose laughter had chorused with her own, and when he related some outlandish yarn, she had no qualms about laying her hand on his forearm and chiding him for his foolishness. The wine, having tinged her cheeks with a rosy glow and filled her head with a fuzzy lightness, had also dulled her sense of reserve.

Jason missed not one word, not one gesture. It chafed him to see her touch another man so fondly. Could she not see that she was arousing Elisha? Even Jason could detect the husky undertones in the man's laughter, the deepened hue in his eyes. Could she be so blind?

He tightened his grip around his goblet. Of course she could be so blind! She knew not the ways of men. But Jason knew—not only because he was a man but also because he was aroused himself. And what man would not be—watching her eyes leap so excitedly, her face flush with the color of strong wine.

Jason heard Elisha's laughter through the web of silent thought he had wound about himself, and at the same time felt a constriction in his loins that nearly tore him from his chair in agony.

"If you were not a married woman, Katy MacAuley, I would steal you from your room some night and hide you aboard my ship bound for the Orient, and the devil be damned!"

"If I were not a married woman, Captain," she teased as she traced one finger the length of his arm, "I would probably go with you. But I should hope that, if you did steal me from my bed, you would have the good sense to steal my shoes also."

A sudden choking sound sent all eyes to the head of the table, where Jason was sopping up the mouthful of wine he had sprayed all over the tablecloth. Lifting his gaze to the shocked faces on either side of him, he set the napkin beside his plate and cleared his throat. "If you are quite through," he said, touching each set of eyes with his own, daring them to utter one word, "I should like to retire to the library. Elisha?" His tone of voice meant that Elisha should proceed to the library by himself; Elisha, however, had a different inclination, so that when Jason left the room, the seaman latched firmly onto Katy's arm and waltzed her into the library behind her husband.

"I hope you don't make a practice of drinking all your claret like that, Jason. Considering the price of things these days, it's a terrible waste."

Jason, who was pouring himself another drink, sneered darkly but nonetheless held the bottle up for Elisha. "You want one?"

As Elisha nodded, Katy pried herself away from his embrace and wandered over to the table where Jason was standing. "I would like some of that too," she commented to no one in

238

particular. She surveyed the decanters at her disposal and selected one which contained a bright red liquid.

Holding the decanter and a glass in the air before her, she started to tip the crystal container over her goblet, when she suddenly found the former snatched from her hand. Rather wobbly but still in command of her faculties, she swung around to be confronted by her husband, who was holding the decanter high above her head.

"If you please, I believe I was using that."

"You have had enough to drink." He replaced the decanter on the table, only to have her reach out her hand for it again. He caught her wrist in midair. "I said, you have had enough to drink. You will only make yourself sick."

Though his hand was clamped like a band of iron around her wrist, she could feel him tremble. "If I want to make myself sick, 'tis my own affair."

"It is *my* affair if I have to hold your head while you heave up your dinner."

"If I have any compulsion to heave up my dinner, I will remember not to ask for your assistance." Her words were angry, but her eyes were not. She had no desire to spar verbally with him, especially in front of a guest, and yet she would not be made to bear the brunt of his wrath simply because he was irate about being made to look the fool.

"Katy," he warned, "do not try my patience any more this evening. You have had so much wine that your nose is lit up like a beacon. I will not abide having the rest of you so illuminated."

He released her hand, half-expecting her to grab for the decanter again, but she did not. Instead, she set her glass gently on the table and looked at him with the slightest trace of disappointment in her eyes. " 'Tis a pity that you have forgotten how to laugh at yourself, Jason. The situation this evening was humorous. If I have embarrassed you in front of your guest, forgive me. 'Twas not my intent. And since you find my mirth so offensive, I shall attempt to act more subdued in the future. May I have your permission to take my leave now? I have not seen your mother since this morning and I would inquire of her disposition before I retire."

So stunned was he by her sudden docility, when he had expected a sharp retort, that when she looked up at him for his assent, he was struck dumb and could do naught but wave his hand stupidly into the air as a gesture of dismissal. He watched in misery as she curtsied and extended her hand to Elisha. He could not hear what she was saying to him, but his head pounded so thickly with regret at having made such a royal jackass out of himself that he did not care to hear. Her stubbornness, he was well equipped to handle—her gentleness, he was not.

When she had gone, Elisha wandered over to the table where Jason was playing sentinel and stuck his thumbs in the waistband of his breeches. "If I reach for that glass of wine you poured for me, will you get the urge to slap my wrist also? If so, I think I'll pass up the after-dinner drink."

Jason, his anger spent, rubbed the back of his neck, airing his discomposure. "I have been a damned poor host tonight, Elisha. I hope you'll accept my apologies."

The younger man swiped the glass from the table and emptied its contents before answering, "Frankly, old friend, I hadn't noticed. Your wife is charming enough for both of you. But I am surprised that you would allow yourself to become so ruffled over some harmless flirtation. You never struck me as the jealous-husband type."

Jason's eyes fled unconsciously to the hall through which Katy had disappeared. "I never thought it of myself! 'Tis frightening, the qualities that marriage can bring out in a man. I thought I knew everything there was to know about women. After three weeks of marriage, I find out that I know nothing—about women or myself! That tiny girl rips my vitals apart with a single look, and then prances prettily up to her room, leaving me to lick my wounds."

Elisha followed the line of Jason's gaze to the hall. "Aye, Jason. But what pleasure to find out about oneself with such a woman. She is lovely as the day is long." Snapping out of his trance, he drew his attention back to Jason and clapped him on the shoulder. "Can you not see that I have turned green with envy? Come"—he tugged at his arm—"let me beat you at a game of chess. 'Tis the least you can do for an ill-treated guest."

12

The towering boughs of the forest that bordered the south side of the house formed a dense ceiling over Katy as she picked her way along a little-used path. Granite boulders and dead tree trunks were strewn like bones, and the air, untouched by the sun's warmth, was cold. She had just about been banished from the house this morning, some conspiracy on the part of Mercy. "Today is thy holiday," the girl had insisted before shooing her out of the house. "Take one of the horses and go riding, or take a book down to the rocks and spend the day reading, but please, just go. Hast been working too hard, and today I forbid thee to do anything."

Katy had acquiesced without much fuss, first because Mercy seemed distraught about the condition of her mistress, and second because she was still rather hurt about the previous night and thought that a sight-seeing tour might improve her spirits. She had gone to the barn to saddle Asticou, but finding him gone, decided to explore afoot instead.

The path she followed swept away from the shoreline and penetrated inland, but after walking for an hour she found herself standing on the edge of a precipice that overlooked a white beach whose sand relected the sun like snow crystals. She shielded her eyes but quickly drew her brows together as she noticed that a horse was tethered to a length of driftwood and that the horse was none other than Asticou.

"Hhmph."

Low, foamy waves washed the sand, depositing long strips of seaweed and kelp along the shore. The water at its shallowest point shone lime green, then melted into a deeper blue that caught the sun's rays and sparkled its brilliance, yet nowhere did a human form stir. Katy frowned as she regarded Asticou once again. How had he come to be here?

A dark form in the water suddenly caught her attention, and she narrowed her eyes for a better view. A head bobbed out of the depths, then disappeared below a wave. When next she spied the form, it had become attached to a body and was emerging from the sea like some proud aquatic god. Only it was not a god.

It was Jason. A very wet, very naked Jason.

As he dashed the water from his face and pushed his hair back, she watched, her eyes clinging to him. Slowly he made his way across the beach toward Asticou. Katy could see that his skin had turned reddish-purple from the frigid Atlantic surf and that between his legs he was full and hard. The blood drained from her face and pumped into her loins. If he saw her . . .

Without thinking, she concealed herself behind a wide-trunked spruce. She did not feel guilty about invading his privacy, rationalizing that anyone who chanced swimming in the nude in broad daylight was in constant jeopardy of being discovered. What she could not admit, even to herself, was that she had no desire to remove her eyes from the man, so great was the pleasure of observing the powerful rhythm of his body.

He grabbed a linen towel from his saddlebag and whisked it over his salty skin till the hair on his chest curled into crisp, dry ringlets. Invigorated, he linked his fingers together and stretched his arms above his head, sucking in his stomach below his rib cage until it appeared that front would meet back. At length he drew on his breeches, but pricked by a strange sensation, canted his head to the side and looked askance at the cliff to his right. Katy ducked back behind the tree and held her breath. For an interminable amount of time she stood with her back pressed against the cool bark, listening to her heart pound in her throat. When she finally mustered enough courage to peek around the tree again, Jason was atop his horse and pacing slowly down the strand. When he reached the opposite end, he nudged Asticou to the right and then both horse and rider were swallowed up behind the dunes and tall grass.

At supper that evening she kept her eyes averted by staring into her plate, for she feared that if she lifted her face to Jason, he would detect the fiery warmth that burned her pupils with the vision of him emerging naked from the surf—a vision that had haunted her all afternoon, dooming her to long lapses of unrest and alternating flashes of hot and cold. Jason mistook her prolonged silence for anger, thinking her still upset over his behavior of the night before, but since it was not his policy to make amends in front of the entire household, he did not try to coax her out of her withdrawal by flowery apologies. He would do that later, in private.

When the meal was finished, Katy rushed up to her room, hoping to avoid any further contact with her husband. In the library, Jason closed his eyes to imagine the activities that would be occupying his wife as the minutes ticked by. When forty-five minutes had elapsed, he rose and mounted the stairs himself, stopping before Katy's door.

From where she stood, peering languidly out the balcony doors, she bade the caller enter, and turning, was instantly taken aback. "Jason!" She blushed, for she had just been dwelling on a most provocative image of him. "I . . . I thought you were Mercy."

"Lord preserve her from becoming the size of me. No man would ever have her." He hesitated by the door. "May I come in?"

"Of course. Come in." She was surprised that her voice reflected an inner calm that was not there, but was worried that her eyes would betray her true feelings. Could unladylike thoughts change the color of one's eyes? For indeed, with the bend of her thoughts today, her irises should be blazing red.

Jason closed the door behind him, then strode casually to the love seat, much the same way, Katy thought, as he had walked across the sand today with the sun beating down on his glistening flesh. The blush mantling her cheeks deepened.

"Come." Jason beckoned to her. "I have need to talk with you."

She hastily flung a wrap over her nightgown before seating herself in a chair opposite him. His voice touched her with its deep resonance.

"Are you still angry with me?"

She looked perplexed. "Angry?"

"You were so quiet at supper. I thought perhaps you were still piqued at me for my behavior last night."

"Oh, that." She stared at his hands. "Your behavior was most ungracious in front of your guest, and you were not overly kind to me either, but I swallowed my outrage at breakfast and spent the rest of the day soothing my bruised feelings. I would venture that I am back to normal again."

"Well, then, I will not detain you long." Already the sight of her lightly clad body was sending erotic messages to his loins. "I have come for two reasons. First, to apologize for making such an ass out of myself last night. I said things to both you and Elisha that I had no right to say, and I'm sorry. It's just"—he clenched his hands into fists—"it just galled me to see Elisha kiss you like that!" He shrugged shoulders that she knew to be smooth and tanned beneath his shirt. "I lost my head."

"And your temper."

"Aye. It seems that has become my destiny. I have become so irascible that I cannot even be sportive around my friends."

She studied the disconsolate look upon his face, realizing that she was the cause of his torment, and inwardly she felt ashamed. "You said there were two reasons you came to see me. I have

243

already forgiven you for making an ass of yourself. Now, for what other deed do you seek forgiveness?''

Her voice was so ridiculously authoritative that he lifted his eyes to her and laughed despite himself. ''The deed for which I would seek forgiveness, I have not yet performed, as you well know. What I came to speak to you about is my leaving.''

The green eyes that had been veiled beneath thick lashes flew open. ''Leaving?'' The blossom of affection which had rooted so fragilely in her heart seemed to wither. ''You . . . you are going back to sea?''

Jason was thunderstruck, for never did he expect so violent a reaction to so simple a statement. Yet he was not displeased. Could she become so distraught at the mere thought of his going away if she cared nothing for him? He thought not. ''I will be gone for four days only, Katy, and if you would care to come along, I need not leave you at all.''

Much relieved, she exhaled the breath she had been holding. ''Where are you going?''

Jason leaned back on the sofa and caressed her with his eyes. ''I have promised to take the women to Boston for their annual shopping spree, and since Elisha is sailing there two days hence, I thought to kill two birds with one stone. We can sail down with him and back with Obediah Breed, and while the women are spreading my money about Boston, I can sell my cargo at the mercantile house and see about procuring staples for the coming year. If you wish to come along, you may find it more pleasant than the previous two times you visited that port. Will you lend us the pleasure of your company?'' He had no intention of telling her that she would be forced to share a room with him at the inn or that she would be sleeping with him again despite any objection she might might raise.

Katy's thoughts, however, had not traveled beyond the room at the end of the hall. ''If all of us leave, who will take care of Clare?''

''Riley will still be here, Abigail Breed has offered to cook meals, and Marian Pettyface, a friend of my mother's from the village, has agreed to sit with her while we're gone. 'Tis all arranged.''

''But, Jason,'' and as she spoke, her mind held an image of pale eyes downcast in the humiliation that comes from having to rely on someone else to perform the most intimate tasks for her, ''Riley cannot change her bedsheets and her clothing after she has . . . well . . .'' How could she phrase it gently? ''Nature still has its way with her. Her bodily functions have not ceased. You cannot entrust such personal care to strangers.''

"Strangers? Abigail and Marian are hardly strangers."

"You don't understand. Your mother is mortified each time one of *us* has to care for her, is still embarrassed when she must uncover the sores which torment her. How do you think she would feel if she were forced to endure such an intimacy from someone outside her family? I would want no one to see me, Jason. I think Clare would feel the same way."

Jason regarded his wife anew, touched by the sensitivity she displayed. "You seem to possess an understanding of things which I would never stop to consider," he reflected. "What do you suggest we do?"

"Is that not obvious? You will take the ladies to Boston and I will remain here with your mother. Mercy can buy the few things that I need."

"Your intentions are commendable, my love, but I don't think you are strong enough to lift my mother and change bedsheets by yourself. Mayhap I can convince one of the girls to remain instead of you."

"You will do no such thing," she protested. "I am perfectly capable of caring for one woman who weighs no more than myself, and I will not have you dampening everyone's spirits by forbidding either Mercy or Desire to accompany you. Allow me to do this, Jason. I am not so frail as you would think."

To grant her request would be to deny his own pleasure, but so intent did she seem upon proving herself that he could not even think about saying no. "Very well, Katy." As he stood up, he raked his fingers through his blue-black hair. "You do both Clare and me a great service by wanting to remain here, and I will not refuse your generosity, but I do insist that Marian and Abigail come to help you."

She nodded her assent. "If you insist," she said, and rising, followed her husband's footsteps to the door. That he seemed both anxious and hesitant to leave was apparent as he massaged the back of his neck.

"I hope the next few days will not be too much of a drain on you, Katy. There are roses in your cheeks now." He brushed the back of his fingers lightly down her face. "I would not want them to fade." His hand came to rest on the soft curve adjoining her neck and shoulder; then, flicking his fingers, he unburdened her shoulders of the wrap and allowed his eyes to dwell on the womanly curves silhouetted beneath the nightgown. He felt the warmth of her body, fought for the iron control which waned more with each passing second.

"Perhaps when I return . . ." He searched her face fully before completing his sentence, but mistaking the tenseness in

245

her posture for fear rather than anticipation, he judged it better to let his thought pass unsaid and dropped his hand to his side, away from temptation. "Never mind. Sometimes I would like to forget that I am a man of my word."

"If you were not a man of your word, I would not be your wife," she murmured.

Jason closed his eyes as if he were concentrating on something too painful to endure visually. When he opened them again, they were opaque and jaded. "Wife," he breathed. "I oft wonder if things would have been different had I bedded you that first night aboard ship and gotten the damn thing over with. Now . . ." He shook his head. "Now the waiting is so intolerable that I have to labor physically from dawn to dusk to keep my hands busy and my mind occupied with anything that will divert my thoughts from you. My resistance is wearing down and I become more irritable with my unsated lust. I snap when I should laugh; I growl when I should console; and now, my love, I leave when I should be easing my passion. You have transformed me into a strange beast, Mary Kathleen MacAuley—one that I am not at all sure I understand."

She would have liked to tell him to stay, to talk with her, to hold her, to explain to her the emotions she was feeling, but he had kissed her softly on the cheek and closed the door before she found her voice.

"If I have tormented you, husband, you are paying me back in kind. I cannot erase you from my thoughts. And I think . . . I think I do not want to." Her voice was barely audible, but this hushed utterance of words she had thought herself incapable of speaking touched her spirit with joy.

The next two days were a blur of activity and confusion in which Katy hardly had time to draw an unhurried breath. While readying Jason's clothes for his trip, she was subjected to Hannah's tart dissertations on what should or should not be done in everyone's absence. Arrangements had been made so that Mrs. Pettyface would remain overnight the three nights that the family was away. Abigail Breed would lend a hand only during the day. Katy agreed to the plans, though she thought them mostly unnecessary, especially after meeting Marian Pettyface, a rotund widow whose birdlike mouth chirped incessantly about the most uninteresting subjects. Katy moaned inwardly, considering what a great injustice they were leveling upon Clare. Poor Clare. Perhaps the woman's constant drone would lull her to sleep.

Jason spent a good part of the same forty-eight hours in town with Elisha, reading cargo lists and estimating prices. When he was home, however, his eyes pursued Katy with an intensity that she found alarmingly uncomfortable. Whether she brushed a strand of hair from her face or reached for something at the dinner table, his eyes were there, watching, haunting.

So it was that on the morning of his departure, as the house echoed with female voices shouting last-minute instructions at each other, he wandered into the kitchen seeking respite from the pandemonium. As he entered the room, he was struck first by the silence and then by the sight of his wife bent over a barrel, groveling into its depths. He laughed to himself, thinking that if he had not ogled this same lovely little rump a thousand times before, he might be in a quandary over the girl's identity. But having done a fair amount of ogling, he crossed his arms and quietly admired the scene.

He heard her mutter something deep within the barrel, then grunt as she yanked herself aright, a half-dozen slimy fish poking out of her hands. She wrinkled her nose and grimaced, then endured a sudden start as Jason's voice rolled into peals of laughter. With her hair pinned in disarray atop her head and her face smudged with what looked like salt, she still appeared quite the most irresistible sight he had seen in a long time. She stared back at him, wide-eyed and perplexed, but looking down at herself and imagining what an unkempt wretch she must appear, she shrugged her shoulders and joined in his laughter.

When at last she set the fish on the sideboard and dried her eyes, her voice still rang with amusement. "If we ate more beef and less fish, you would not have to see me like this."

"We eat what is readily available. Besides, who else would provide me with such entertainment if it were not for you sticking yourself into a hogshead of cod?" As he brushed his sleeve across his eyes, he was aware that this comic outburst had relieved much of the tension that had been strangling him for the past few days. He also became keenly aware of the serenity that surrounded his wife and how her tranquil mood differed from the bedlam in the rest of the house. Here he had found a haven. She exuded quiet dignity and seemed completely impervious to the bustling sounds outside the kitchen—twittering sounds which made him impatient for the company of men. He was impressed with her cool manner and smiled to think that this gentle beauty might someday come to love him.

At this thought, the amusement in his eyes faded, and in its place was kindled a spark of light that flamed slowly yet steadily. Elisha would want to leave soon to catch the tide. Too soon for Jason's purposes.

"Wipe your hands, love. I want to show you something."

" 'Tis time for you to leave, is it not? You don't have time to—"

"Please, Katy. Just do as I ask."

It was the gentle, pleading quality in his voice that caused her to frown as she rinsed her hands and wiped them on her apron. But if she was confused by his request, she was even more confused when he took her hand and led her out the back door toward the stand of pine that separated the house from the barn. She ran behind him, unable to keep pace with his long stride, and wondered what he could possibly want to show her at this moment that he had not thought important enough to show her before.

As they entered the forest, she tugged at his hand, implying that he should slow down, but he did not slacken his step and continued along the well-worn path.

"The cows have already been milked, Jason," she panted, thinking that it was to the barn he led her, but no sooner had she verbalized her thoughts than he swung away from the trail and into the denser part of the wood, her hand still firmly in tow. Her eyebrows drew into a V as she peered about her. "Just where are you taking me?"

In answer he thrust her against a tree and pressed his body into hers. Of a sudden his hands were everywhere—loosing the pins from her hair, dropping them to the ground, weaving his fingers through the heavy, unbound tresses that fell around her face.

"Jason!" She squirmed, trying to free herself, but found that she was solidly wedged between the tree and her husband's lean muscles. "Someone might see us!"

"Let them." The huskiness in his voice left no doubt as to the desire that raged within him. He kissed her ungently, his mouth crushing hers with a brutality that caused his body to tremble, his breath to come in uneven pants. Released from her initial fright, she responded slowly to his passion, testing her willingness in his arms. That she had ceased to connect her husband with the man in her nightmares was an idea newly formed in her mind, yet one which allowed her to separate fantasy from reality and to realize that Jason was flesh and blood, not the ephemeral madman who haunted her dreams.

Forcing her lips apart with his mouth, he pressed the hardness that swelled between his thighs into her hip, and she could do naught but yield to his superior strength. Their tongues touched in tender union. A delicate sensation of warmth and moisture impressed itself upon Katy. She fondled the back of Jason's neck with timid fingers, not knowing what else to do or where else to touch him, in awe of his power.

Hearing her moan softly, Jason embraced her face within his hands and eased his lips away from her. A fine veneer of perspiration glossed her cheeks and forehead, her lips parted invitingly, and Jason, afraid that this could be some malicious trick to repay him for his numerous misdeeds, wrapped her hair around his hand and pulled her head back to search her beautiful face with an intensity that would have made the stoutest of men cringe.

"Katy"—his voice was low and grave—"do you play me false?"

She returned his gaze, and in the purity of her eyes he saw her innocence and confusion and knew that her response was no jest. His loins tightened in anticipation. "Can you love me a little, lady? You are my wife. Will you not let me love you?"

He leaned over and heard her breath quicken as he grasped her earlobe softly between his teeth and drew the lobe into his mouth, stroking it with the tip of his tongue. With one hand caressing the back of her neck and the other at her hip, he brushed his lips across the smoothness of her cheek, quieted her mouth beneath the firmness of his own, and ever so slowly lowered her to the ground, pillowing her head on his forearm. Above her she saw a tapestry of evergreen boughs, a flash of blue sky, and then the dark handsomeness of her husband as he lowered his face to hers. His lips were tender, probing. His fingers slid from her cheek to the base of her throat, where he began to unloop the tiny buttons of her gown, laying bare skin that was cool and satiny, like polished marble. Parting the material, he enclosed his hand around the fullness of her breast, then traced a hot path from lips to throat, and as she held his head, he found her soft crown of damson-colored flesh with his mouth and kissed it slowly, sensuously, feeling her shudder beneath him. As he plied and excited, her breath started to fray, coming in short, quick pants. Delicious sensations rooted where his tongue was stroking her and spread across her breasts and down her legs. She clawed at his back, at the ridges of muscle that flexed beneath his skin. He eased one of her hands away from its pursuit and cupped it around the bone-hard muscle between his legs.

"I love you, Katy." His breath was warm against her. Her head felt thick, as though it were veiled in mist. "Say you love me." His face was above hers again, his lips tasting the corners of her mouth. "Say it."

But she could say nothing. She was shrouded in a web of fine golden threads, and in this ethereal floating world, words were elusive. Her mouth was dry and parched. Her lips throbbed sweetly. Somewhere she heard her husband's voice, soft, like a lullaby, but unintelligible.

"Say it," he pressed.

Their mouths fused in a clash of tongues, teeth, and lips, and Jason's presence of mind melted with the fire. With a singleness of purpose he slid his hand beneath the hem of her gown to find soft, downy flesh, unencumbered, virginal. The hand moved of its own volition, caressing the curve of her calf and thigh, upward toward a round hip and a silky smooth stomach, then downward. She felt a sudden dampness where he touched her, and although his mouth consumed her with a burning beyond imagination, the hand that rested motionless on her soft rise of maiden flesh hinted at sensations of a far more consuming nature, and she held her breath.

"Tell me, Katy," he rasped. "Tell me you love me."

In the distance a door banged loudly and Mercy's voice drifted out to them. "Captain! *Caaptainnn!*"

Jason's hand tensed. Damn. He had known this would happen.

"*Caaptainnn!* The buckboard is ready! Riley says we must be leaving! Captain!"

Reluctantly he withdrew his hand and looked down at his wife. Her lips were red and swollen, her cheeks tinged with a sensual flush, her feathery lashes dark against her skin, her breathing shallow as a kitten's. Bending his head, he kissed her forehead protectively.

"Katy?"

She fought the sopor that transformed her bones into lifeless rags, and willed her eyelids open. Her green gaze fell seductively upon her husband, who caught the hand that she extended to his face, kissing the palm tenderly.

"I must leave, Katy. Mercy will be beating a path through here any moment if I don't make a swift appearance. But perhaps when I return . . ."—he paused, his voice tenuous—"we can resume where we left off today."

She smiled, placed a fingertip on his lips. "When you return . . ." she whispered.

Much encouraged despite the fact that she had not professed her love, Jason cupped the breast that was still exposed to him and placed a scalding kiss in the hollow of the girl's throat. "Lady," he groaned as he unfolded himself from around her, his unflagging lust still readily apparent, "this is sheer hell. I pray the next four days will pass quickly." When he had stood and brushed the pine needles from his clothing, he cast a wistful look at his bride and rubbed his neck with a heavy hand. "Four days," he anguished. "Just four days. Do not move from that spot." With that, he started in the direction of Mercy's shouts and soon disappeared from sight.

Katy stretched like a tamed feline and wiggled her toes and fingers. *Four days*. She dropped her hand to her abdomen, wondering at the quivering contractions there, and pondered what magnificent things Jason would have wrought with his hand if Mercy had not beckoned. *Four days*. Bracing an arm behind her head, she smiled at the verdant bower above her. Four days might pass quickly. But not quickly enough.

In the days that had passed since Jason's departure, Katy had thought she would burst from the joy that bubbled within her. Even when she attempted to be serious, she could feel a smile crawling across her lips, and although she could tame the upward curve of her mouth, she could not disguise the buoyancy in her eyes. No task was too great for her to perform, no detail too small for her to devote her attention to. She felt herself imbued with an infinite reserve of energy and knew that if she were called upon to do so, she would be capable of moving mountains.

She saw to Clare's needs as if she had been reared from childhood to perform this one function, and always with a smile lighting her face and a cheery tune on her lips. Having accepted the burden joyfully, she was not aware of its weight, so while others might have complained, she thrived.

She was in love, and the world became a touchstone for new perceptions. She was finding that there was much beauty even in the meanest of creatures—beauty which she had never seen before. She even learned to tolerate Mrs. Pettyface's mindless prattle at the dinner table. Marian's steady buzz served as a backdrop for Katy's thoughts, and these thoughts always focused on one thing—Jason. His taste. His touch. His extraordinary capacity to love her, wholely, as no one had done before—to love her as she had never loved herself.

Aboard the *Minotaur*, Jason had withdrawn into a euphoric state of reticence that prompted more than one person to look askance at him. Elisha could not fathom the reason for his friend's preoccupation. Although Jason was quiet, he was not in a foul temper, and usually with Jason, one accompanied the other. He had spent the entire journey to Boston in the bow of the ship, staring silently out to sea, and no one had dared disturb him. In Boston he had transacted business at the mercantile house with his customary aplomb, obtaining a veritable fortune from his cargo, but when Elisha suggested celebrating their windfall in one of Boston's finest brothels, he had politely refused.

On the day before the family was expected to return to the island, Katy stood smiling over two dozen cod she had just finished scrubbing—not with satisfaction at having completed a messy job, but from the fluttering that beset her stomach at the thought of her husband's return. She glowed with an inner warmth, and Abigail Breed could not help but notice. The girl was obviously so much in love that she had been able to think of nothing else for the past three days except the husband who was not here. It was not difficult to discern the thoughts masked by the girl's lovely face, for she was radiant in every respect, as only new brides are.

"I have never seen anyone smile quite like that at a bunch of cod before," Abigail teased.

Katy, feeling her cheeks darken with red smudges, picked up another cod and started scrubbing it self-consciously. " 'Twas not of the fish I was thinking."

"So I gathered. You miss him very much."

"Is it that obvious?"

"Aye. Anyone who can smile at both a dead fish and Marian's narrations has to be thinking about something else. And you needn't blush in front of me. I know many women who would love to get their hands on Jason MacAuley. 'Tis only fitting that his wife should want to."

As the fluttering in her stomach persisted, Katy took a deep breath, trying to compose herself. "Have you any idea when they'll be back tomorrow?"

"Sometime after sundown, I suppose. With Hannah aboard ship, Obediah will not dare to fly full sail."

From the backyard a sharp wail sounded from Abigail's youngest son, David. The woman shook her head as she wiped her hands on her apron. "How many times does that make today?" Winking, she opened the door and disappeared into the backyard to soothe her three-year-old's wounds, but Katy had suddenly become distracted by another sound—horse hooves and . . . wagon wheels? Had they returned early? And she looking like one of the fish she had been scrubbing!

Ripping her apron off, she ran to a basin of water and rubbed her hands fiercely with a bar of lye soap until the slime that scabbed her skin peeled off. She had wanted to smell like wildflowers for him today, not salt cod. Bosh! Outside, the wheels had stopped, and unable to contain herself any longer, she lifted her skirt and dashed through the hall, opened the front door, and ran headlong into a body that was hard as a brick wall, but not her husband's.

She looked up. "Fergus!"

252

The man swooped her off the floor and into his arms in one movement, hugging her like a great bear. She threw her arms around his neck. "You've been gone so long! I thought you were never coming back!"

"But I told you I'd be back. Do yer think I'd be one to break my word, lass?" He laughed his low, grumbling laugh as she squeezed him. "And if you don't let go my neck, you'll soon have it broken!" Unwrapping her arms from around him, he set her back on her feet. "Now, let me have a look at you. 'Tis Mrs. MacAuley I am addressing, is it not?"

Twirling around briefly as Fergus indicated with his finger, she stopped and laughed into his eyes. "I have been Mrs. MacAuley for one month now."

"And you áre happy, Mary Kathleen?" he asked seriously.

"Can you not tell?"

Fergus lowered bristly brows over his eyes and scrutinized her. "I would say . . . that you are happy. That miserable husband of yours is treating you well?"

"Not so well," she confessed. "He has left me."

Fergus' chest puffed up to twice its size as he bellowed out, *"Left you?"* But Katy grabbed the fist he had made and smoothed it out within her own gentle grasp before he had a chance to yell again.

"Not permanently," she amended. "Only for four days. Did you not see him in Boston?"

"Nay. We left Boston five days ago." In answer to Katy's puzzled look, he continued. "You'll be wondering why it took us five days to reach home. Well, we stopped at several places along the coast on our way back. Boston is not the only place where a man can strike a bargain. Isn't that right, Daniel?"

As he moved his great hulk of a body to one side, Daniel English stepped onto the porch, and Katy felt her knees begin to shake. "Daniel . . ." Although her voice was no more than a brittle whisper, the soft tone could not dissemble her unease. The boy's thin lips turned upward into a smile, but there was no humor in the hazel eyes.

"Hello, Katy. I suppose congratulations are in order."

"Daniel . . . 'tis . . . 'tis good to see you again."

Fergus frowned at the ensuing silence with fatherly tolerance but was quick to take up the slack. "Have both of you reached the limits of your conversation? One would think you were strangers. You have a new bride standing afore you, Daniel. The least you can do is shake her hand to wish her luck, or have you forgotten every bit of courtesy that was ever taught you?"

The blond sailor flung a cocky look at the Irishman before he clutched Katy's forearms, pulled her to him, and kissed her so roughly that tears welled in her eyes. Even Jason had never kissed her with such anger. Deep within her the old fear returned and riffled through her bones. Frantically she pressed her hands against his chest and pushed herself away from him. She drew her hand across her lips and narrowed her eyes. "Do you favor all your old friends with such a greeting?" Her voice was caustic.

Daniel stepped back. He had been living with his hurt for so long that he had been blinded by it. Now, as he saw the tears glistening in her eyes, he realized what he had done and he was ashamed. "I'm sorry, Katy." He reached a suppliant hand toward her, but when she refused to accept it, he let it fall to his side. "I'm sorry."

Looking grimly at the pair, Fergus moved toward Daniel and placed his large hand on the boy's shoulder. "You must forgive him, Mary Kathleen. I think he is still bruised from having you stolen from under his nose. But he will get over it." Holding the hazel eyes to his own, he added with a warning smile, "He had better get over it."

Collecting her scattered wits about her, Katy remembered her duties as hostess and gestured the men into the house.

Between bits of cheese and gulps of ale they listened to Fergus relate his adventures of the past month. Katy related only the barest details of her marriage ceremony, but dwelt more on how she had found Ian and Elizabeth and how she had been occupying herself since arriving on the island.

"So what do you think of our paradise here? Is it not the most beautiful place on earth?" Fergus asked.

Katy hesitated to answer. "I have not seen much of the island," she admitted. "You told me that you would guide me personally throughout the area when you returned, so I have waited patiently for your escort."

Fergus' brows drew together in a bushy ridge. "You mean to tell me that Jason MacAuley did not insist on giving you a tour of the island and introducing you to his friends himself?"

"Oh, he insisted, but I was quite adamant about waiting for you."

"Indeed? Well, I imagine he will have a few choice words to say to me when he returns. But now that *I'm* back, we needn't postpone our excursion any longer. I'll be by for you early tomorrow morning and treat you to your first thorough glimpse of paradise. When do you expect your husband back?"

"Tomorrow sometime."

"Good. That will leave you free this afternoon."

Katy wrinkled her slightly upturned nose at him. "Free for what?"

"For you and Daniel to run an errand for me while I'm passing the time of day with Clare."

"Mrs. Pettyface is with her now."

"Oh, Lord." He laid the heel of his palm against his forehead and grimaced. "I have known men's hair to turn white waiting for Marian to finish saying hello. I do not have an entire week, only an afternoon, and I have no desire to have my time monopolized by Magpie Marian." He scratched his head thoughtfully. "Is Riley here?"

She nodded.

"I'll have him hitch up the buckboard, and you be telling Marian that Jason will be back soon and you no longer require her services. I'll make myself scarce, and don't you dare tell her where I might be hiding. While you and Daniel are gone, I'll see to the lass upstairs. Understood?"

Within the hour Marian Pettyface was seated on the buckboard beside Riley, heading back to Cromwell Harbor. She had been thanked and paid generously by Katy who insisted that the woman return soon for a visit, and much to the girl's dismay, Marian agreed, saying that she would call again one week from today, on July 15. But Hannah would be home then, Katy thought, and Hannah would surely have no problem entertaining the village magpie.

With Marian gone, Fergus came out of hiding and hurried Katy and Daniel into his buckboard so they could be about his errand. Once on the carriage path, Daniel drove the team so recklessly that Katy bounced out of her seat. She threw a scathing look at him as she crawled back onto her perch. She already felt battered, but if she was visibly bruised when they returned to Oak Hill Cliff, Fergus would definitely hear about his fair-haired boy.

Almost as if Daniel could sense her intentions, he slowed the two horses to an even pace, then cast a sidelong glance at his beautiful companion. "Is *that* more to your liking?"

Katy sucked in one side of her cheek. "*That* is, but your attitude is not. Is this the kind of behavior I can expect from you from now on? Because if it is, I don't think I care to see you again."

He stared ahead woodenly. "Does it mean nothing to you that I love you?"

"Of course it means something to me! And I am deeply touched, but, Daniel, I cannot return your love. I . . . I love my husband." She had never admitted it aloud before. How strange it sounded coming from her lips.

"You can love him knowing what kind of man he is? After he ran off with that prostitute under your very nose in Boston?"

Yes, that had bothered her, just as his episode with Desire had infuriated her, but she was willing to forget all that now. "He is a man." She shrugged. "Is it not common for men to indulge in such pleasures?"

"You have acquired a strange sense of morals, Katy."

"And you have acquired a strange sense of justice."

They rode for a while in contemplative silence before Daniel spoke again. "If you truly love him, then I have lost all."

"Nay, Daniel." She laid her hand on his arm. "Can we not share each other's company as one friend to another?"

"I doubt that your husband will condone the arrangement. If you were mine"—he looked at her then, and his eyes mirrored the pain in his heart—"I would let no man near you."

"Well, thank goodness I am not yours." She laughed. "I should become most ill-natured if I were locked in an ivory tower."

Daniel grunted feebly and stared at the reins in his hands.

"Friends?" The light green eyes that questioned his were so captivating that he could do naught but sigh in defeat.

"Friends," he conceded.

By this time they had reached Fergus' property, and as Daniel turned down the drive to the house, Katy found herself becoming curious. "Fergus did not tell me the reason for our errand. I assume *you* know?"

"Aye."

She waited for the answer, which did not come. "Well?"

"You will see." He grinned.

Daniel drew up rein before a dark brown saltbox that was not so grand as the stone house at Oak Hill Cliff, but nonetheless imposing. It was almost crude in its simplicity, yet there was latent strength in the way the clapboards were fitted and meshed, almost in defiance of nature; it reminded Katy very much of Fergus himself. Daniel helped her to the ground, then led her through the front door of the two-story structure. " 'Tis so quiet," she breathed. The smell of stale air permeated the house, affirming the fact that neither doors nor windows had been opened in over a year. Sheets blanketed every stick of furniture, and a narrow shaft of light punctured the dimness through a single small window, illuminating motes of dust.

"William must be out back."

"William?" Katy followed him through the dining room and into the kitchen.

"Aye. William Briggs. Fergus brought him back from Boston

to help us with the repairs to the house. Nice-enough sort. Doesn't say too much.''

''He must be related to Riley,'' she mumbled to herself. Surveying the barren kitchen with a woman's eye, she shook her head hopelessly. ''I think you may need all the help you can muster to clean this place up. Perhaps I'll come by to lend you some assistance.'' She traced her finger through the dust on the sideboard, then blew the particles off her fingertip. ''Men know nothing about housework.''

''Be my guest. And by the way, men know nothing about cooking, either.''

''That, Mr. English, you may learn for yourself.'' Her attention was suddenly drawn to the back door as it was kicked open to admit a man whose torso and face were hidden behind an armful of firewood. When the man stumbled over the threshold, Daniel ran over to lend some asssitance.

''Thanks,'' the man rasped as he emptied his arms of their burden on the hearthstones. Turning, he brushed himself off with a few rough gestures and was about to say something more to Daniel when he became aware of another presence in the room.

Katy masked her shock with difficulty. The man's complexion was the color and texture of lumpy gruel—shiny where the skin was stretched tautly over thick ridges of scar tissue, puckered where one ridge dipped to another. Above one eye the lid drooped lifelessly over an iris of indistinguishable color. The man was neither young nor old, the cruel mask of his face either chopping years off his age or adding years to it, she could not tell which. Yet he was scrutinizing her as if *she* were the spectacle, making her feel much like an exotic insect in a glass jar. Had Daniel not been within sight, she would have bolted.

''Your wife, Daniel?'' William Briggs grated. The quality of his voice was so abrasive that Katy felt chilly cat paws race up her spine at the sound.

''I am not that lucky a man, Will,'' Daniel replied as he sauntered to Katy's side. ''This is Katy Ry . . . Katy MacAuley. *Mrs.* MacAuley.''

A sentiment other than pleasure flickered in Briggs's muddy eye as he tipped his head to her. ''Fergus' Mary Kathleen. My pleasure.''

''Mr. Briggs,'' she managed to choke out by way of greeting. Daniel should have warned her about the man's appearance. But would any amount of warning have prepared her to meet this man and not react so violently? What horrible thing had befallen him? ''Uh . . . Daniel tells me that you are here to help Fergus with the repairs to his house. It seems you may have taken on

257

more than you bargained for." She indicated the chaos surrounding them.

"A man in my situation takes what he can get."

"Your situation?" she asked, confused.

"There aren't many people around who'll hire a man with a face pretty as mine. Would you want to look at me all day, Mrs. MacAuley?"

Her mouth opened, but words did not form. "I . . ." Why had she been gawking like a goose? Of course he had noticed.

When it became apparent that her tongue was in irons, Daniel slid an arm around her shoulders and squeezed tightly. "If you proved yourself worth your mettle, I warrant Katy would be delighted to look at you all day, Will. Actually, your face isn't that bad. I've seen fish who looked worse!" Daniel chuckled at his own clever attempt to mitigate tensions, but when he saw that William Briggs was not sharing in the humor of the comment and was staring at him oddly, Daniel wiped the smile from his mouth.

"You'll excuse me now," Briggs said in his scratchy voice. "I need to see about hauling the rest of that wood in here."

Daniel motioned for him to stop. "Before you go, would you mind helping me load that trunk that's in the parlor onto the buckboard? I think Fergus has crammed too much into it for me to handle alone."

"Sure, if you can take your hands off Mrs. MacAuley long enough to come into the next room with me." He twisted his mouth into a cruel smile as he headed toward the parlor. Daniel followed, having dropped his hand self-consciously from around Katy's shoulder.

Outside, Katy stared at the large leather-bound trunk that had just been hoisted onto the buckboard. "What's in it, Daniel?"

"Things. For you."

Her eyes leaped with childish excitement. "For me? What?"

Waving his hand toward the chest, he laughed. "Why not see for yourself? 'Tis not locked." She did not need to be asked a second time. Daniel boosted her up on the back of the wagon, and with deft fingers she loosened the leather bindings and flung the lid open, her eyes becoming wide at the array of finery that stared back at her.

"Oh, Daniel!" She brushed her fingers across the rainbow of materials packed within—Moravian worked muslin, clear French lawns with elegant figures and spots, cambric and calico, muslins painted with chintz patterns and worked in colored sprigs, dresses in shades of pale canary, sky blue, dove pearl, lemon and lilac, pomona green. "How did you come by these things?" she gasped. "There must be . . . a dozen dresses in here!" And not only dresses, she discovered, but frilly lingerie, chemises, nightgowns and wraps, bonnets, cloaks, kid and satin slippers. She searched Daniel's delighted face. "I don't understand. How did you know what . . .?"

He motioned her to silence with a gesture of his hand. "We only bought what the message said to buy."

"What message?"

"I believe it was on the morning that you people arrived in Boston last month. There was a note in Fergus' cabin instructing him what he should purchase for the new bride and what sizes to order, handwritten by your husband."

"Truly?" Removing a narrow black leather case from the trunk, she unlatched the cover to find an Augsburg three-barreled flintlock pistol nestled in red velvet. Folded within was a note from Fergus explaining the purpose of the gift: "To Mary Kathleen—If you take another ocean voyage, you should learn to shoot this little beauty, and learn to shoot it well."

Anxious to arrive home so she might browse at length through her newly acquired treasures, Katy reclosed the trunk and scurried onto the front seat of the buckboard, then craned her neck to where Daniel still stood. "God's bones, are you still standing there? Hurry up, Daniel!"

The boy laughed at her well-intended cajolery. "Ah, what a greedy wench you become for a few silken threads." Jumping in beside her, he grabbed the reins and spurred the team forward.

"You'd become greedy too, if you had been condemned to wear the same gray gown day after day." She shouted to be heard over the din of horse hooves. He laughed again.

"If I were to don a gown, I would have more to worry about than the color!"

They completed the journey home in the best of spirits, Daniel cleverly imitating several Bostonian dressmakers and Katy holding her sides with laughter at the pinched and prunish faces he was making. He had forgotten how her eyes gleamed when she laughed, how sultry she looked with her hair blowing loosely in the wind. If he could not marry her, he could at least play the hospitable neighbor and visit her often, perhaps take her on rides such as this when Jason was at sea. If he were honorable and yet persistent, anything might happen. After all, it was not uncommon that men drowned at sea, even seemingly indestructible men like Jason MacAuley.

When they arrived back at Oak Hill Cliff, they were surprised to discover the three Meacham women bustling about in the foyer, their bags and baggage strewn from one end of the hall to the other. With the anticipation born of first love, Katy stood amid the confusion and quietly awaited the appearance of her husband. She wanted to run into his arms, to thank him, to love him, but Mercy's first words foiled all her expectations.

"We completed our shopping so quickly, mistress, that the captain sent us home a day early, but he instructed me to give thee his regards and to tell thee that he would see thee on the morrow. I hope my tidings have not disappointed thee too sorely."

It was a common enough statement to make to a person whose face had just registered the loss of her deepest wish.

13

Fergus arrived at seven o'clock the next morning to find Katy attired in a deep-necked, puff-sleeved muslin dress at which he could only shake his head. "I suggest that you march back into the house and get some fly dope from Hannah," he said as she led Asticou from the barn. "We may be around fresh water today, and I think the mosquitoes will find all that exposed flesh of yours much too tempting to resist."

"Fly dope?" She laughed.

"Aye. Doesn't smell too good, but it beats playing dinner to those damn insects. 'Tis a concoction of pennyroyal oil, tar oil—"

"Tar! Oh, no, Fergus," she choked, waving off his suggestion. "I will not paint myself black with tar just to ward off a few insects."

" 'Tis not black," he contradicted her. " 'Tis clear." Plucking Asticou's reins from her hands, he scooted her toward the house. "Now, be off with you to get that ointment. If we visit Prettymarsh, you'll be thankful for it."

Unconvinced but obedient, she ran on ahead of him to the house. Not finding Hannah, she had to swallow her pride and make her request of Desire instead. Desire rummaged about in the pantry for some time before emerging with a small bottle filled with a pale yellow liquid.

Although the day held a promise of warmth, the wind blew hard from the northeast. Fergus led Katy south on a little-used path through the island's forest of larch and red oak, paper birch, and quaking aspen. The cool shadows sent chill tremors racing across Katy's flesh but had scant effect on Fergus, who rode beside her, pointing out low-bushed blueberries and blackberries and pendant cones that littered the base of tall white pines. Occasionally a sliver of sunlight pierced the thicket of branches and fell upon a blushing wood lily.

They skirted around the mountain to the east and followed a narrow trail that gradually sloped upward. In the distance the roiling Atlantic lay in wait. To Katy's right, more granite peaks rose; to her left the terrain ceased abruptly and fell to a marshy hinterland at sea level. She recognized this sweep of land, however, and knew that beyond the brow of sand dunes on its southern flank, there was a well-remembered white-sand beach. The sudden memory of what she had seen that day dyed her cheeks a deep red.

Beyond the beach the island's granite ribs jammed together in a rugged bulwark against the sea, while overhead, herring gulls performed their aerial acrobatics. To the right of the path, a border of pitch pines twisted their knobby limbs into impossible contortions. And everywhere, there was granite: pink, gray, golden in the sun, black beneath the surf, green and gray with lichen.

They traversed the shore path at a leisurely pace and were soon ensconced in a dense forest of red spruce and blue-green balsam firs from whose boughs hung cobwebby lichens—called prophet's beard, Fergus said. Climbing a slight incline, they emerged from the woodland to be confronted by a frothy geyser that spumed high above the lip of the precipice before them, drenching them with salty rain. Katy steadied Asticou with a firm hand, then stared about her. Below them she could see the island's rocky flanks, a continuous ledge of granite that had been scored with long parallel cracks that seemed more the handiwork of a master sculptor than of nature. Otter Point, Fergus named the promontory.

They proceeded westward through the cool and fragrant evergreen forest that encompassed the Otter Cove inlet, and eventually passed by Hunter's Beach and Bracy's Cove.

Wending their way two miles to the north, they came upon a broad finger of sparkling water nested in a valley that was dwarfed on three sides by granite highlands. From the banks of the pond a lush forest marched upward to swathe Pemetic Mountain on the east and Penobscot Mountain on the west. At the northernmost tip of the tarn, two gently contoured bubble-shaped mountains burst forth from the landscape like Mother Nature's milk-laden breasts, and it was to these that Fergus directed his comment.

"They're called North Bubble and South Bubble, but I always had another name for them that no one ever seemed to appreciate."

Katy waited for a moment, then laughed. "Well, aren't you going to tell me?"

"Tell you? Mary Kathleen, 'tis not fit for such tender ears as yours."

Shaking her head, she slid down from Asticou and trailed her hand through the water.

"You ever get the impulse for a swim, lass, you come here to Jordan Pond. No one would ever bother you. People don't come here much, and it would be a lot safer than swimming where an undertow could drag you out to sea. Probably a helluva lot safer than bein' in the same room with that husband of yours when he's in a vile temper.''

She turned her face slightly to hide her blush, and quite accidentally noticed a small cabin hidden within a copse of maples. "What's that?" she asked, gesturing toward it.

Fergus peered over his shoulder. "Hunting camp. Used it lots when I was younger, but haven't used it much since then. Guess in my old age I enjoy being around people more than I enjoy traipsing about the woods with my flintlock.''

"Does anyone ever use it anymore?"

"What? The cabin?" He shook his head. "Naw. People this side of the island are too damn busy to hunt, and people the other side have their own forests and lakes. This place is about as private as they come.''

Katy made a mental note of the placid mountain lake, for if she ever sought respite from the Meacham women, this would be the place to come.

As they headed northeast toward Cromwell Harbor, Fergus stopped at various farms along the way to introduce Jason's wife to some of the island residents. She met more people that day than she would ever remember—the Manchesters, Higginses, Gilpatricks, Murphys, Savages, Obers, and Bartletts—each boasting large families with fine, strapping youngsters and each more curious than the other about the new MacAuley bride. Fergus whisked her in and out, but even during her brief visits Katy was impressed with the eloquence of these people's speech, with their dignity and sense of propriety. They were a self-sufficient and vigorous people, as rugged as their coastline and as independent as the birds that roamed the skies.

In Cromwell Harbor the putrid smell of fish was overpowering, but they lunched on a knoll overlooking the placid harbor, then headed northwest until they reached the rocky beaches of Hull's Cove, where the skeletons of sailing ships rested on massive ways high above the tidal waters, waiting for the skillful stroke of the master shipbuilder's chisel. Saws ground, adzes scraped against wood, hammers smashed against planks and reverberated within the curved ribs of the tall oak giants. The smells of pitch, tar, and freshly sawed lumber permeated the air.

Katy inhaled deeply. "Who owns all this?"

Fergus grinned. '' 'Tis yer husband's shipyard, Mary Kathleen. Has the lad not told you that you married a very wealthy man?''

Her mouth opened, then closed. "He . . . implied it once. I don't think I quite believed him.''

263

This tickled the Irishman, whose booming laughter continued for a long time after that.

The landscape on the western side of the island was not so dramatic as that on the eastern side. The land was flat, less rocky, and the air was filled not so much with a fresh salt tang as with the fetid smell of the muddy tidal flats. "Always smells this way at low tide." Fergus laughed as he noticed her wrinkling her nose. "You won't be noticing it so much on the other side of the island, because the water's deeper there. We dig for clams in those mud flats. I'll be having to show you how it's done, one day when Jason is out fishing."

While exploring this part of the island, she was surprised to discover that nearly every cove and inlet was the site of a ship-building operation of one kind or another. There were a great many more hayfields here than she had seen elsewhere, as well as smokehouses for herring, try houses for extracting oil from porgy and menhaden, and icehouses where huge blocks of ice cut from lakes and ponds during the winter were stored for summer refrigeration.

"You don't allow anything to go to waste, do you?" she quipped.

"Everything has some use, Mary Kathleen. Problem is discoverin' what it is."

As the late-afternoon sun cast orange highlights upon the earth, they reached Prettymarsh and from there set a course back through the interior of the island. Fergus seemed enormously content. "Well, what do you think of our little island?"

"Lovely, but by no means little. We still have more to see, don't we?"

"Aye. Another time we'll start at Prettymarsh and head south. Right now I think you must be tired."

"A little," she confessed.

After they had ridden some time in silence, Fergus asked, "Have you ever picked blueberries?"

"Blueberries?" She shook her head.

"Well, no tour of this island is complete until you've picked blueberries. Bring some back to Mercy and she'll show you how to make blueberry pie, blueberry cake, blueberry muffins, blueberry—"

Katy laughed at the man and his obsessive preoccupation with all things edible. They stopped at one of the salt marshes where Fergus was sure he had seen the berries flourishing at one time. After dismounting, he helped her down and dug the bottle of fly dope out of her saddlebag.

"Mind you, now, lass, put this all over your face and chest

and arms. This place is a breedin' ground for mosquitoes and blackflies, and they're not particular about where they bite you. I'll go on ahead to see if I can find a patch of berries."

"Don't you want any?" She removed the cork and held the bottle out to him, but he dismissed it with a gesture.

"My skin's too thick. They'll not bother me."

As he disappeared into the tall grass and reeds, Katy began to smear the ointment over her body, grimacing at the viscous substance. Something seemed not quite right, though. The ointment was just *too* gooey. Shrugging, she placed the bottle back in the saddlebag and headed off after Fergus. She found him crouched down in a section of short, weedy grass on the periphery of the swamp. She had already removed her hat, fanning it violently to cut a path through the insects that were buzzing around her.

Fergus heaved himself to his feet, laughing. "Told you you'd need that fly dope."

Having found a thicket of blueberries, Fergus picked several and rolled them around in his hand for her scrutiny before popping them into his mouth. "Delicious. 'Tis the best part of New England summers, these little berries. Almost makes our other nine months of winter weather worthwhile." Handing her one of the small sacks he had brought along with him, he indicated where the picking was best and said he would pick in a thicket a short distance away. When he had gone, Katy bent down and started plucking the berries from their stems with one hand and swatting mosquitoes with the other. The insects seemed to be increasing in number as the shadows lengthened over the land, and rather than deter the little devils, Hannah's fly dope only seemed to be attracting them. Hungry battalions swarmed about her, flying into her eyes and nostrils, buzzing in her ears, sinking their needles into her bare flesh, striping her with a mass of angry red welts. She scratched, batted the air, scratched again. The blackfly bites welled with tiny pools of blood that streamed across her skin. The mosquito bites swelled and became more inflamed. And still they swarmed about her. Buzzing inside her ears, around her mouth, in her hair, buzzing, stinging. . . .

"*Ferrrgusss!*" she shrieked, and dropping the sack of blueberries, clapped her hands over her ears and began to run toward him. "*Ferrrgusss!*"

Hearing her scream, Fergus dropped his sack and for a brief moment felt his heart stop. If anything had happened to her . . .

He let the thought go unfinished as he bounded back through the thickets toward the sound of her screams.

"Fergus!"

A deathly pallor entered his face when he caught sight of her, for she was scratched and bleeding and her eyes were wildly insane. She ran into the arms he opened to her and tried to bury her head beneath his waistcoat.

"They're eating me alive!"

Yanking off his coat, he wrapped it around her head and shoulders and swept her up into his rugged arms. He beat a path swiftly through the grassy marshland and within a matter of minutes had delivered them out of the realm of swarming insects. Setting her on her feet beside Asticou, he lifted his coat from her and stared ruefully at her wounds.

"How . . . ?" The word hung in the air. "Oh, Mary Kathleen, lass." He dug a handkerchief out of his waistcoat and began to dab at the bloody welts on her face, then fumbled for her hand as she raked her nails down her arm. "They'll only bleed the more if you scratch them. Rub gently if you must, but don't be scratching."

As he held her, he noted that his hand was sticking to the goo on her skin. "What in the bloody hell is in that fly dope?" He sniffed his fingertips suspiciously, then brought them to his tongue. "Honey. 'Tis naught but honey! You tell me how Hannah could mistake this for fly dope?" he raged. " 'Tis no wonder those damn insects attacked you like they did!"

Honey? She felt the heat mount in her face. Nay, Hannah would not make such a mistake. But Desire . . . Her clear green eyes slitted and smoldered with fire. Desire would do such a thing apurpose. The malicious bitch! Her outrage flamed as she scraped her knuckles against her tortured flesh. She would tear the bitch's hair out by the roots. She would . . . she would . . .

"Come about, lass." Without waiting for a reply, Fergus lifted her onto her saddle. "We've got to get something on those bites before the itching drives you mad, and then I aim to have a talk with Hannah Meacham."

"That will do you little good. 'Twas not—"

"Do not try to defend the woman," he cut her off. "I will speak my mind, and that's that."

"But, Fergus—"

"Say no more, Mary Kathleen. The matter is closed. Now, follow close behind me. We'll take a shortcut home."

By the time they arrived at Fergus' brown saltbox, the sky had become rippled with layers of deep golden clouds, thick and billowy like the froth of waves. Fergus tethered the horses, then led Katy through the back door into the kitchen, where William Briggs straddled a chair and whistled a strange tune as he carved delicate intricacies into a chunk of wood. The vision triggered a memory in the recesses of Katy's mind—long forgotten and obscure—of a steel blade biting into wood in another time, of hands working quickly, cruelly. Then, just as suddenly, the image dissolved into oblivion, and she shuddered.

Daniel stood beside a kettle on the hearth, cursing under his breath. As they walked in, he looked up, caught sight of Katy, and stared at her in mute horror. "Katy! What happened?"

William Briggs looked over his left shoulder and appraised her with a calculating eye.

"Those ornery insects in the salt marsh," Fergus barked as he settled her into a kitchen chair. "They damn near ate her alive, thanks to Hannah Meacham, who's needin' a pair of spectacles in her old age. Daniel, run up to my room and fetch the witch hazel and some cotton-wool from my dresser and a clean sheet from the linen chest. And, Will, I'd appreciate your rubbin' our mounts down and then stablin' Katy's in the barn. I'll be givin' her a ride home in the buckboard later."

When they had gone, Fergus retrieved a basin, cloth, and soap from the sideboard and walked over to the hearth. As he poured warm water into the porcelain bowl, he peered into the iron kettle and sniffed disgustedly. Blackened potatoes and carrots floated in a swill of grease thick as whale blubber. His eyebrows drooped at the grotesque concoction. "Someone ought to teach him how to cook," he muttered as he returned to Katy's side.

Katy touched a swollen ridge on her eyelid and rubbed it furiously. "Cooking is not man's work."

"It is when you have no one else to do it for you!"

He lathered the cloth and proceeded to wash the honey from her face.

"Why don't you get married?" she mumbled around the soapy cloth. "There are plenty of available women . . ." She closed her mouth as he rinsed her face, but continued as he began to scrub her arms. " . . . on the island—Hannah, Marian Pettyface . . ."

"Clare," he added softly in what might have been a thought that escaped accidentally to his lips. His eyes were hidden beneath the silvery thatches of hair at his brow, so Katy could not see the anguish in their blue depths but could sense it in his voice. Slowly she recalled the doleful expression he had worn after he had visited Jason's mother yesterday. And then she saw the truth. How could she have been so blind?

"You love her!" she whispered.

"Always have. Probably always will."

"After her husband died, why didn't you—?"

"Couldn't. With Clare I could never find the right words to

tell her how I felt about her. She was a grand lady, and me nothing but an uncouth Irish tar too big to get out of his own way. Oh, I tried to ask her once, even went to Yorktown to do my proposin', but my tongue just wouldn't work. So here I sit, and there she sits, and that's the way it'll always be. But at least I can visit her when I want to. 'Tis better than nothing.''

Katy regarded the lumbering sea captain through a sudden mist that glazed her vision. Undaunted by man and sea, yet overawed by one frail woman. "Does anyone know?''

"Me.'' He studied her face with a relieved grin. "And now, you.''

Into this scene of quiet camaraderie Daniel bounded, breathless and anxious to be of help. "Everything you wanted,'' he assured them as he set an armful of cloth and bottles on the table. "Only I wasn't sure which bottle contained the witch hazel . . . so I brought all of them down.'' He shrugged innocently as Fergus came up beside him.

"Aye. That I can see.'' Unraveling the sheet, he handed it to Katy and gestured toward the adjoining room. " 'Twould be best if you got out of those clothes and wrapped that around you, lass. I wouldn't want your new dress to get stained.''

She looked apprehensive as she gathered the sheet in her hands. "You want me to remove . . . everything?''

"Everything that you don't want ruined.'' Detecting her reluctance, he laughed in an attempt to assuage her nervousness. "Come now, lass. You have nothing to fear from us. Quickly, before you start scratching and make them bleed again.''

Obediently she hastened to the next room, stripped the clothes from her body, and wound the sheet securely around herself. When she reentered the kitchen, Fergus motioned her to a chair. He sprinkled a greenish liquid onto a square of cotton-wool, then pressed the swatch to a puffy mound on her neck. She winced as a stinging sensation erupted beneath the cloth, but relaxed as it dissipated, leaving in its stead a refreshing coolness. He followed the same procedure for each bite on her chest and arms until he had run out of cotton-wool. The burning and itching having miraculously disappeared, Katy leaned back in the chair and breathed deeply. "Oh, Fergus. That feels wonderful.''

"I'm hoping that you'll never need it again.'' He patted dry the greenish streams of liquid that had trickled down her arms. "Now what about your legs?''

As she lifted the sheet to her knees, Fergus grimaced. There were as many welts on her legs as she had on her arms. "Good God, lass, 'tis a wonder you escaped with your life. We'll be needin' more cotton-wool. I'll rummage upstairs to see if I can

268

find some. Lord only knows where I've hidden it. Meantime, Daniel, you see to the bites on her face and make sure you don't let any of that stuff ooze into her eyes. Think you can handle that?"

Daniel, who had been sitting in a chair at the opposite end of the table contemplating Katy's bare shoulders, jumped up and darted to her side. "Of course I can handle it," he snapped in annoyance. "What do you think I am?"

Fergus scratched his head, screwed his mouth to one side. "I can tell you what you're not." He glared at the kettle on the hearth. "A cook."

When he had disappeared into the next room, Katy laughed aloud. "Oh, Daniel, he is not at all pleased with you. Perhaps you should come to our house for supper tonight."

"If your husband will be dining with us, then I respectfully decline." His ego still smarted from his last encounter with the man. Splashing more witch hazel onto the cotton-wool, he held it to the side and asked her to lean her head back and close her eyes.

"I apologize for Jason's treatment of you aboard the *Ugly*," she said as she followed his instructions. With her eyes closed she was spared the ordeal of having to behold the face of the man who had once looked upon her so torridly. "He can be so grisly at times but doesn't mean half of what he says. I hope you understand. He merely has a hasty, irascible temper. What more can I say?"

Daniel bent close to her face and dabbed at the bite on her eyelid. "Say you will grow tired of his temper and run away with me. Tomorrow. Next week. I don't care when, just say you will."

Katy laughed. "You are much too trustworthy to ever run off with another man's wife, Daniel English."

"Do not be so sure."

As he bent over her, the back door rattled open and then closed. Katy shifted uncomfortably in her chair, not wanting to be scrutinized in her present attire by William Briggs. "Are you almost through, Daniel?" she whispered.

"Aye, love, just let me—"

He never finished his sentence. A large hand shot out, caught him on the shoulder, spun him around, and smashed him solidly in the face. With her eyes still closed, Katy heard the sound of flesh hitting flesh. When she heard what sounded like a body being hurled across the room into a piece of furniture, and a pathetic groan as both furniture and body crashed to the floor, she wiped her palm across her eyelid and peered in that direction.

Daniel lay in a crumpled heap beneath one of the kitchen chairs, blood oozing from his nose; unconscious. Towering above him stood Jason, kneading his fist into his palm.

Katy stared in sickened disbelief. "My God," she breathed. "Daniel!" She ran over to his inert form and removed the chair from across his body. Rolling him onto his back, she tilted his head back in an attempt to stanch the flow of blood from his suddenly misshapen nose. She looked up at Jason accusingly. "What did you do that for?"

He returned her stare with eyes hard as flint. "I do not take kindly to being cuckolded, lady."

"Cuckolded!" she screamed. "He was only trying to—"

"I *saw* what he was trying to do." His voice swelled, rolling deeply through the room. For four days he had been able to think of nothing except Katy—the dark passion in the depths of her eyes, the sensuous pleasure of her lips yielding beneath his. Had she enjoyed his loveplay so much that she had decided to experiment with the first man who happened by? She had once agreed to marry Daniel. Did she still feel something for the boy? As his anger fed on his jealousy, he clenched his teeth together. He had expected to come back to a willing bride, but not one who was willing in another man's arms. "For a woman who was so frightened at the mere thought of a man's touch, you have turned into quite the brazen hussy. Do you enjoy peddling to others what I have been denied? How many have crawled between your thighs in my absence, madam?"

The words pierced her like thorns. A hush descended upon the room—a hush that numbed her senses and thickened around her head. She looked from Daniel's body to the powerful man looming before her. He could not have spoken those words. No man who loved her could say such things. But he had. And he meant every word of it.

Slowly she rose to her feet, walked to her husband, then drew her hand back and hit him full across the face. "Your mouth is as foul as your thoughts. Daniel is my friend. How *dare* you hurt him!" Her anger dancing like sparks of fire in her eyes, she stood before him, nostrils flaring, daring him to voice one more insult. Ready to match wits with him verbally, she was totally unprepared for what followed, for as Jason recovered from the shock of her slap, the maelstrom of shattered emotions and frustrations within him exploded, and before he realized what he was doing, he raised his arm and struck her across the cheek. Reeling backward, she fell to the floor and covered her bruised cheek in astonishment. With an effort of will she held back the tears that formed in the corners of her eyes.

"I dare anything, lady. Don't ever raise your hand to me again." With his fury allayed by the blow he had inflicted, he leveled his gaze on her slight figure and only then noticed the terrible swellings on her flesh. Beneath his rigid exterior he flinched. He had observed her when she bent over Daniel, but in truth, he had not really *seen* her. A twinge of conscience made him relive the moment when he had stepped through the door. Daniel hovered over Katy. Locked in a lovers' embrace? His eyes wandered to the table. Witch hazel and cotton-wool.

He returned his gaze to her puffy skin, to the welts on her face and arms—mosquito bites. He indeed might have been too hasty in his judgment of the situation, but he could not back down now. She had to learn what was proper conduct for a New England wife. But . . . He stretched his hand guiltily; he should not have struck her. Nay. He should not have struck her.

"Your clothes, madam. Where are they?"

Her countenance froze in a mask of repugnance. Disregarding his question, she gathered the sheet about her knees and made to slide across the floor to Daniel, only to have Jason halt her advance by planting his six feet, three inches between her and the boy's body. "I said, where are your clothes?"

She answered him with a silent stare.

"Katy!" he bellowed. Leaning over, he shackled her upper arm within his hand and started to yank her to her feet, but she, thinking that he intended to hit her again, twisted her body around so that she was facing in the opposite direction.

"Nay!" she screamed as she huddled close to the floor. "I will not turn the other cheek so you can bloody that one also!"

Beneath his hand he felt her trembling, and instinctively he loosened his grasp. He should never have struck her. "Do you wish to ride home in a sheet?"

Silence.

He swore, then stormed into the next room, returning in a moment with her clothes rolled up in a ball. She remained prostrate on the floor, her head bent, her hair fanning her back in an ebony cape.

"I will not leave you here, Katy. Like it or not, you're coming home with me."

The almond shape of her eyes lengthened, turned to slits. She could not swallow the gorge in her throat. As she looked up at her husband's imposing physique, she vowed he would never hit her again. Untwisting her body, she rose to her feet, brushed herself off, and headed out the door. Asticou was nowhere in sight, only Jason's black stallion remained tethered to the hitching post, and she had no intention of sharing the same horse with

Jason on the trek back. She stalked off toward the barn and heard her husband call out behind her.

"Where do you think you're going?"

Silence.

Jason cocked a brow in irritation. Damn stubborn female. Stuffing her clothes beneath his arm, he mounted the black and reared him toward her retreating figure. As she neared the barn, Katy began to run. She heard the stallion's hooves pounding behind her and had just looked over her shoulder to gauge the distance between them when the steed was suddenly upon her and she shrieked in fright. With his free arm Jason seized her around the waist and swept her into the saddle before him, never breaking stride.

They were halfway home when Jason turned from the road onto a path that zigzagged through a copse of spruce. Stopping, he wound his arm around her waist and let her slide to the ground.

"Get dressed," he said as he shoved her clothes into her hands. "I would not want to have to explain your present attire to Hannah."

Sucking on the inside of her cheek, she spun around and started to walk away from him. Hannah. Hannah. Hannah. Perhaps he should have married Hannah.

"And don't think about running away," he added. "I know these woods far better than you do."

They completed the remainder of their journey in absolute silence. At the house Katy squirmed down from the horse and ran into the front hall, past a bewildered Mercy, up the stairs and into her room, slamming the door behind her.

Three days later, Katy sat in her bed hugging her knees to her chest and glaring into the darkness. She touched a finger to her cheek and in her mind's eye saw the ugly bluish-yellow bruise that covered an area the size of an egg. He would be sorry. He would be sorry he ever raised his hand to her. In the diminishing darkness her eyes sought out the flintlock pistol that rested on the table beside the bed. For the past three days she had ridden out to the cabin at Jordan Pond, as much to escape Desire's sniggers as to hide her face until her bruise healed. But while there, she had begun toying with the pistol, experimenting with powder and shot that Riley had provided. She was convinced that she would never become a master marksman. She merely wanted to acquire a working knowledge of the gun, or at least look like she knew what she was doing. Jason would probably try to take it away from her if he knew, but she had no intention of giving anything up to Jason. If he attempted to harm her again, he would be looking down the muzzle of three loaded barrels of shot. Let him try. A hole between his eyes might improve his vision.

While Katy fantasized her revenge, Jason sat hunched over the edge of the bed in the next room, his elbows propped on his knees, his forehead pressed against the heels of his palms. He felt sick inside.

If only he had not hit her.

The guilt from his deed weighed so heavily upon him that he could not bear to face her, to see the purplish bruise on her cheek, knowing that his hand had put it there. Her eyes would be accusing, filled with hate. Damn. Why had he hurt her?

Jason sank his fingers into his scalp. There was no sense in agonizing over his decision any longer. He wouldn't bother to assign another man to command his ship to the West Indies. He would go himself and be gone from here in four days' time. Katy would be much happier with him gone. Then she would be able to entertain Fergus and Daniel and Elisha without fear of having her jealous husband break any more noses. When he returned . . .

He suffered a tightness in his chest.

When he returned, he would have the marriage annulled and would send Katy back to Spain or Yorktown or anywhere else she wanted to go. *There.* He had finally admitted to himself the only course of action left to take. But it did not make him feel better.

With her beside him he could have forgotten the sea, but now he would be forced to seek refuge within that watery domain again, just to forget about her. Yet he knew it to be an impossible task. One does not forget a woman that easily—especially a woman that one loves. Slowly he rose from the bed, poured himself a drink, and gulped it down in one swallow. He told himself that the tears that stung his eyes were a result of the alcohol, but he knew better.

After three more days of healing, the colors in Katy's cheek faded to a sick yellow, which was fortunate, because this was the day that Marian Pettyface had promised a return visit, and Katy did not want to have to explain the origin of the bruise. It was bad enough that she had had to lie to Mercy, telling her that she had run into a branch while riding with Fergus. She didn't want to have any more lies on her conscience.

Leading Asticou to the back of the house, she tethered him to a sapling. It was still early, so she planned to ride to Jordan Pond and indulge in some further target practice before the remainder of the day was consumed by Marian's endless chatter. But first she wanted to sneak into the kitchen and pilfer a few confections. Hoping that no one would be inside, she opened the back door.

Only minutes earlier Jason had awoken feeling like the inside of his mouth was full of sand. His brain hammered against his skull as he rubbed his eyes and squinted painfully into the bright sunlight. One too many, he groaned, but as he sat up and felt the queasiness in his stomach, he revised his judgment. *Several too many.* He dressed in slow motion, fearing that any sudden movement would send the contents of his stomach lurching upward. Hannah would simply have to mix one of her restorative concoctions for him to drink. He grimaced, remembering its vile taste.

When Jason entered the kitchen, Desire was dabbing a pasty substance on a silver candlestick to restore the shine. He acknowledged her briefly with a nod of his head, but it was evident to her that it was not her he sought. His eyes came to rest on her only when he had completed his survey of the room.

"Where is your mother?"

Desire smiled, relieved that it was not his wife he sought. Katy had made herself scarce ever since her mishap in the salt marsh, and considering Desire's own part in that misadventure, she was just as glad that she did not have to look at the chit.

"She is upstairs with Mrs. MacAuley. May I be of service to thee?"

"Oh. Damn." In his abstraction to think of what to do next, he rubbed his neck and stared at nothing in particular. Desire's gaze, however, could not be so easily diverted. Her eyes slid down the length of him. He had not shared his wife's bed since he returned from Boston. Such continence! Mayhap it was a propitious time to end his celibacy.

"Oh!" she sniffed. Jason focused on her again as she rubbed her forearm across her left eye. "I have something in my eye, Jason. Wouldst get it out for me? My hands . . ." She held up her gummy fingers as evidence of her plight, then dug her wrist into her closed eyelid.

"Here, let me look at it." He walked over to where she stood, and placing one thumb on her upper lid and one thumb below, opened her eye wide and searched for the source of the irritation.

"I can see nothing. Is it still there?"

He let go the skin around her eye but continued to cradle her head as she blinked experimentally. "It feels like a stick of driftwood. Canst not see something?" As she spoke, a single tear managed to trickle down her cheek. Jason tilted her head back and scrutinized the beautiful brown eye more carefully.

With his face only inches above hers, his lean body pressed the full length of her own, she concentrated her attention on the flawless line of his mouth and suddenly threw her arms around his neck and bent his face down to meet her lips. The embrace, though quite accidental on Jason's part, was most convincing. The two bodies were angled into each other, their limbs intertwined, their lips meshed solidly.

The back door opened, and Katy entered the kitchen.

Wide-eyed, she stood for just one moment, then clenched her fists and spun on her heel. Jason, having lifted one eye in her direction when the door opened, was struggling to detach himself from Desire's clutches when the door slammed shut again.

"Katy!" But it was no use. She had already fled. Fanning his fingers through his hair, he muttered a graphic obscenity, cast a malevolent look upon Desire, then raced toward the rear exit himself. Desire rubbed her wrists lovingly and looked askance at the door. Mayhap if Jason did catch the little ninny, he would bruise her other cheek for her. Aye. It would suit her coloring well.

Outside, he watched Asticou's pounding hooves kick up clods of earth as the great stallion galloped across the lawn, and despite his shouts, Katy continued to flee, neither breaking her pace nor turning her head. As his last invective pierced the air, she had already reached the road and was heading north, her braided hair having tumbled down to stream wildly behind her. Forgetting the pain in his head and stomach, he ran toward the barn. By God, he would catch her, and when he did, she would listen to what he had to say. He did not even hail a greeting to Riley as he stormed through the barn gathering the gear to saddle his horse. When he had completed his task and mounted the bay, he stared stupidly at Riley, who had not bothered to look up from his work. Hell, Jason mused to himself, he didn't even know where to look for her. As Riley pitched another forkful of hay into the feed trough, Jason narrowed his eyes and posed a question. "These jaunts that Katy takes during the day, Riley. Do you know where she goes?"

The small Irishman stabbed his pitchfork into the hay as though he were killing a serpent. "Eayh."

Jason waited. Riley continued to fill the trough.

"Well, where does she go?" Jason snapped impatiently.

"Reckon that's her business."

" 'Tis my business now!" he barked, tightening the reins as his horse reared. "I have need to explain something to her . . . something"—and his voice softened at that—"which she should not have seen."

Riley thrust his fork into the ground, leaned his arm on the handle. The eyes which he cast upon Jason were steady but held a trace of suspicion. He had talked to Fergus, had heard about Daniel's broken nose, and knew that Katy hadn't run into any tree limb. If Jason had been angry enough to break the lad's nose, he could have been angry enough to strike his wife. And that did not sit well with Riley. Nope. It did not sit well at all.

"Well? Need I beat the information out of you?" Jason's tone was fast becoming less anxious and more volatile, and Riley realized that it would be wiser to divulge his information than to be beaten to a bloody pulp, but first there was a certain guarantee he wanted.

"She won't be runnin' into any more tree limbs if I tell you, will she?" Riley discerned from the guilty look on Jason's face that he had indeed hit a sore spot.

"I . . . I didn't know what I was doing. It was a fluke."

"Pretty ugly fluke."

"Aye." Jason's expression became so tortured that Riley could almost feel his discomfort. Clearing his throat, he spoke quietly, casually. "Jordan Pond's mighty nice this time of morning."

A strained smile flickered across Jason's lips. "Thanks." As he started to spur the bay forward, however, Riley called out after him.

Jason looked over his shoulder.

"Anything bad happens to the girl, you'll be answerin' to me."

He made no answer to this but sped out the wide door. Mentally he added another notch to the long list of Katy's conquests—Madison, Daniel, Fergus, Elisha, and now Riley. But not her husband. No, never himself.

14

Katy sat beneath a tree overlooking the pond, ripping single blades of grass from the ground and tossing them before her. She licked her lips, tasting the salt from her dried tears, and rubbed her hand across her nose. He dared shout at her of cuckoldry, when all the time he was enjoying lewd dealings with that slut. Is that why he had taken her to Boston with him? So they could have a bawdy interlude without fear of being discovered by someone in the house? The thought of Boston stirred other memories, and she reddened when she remembered how receptive she had been to Jason's caresses that morning in the forest. She touched her hand to her cheek. This was how he displayed his love for her—by striking her—while Desire received soft kisses and embraces. Bastard. Whore! They had undoubtedly been fornicating since that first morning she found them together. Her husband's duplicity left a strong taste of bile in her mouth. She knew him not at all, for surely the man who was so considerate of his mother was not the same man who had slapped her face or taken his mistress to bed under her very roof. The image of the tender embrace in the kitchen clouded her vision. She hated them. She hated them both. But before she had a chance to vent her spleen in some significant way, she heard a commotion in the distance and turned her head to find Jason riding at breakneck speed into the clearing surrounding the pond. With a swiftness born of loathing, she quit the ground and mounted her stallion.

Jason dismounted by the water's edge. He stood silently for a moment, listening, searching. Lulled almost to despair by the apparent absence of his wife, he was startled when he looked over his shoulder to discover her sitting astride her horse some paces back from him. She held the reins steadily with her left hand and concealed her flintlock beneath a fold in her skirt with her right. Her throat was dry. Her face registered cold determination.

Already Jason could sense that his task would not be an easy one. "Get down from your horse, Katy."

"Nay."

Her denial was so unexpected that he allowed an incredulous grin to touch his lips. "Did you hear what I said?"

"Did you hear what *I* said?" she retaliated.

Jason wound his horse's reins more tightly about his wrist as the animal snorted testily. So it was a battle of wills she desired. He could oblige her. In soothing the stallion, he took a discreet step closer to his wife.

"It would be easier to explain if you would come closer. I have no wish to scream at the top of my lungs."

"No need to shout. My hearing is excellent. Do explain, Jason, and I shall listen to you, as you were wont to listen to me when you found *me* in a compromising position."

Her words smacked him roundly, for, as her sarcasm implied, he certainly had not been receptive to her explanations concerning Daniel. But that, he reasoned, was different.

"I have never alleged that I am overly patient or tolerant."

"And justly so. Indeed, I have found you to be completely lacking in both qualities."

His face hardened at her slur. She was making it damn hard for him to retain an even temper. Venturing another step forward, he halted suddenly when he realized that she had produced a three-barreled flintlock pistol out of thin air and was aiming it squarely between his legs. "That's far enough."

He could not begin to mask the horror in his voice. "Where did you get that?" he rasped.

" 'Tis none of your concern where I got it. What *should* be of your concern is that it is loaded and I know how to use it, whoremonger." She observed his reaction keenly, and when he stopped, as she had bid, she continued. "Did you think that I would so fear your displeasure that I would accept your lies blindly? How long have you been crawling between that bitch's thighs, husband? Surely the morning that you were chopping wood was not the first time."

Jason's eyes narrowed. The muscles in his jaw bunched with tension. "What are you talking about?"

"Do not play the innocent with me, my dear captain. I saw you quite distinctly and you did not appear an unversed babe in the art of whoring, or will you try to tell me that it was she who seduced you? Either way, you have proved yourself a most willing participant. What I want to know is how you found the gall to profess your love for me with the same mouth that drooled over that . . . that slattern."

Jason did not even hear her last question. So she *had* seen him that morning when he was chopping wood! The events of that day suddenly tumbled into his mind, and he saw with astounding

278

clarity that many of their problems had taken root that day. Of course! She was so outraged at the thought of his unfaithfulness that she wanted nothing more to do with him. And from that point everything had mushroomed, going from bad to worse. The source of their misunderstanding found, Jason rumbled with laughter. To what depths they had fallen to arrive at so simple a solution!

Katy watched the absorption behind the brown eyes with wary interest, winced as his laughter increased in volume.

"Katy!" He chortled. "We have been the victims of a terrible misunderstanding." The relief in his mind having sent a similar message to his feet, he started to walk briskly toward his wife to explain the circumstances that had led to their dissension. What he failed to notice was that Katy's finger had tightened around the trigger.

In the next instant an ear-splitting shot rang through the air and Jason froze as he marked the entry of the lead ball into the ground at the tip of his boot. Startled by the sound, his horse reared violently, and it was only after Jason had steadied him with a firm hand that he clenched his teeth and looked back to his wife, who had quickly primed, cocked, released the lever on the second barrel, and taken aim once again.

Their eyes locked.

"I warned you," she snapped. "I must also warn you that, never having held a man at gunpoint before, I am a trifle nervous. My finger might slip and my aim be a little high . . ."

He felt the skin prickle at the nape of his neck as she waved the gun dangerously at some point between his ears.

". . . or it might be a little low . . ."

The weapon danced in her hand, coming to rest at an angle that was in a direct line with his groin.

". . . and wouldn't your slut be disappointed then. Tempt me no more, Jason. My finger is itching to do away with you."

If Jason had any doubts about her ability to pull the trigger before, he had no doubts now. "For Chrissakes, Katy, put that thing down and let me explain."

"You may explain all you like. The gun remains where it is."

His breath hissed through his teeth like fire. "Despite what you think you saw, I have never bedded Desire Meacham."

"Liar!"

"I have never lied to you!"

"Huh!"

His chest heaved in anger. When he got his hands on her, he would flay her alive. "I have digested all the insolence that I care to digest today. Get off your horse so we can talk."

"Pray tell, what are we doing now?"

"Damn your hide!" But as he made a move toward her, she pointed the gun steadily at his loins. He paused, unsure of the woman he thought he knew so well.

"You forget who has the upper hand," she snarled. "I have two bullets left, and absolutely no qualms about using them."

Watching the expert way she handled her weapon, he cursed to himself. What other surprises did she have in store for him? "You're mad."

"Only a little." She laughed. "But I *have* thought of a fine jest. And I think we will start with . . ."—her eyes ranged up, then down—"your boots."

"My boo . . .?" Reading her purpose, he shook his head. "Nay, lady."

She smiled at the thunderbolts his eyes were flinging at her. "I see you are not amused." Lifting her shoulders indifferently, she jabbed the gun into the air. "Nonetheless, take your boots off."

When his only response to her was a hand balled tightly into a fist, she determined that a bit of persuasion would be in order.

"I give you to the count of three. One . . ."

He squinted uncertainly.

". . . two . . ."

She wouldn't deliberately . . .

". . . three!"

Seeing her hand flicker, Jason threw off the reins of the bay and dived to his right. The air exploded. The space Jason had just vacated smoked white with haze, and from where he lay he heard the bay charge southward across the meadow, away from the shrill sound of bullets and the acrid smell of gunpowder. He pulled himself to a sitting position and of a sudden suffered a lightness of head, not from any physical injury, but from the measure of her hatred. When he stared up at the girl who sat with such cool immutability atop her steed, his insides numbed. Good God, she really did want to kill him!

"You have dallied long enough, Captain. I suggest you do as I say before I am forced to waste another bullet on you."

This time Jason had no taste for challenging her order. He heaved off one boot, then the other, and when he held them up for her perusal, she looked thoughtful for a moment, then smiled. "Throw them into the pond."

The horror on his face was readily apparent. To walk back to the house in bare feet was one thing, but to destroy a perfectly good pair of leather boots was an abomination that his New England practicality could not abide. "You go too far, lady."

"Your boots," she threatened.

Realizing that her resolve had not diminished, and knowing that he had no other choice, he hurled the boots, one at a time, into the pond, his anger emerging from his throat in an ugly growl. When he turned back to his wife, the muscle beneath his eye was twitching irrepressibly and his gaze had blackened, for he was planning his revenge. No punishment would be too great. He would strangle her, beat her black and blue. Aye, she would rue her actions this day.

When she was sure her voice would not betray her inner fright, she angled the muzzle of the pistol at him. "Now the breeches."

"The hell, you say."

"But, Captain, since you are so proud of the implement which you wield between your legs, I have decided that you should display its magnificence to the entire community."

His scowl became ominous. "The only way these breeches will come off, lady, will be for you to tear them off my body. You'll have to kill me first." A fierce smile twisted his lips. "And I warn you, should your bullet go awry, you had better be able to ride damn fast."

She tried to close her mind to her husband's intimations, but he was too enraged for her to ignore. Her courage flagged, and the finger that was itching to do away with him slackened. Jason detected the change in her posture and with a burst of adrenaline lunged toward her. Unnerved, she jolted, and her finger slipped. Jason flew onto his stomach as the bullet whirred overhead. When Katy realized she had no ammunition left, she reared the stallion and raced toward the open field, looking back over her shoulder to find Jason hopping one-legged and clutching his opposite foot in pain. Either he had stepped on something or she had blown his foot off. She didn't want to stay to find out which.

She arrived back at the house knowing exactly what she must do—pack her clothes, then seek refuge with Fergus whose size, she hoped, would be formidable enough to protect her from Jason's rage. But as she crept through the front door, Mercy flew at her like a dervish.

"Oh, mistress! 'Tis glad I am to see *thee!* Mrs. Pettyface has been here forty-five minutes and has been pondering thy whereabouts for forty-four. Wilt go to her now to appease her curiosity?"

Katy's brief hesitation provided just enough time for Mercy to note the high coloring of her mistress's fair complexion. "Has aught befallen thee, mistress?"

Katy's laughter gushed forth more from nervousness than from levity of spirit. "Nay, nothing has befallen me, but I have need

281

to ride out again.'' The girl's crestfallen reaction prompted her to add, "After I have appeased Mrs. Pettyface's curiosity, of course."

That is exactly what Mercy had wanted to hear. She scurried her mistress toward the parlor. "Desire is sipping cider with her at the moment." In her excitement, Hannah's daughter failed to detect the stiffening of Katy's back or the uncompromising expression that flitted across her face, but at the entrance to the parlor she did note that Katy's eyes were bright, as with fever.

"Mistress, thy eyes are so—"

Katy dismissed her with a quick wave of her hand. "I feel fine. Now, off with you."

Mercy did not have to be told twice.

Marian's chatter drifted out to the hall like the clucking of a hen. Gritting her teeth, Katy swooped into the room. Mrs. Pettyface bounced out of her chair and waddled over to extend a greeting.

"What a pleasure it is to see you again, my dear," she twittered, but stopped mid-stride as her nearsighted eyes focused more closely upon her. "Whatever has happened to your face, child?"

Katy's hand flew to her cheek. "Oh, that." But as she beheld Desire's smug countenance, she realized that she had no wish to gloss over the facts. Smiling, she caught Marian's plump hands and laughed. "Did you not know that my husband beats me?"

The old woman's lips had formed around a horrified O before she perceived that Katy's comment had been in jest. "Oh, tush," she scolded. "Jason MacAuley would sooner cut his hand off than strike a woman. Now, come and sit beside me so I can tell you what magnificent plans I've been making. If no one here is anxious to show you off, *I* certainly am!"

Katy allowed herself to be swept into the whirlwind created by Marian's zeal, and, finding herself planted next to the woman's abundant form on the sofa, she dulled an ear to the monologue on how best to introduce Katy to the community at Cromwell Harbor. All her powers of concentration were centered on Desire Meacham's lofty demeanor and how pleasant it would be to temper her queenly affectations, revenge herself for the insults, the injuries. It was high time Mistress Meacham was brought to task. Behind the demure mask that Katy's face had become, her brain worked feverishly. Her eyes focused on the tall pitcher of cider, absently at first, then with fondness.

". . . so, my dear, does that meet with your approval?"

"Hmm." Katy rubbed her nose distractedly before popping up from the sofa and wandering over to the table where the pitcher sat. Lifting it, she turned, a virtuous smile touching her lips. "More cider?" she asked.

As she filled Mrs. Pettyface's glass to capacity, Katy's idea crystallized and she nearly laughed aloud.

"Will you have some also?" she cooed, turning toward Desire.

Had Desire considered Katy as something more than a mousy child, she might have kept her distance from her adversary. But thinking Katy too mealymouthed and spineless to fight, she took advantage of the situation and smiled as employer offered to serve employee. "By all means," she said airily, holding her glass out to have it freshened.

Marian watched the encounter with little interest until Jason's wife overshot the proffered glass and Desire began screaming.

"Oh, how absolutely clumsy of me!" Katy hugged the empty pitcher to herself while Desire shot out of the chair, choking on her rage.

Katy eyed the spreading stain on the girl's lap with a simple smile. "Do change your clothes, dear. You're dripping all over the floor."

Desire favored the captain's wife with a vicious look, but knowing the widow's love of gossip, had to forgo further retaliation. She stalked from the room, her back stiff and her indignation apparent.

"I trust I have not inconvenienced you too greatly," Katy called out after her. "I know how infatuated you are with taking your clothes off!"

Marian Pettyface subdued a giggle, and when Katy turned around, looked at the girl with new eyes. There was much more to Jason's wife than met the eye. Perhaps she was not the obedient and demure child that she had seemed at first. No, beneath the gentle facade there was a woman of considerable substance.

"Now, Mrs. Pettyface," Katy said. "Where were we?"

As the minutes dissolved into the quarter- and then the half-hour, Katy became acutely aware of the clock's chiming the passage of time. It would not take Jason the remainder of the day to walk home, even without his boots. And if he happened to run across someone who would give him a ride, he would arrive home that much sooner. The prospect of such an occurrence twisted her stomach into knots. She could not be here when he came home!

Another half-hour passed. Mercy padded into the room, curtsied. Katy sighed in relief.

" 'Tis nigh on one," Mercy announced. "Wouldst have me prepare a tray and serve thy lunch in here?"

"That won't be necessary," Katy burst out a bit loudly. "
must be—"

"Oh, how delightful!" Marian clasped her hands, looking
euphoric. "Yes, a light lunch would do nicely."

Mercy looked to Katy for approval. "Mistress?"

Katy swallowed hard and nodded, not having the wherewithal
to do anything else. By the time Marian finished eating, they
would be halfway into tomorrow! Yet how could she unbridle
herself of the woman's company without appearing rude? She
certainly could not dump a pitcher of cider in her lap also!

Mercy curtsied again and disappeared. Mrs. Pettyface continued at double speed the monologue she had left off, while Katy
listened for the chimes of the grandfather clock and wrung her
hands. She sank her teeth into her bottom lip with nervous
apprehension as the clock struck the hour. Three hours! Three
hours had elapsed since she left Jason. She had to escape quickly

It was at that precise moment that Mercy, tray in hand, made
her way into the hall. It was also at that same moment that the
front door crashed open, shaking the very timbers of the mansion
Katy went dead white, her breath catching somewhere in her
throat. From the hall a cacophony of sounds exploded: a terrified
scream accompanied by a more frantic "Captain MacAuley!"
. . . heavy silver clanging against wood . . . porcelain and china
shattering.

"Where is she?" Jason roared, his lungs so swollen with
anger that the sheer force of his voice rattled the windows.

Katy's skin prickled and rose like goose flesh. She sat transfixed
paralyzed by fear, and knew that even if she could stand, her
knees would buckle beneath her. More sounds erupted in the
hall. A high-pitched, incomprehensible utterance, the scudding
of feet, the kitchen door banging shut. Impervious to Marian's
befuddled expression, Katy held her breath and gnawed on her
lower lip.

More footsteps, but not booted. Bare. And fast-paced. She
heard his gravelly breathing deep within his chest before she saw
him, for she dared not shift her gaze to the doorway.

"Excuse yourself, Mary Kathleen," he ground out.

Hesitantly she inched her head around. His big body filled the
doorway like an effigy of Samson about to topple the pillars of
the temple. His breeches were muddied and torn indiscriminately
he had parted company with his shirt some time ago and his arms
were scored with so many scratches that he looked like he had
just fought his way out of a briar patch. But his face was worst
of all, because he was wearing a scowl as black and as frightening as a sentinel to the gates of hell.

At the sound of Jason's voice Marian had started to set her mouth in motion, only to have the words freeze on the tip of her tongue at the sight of him. He was practically naked! Eyes bulging and jaw slack, she squinted for a better look, then did what any other self-respecting New England lady would have done. Gasping in shock, she keeled over in a dead faint.

"Mrs. Pettyface!" Katy shrieked. Sprinting over to her side, she grabbed the woman's limp wrist and slapped it gently. "Mrs. Pettyface?" Jason stormed into the room at the same time, but with no thought of administering to their guest.

"Ohhhh . . ." She slapped harder. "Please wake up. Mrs. Pettyface? You have frightened her half to death, Jason. Now what am I to do?"

"Do?" he barked. "You will do nothing. She will wake up. Right now you're coming with me."

In her concern for Marian she had almost forgotten her own fear. Now, as her husband towered menacingly above her, it rushed back full measure. "I . . . I must stay here with her . . ." She faltered. "She is an old woman, and there is no telling how serious—"

"Katy!" he blazed, his voice commanding her attention. Involuntarily she looked up. "It matters little to me where I deal with you. Here is as good a place as any, but for what I intend, you may prefer the privacy of your own room. I allow you that courtesy."

No sooner had her sense of survival, which urged her to flee, overcome her sense of reason, which urged her to stay, than Jason clamped his hand around the back of her neck, easing her to her feet.

"Nay, lady, put all thoughts of running aside. You will not escape me this time."

She glared at him, unable to wrench free from his grasp. "Shall I turn the other cheek?" she hissed.

"You'll be turning a cheek, all right"—he laughed cruelly—"but not in the way you have in mind."

She trembled beneath his grim smile, but before she could form a retort, he lifted her up and tossed her over his shoulder.

"Let go of me! I will have no part in your perversions! I will kill you!" she screamed, pounding his back with her fists.

Jason's long strides took them swiftly across the room. "Quiet!" he snapped. "Unless you want to discover just how perverted I can actually be."

If either of them had thought to look back to the sofa at that moment, they would have noticed a pair of close-set eyes peeping over the top and twinkling with excitement. Covering her mouth to contain her giggles, Marian studied the two MacAuleys with curiosity. Why, the idea! New wife or no, it was *Sunday*, and simply unheard of to drag your wife off to . . . Well, it was only too obvious where he was taking her and what he intended to do. Muttering a few disjointed thoughts about the frivolities of youth and wishing she were forty years younger, she rolled onto her feet. Katy's caterwauling floated back to the parlor and bounced off the walls. Most peculiar. Best to stop by Abigail's and hope they had not eaten yet. Even with six male children it was bound to be less hectic there than it was here!

On the second floor landing Jason stalked past the shocked faces of Hannah and Desire, kicked open the door to the bedchamber, then turned, scowling. "I will not be disturbed. And get *her*"—he glowered at Desire—"out of my sight." The door slammed shut with a reverberating bang.

Hannah gawked at the portal, then at her daughter, suspicious of the nervous alarm she saw leap into the girl's eyes. "I think it's time we had a talk, missy, a long talk."

Within the bedchamber Katy's scream became muffled in the bed quilt as Jason threw her onto the mattress. Once free of his grasp, however, she scrambled toward the opposite edge, only to be dragged back to him by her ankle. "I have no intention of chasing you around this room, girl. If you know what is good for you, you'll be still."

"I wish I had aimed for your heart!" she raved as she tried to kick her foot free.

If she had to say anything, it should not have been that. Jason pulled her roughly to her feet and dug his fingers into her shoulders. "Virago! When I finish with you, you'll wish you *had* killed me!"

"I am already sorry I did not!" Her yells had reached a level equaling the volume of Jason's. "Go ahead! Hit me! You are so skilled at beating women, you should not have to exert much effort!"

His only reply to that was to rake his darkened eyes over her body. The pulse in his throat throbbed convulsively. "You leave me no choice. 'Tis your turn now, madam. Take off your clothes."

His words turned her knees to jelly and she could do naught but shake her head in refusal.

"Must I do it for you?"

"Nay!" she gasped, and realizing what her fate would be once disrobed, she began to assail him in earnest. She succeeded in clawing his forearm before he was able to fetter both her wrists in his one hand and whip her around so that her back was

286

facing him. With his free hand he flung her hair over her shoulder and grappled with the hooks at her neck. Enraged, she shifted her weight to one side, and stepping back, drove her foot so hard down on his instep that the air rang with an entirely new barrage of vituperations. With the cursing came another sound as Jason, goaded beyond reason, yanked downward on the collar of her dress, splitting it from neck to waist. Her terrified shriek fell on deaf ears as he tossed her facedown on the bed and with his knee pressed into her back tore the remainder of her dress and chemise from her body. Her fists struck his flesh more than once, as did her thrashing feet, but against his solid limbs her blows fell with little impact. Having rid her of her garments, Jason sat on the edge of the bed and pulled her across his lap. For a brief moment he allowed himself to stare at the perfection of her rounded buttocks, pale, like half-moons. In the next he had brought his large hand across their width with a resounding smack. Katy bucked from the shock but did not cry out.

"This," he ground out as his hand came down hard again, "is for the first bullet that missed."

She clamped down so violently on her tongue that she thought she would sever it. She would not cry out! No matter how much . . .

"And this . . ." Darts of pain shot through her back and legs. Her abused buttocks tightened. Her body shivered. ". . . is for the second and third!" Katy winced with each successive crack, but still she kept her silence.

"And for the destruction of a perfectly good pair of boots . . ." His hand gained momentum with each downward stroke. The power behind each slap increased, stinging her unmercifully. Tears formed in the corners of her eyes and flowed down her cheeks as his repudiation continued with no sign of letting up. "The walk home was not pleasant, Katy!" he shouted. He smacked the rounded flesh again and again. "Even a horse is allowed shoes on such roads!" His gaze wandered to the smooth curve of her back, and it was then he became aware of other sensations—the undulation of her breasts against his thighs, the warmth of her body pressed against his own. Just as her mind screamed inwardly with pain, he slammed his hand down again, but stopped short of his target. She had had enough. *He* had had enough.

Katy, expecting another blow to fall, tensed, shivered. Tears streamed down her face, and when his hand did not strike, her breath escaped involuntarily in a tremulous sob. She hurt. Every muscle, every bone.

Loosing her wrists, he lifted her gently to the bed, but once freed, she scrambled across the disheveled bedcovers, hopped to the floor, grabbed the candle sconce, and flung it headlong at his skull. Jason ducked. The sconce whizzed past his head and crashed into the wall. With the sound still ringing off the walls, she ran to the dresser and hurled a succession of objects across the room at him.

"You hellcat!" he raged. He took long, deliberate strides toward her, fending off the onslaught of makeshift weapons, till he stood awesomely before her. She cowered in his tall shadow, her arms crossed protectively over her chest. He spoke not with his lips but with eyes that shone with the reflection of a coil that had been wound too tightly and was about to spring. The steady pulse in his neck, the unwavering stance of his big body—both clarified his intent.

"I would harness your spirit for other purposes." Reaching his hand behind her head, he pulled her to him. His strong hands cupped her face. He centered his thumbs on the soft crest of her lips, and behind his eyes felt the burning pressure of his anger and desire mount.

Sweeping her into his arms, he strode across the floor and deposited her none too gently on the bearskin pelt before the hearth. He shed what was left of his breeches as she thrashed about, and then he was stretched out beside her, stilling her legs beneath the weight of his leg, her hands within the vastness of his hand, stiffly, above her head. He took measure of her slowly, deliberately, as if he were charting the waters for his next voyage. Katy turned her face away, bucked and strained against the burden of his limbs, but with little result. She felt her hair being brushed back from her face, his lips grazing her ear, his breath touching her with its warmth. With his fingertips he traced the smooth underside of her arm downward, rested his thumb in the long recess where arm blended into chest. As he drew her earlobe into his mouth, his hand moved to form itself around the soft span of her breast, shaping its wide circumference into exaggerated fullness. His mouth left her ear. She felt his lips, warm against her breast, and she steeled her body against him. The man touched his tongue to the sensate bud of dark flesh, then pulled it greedily into his mouth as if it were a sweet summer berry and he a starving man. With flawless rhythm he elongated the nipple, then released it, elongated and released, making Katy aware of nerves she had never known existed. His hand slid downward. With the tips of his fingers he numbered each of her ribs, with his palm he traced the surface of her skin, each depression, each rise, until his long fingers found the tongue of virgin flesh he had been seeking and he began to stroke her gently. Within her a throbbing constriction bathed her

288

loins. Jason felt her readiness, moist upon his fingertips. Moving his leg, he lowered himself atop her. His eyes bored steadily into the green of her own.

"I never intended to take you this way, lady, but you leave me little choice."

His dark visage descended upon her as if in a dream. His lips met hers in a hard, dry kiss, and as she pushed against his broad expanse of shoulder, she felt his muscles flex beneath his flesh and was reminded of the power of the man above her. This thought, more than the kiss, warmed her, and in her mind's eye she saw the image of his body, naked and golden in the morning sun at Newport Cove. Reluctantly her lips parted. The hard pressure of his mouth increased. The tip of his tongue caressed the soft underside of hers. The heat in her loins spread and coated her skin with a thin film of moisture.

Jason arched his back upward, and with his arms braced like columns on either side of her, wedged his legs between her thighs. The sooty glow in her eyes turned to terror, and he knew she would derive no pleasure from what he was about to do. Supporting himself on one elbow, he slid his other hand over the bud whose membrane Molkeydaur had sought to rend and thrust himself gently into the tight opening.

Her eyes widened at the pain. She gasped on a breath that caught in her throat and bit down on her already swollen lower lip. He remained motionless within her, waiting for the tortured look on her face to subside, but seeing that it persisted, he bent his head down and kissed the perspiration from her temple, the salt from her cheek. "Katy," he whispered, "it would not hurt so if you were less wooden." Her answer was a groan that escaped as she strained beneath him. Firmly cushioned within her now, Jason gave in to his frustrations, and as she cried out, thrust himself deeper with one powerful movement. Conscious of her pain, he moved slowly at first, but with his passion heightened from long months of abstinence, the tempo of his thrusts increased so rapidly that he spilled his seed into her with premature suddenness. He frowned to himself, concerned at his inability to prolong the act. It was as if he were fresh out of puberty and this his first time with a woman. Rolling over on one elbow, he slid his hand the length of his wife's body. Her face was turned away from him, her hair masking her features. If she had had cause to hate him before, she had even more reason now.

Reaching out his hand, he turned her face toward him. Her eyes were glazed with tears, her expression devoid of emotion. "Listen to me, Katy," he whispered. "What you saw this morning . . . Desire asked me to get something out of her eye, and when I tried, she . . .'' He stopped mid-sentence, realizing how flimsy his excuse sounded. "Dammit, Katy, she muckled onto me like a bloodsucker. She has some crazy notion that she's in love with me. When you walked in on us, *I* wasn't even sure yet what had happened.''

Her steady eyes peered through him as if he were not there.

"And that morning I was chopping wood, when this whole misunderstanding began,'' he continued urgently, "I was so hot after you by that time that when I closed my eyes I imagined Desire to be you. If I had not come to my senses when I did, I might have . . .'' He stopped. Her silence was unbearable. "But I *did* come to my senses. *Nothing* happened! Though Lord knows I would not be in so foul a temper all the time if it had. You have left me a pitiful excuse for a man.''

Her eyes fell instinctively to the hardness that persisted between his thighs. Not so pitiful, she thought, as tears blinded her vision.

"I have hurt you.'' Tenderly he brushed the tears from her cheeks, and rising, lifted her into his arms. He laid her on the bed, covered her with a quilt, then slid beneath the cover himself, drawing her into the crook of his arm, her head resting against his shoulder. His breathing was less heavy now. His passion sated for the moment, he was content to hold her protectively against him.

"The pain . . .'' he began apologetically. "I am told it does not last long.'' He kissed the top of her head, felt her tears like dew against his side. "Sleep now.''

She lay quietly in his arms, fearful that her slightest movement would further arouse him.

Minutes passed. His chest rose and fell in the even rhythm of sleep and exhaustion. No sound met her ears save for the distant rumbling of the ocean and Jason's steady breathing.

He had not hurt her. Perhaps a little at first, but only for a moment. Her tears had been tears born more of fright than of pain, for even in his anger Jason had been gentle. It had not been like that ugly time with Molkeydaur. The thought making her shiver, she drew closer to her husband. Molkeydaur had wanted to hurt her, to tear her asunder with his grotesque mauling. Today the memory of that nightmare vanished behind the image of Jason's big body kissing her, caressing her, avenging himself upon her with a love that left a sudden emptiness in her loins. It had happened so quickly. Was the act of love always so brief? Other than the initial pain, she had felt virtually nothing, only an awkward gnawing that rooted in the place where he had entered her. Was that all there was?

She laid her fingers delicately on his bare chest. Could she believe what he had told her about Desire? Yes, she wanted to believe him, but more to the point, she could believe that Desire would deliberately flaunt herself before him, tempting him with the seductive movements of her body. In fact, the more she thought about it, the more she realized how difficult it must have been for Jason to avoid the little slut. He said that nothing had happened, and she found herself embracing his explanation and transferring all her distrust and wrath to Desire. She loved Jason. Yes, despite her threats and her oaths, she loved him very much. And she would show him that she was just as much a woman as Desire Meacham.

She slid her hand across his chest, tangling her fingers in his crisp black hair. She would prove her worth . . . and her love.

Jason awoke first, thinking he had heard a faint noise. He looked down at Katy, who still slept peacefully cradled in his arm, her hand stretched lazily across his breastbone. Cool light streamed in through the French doors, and he suddenly realized that he had slept away most of the afternoon.

The noise sounded lightly again, and he trained his eyes on the door. If it was Desire, he would put an end to her nonsense once and for all. Reluctantly he removed Katy's hand from his chest and eased himself from the bed so as not to wake her. He grabbed a small towel that was draped over the Oriental screen in the corner and pulled it around his waist, holding the ends together behind his back.

Balancing the supper tray on her knee with one hand, Mercy had just raised her other hand to try knocking once more when the door flew open before her. "Oh!" she squealed, and frightened by both Jason's abruptness and his scowl, felt the tray totter precariously on her knee. Jason saw it too. He reached out to grab it from her and at the same time felt the towel slip from his waist. "Oh!" she cried again, her eyes riveting on that which the towel had concealed. Blushing to the roots of her hair, she covered her mouth and ran in the opposite direction.

Jason shrugged. Poor Mercy would probably never be able to look him straight in the face again. Smiling wryly at the tray of food in his hands, he kicked the towel out of his way and quietly closed the door with his foot.

Katy's tiny form remained an inert lump in the middle of the bed. Jason set the tray down on the night table, then lowered himself to the edge of the mattress. Linking his fingers together, he stretched his arms out before him, forcing the sleep from his limbs and wincing at the multitude of scratches marring his flesh.

Katy's warm breath touched the middle of his back in a hesitant kiss. Jason's face restructured itself in a mingling of shock and wonder. "Katy?" Before he could turn to face her, she threw her arms around his neck, thinking to hug him—in reality choking him. Intent on mimicking his earlier lovemaking, she lapped his ear, but when this elicited no response from her husband except strange gagging sounds, she snatched her arms away from him. Able to breathe once again, Jason turned his face, flinching as the point of her retreating elbow drove itself into his cheekbone. His eyes smarted as he held the palm of his hand to his cheek, and amid this sudden gathering of tears he saw his wife, leaning back on her heels, her hand extended outward.

"I . . ."

She had just demonstrated the full scope of her carnal abilities and realized how utterly lacking her efforts had been. Angered by her ineptitude, humiliated by her awkwardness, she touched the man's face where she had struck him, and mustered a sad smile that engendered her willingness and her plea for help. Jason pressed her fingertips to his lips, reached his hand out to stroke the soft curls circling her face. And they remained like that for a long time, connected by eyes, and limbs, and fingertips, until he hinted gently with his eyes and Katy leaned back into the pillows, awaiting her husband. He placed a hot kiss in the hollow of her throat, then worked his way unhurriedly to her lips. With his hand he caressed and explored the body he had so often dreamed of, and when she was prepared to receive him, he lifted himself above her. She moved her legs to accommodate him, tracing her fingers downward through the hairs of his chest.

He probed gently for her opening, then, finding it, guided himself into the soft recess of her body. She felt him grow within her, slide back, then thrust again, slowly, purposefully. Each movement was a caress, each thrust drawing her more deeply into a sphere of sensation that blotted out all conscious thought except the feel and taste of Jason. Within her every nerve twitched, every muscle pulsed. Jason's breathing quickened. Grasping her hand, he cupped it around the soft swelling beneath his phallus, then watched the initial shock on her face melt into a warm glow. The tempo of his thrusts increased with a gentle fervor. As the rhythm of their movements became as one, so also did their breathing, their passion. His mouth consumed her; her lips throbbed in response to his bruising kisses. He drew a deep labored breath. Shuddered. Katy held him greedily to her, trembled beneath him, unable to distinguish where her body ended and his began. As Jason gasped with his release, she felt a constriction in her loins like a thousand tiny heartbeats exploding and flooding her with exquisite sensations. She arched her back, caught her breath, and then she was no longer of the earth. She was flying, spiraling upward, warm and secure and loved.

Still within her, Jason rolled onto his back, wrapping her solidly within his embrace atop him. He fondled her buttocks in his large hand as she nuzzled against his neck. His lips curved upward, surprised and bemused. "Katy?" he whispered as he looped a strand of her hair around his finger. "Are you all right?" She was so quiet that he began to wonder if he had hurt her. After all, he was no lightweight.

"Mmmm."

A smile broke across his face. "I think, if given the chance, you could be a very lazy chit."

"Mmmm."

He stroked her hair for long minutes, then kissed the top of her head. "I love you," he breathed. But she was already asleep.

She awoke to find his hand sliding over her hip. Her back was pressed against his hard body, his lips were warm at her ear, and she could feel his readiness full against the small of her back. The room was black as pitch.

"Jason!" She sat up, horrified. " 'Tis dark! Riley. The cows!"

The weight of his hand forced her back into the pillows. "No Riley. No cows."

"But—"

He kissed the corner of her mouth.

"But he'll wonder where I am!"

"You think he does not know where you are?"

She blushed at the thought of what the family must be thinking. "I can imagine the look on Hannah's face right now." She chuckled. "We've been in this room all day, Jason."

"And half the night."

"Good Lord, you must be famished!"

His lips touched her gently. "Aye."

"Let me go downstairs and find you something to eat." She made to get up, only to find his hands set firmly on her shoulders. "I cannot satisfy your hunger unless you let me go," she coaxed.

His husky laughter rumbled in his throat. "On the contrary." He bit her shoulder and worked downward from there.

She did not hear him rise before dawn the next morning, nor did she feel his eyes devouring her as he stood beside the bed. "I could not tell you, Katy." His voice was an undertone. "I could not. Forgive me."

When she awoke several hours later, she stretched her arm out expecting to find a warm body. What her hand fell upon was a tangle of sheets. "Jason?" She snapped her head around.

Gone.

Peering from beneath her covers, she propped herself up on her elbows and made a cursory survey of the room.

Still gone. But where? . . .

She fell back onto her pillows with a smile lighting her face, closed her eyes, recapturing the feel and smell of him, the pressure of his loins against her. Light-headed and drowsy with physical satisfaction, she forced herself to her feet, rubbed her backside as if to warm herself. The gesture caused her mouth to form into a silent circle of pain. Looking behind her, she frowned at the blue-green mottled skin and remembered her punishment of the day before.

"A fine thank-you, Jason MacAuley," she said aloud. "Mayhap this will put a dent in your lusty games for the next few days." She winced as she touched the tender flesh again, confident that her condition would not deter him. As he had demonstrated last night, there were ways, and then . . . there were ways.

Dressing quickly, she rushed downstairs, but was surprised to discover that each room was as empty as her own. With a dark foreboding gnawing in the back of her mind, she wandered into the kitchen. Hannah and Desire looked up briefly, then went back to their chopping. Mercy alone flashed a bright, knowing smile.

" 'Tis good thou hast finally allowed thyself the luxury of sleeping-in one morning, mistress," she chimed. "Thy face is positively radiant this morning!" This last she directed in an exaggerated tone at her sister's back. "Might I prepare some breakfast for thee?"

"Has . . . has Captain MacAuley already eaten?" She removed an orange from the basket on the table and fondled it between her hands.

Hannah shot a queer look at her older daughter before answering. "He ate hours ago. Then he left."

Katy's fingers moved lightly over the surface of the orange, stroking it with rhythmic motions. "Left?"

Hannah's eyes took on an incredulous glint as she stared back, but Mercy found a reply before her mother could formulate an answer that would embarrass Katy.

"Thy long sleep has made thee forget what day it is. Dost not remember that the captain leaves for the West Indies today? A short trip, though—only till October."

The shock of Mercy's announcement stained Katy's cheeks with a rush of blood. "I . . . I had forgotten. How . . . silly of me." Breathless, she clutched the orange to her side as if she would squeeze it into pulp, and backed toward the door. "Excuse me."

She ran blindly, neither knowing nor caring where her feet carried her. How could he leave after what they had shared? He could not be gone. He could not do that to her! In the barn she led Asticou from the stall and hoisted herself onto his bare back. They were lying to her. All of them! They had to be lying! Clinging to the stallion's silver mane, she dug her feet into his sides and crashed headlong through the forest to the road that Fergus had shown her. Otter Point. Would she not see his ship from that vantage point?

But when she drew her horse to a halt on the edge of the precipice, she compressed her lips and blinked against the wind.

Nothing.

Not a ship. Not a sail.

He was gone.

She shivered with a pang of loneliness that she would come to know vividly in his absence.

15

It was four days after Jason's departure that Hannah Meacham put her elder daughter out of the house. So incensed was the woman when she learned of Desire's unhealthy absorption with the captain that no amount of pleading on the daughter's part would alter the mother's decision. The situation might have been different had Jason been unwed, but he was married, even if it was to a woman Hannah despised, and the housekeeper's rigid code of honor and loyalty to her employer far eclipsed the thought of the loss of a daughter.

On July 19 Desire Meacham sat beside Riley on the buckboard, her possessions crammed into a solitary traveling chest, her beautiful face cold and implacable. She was to be shepherded out to the Breeds to assist Abigail with her brood of screaming little boys and in return for room and board would be expected to submit herself to common servility. But she had no intention of remaining there till her hands were as raw as a fishwife's. . . .

With her favorite child outside her domination, Hannah's already acerbic temper became actively nasty, so to spare Katy the housekeeper's unpleasantness, Fergus rode by often to spirit the girl away to other parts of the island. On days when the sea was calm, he would outfit his own sailboat and navigate the waters of Somes Sound, one hand attendant upon the boom, the other wrapped protectively about Mary Kathleen. From the bay they watched sunsets in flame and coral fire the mountainsides; inhaled air thick with the aroma of offshore fog; scudded through low-lying mists that enveloped their boat and slithered serpentlike into every harbor. With Daniel they plodded through the black tidal muck to dig clams, Fergus unable to believe that any one person could attract as much mire as Katy. He surmised that Jason would not be pleased to learn how much time his wife was spending with Daniel and him, but, he reasoned, if Jason wanted to chaperon her activities, he should not have gone off to the West Indies. It was beyond the Irishman's comprehension how anyone could abandon so lovely a bride as Mary Kathleen after only six weeks of marriage. The man had to be insane!

Having learned of Jason's abrupt departure, Elisha Hastings, running between Boston, New York, and Philadelphia, cultivated the dangerous occupation of escorting the captain's wife when he was in port. Hoping to be awarded the captaincy of the vessel being constructed at Hull's Cove, Elisha oftentimes stopped by Jason's shipyard to check on the wainwright's progress—and to avail himself of the pleasure of Katy's gentle company. It never ceased to amaze him how Daniel English always managed to find them. Elisha pondered various ways to discourage Daniel's continual interference. He wondered if breaking his neck would be too harsh.

The intense heat of summer mellowed as August blended its warmth with the coolness of September. Fat and succulent with autumn ripeness, the bountiful harvest from the earth was gathered and stored in root cellars for winter consumption. Night descended earlier. Predawn temperatures dipped to freezing, the union of frigid air and warmer ocean water producing a flowing current of sea smoke that hovered and swirled above the surface of the Atlantic like steam. Katy dug out her woolens to offset the drop in the temperature, and as she trudged about the house in layers of shawls and stockings, began to covet the sweltering Spanish weather she had grown up despising. They had received only one letter from Jason since July—a short missive for Hannah, advising her of some business to which she should attend and informing her that there was a possibility of his being detained till November or December. At the end of his correspondence he had added a solitary sentence. "My love to Clare and Mary Kathleen." Nothing more. She longed for some personal message that would engender her own cherished thoughts of their first coupling, but nothing ever came. She hardened herself to the torment of ten to twelve more weeks without him.

Ten to twelve weeks.

Forever.

The fog that hemmed in the harbor did not slow the steps of Jason MacAuley as he beat a path along the waterfront of St. Eustatius. Neither did it stop a buxom tart from grabbing his arm as he passed a deserted alley.

"You're a pretty one, ain't ya?" Her eyes traveled lower. "And it looks to me like you got enough in there to hoist a sail on. How about if we . . ."

But he had freed himself and was gone before she could finish her sentence.

Jason would have considered the situation humorous had it not been for the fact that only last week he had fortified himself with a bottle of whiskey and roamed the docks to find a whore to ease himself upon, only to discover that once he had the woman abed, he had been unable to sustain his arousal. He had blamed his non-performance on the liquor, but he knew the real reason was guilt. The thought of easing himself on another woman made him feel guilty. Mary Kathleen MacAuley had shackled his loins. Damn her.

When he had left Frenchman Bay that morning in July, he had been euphoric—his marriage had been consummated and Katy had even seemed to delight in his lovemaking. But the more he remembered of that day, the more disquieting the memory became. For Katy had spoken no words of love, and somehow that was significant. What game did she play?

As the days at sea had lengthened into weeks, Jason's euphoria became victim to his own constant cross-examinations. His elation was replaced by disenchantment, then by apprehension, then by a gnawing fear that she would not even be there when he returned to the island.

And now, he could not even relieve his frustration without having his ardor cooled by guilt.

Well, he was a man, and no wife was going to shackle his loins. Perhaps he had had trouble mounting a whore when he was dead drunk, but tonight he was stone sober. Tonight he would have no trouble.

Even hindered by the thick fog, it took Jason no time at all to find a respectable brothel and even less time to tell the madam what he wanted. Once closeted behind the doors of one of the bedchambers, he dragged off his boots and stretched out on the bed, thoughts of his wife firmly planted in the back of his mind as he anticipated the night's fare.

The door to his room opened and closed. The girl was tall, with platinum blond hair that fell to her waist and brown eyes that appraised him with more than a lusty interest as she padded softly toward him. He felt his desire take flesh as she smiled down at him, and he could not help but think how very tall this girl was—as tall as Desire Meacham. And he noticed that her hair was long and straight—like Desire Meacham's. And her eyes were the same color brown as Desire Mea—

Thoughts of Desire Meacham suddenly evoked images of Frenchman Bay, and thoughts of Frenchman Bay evoked images of that morning back in July when he had sailed from the island, leaving Katy all warm and soft—

"Aw, hell."

Soft suddenly described more than just Katy.

* * *